PRAISE FOR *EDEN*

"*Eden* is not just another farewell-to-the-summer-house novel, but instead a masterfully interwoven family saga with indelible characters, unforgettable stories, and true pathos. Most impressive, there's not an ounce of fat on this excellent book."
—ANITA SHREVE, NYT best selling author of *The Pilot's Wife* and *The Stars are Fire*

"*Eden* is a heartbreaking novel about the wounds that are passed down through generations. Blasberg's voice is strong and clear, and her characters are so real—with their ambitions and their weaknesses, their good intentions and their resentments—that no reader is likely to forget them."
—IVY POCHODA, author of *Wonder Valley* and *Visitation Street*

" . . . a beautifully written masterpiece that takes you on a historical journey. . . . "
—*BOSTON HERALD*

"Blasberg's evocative prose captures the place and atmosphere.... An engrossing, character-driven family saga."
—*KIRKUS*

"A stirring historical novel perfect for women's fiction fans."
—*BOOKLIST*

THE NINE

THE
NINE

A NOVEL

JEANNE McWILLIAMS BLASBERG

SHE WRITES PRESS

Published August 2019
Printed in the United States of America
Print ISBN: 978-1-63152-652-7
E-ISBN: 978-1-63152-653-4
Library of Congress Control Number: 2019935719

For information, address:
She Writes Press
1569 Solano Ave #546
Berkeley, CA 94707

Interior design by Tabitha Lahr

She Writes Press is a division of SparkPoint Studio, LLC.

For my children, Jack, Charlie, and Annie

"*And now that you don't have to be perfect, you can be good.*"

—John Steinbeck, *East of Eden*

PROLOGUE

Sam trod carefully on the narrow sidewalk, which, despite constant salting and plowing, would not regain the texture of asphalt until well into springtime. Hemmed in by knee-high snowbanks on either side, he caught up with Raymond and Saunders, his skin tingling with anticipation, his breath rising in plumes of white vapor. The hood of his black sweatshirt hampered any reliable peripheral vision, but the full moon illuminated a clear path ahead.

As promised, Gary, their collaborator from Maintenance, had left the padlock to the shed behind the gym hanging loose, and the boys found three cans of blood-red paint waiting in a corner. They each took one before Sam ushered them out and secured the door. The can's cold metal handle dug into his palm, and its weighty cylinder swung against his thigh.

Sam sped in front of the other boys, creating a tight triangular formation. Steering them clear of the security cameras that had recently been installed on various lampposts, he checked that his paintbrush and screwdriver were still in his pocket.

Raymond tapped Sam's shoulder, then split off and headed to the football stadium. A few moments later, with a soccer player's explosive instinct for the open field, Saunders cut toward the academy building.

Silence enveloped the campus as Sam proceeded alone, making his way to Headmaster Williams's house on a section of path that was better salted than the rest. Despite the care that had been taken around his entryway, the headmaster's roof was heavily laden with winter. Icicles hung from its eaves, daggers shining silver in the moonlight.

No matter the season, Sam's mother had always trilled about how "lovely" the house was, pointing to the gingerbread detail and scrolled pillars on the porch. Her remarks were usually followed by a question about Williams's daughter, who happened to be in Sam's class, and whether they'd become friends. Sam never dignified his mother's prying with a response, even though he'd witnessed Mary Williams plenty of times over the years, emerging from the back door during the middle of the day with cookies, Diet Cokes, and other homey comforts for her girlfriends.

Sam looked up at the large white Victorian, with its black shutters and wraparound porch. It sat on the road that bisected the campus, and its prominence on the main green was emblematic of the headmaster himself. He'd been a fixture at Dunning Academy since the days when teachers used purple ink to mimeograph handouts.

Stretching the sleeve of his sweatshirt to muffle the sound of metal on metal, Sam popped the lid off the paint can with the screwdriver. He dipped the brush in the gooey pigment and recalled the summer he'd painted the garage with his father, a man who would have winced at the idea of sloshing a brush into a can that hadn't been properly mixed.

He stepped off the walkway, carefully placing his feet on the crusty top layer of snow. He crouched low as he began painting, having rehearsed the choreography that morning. The cold air quickly stiffened the brush's bristles and numbed his fingers, but the glossy red design contrasted with the sparkling white canvas in a way that elicited unexpected pleasure in Sam and thawed whatever tension had built up in his shoulders.

He had just finished the last stroke when his Converse All Stars broke through the snow with a percussive pop. Cold powder filled his shoes and numbed his ankles. He held his breath and searched the headmaster's windows for several seconds. They were dark, with the exception of one which glowed amber. Sam bit down on his lower lip, trying to recall whether it had been on when he had arrived.

When there was no visible movement from inside, he exhaled, tiptoed back to the path, and admired his work. He knew that early-morning commuters driving past would see a giant number six, but there was no doubt how it would look to Williams when he opened his front door to collect the *New York Times*.

Sam ditched the empty paint can and his tools in a Dumpster behind the dining hall, then made his way to the academy building, where he reunited with Raymond and Saunders. They bumped fists—mission accomplished.

Elkinah knew his wife Hannah and the Lord remembered her. Hannah conceived, and at the turn of the year bore a son. She named him Samuel, meaning, "I asked the Lord for him." And when Elkinah and all the household were going up to offer to the Lord the annual sacrifice at Shiloh, Hannah did not go up. She said to her husband, "When the child is weaned, I will bring him. For when he has appeared before the Lord, he must remain there for good."
—Samuel 1:19

CHAPTER 1

The first time I heard Headmaster Williams speak the foreign phrase, I took it as a promise from one parent to another. Later, I'd learn it was the law, but on that very first day, when he touted *in loco parentis* as one of the academy's primary responsibilities, I gave the man credit for comprehending a mother's pain.

Even though I'd turned Sam over to Dunning Academy five years prior, I recalled the headmaster's speech like it had happened yesterday: the way the Latin rolled off his Brahmin tongue, the way he pushed his round tortoiseshell glasses high on the bridge of his nose, and the way his tweed jacket stretched across the remnants of an athletic build. I see now how clinging to his every word was a little ridiculous, but back then I craned my neck, peering above the crest-adorned podium, to fully absorb his booming wisdom.

Even though I'd packed away my blind worship of the man along with everything else from my old life, that memory of him was back.

You see, my new life was only recently planted, hadn't yet established deep roots, and I was vulnerable to storms and floods, to the slightest gusts of wind. My safe harbor was work, and a recent promotion to executive director of the Boys & Girls Clubs had become an all-consuming endeavor. Thanks to the Internet, however, even that couldn't protect me.

....

I was thumbing through insurance policies, waivers, and program schedules when my assistant popped her head through the door. "I'm heading home now, Hannah," she said.

I looked at her over my reading glasses, then checked my watch. After conducting story time for our youngest campers, I'd gotten lost in a pile of paperwork, hoping to make a dent before the weekend. "Is it that time already?"

"Yes, it is," she said, with a wink, before rustling her purse from a file drawer. "You should cut out soon too." Not long after, her footsteps faded down the hallway, and the only noises left were the kids' cheers in the gymnasium. The club served students who needed its supervised recreation desperately. They didn't have mothers waiting at home to greet them after school.

I brushed my unruly hair into a clip and dug my yoga gear out of the closet. Joy and I had plans to meet at a six o'clock class and then go to dinner. It had become our standing Thursday date, one that I looked forward to not only for the companionship but also for the benefits to my fifty-eight-year-old, deskbound body.

Before shutting down my laptop, I checked email one last time, hoping for something from Sam. Instead, a message from his former dorm parent, Shawn Willis, caught my attention. The subject line read:

Re: Dunning, wanted to make sure you saw this.

My hand floated back, seeking the stability of my armchair as my body sank down into it.

Hannah,
Lou forwarded this to me. It was sent to the Dunning Academy community yesterday. Be glad that it's all behind you.
Best,
Shawn

My eyelid resumed its rapid twitching of the prior year, as if preparing for an onslaught of debris. The email Shawn forwarded was addressed to Dunning families, past and present. That we weren't included on the original distribution was yet another sign that the Webbers had been wiped from the school's system.

I skimmed the words, my vision dancing, wanting to take in the email's whole meaning in one gulp. I finally focused, drawn to the last paragraph:

As the Board of Trustees, we accept full responsibility for the failures of those whose duty it was to protect the students. We recognize the enormous violation of trust and the lasting wounds inflicted and endured.

I couldn't believe it. An admission of guilt by Dunning Academy?

My mouth turned dry, and I reached for the water bottle in my yoga bag. I read the letter again. It wasn't signed by Headmaster Williams. He was long gone, and besides, he would never have conceded such a thing.

That first afternoon in the Dunning assembly hall, I had been mesmerized by his charismatic Kennedy style—that toothy smile, his slicked-back dark hair, his wise expression—welcoming us to some sort of Camelot. His assurances had allayed my fears as I stood at the sink over the next three years, hands submerged in sudsy water, my deepening worry lines reflected in the blackened bay window. Although the thing I loved most about my old, simple kitchen was the doorframe where I'd etched lines and penned dates chronicling Sam's growth over the years, I always remembered myself at that sink. Every Sunday evening, I'd be scrubbing chicken drippings from a roasting pan and waiting for the phone to ring.

Sam conditioned us with well-spaced contact, our relationship hanging on a lifeline of weekly phone calls. I'd kidded myself they were enough, and what a laugh that would prove to be. I'd carry the phone past the space station model he'd left half-finished in the family room, so that Edward and I could talk to him on the speaker. I'd saved up so many topics for those calls and had needed, I realized now, so much in return. I'd needed Sam's happy voice to confirm that Dunning Academy had been the right decision, to lighten the weight accumulating in my chest.

Yoga. I closed the laptop and left my office. On the car ride over, I recounted a guided meditation and wondered if I might let my anger toward Headmaster Williams float away like a helium balloon. It was a visual that had proved successful over time with regard to my feelings for Edward, but I doubted there was enough helium in the world to lift my resentment for the headmaster. And I vowed not to bring it up at dinner either. Joy was a good friend, but I couldn't burden our Thursday night with any more of my history.

We'd met at the yoga studio years earlier, and she'd come to my rescue after the divorce. She'd pulled me from the deep recesses of my hard drive, a place where I stored pictures of happier days, when Sam's voice rang through the house and he needed me to shuttle him to early-morning swim practice.

I'd fallen into the habit of sifting through pictures, sometimes all the way back to the day my miracle baby was born. I'd gotten pregnant right after our wedding, then miscarried twice. We'd tried for many years before Edward agreed to see a fertility specialist. Before our initial evaluation, however, I missed my period. Edward attributed the healthy pregnancy to my leaving the bank, and to reduced stress, but I was convinced it was prayer.

Sitting at a traffic light, I wondered if somebody had forwarded the email to Sam as well. I squeezed the steering wheel with one hand and twisted a loose strand of hair with the other, recalling the gleeful afternoon when an email from Dunning signified his acceptance. I'd gone so far as to pop champagne before supper, celebrating not only his entry into an elite, rarefied world but also my job well done. It had been me, after all, who had taken him to the library every week and quizzed him with flash cards before vocabulary tests.

A week after we celebrated, another email arrived from the school, to Edward's address this time, saying Sam hadn't qualified for financial aid. Truth be told, I was secretly pleased Dunning hadn't lumped us among its neediest families. My parents' finances were the reason I'd remained in state for college, and it was nice to think that, in Dunning's opinion, at least, we had means.

Edward explained it had nothing to do with our cash flow and everything to do with our balance sheet. "It's our zip code, Hannah." If his parents hadn't helped with the down payment, rooting us in one of Boston's western suburbs, we would never have owned a home with so much value. I pleaded with him to figure something out. His parents had seemed impressed when I'd called to tell them about Dunning. "Maybe they'll help with the tuition?"

Edward shook his head at that idea, instead spending several nights armed with pad and calculator beneath the glow of his desk lamp. He finally jostled me awake, having determined we could swing it if I tightened things further and worked additional hours. I wept into the pillow, forgiving him, if only momentarily, for having never become the provider he could have been.

Edward grumbled when it was time to send in the tuition deposit, but I shushed him, not wanting Sam to carry any added pressure. How foolish I'd been back then, thinking our biggest sacrifice was financial.

As I prepared for his departure, I ignored the naysayers. There were my sisters back in Ohio, conservative Jews with ten children between them, mystified about why I'd send Sam away, especially after how hard it was to have him in the first place. They never understood how things were done in this educated corner of New England.

"It's Dunning," I explained. "When one has an opportunity to attend, one doesn't decline." It was a phrase I'd overheard while waiting for our interview in the admissions office. What I'd never voice was my premonition that Sam was destined for something extraordinary and that it was my duty, as his mother, to set him on the right path.

The mothers of Sam's middle school classmates didn't know what to make of me either; I was a decade older because of the trouble we'd had conceiving. They never invited me to their girls' nights or book clubs, or whatever excuses they came up with to drink wine away from their children midweek. Still, their doubting expressions sometimes gave me pause. I had to remind myself of Dunning's place in history, the caliber of men counted among its alumni—Supreme Court justices and US senators, for goodness' sake.

"Inhale, exhale, inhale, exhale." The yoga teacher chanted her prompts. "Let go of your day. If your mind is racing, come back to your breath." I filled my lungs, then emptied them through my nostrils, wrestling with the hold Williams had on me. It was as if he'd looked directly into my eyes the day Edward and I dropped off Sam and sat among the two hundred other parents who'd bought into a name-brand education, and delivered a personal message to me.

He'd said his daughter, Mary, would be a member of the class as well, as if that meant he would pay extra attention to this crop. He said it was time for us to wean our children, that, despite our belief to the contrary, they were ready to get on with their promising futures. It was time to stop helping with their homework and reviewing their essays. He also pressed us not to fall prey to their homesickness, their inevitable frantic calls. "You mothers will be particularly vulnerable to the distress in their voices," he warned. "But don't you worry—we are experts in the business of teenagers. Give us six weeks, and they'll be well on their way."

When he remembered my name, I was convinced. "Thank you for entrusting Sam to us, Mrs. Webber," he said, holding my gaze for an extra beat before Edward guided me out, his hand on the small of my back.

On the drive home, I double-checked the literal translation of *in loco parentis* with Edward. "In place of a parent," he told me. Headmaster Williams never specified, I realized later, which kind of parent—the kind who gets down on the floor and puts on puppet shows or the kind who forgets her child in an overheating car.

....

Not until later would I recall the way Edward winced when I portioned out the three flutes of bubbly to celebrate. The problem was, he never articulated his concerns. I chalked up his lack of enthusiasm to the fact that he'd also come of age in these East Coast prep schools and couldn't truly appreciate what a leg up he'd been given. I assumed it was the money and that he'd miss having another man around the house. I can't help thinking now that there was something else he knew, something I'd have no way of understanding, about the enigma of boarding schools, how strange they could be. Now that they are in the news day after day, featured in more stories of misconduct and cover-ups, I wonder what he chose to keep private.

But I can't cast the blame on Edward. When I put my mind to something, there's no stopping me. I saw the *Forbes* ranking of the best high schools in the United States, and I wouldn't settle for anything less than Dunning Academy for my Sam.

....

When the yoga class ended, Joy and I dressed in the changing room. I followed her car to the restaurant, and when we entered, she cast animated eyes toward the active bar. It wasn't until we were seated that she furrowed her brow with concern. "Okay, what's going on?" she asked. "You're in another world."

A server stopped at our table. "You ladies want the usual?"

"I'll need a minute," I said, holding my menu. When she moved along, I said to Joy, "I'm sorry. I got an email before leaving the office."

"Edward?"

"No."

"Sam?"

"No."

"What, then?"

"Never mind."

"Just let me see." Joy held out her hand for my phone, as if she'd be able to read it, decipher its meaning, and categorically dismiss whatever was bothering me so we could get on with our evening.

"No, it's okay. I'm fine." I couldn't explain that it was Dunning and the headmaster again; it was the damned hypocrisy.

"Fork it over," she insisted.

I felt around in my purse, knowing she wouldn't back down. Pulling out my phone, I noticed Sam had texted: "Call me when you can."

The hairs on my forearms stood straight up. It wasn't Sunday. He must have seen the email too.

"I'm so sorry, Joy. I need to go out to the parking lot to return a call."

I navigated the crowd at the bar toward the exit, dialing Sam's number en route.

"Mom?" He picked up immediately.

"Sam? Are you okay?"

"Sort of."

My heart cratered at his crackling voice, at the distance between us. I leaned against the hood of my car and asked, "Did you see the email?"

He cleared his throat. "Yeah. That's why I texted."

"Shawn forwarded it to me. I read it briefly on my way out of the office." I couldn't predict whether he would feel angry or vindicated. Likely both.

"They've hired a special counsel and set up a process where victims can come forward to make reports."

"But not you?"

"No, Mom. Nathalie and Astrid and some of the other girls in Bennett want to."

Why was this an acceptable time to come forward? Just a year earlier, when Sam had had something to say, it had stirred up a tsunami.

"Mom?"

"Right. Of course. Of course they should make a report. Absolutely," I stammered. "But . . ."

"But what?"

"I worry about you. Opening old wounds after you've come so far."

"I know, but it's time for the girls to seek justice."

I put my hand to my temple, remembering how, not so long before, Dunning's lawyers had browbeaten us. Would they really receive Nathalie and Astrid any differently?

"I might be called on to make a statement."

"And the Crandalls?" I asked.

After a brief pause, Sam chuckled. "I never thought I'd live to hear you concerned about them."

CHAPTER 2:

FIVE YEARS EARLIER

Nudging the door open, Sam bumped into his roommate, stretched across the carpet, doing push-ups. After a full day of classes, swim team practice, and a harried dinner, all he wanted was to seek solace in his room in Wilburton Hall.

"Ethan, what's up?" he mumbled, skirting the boy's planked body and scattered clothes.

Ethan's loud exertions suggested there was some frustration he needed to work out. These first weeks of school had awakened both boys to the disappointing reality of their athletic prospects at Dunning. The swim coach had told Sam he shouldn't ever get his hopes up for varsity, and even though several first-year standouts on the soccer team had been promoted directly to the premier squad, Ethan hadn't been one of them.

Sam and Ethan had bonded on move-in day while their mothers made their beds and folded clothing away into drawers. They were from similar middle-class backgrounds; Ethan's father owned a John Deere dealership in Burlington, Vermont, and his mother had recently retired from teaching school. Sharing a room had accelerated their mutual understanding, and this seemed like one of those times when it was better to leave Ethan alone. Sam sat down at his desk and opened his copy of *Hamlet*.

When Ethan's alarm sounded at 9:45 p.m., marking the end of study hall, he slammed his textbook shut, and the two boys burst into the hallway. Their fellow first-years (nicknamed preps, formally known as Class Four) were already sitting with backs against the walls and their legs splayed across the carpet. Their desire for connection had taken on a primal urgency, as it had become increasingly clear that they occupied the lowest rung on the Dunning social ladder. Girls looked right past them, and the upperclassmen were having more than a few laughs at their expense.

Their dorm, Wilburton Hall, like the others in the quad, rose four stories, providing a natural segregation of the classes. While Headmaster Williams professed that the arrangement fostered class unity and the "lifelong bonds only living together can achieve," their proctor claimed preps were kept a good distance from the older boys to postpone, for as long as possible, their debauchery.

Burrowed away beneath the dormers, Sam and his classmates broke out into spontaneous wrestling, laughing, sharing, embellishing, and, in one way or another, reinventing themselves. Having mastered things like Rubik's Cube or spelling bees in middle school, they saw boarding school as an opportunity to adopt a new, "cooler" identity. Their horseplay also weeded out who was game and who was a jerk, who was decent, and who could carry things a bit too far.

From his spot in the middle of the group, Max explained to the redhead from Chicago, "You shouldn't have aced the placement test; now you're in one of the hardest math sections, and there'll be no way to get a good grade."

The redhead frowned and nodded, sinking back against the wall.

"Enough talk about classes. Is there a dance in the student center this weekend?" Ethan asked. He already had his eye on several first-year girls.

"Yes, there'll be a dance in the student center, like every weekend," Max answered. He had a father and two brothers who'd graduated from Dunning and was a fountain of information.

Sam listened and observed. He didn't talk much about himself, instead using those first weeks to try on his new independence. He could go to the student center whenever he wanted and ruin his appetite on the free popcorn. He could wash his face or not, eat his vegetables or not.

Although he was glad to be out from under his mother's constant watch, he did shed an occasional tear into his pillow. He hadn't expected to miss the way his father poked his head through his bedroom door, speculating about the Red Sox's chances, or how his mother's floral perfume clung to her hair and filled his lungs when they hugged. Even though his parents were mortifying, Sam missed their proximity, their familiarity with the characters in his life. They had no idea about the odd sorts he was coming across at Dunning, and even if he had wanted to explain during their Sunday phone calls, he wouldn't have known where to start. They were only an hour away by car, but the distance between Dunning and home was immeasurable.

There were all these traditions, for example, which legacies like Max had to explain, such as where to sit at all-school assembly, and sacred spots on which one should never set foot. And Sam wasn't the only first-year still trying to figure out the place, as their evening bull sessions in the hallway indicated.

"Mrs. Stillman said one more tardy and she'll have Willis put me on restrictions. Can she do that?" a boy from California asked.

"They can do whatever they want," Max said.

"But what about Dean Harper at assembly this morning?" Ethan laughed recounting the dean of students' tirade. He had dimmed the lights to project a brief instructional on emergency protocol, but a crudely shot video had blanketed the screen instead. At first it had been hard to tell what they were watching, until the white skin of rear ends had become decipherable. Laughter had pealed through the auditorium while the dean hollered to cut the projector.

"Was probably the Nine," Max said.

"Who?" Ethan asked.

"The Nine," Max repeated. All the faces turned to listen. "The elite of the elite. You know, it's, like, the highest honor at this school."

"Like a classics diploma?" Ethan asked.

"No," Max said, shaking his head. "Anybody can work hard and study Latin; the Nine are chosen." He went on to explain how the underground group was supported by legions of alumni and how its members received special treatment when registering for classes, drawing room assignments, even with college admissions.

Sam wanted to ask Max more about it but held his tongue in front of the group. He found it hard to believe a power-wielding secret society could exist in a high school.

But the evidence mounted. Throughout the autumn and into the winter, the audacity of anonymous pranksters kept Sam and his classmates amused. When schoolwide emails were sent from Dean Harper's account announcing pajama days, when a cow was marched up to the second floor of the academy building, when a pyrotechnics spectacle scorched a phallic image across the football field during homecoming, they cheered from the sidelines. They rehashed the genius acts at dinner, then speculated over breakfast, across long wooden dining tables, how the Nine might strike again.

They remained stone-faced and silent, however, when Mr. Willis, their dorm parent, delivered warnings of severe punishment if any of them were stupid enough to be discovered out of the dorm after check-in. But as soon as he retreated down the stairs, the boys broke into more laughter, this time at the administration's frustration.

"Meep-meep," Sam said. Everyone laughed even harder. "It's like watching the Road Runner and Wile E. Coyote."

This type of antagonism wasn't the dynamic he'd envisioned when applying to Dunning. The tour guide had romanticized life on a campus that blended pastoral New Hampshire with classic Harvard Yard, and, while his father had driven them home, his mother had read aloud from the catalog: "In 1839, Ezekiel Dunning bequeathed five hundred acres to found an academy to educate the finest young men of New England. Its future buildings would be interspersed with expanses of green lawns, playing fields, and woods stretching to Miller's River. One of the few secondary-school campuses designed by Frederick Law Olmsted, it has well-appointed dormitories demarcating residential quadrangles, and its paths meander beneath great oaks and maples, past a white clapboard chapel and granite academy buildings."

"All right, Mom. I get it," he'd said, not caring as much about Dunning's history as he had about the Olympic swimming pool, a far cry from their local YMCA; the make-your-own-sundae bar in the dining hall; and that sleek robotics lab.

"It's not about the buildings, Sam. You'll see—it's all about the friends you'll make," his father had said, with a nostalgic smile.

When Sam had sat at the kitchen table, working on his Dunning application, he'd flipped through the pictures in the glossy admissions catalog. On the page exalting Dunning's residential life was Wilburton Hall, an iconic redbrick structure set off against a crisp blue sky with orange foliage in the background. A group of students emerged from its doors, smiling and laughing, clutching books to their chests.

As his first year unfolded with a cold north wind prematurely blowing the leaves from the trees, Sam's experience was colored with an altogether different hue. *His* New Hampshire sky seemed terminally gray, the ancient inner workings of Wilburton meant the showers spat meager streams of lukewarm water, and the old, clanking radiators hissed the type of dry heat that made his nose bleed.

He attempted to familiarize himself with the 150 kids in his entering class, meeting others like him, admitted for their scholastic achievement, excellent test scores, and well-roundedness. Still, legacies of "old Dunning" were prevalent. In addition to kids like Max who assumed a Dunning education as their birthright, fixtures of the past were everywhere: oil-painted portraits, statuaries, and gold-leaf plaques harkened back to prior generations, before Dunning was coed, before it offered financial aid and imported students from Asia, and definitely before a left-leaning faculty made it a bastion of political correctness.

"Hey, Webber," a tall, blond sophomore yelled across the locker room before swim practice.

Surprised to hear his name, Sam looked up to see Justin Crandall, a towel wrapped around his waist, smiling in his direction.

Descended from a prominent family of alumni, Justin was an in-the-flesh portrait of the quintessential Dunning boy—handsome, athletic, and effortlessly smart. There had once been a life-size bronze statue representing the school's ideal atop a pedestal overlooking the entrance to the dining hall. Headmaster Williams had had to remove it, however, after the Asian Student Alliance had threatened to topple it.

"How's the crew on the fourth floor?" Justin asked.

"They're all right."

"I hear there are some weirdos this year."

Sam shrugged off the slight. "I guess I'm one of them."

Justin laughed. "Yeah, I guess you are."

In addition to feeling at home with Ethan and the others on the fourth floor, Sam was embraced by older boys on the swim team. He didn't brag, he was self-effacing, and he was generous with his mother's care packages. He was tall but not too tall, was not too thin or too fat, and although his dark brown hair was nothing special, he liked the way it curled around his ears. He was the type to listen until there was something to say; then he usually made a relevant comment. He had a dry sense of humor and good timing honed from years of watching classic comedies with his father.

Justin liked to hold forth at meals, the kind of kid who made room for Wilburton first-years at his table in the dining hall. Sam joined in the conversation and laughed on cue. While the others spoke in the parlance of the Manhattan elite, dropping the names of European ski resorts their families patronized and nightclubs they planned to frequent once they acquired fake IDs, Sam was unique in his humility.

Hanging out with Justin's crowd, Sam concluded he might never be the most popular kid in school or receive the best grades; he'd never "belong" at Dunning like the kids whose fathers and grandfathers had paved the way. He realized something during those first weeks it would take his mother a long time to understand: the only way he was going to master Dunning Academy would be through a side door.

Upon returning from the pool one afternoon, Justin grumbled by the bike rack outside Wilburton, "My idiot brother locked this here on drop-off day without giving me the combination."

Sam looked over his shoulder. "If it's one of those four-digit cables, I can probably figure it out."

"Yeah, but that would take all night."

"Let me have a look."

Sam bent over the lock, aligning the numbers, spinning one digit at a time, pecking and tugging, until the lock came loose in his hands. It took about thirty seconds.

"Awesome," said Justin. "Are you a bike thief or something?"

"Nah, I've just got lots of forgetful friends."

Justin smiled. "Hop on the handlebars, Webber. I'll give you a ride to dinner."

CHAPTER 3

Shawn Willis drove the thousand miles from Wisconsin in his rusted-out Datsun, which choked out just enough fumes to deliver his weary body and worldly possessions to the Wilburton parking lot before it died with a final, steamy cough.

His father had emphasized the "coup" of adding Dunning Academy to his feeble résumé. It had a reputation for being a cutting-edge teaching environment where young idealists launched promising careers, as well as providing a bucolic setting where revered academics could finish theirs in comfort. What existed in the middle may have been a murky combination of disillusioned professionals and disgruntled victims of departmental politics, but it was a terrific first job for Shawn.

What was more, the board of trustees aimed to keep the teachers happy. Each time a rising star threatened departure to a rival school, the board answered with a wage increase. Even though a handful of teachers came and went, there was a loyal contingent that dug in, planted roots, and made Dunning their home.

Shawn dripped with sweat that first afternoon, unloading his car and setting up his dormitory apartment. Given the latitude of Dunning, New Hampshire, the heat and humidity would last about as long as the quiet on campus, but it was turning his move-in day into quite a workout. He opened all three windows and turned on the electric fan he'd been issued. He found an outlet for his old TV and set it on top of a bookshelf, and then another by the bed for his alarm clock. He stood in the middle of the kitchen-dining-living area and admired the space. It was the first home he could call his own.

The architectural features were classic: large mullioned windows, moldings, and a fireplace with an intricately carved mantel, although he'd been warned not to have any fires. Dunning had also issued him an upholstered sofa, coffee table, and kitchen table with four wooden chairs. He assumed, as had all eager new dorm heads before him, that it was for hosting the boys, that his apartment would become a venue for camaraderie.

Shawn debated the finishing touches, similar to the way students considered which posters to tack up on their walls. One had to be careful with how much of one's personality to broadcast. He thought about hanging some curtains, the kind of thing his mother might have suggested. Every little ramshackle place they'd moved into, she'd brought her curtains along.

He studied his framed photo of his Wisconsin hockey team celebrating on the ice after winning the national championship. Shawn was the guy in the picture wearing street clothes, leaning on crutches. He considered the blank spot on the wall, then wondered what other faculty members hung on their walls, before stowing it under the bed.

He'd been hired as an assistant hockey coach and dorm parent, a job that had materialized after his father scoured his Rolodex. The prior winter, Shawn had done his knee in for good. At least he'd been able to stay at school and earn his degree, but his dreams of pro hockey were dashed; he was a washup at twenty-four. "A job in coaching," his father had said, "is the next best thing. At least you'll still be around the game." But that was his father's life. Shawn had always seen himself as a player.

He had to be grateful for the help, however. Having taken to drowning his sorrows after the injury, Shawn had been in no shape to get a job on his own. He saw housing and meals as a perk: he'd save money and wouldn't have to eat his own cooking. What nobody had counted on was the head coach dropping dead while mowing his lawn over Labor Day weekend, catapulting Shawn to interim head coach, whether he was ready or not.

When Shawn's father heard the news, he shouted into the phone, "It's just the break you need. Now, go in there and ask for the permanent position."

It took a few weeks for Shawn to muster the courage. The athletic director smiled at his spunk, looking him up and down. "Sure, kid. I'll put your name on the list."

"Thanks," Shawn nodded. Despite the AD's amusement, Shawn reasoned, he'd be easy on the payroll.

"Probably too late to find a replacement for this season anyway," the AD said, looking down at the papers on his desk. "Consider it a tryout."

It was a long shot. The hockey team was, after all, a high-profile source of great pride. It had won a string of championships in the formidable New England Prep School League and seven out of the past ten contests against its archrival, Easton Academy. Its success was attributed to its stacking the team with postgraduates, eighteen-year-olds who attended Dunning as an intermediary step between high school and college. Shawn had been impressed reviewing the films, the soundtrack of fans' cheers echoing off cinder-block walls as players celebrated goals with the flair of high school stardom.

....

Dean Harper had asked Shawn to be freshly shaven the morning the first-years arrived. He usually wore two days' growth in order to add a few years to his youthful appearance. Although he could mask his baby face with whiskers, there was nothing to be done about his height—five feet, eight inches—and the way people looked down on him.

Finishing breakfast, Shawn glanced out the dining hall window to see a stream of cars already coming up the drive. Dean

Harper had warned there were always eager parents who arrived before the nine o'clock registration. He advised Shawn to welcome families in the morning, then make himself scarce later on. "You don't want to get in the middle of those first-years saying goodbye to their parents. It's awful."

Shawn cleared his plate and walked across the quad to his post by the front door of Wilburton. He resisted hurrying, as he'd never completed the physical therapy prescribed after his knee surgery and rushing made him limp.

As he walked on the path from the dining hall to the dorm, a Subaru wagon drove past, a little too quickly, and turned into the Wilburton lot. The driver cut the engine, and the brunette in the passenger seat flipped down the visor mirror and applied lipstick. She opened her door and stretched out her long legs, one at a time, before smoothing the front of her skirt. Shawn wondered whether she was a parent at all—she seemed a little overdressed to carry luggage up three flights of stairs. When a heavyset man and a teenage boy opened doors on the driver's side, however, it was clear by the way she gave them instructions that she was the mother.

The trio eventually approached him, the father carrying a laundry basket filled with sheets and blankets, the boy clutching a pillow. Shawn was about to introduce himself to the boy when the mother took his outstretched hand in hers. "Hello, I'm Hannah Webber. We're looking for Wilburton Hall."

"Well, you found it," Shawn said, taking a step backward. "I'm Shawn Willis."

"Hello, Shawn. Can you tell us where we might find the teacher in charge?"

"That would be me."

"Huh?" The woman made no effort to mask her disappointment.

"I'm the dorm parent of Wilburton."

"You?" she asked, shooting a glance at her husband, who stared into the laundry basket. "Oh, I'm sorry—it's just that you look young enough to be one of the students."

"I know." Shawn tried to brush it off. "I get that all the time."

"Excuse me. This is my husband, Edward. And this is Sam!" She pushed her son toward Shawn with both hands.

The boy and the father each shook Shawn's hand, exchanging pleasantries before the mother launched into a second round of questions. "So, Mr. Willis, what subject do you teach?"

"Oh, I–I'm the boys' varsity hockey coach."

"Hockey? And how long have you been doing that?"

"Um, well, this will be my first year," he answered.

"Really," she said, arching one eyebrow.

"I'm new here, just like Sam. Hoping you boys take it easy on me." He expected a little laugh from that comment, but there was nothing.

"And how many, uh, boys will be living in the dorm?" She kept it coming.

"Sixty-five."

"Really?" She raised that eyebrow even higher.

"But other faculty members help out. Dean Harper is on duty twice a week, as well as a few others."

"Are the others real teachers?"

"Hannah," said the father.

"Wait, Edward. I'm asking because they made this big deal about first-year study hall, and I want to make sure that if Sam needs any help, he gets it."

The boy cut in. "Mom, there are proctors for that. C'mon." He looked at the ground, his dark brown hair hiding his eyes. Hannah headed back to their car. Opening the hatch, she seemed to hang on it, breathing deeply, having lost her big pink smile. She pulled her dark hair from her neck and knotted it on top of her head, then reached into the back for a bag.

Shawn turned his attention back to the boy. "So, where you from?"

"Boston. Well, outside Boston."

"Cool. You a Bruins fan?"

"Not really. I've watched them on TV, but I've never been to a game."

The father shrugged. "I guess that one's on me," he said, placing the laundry basket at his feet. "We're baseball fans." He removed reading glasses from his breast pocket, perched them on his nose, and unfolded a campus map.

Hannah returned with a duffel bag. "Okay," she said. "Let's not waste any more time; we should get the car unloaded. Mr. Willis, can you show us to Sam's room?"

"Have you picked up his registration packet and room key?" he asked.

"No, we came straight here."

Shawn checked his watch. "You need to go over to the academy building basement to register and get his key. They'll be open soon."

She looked at Shawn as if she'd just been sent to the end of a long line at the post office.

"But feel free to leave your stuff," Shawn offered. "The academy building isn't too far. The packet will also have Sam's course schedule, and you might think about stopping at the bookstore to buy everything he needs for class. I'm told they sell out, so it's a good idea to go early."

Hannah looked over her husband's shoulder at the map before starting across the quad. The father followed with Sam, a little hunched in the shoulders, scuffing his big feet behind them. Shawn was opening the door to the dormitory when Sam turned back to face him. His hair caught the breeze and swept aside, making his entire face visible for the first time. He was frowning, pointing to his parents, silently apologizing for his tightly wound mother.

....

Shawn drew the rookie assignment of administering the mandatory swim test for new students. He wasn't meant to judge technique, just whether the student could get up and back without stopping. Still new to the ways of teenage melodrama, he'd expected the afternoon to be no more than a formality. The shivering nerves he met up with on the pool deck, however, caught him by surprise. Pale and gangly, in varying styles of swimsuits, with acne on their backs and cheeks, the students were a huddle of pubescent hormones that triggered the aching memory of what it was like to be fourteen. They all clutched towels. The boys, for the most part, seemed skinnier than they'd like, and the girls, for the most part, seemed chubbier than they'd like, constantly tugging at the nylon that crept up their backsides.

Shawn would eventually lament over the role he was required to play, inflicting humiliation on kids for the sake of an antiquated rule stating that every Dunning graduate must be able to swim. Over time, he'd check a name off for the hell of it, just to give a kid a break. He'd never witnessed so much stress in his life. But that first day of his first year, he was still following orders, so he blew his whistle and lined them up. Some pushed to the front, wanting to get on with their free period, while others lingered toward the back, arms crossed tightly over their chests, squinting to see without their eyeglasses.

Thirty minutes in, he was barely halfway through the line, and the chlorine was going to his head. It was at this moment that Coach Schwartz lumbered through the tiled echo chamber, waving his clipboard and bellowing, "Don't be shocked. Always a few who can't pass."

A heavyset girl stared down at her feet while Coach Schwartz laughed at his own callousness. He was a giant of the athletic department, the head football coach and assistant baseball coach, as well as the late hockey coach's best friend. Even Shawn had enough sense to know that befriending this man would only help his chances at securing the head coaching job.

"Yeah, maybe," Shawn said, nodding slowly. "But I think this group is going to do just fine."

Coach Schwartz chewed on that retort. "Anyway, a bunch of the other coaches come over to my place on Fridays after practice. Want to join us?"

Shawn had worried it would be slim pickings when it came to socializing, not to mention dating, in rural New Hampshire. He smiled and nodded in response to the invitation. It would be nice to have plans for Friday night, even if it was with a bunch of middle-aged coaches.

CHAPTER 4

Sam and Ethan chatted from the safety of their bunk beds after lights out. Nestled in the top berth, his voice bouncing off the ceiling, Ethan shared what he'd learned about partying on campus. "Besides weed, some guys cut Adderall into lines, and I've heard girls sneak vodka on campus in Nalgene water bottles."

"That's cool." Sam humored Ethan, but Dunning's pranking culture and the Nine's underlying disregard for "the man" had ignited more of a spark in him than any illicit substance ever could.

"So, like, do you want to go in on something with me?" Ethan asked.

"I don't know, Ethan. That's not really my thing."

"What *is* your thing?"

It wasn't the answer Ethan was after, but Sam loved building robots. It inspired the same childhood excitement as diving into the bins of colorful Legos his mother stored in their family room once had. The Roland Center for Robotics, the core of Dunning's new, state-of-the-art science center, had become Sam's playground. It was sleek and white, designed with a Steve Jobs aesthetic, housing all the computing power, circuitry, plastic components, and motors an aspiring engineer could wish for.

He was currently building a remote-controlled device that

would be able to roll beneath his hallmates' desks during study hall, pecking at their feet and emitting mouselike squeaks.

"I don't know, Ethan," he replied. "I'm just figuring things out here, but I like robots."

Ethan was quiet, and after a few seconds, Sam heard light snores coming from above. His thoughts drifted away from pranking and robots to the realm of girls. Sure, he'd taken part in the requisite middle school flirtations, but he'd never before experienced the powerful combination of physical attraction and intellectual connection that he felt for Nathalie de Witt.

"Is this seat free?" Nathalie had asked, pointing to the space next to him their first morning in Precalculus.

"Sure," he'd said, barely looking up.

It wasn't until she sat down that he noticed her cropped hair and multistudded ears, an unconventional look at Dunning, where the mainstream wore long, straight tresses highlighted in varying shades of blond. Nathalie's buzz culminated in a V of baby-like peach fuzz on the nape of her neck. It was all Sam could do not to run a finger across it when she leaned over to work on a problem set.

First period became the highlight of his days. He'd confer with Nathalie over their homework, her concentration accentuating her dimples. Looking down into his backpack to grab a book became an opportunity to admire her petite ankles and sockless feet slipped into a pair of flats. Sam made the most of every interaction, anticipating that this smart girl would surely be transferred to a faster-paced section after the first quarter.

Lying in bed and thinking of Nathalie, he felt his penis harden. He rolled onto his stomach, biting the inside of his cheek, having not yet learned the boarding school technique of masturbating in silence.

Sam couldn't help compare himself to Nathalie or other brainy kids in their class, even the anonymous faces who carried around violin cases and studied Mandarin. It was in the moments just before sleep when he wondered whether, when it came to him, the admissions office had made some kind of mistake. He'd always done very well in school, but the teaching style at Dunning left him uncertain about being up to the task.

Classes were arranged around oval tables, the dimensions of which resulted in each face being visible to every other. There were no lectures, just discussions. Teachers said frighteningly little, steering the conversation only when it went off track and interjecting questions every once in a while. Sam had been reticent to speak up, not wanting to sound stupid, especially not in math class in front of Nathalie.

But at Dunning, being vocal was an important part of every student's grade. It became clear, around those tables, how much some of the kids knew, and how much they liked to show it. Trying to find a way to insert a relevant comment exhausted Sam. By the afternoon, what he looked forward to most about swim practice was being underwater, where he wouldn't have to talk to anyone.

....

Early in the school year, the boys in Wilburton came face-to-face with their first disciplinary action. Dean Harper and Mr. Willis assembled the first-years in the common room, where Vlad Grabowski, a classmate who'd been labeled early on as an outcast, was already seated on one of the long couches. Vlad was tall, overweight, dressed in an off-brand way, and clearly one of the kids who'd gotten into Dunning on smarts alone. He was also a computer science friend of Nathalie's.

Sam and Ethan had whispered about Grabowski's having found a way around the school's Internet firewall with an anonymous IPN, allowing access after 11:00 p.m. He had shared his hacks with Harold Chu, a kid from China who occupied the room at the farthest end of the hall. Harold had paid Grabowski good money to help accommodate his gaming addiction, but he had also used the hack to visit porn websites, and when word got out, other boys had purchased the hack as well.

Chu was the one who got caught. Mr. Willis burst into his room after midnight to find him with his screen open and his pants down. Harold would be the first in their class to get into real hot water, not just a lecture from Dean Harper but an actual face-off with the disciplinary committee.

"Now, boys," Dean Harper said, rocking back on his heels, "you think we don't know what you're doing when you're alone in your room. But we can find out. Eventually, we can find out everything."

Sam caught a glimpse of Ethan's quizzical brow and Max's unfazed expression. Vlad and Harold looked down at the floor.

The dean continued, "Sexual urges exist. No secret there— basic biology. But, as part of the Dunning community, you need to show restraint."

The dean turned toward Harold and Grabowski. "Harold is very lucky. We won't ask him to withdraw. But let this be a warning to all of you. In your rooms and lights out at eleven—and no Internet."

Sam glanced at Grabowski, who he worried might go down as a result of all the interrogations. He had started it all, but after forty days at Dunning, Harold Chu had absorbed enough of a sense of loyalty on the hallway to understand the honor in keeping his mouth shut and taking his punishment alone.

After the dean's lecture, Max denounced Grabowski as the type better suited to befriend gamers across the globe than to connect with human beings in the dorm. But Sam argued that Vlad was okay and that when it came to the world of computing, he was more of a programming architect than a mindless consumer of video entertainment.

That night, during the golden hour between study hall and lights out, their faces sullen and grotesque under the orange glow of new, energy-saving lightbulbs, Sam tried to sew the group back together. He lured Grabowski out of his room with a chessboard and chocolate chip cookies his mother had sent. He patted a space on the carpet for him to join them.

Sam and Vlad set up the chessboard amid the usual banter. Sam was steeped in concentration over his opening move and barely caught the tail end of Max's story.

"If the Nine are so secret, then how do you know about them?" Ethan was asking.

"How do you think?" Max said, implying that, yet again, his answer had to do with the fact that his family was Old Dunning. "Not everyone knows, stupid."

"There are actually two underground groups at Dunning," Vlad said, before picking up his queen and moving it across the board. He rarely spoke in these raucous forums, so his comment caught Sam's attention.

He went on. "There are the Nine, and there's a new group that transcends campuses. It's a hacking community with members at Dunning and elsewhere. They operate online, a bunch of vigilante-justice types."

"Whoa, Grabowski, are you serious, man? Like, freakin' cyber-terrorists at Dunning?" Ethan asked.

"Not terrorists; they're more in it for the thrill of giving jerks what they deserve. I'm surprised you haven't heard of them. There's been a ton of blogging about it."

"Like we sit around reading fucking blogs," said Max.

Grabowski pushed his thick, black-framed glasses back up onto his nose. "It's called Faceless," he said, with an authoritative nod. "Harold Chu knows about it too. Someone contacted him. I guess they liked his disregard for the rules."

Sam was quiet. It made sense—Dunning was the perfect birthing ground for a group of young hackers, a new generation of students who didn't personify the Dunning ideal. He had to think no further than kids like Nathalie and Grabowski, two among the school's growing population of coders who'd invented apps on the side. He'd watched in admiration while Grabowski talked coding lingo with Nathalie. Her fluency implied an intelligence that surpassed even what he witnessed in math class.

"I've never heard of Faceless," said Max.

"Well, maybe you haven't heard of everything," Ethan said.

Sam worked hard to forge camaraderie among the Wilburton first-years, steering their hallway conversations toward topics they could all relate to.

He took it upon himself to pay the guys the compliment of a nickname. "You are hereupon Grabs," Sam declared one night, anointing Vlad's shoulders, as if bestowing knighthood. The older boys took to the monikers, appreciating that Sam intuited how it worked, that nicknaming was one way they showed affection for one another, and that a good nickname could stick for life.

As his friendship with Grabs evolved over the chessboard, Sam marveled at his classmate's mastery of the game. It was emblematic of life at Dunning, where he was often outwitted and overmatched. Sam had been one of the smartest kids in his eighth-grade class, but at Dunning, his classmates were off-the-charts, Russian-chess-genius smart.

This was not the case, however, with many of the Dunning staff and administrators. Mr. Willis, for example, was the opposite of intellectual, avoiding academic conversations with the boys at all costs. "If you want to talk hockey, on the other hand . . ." was his comeback. When he came up to the fourth floor to do his nightly rounds, they tried joking with him, offering him cookies or a slice of pizza, but he'd just pester them to turn their lights out. He claimed he was fed up by the late hour and by the crap the upperclassmen were pulling down on the first floor. And so, instead of befriending their young dorm parent, as they had expected to, the boys in Class Four made cracks about him behind his back.

"Yeah, seems like he should be fun, but what a short fuse," Ethan said.

"He's in way over his head," said Max. "My father wasn't impressed."

"Easily intimidated," said Grabs.

Sam laughed. "To say the least," he said, recalling the third degree his mother had given Willis on move-in day.

Their proctor filled the void, explaining how first year was considered a relative layup, academically speaking.

"So enjoy it now," he grumbled, before slamming the door to his room, where a pile of college applications awaited. It wouldn't be until late into sophomore year, when transferring was too much of a hassle, that the teachers would turn up the heat.

Before their first class in the morning, Sam walked with Ethan, Grabs, and a few others from Wilburton to the dining hall, an austere, dark-paneled space where every graduate's name was inscribed by class in gold-leaf calligraphy. The shimmering script was dizzying in the cacophony of the morning rush. The first time Sam had seen Max swipe his finger across a name, he'd been confused, but Max had eventually explained that that was how legacies paid tribute to their ancestors.

It was another one of those customs that polarized the campus, dividing the legacies from everyone else. Sam had shaken his head when Headmaster Williams had encouraged students who were not descended from alumni to honor graduates of their choosing; there certainly were many famous ones to pick from. But after that speech, Sam, Ethan, and Grabs made a pact: not in a million years.

They tossed their backpacks on the floor between the dining hall's grand double doors and the food line. In the midst of the melee, the boys found solace in routine. Sam pushed a scoopful of powdered eggs around his plate with a hardening piece of toast, Ethan stirred packets of sugar into a cup of coffee, and Grabs slurped up cereal and perused Wired.com on his phone.

After winter break, the upperclassmen formalized a dorm grill in the common room, reselling slices of pizza they ordered from a local restaurant. When Sam lined up with the other first-years, out of both late-night hunger and a desire to be in the older boys' presence, he almost choked when he saw the price: $5 a slice. Sam and a boy from Atlanta stepped out of line, having stuffed only a couple of singles in their pockets.

We're happy to extend credit," said a big lacrosse player, laughing at the usury practice they'd formalized."

"Don't worry—I gotcha, Webber," said Justin, handing over a $10 bill. Sam was learning the disparity between what was considered adequate spending money at Dunning and the $100 his parents expected to last a month. He exchanged an uncomfortable glance with the boy from Atlanta. Buying pizza at the dorm grill was a mistake Sam would never make again, but he got back in line, nauseated by the smell of greasy cheese.

The seniors spoke a lot about dorm unity even as they took advantage of the first-years. To compensate, however, they orchestrated hookups for the younger boys and let them in on the Laundry Room Challenge.

Sam's stomach twisted when he learned the contest rules: a bottle of detergent atop the far-right washing machine meant the space was already reserved for the evening; if the door was closed, under no circumstances should it be opened; before underclassmen accumulated points on the scoreboard, they needed further tutelage in what qualified as a "score"; and—this one was offered more as advice than as a rule—it was best to leave the fluorescent lights on over the dryers, as it was seriously like operating blind when it was totally dark down there.

CHAPTER 5

The growing number of commuters living north of Boston in tax-free New Hampshire often snarled the drive to Dunning. It was during those stop-and-go journeys that the landmarks along the route between our home and Sam's world became ingrained in my mind. The larger-than-life steak restaurant, awash in neon, glowed from the top of a hill on Route 1, signaling my departure from the metropolitan area. It was the type of place I saw us stopping at to celebrate an achievement or a birthday. There was the New Hampshire state liquor store, just over the border, my go-to bathroom break and a place to pick up a few bottles of inexpensive wine. Once we exited the highway and began winding around local roads, there were fewer commercial establishments, although one billboard advertised factory outlets, which I had intended to visit at one point.

Four years sounds like a long time, but Sam's high school career sped by without our ever getting to those outlets or raising glasses over a steak dinner. Because when I got behind the wheel, I drove toward Sam with the same urgency that consumed me the night I rushed back to Ohio after my mother's stroke.

During the winter of Sam's first year, I snuck out of work early on Wednesdays to attend his swim meets. Same thing on Saturdays, although Edward was able to join me then. I'd hop in the car, avoiding his bicycle and carton of bats and baseballs against the wall in the garage. Once in the car, my internal compass pointing north, I'd lighten up, knowing I'd soon be laying eyes on my boy. I'd tick off our progress as the honey-baked-ham store and the ice-skating emporium flew past, eventually leading to the entrance ramp and the interstate.

I'd review the topics I wanted to discuss with Sam. I'd kept a list in my purse and once made the mistake of letting him see it. "Mom's agenda" become his running gripe, a nod to the fact that my questions were never-ending. So I committed several casual inquiries to memory: Did they serve enough vegetables in the dining hall? Did he need a new toothbrush? Had he become friends with the headmaster's daughter yet?

Facebook offered a teeny glimpse into Sam's life. I hadn't allowed him to use it in middle school, but it was the first thing he'd asked permission for at Dunning. "The other kids think I'm a freak," he'd said.

"On one condition," I'd relented. "You have to friend me." His occasional posts and tags, combined with infrequent texts and weekly phone calls, became the data with which I filled in the narrative of his life. I pictured him waking up, going to class, eating meals, swimming, and studying, comforted by the notion that what little else he might have time for was easy to piece together.

There was no substitute, however, for seeing him in the flesh. One Saturday toward the end of his first swim season, we hopped in the car to attend the big contest against Easton, Dunning's archrival. Sam was on the junior varsity squad and used to spotting me in the bleachers. Despite the freezing outdoor temperatures, the pool was a hothouse, and Edward and I shed our winter coats quickly. When Sam climbed up into the stands to greet us during a break in the action, he brought Justin, a sophomore in Wilburton who swam varsity breaststroke and had a spot on one of the relay teams.

"Pleased to finally meet Sam's parents," he said, and beamed, all manners and good looks. We were chatting about how the meet was going when he pointed toward a woman in a fur-trimmed down jacket hurrying across the pool deck. "And here comes my mother, the infamous Mimi Crandall—on time, as usual," he said, smirking.

When she reached us, mildly out of breath, she smiled and extended a hand. "Hello, I'm Mimi, Justin's mother."

"So nice to meet you. I'm Hannah Webber," I said. Finally, another mom I might connect with. I'd been traveling to these meets all season, only to find myself among a few fathers of day students.

After the boys returned to their poolside huddle, Mimi sat next to Edward and me. My pleasure in making her acquaintance quickly disintegrated into nerves as I eyed her blond hair swirled back into a twist, her leather handbag and matching boots, and the expert knot in the silk scarf around her neck. She had a bronze tan, despite its being winter, and chunks of gold on her ears and around her neck. She was *Town & Country*, and I was an unsophisticated suburban Jewess. Her ensemble spoke of a high-powered career or a high-powered family, most likely with a Dunning tradition, and mine pointed to the fact that we were lucky to be here and just passing through.

"So, how is he adjusting?" she asked, pointing to Sam.

"Fine," I said with a ring of pride.

"Don't be surprised if he struggles from time to time. I'm always having to convince Morris we should visit more often. Sometimes Justin just needs bucking up."

This divulgence sparked the thrill of connection, but I had no intimacy at the ready to share in return. "Is Justin your only son?" I ventured.

She chuckled. "Oh God, no. The last of four. My baby." The last part was in air quotes, as if any of these boys, with their manhood bulging against their nylon swimsuits, could be considered such a thing.

"Four children, my goodness. Sam is our only one."

Mimi sighed. "We've got two boys and two girls. They've all gone through Dunning."

"Wow, I can't imagine. Do you live nearby?"

She shook her head. "Manhattan."

We continued with the small talk, registering vital statistics, while Edward edged poolside in anticipation of Sam's one event. Large windows divided the enormous wall across from our seats, allowing in plenty of natural light, even as they were fogged and dripped condensation. The chlorine in the air was starting to irritate my throat.

After a few minutes of silence, Mimi rolled her sleeves above her elbows and asked, "So, how do you pass the time now that your only child is gone?"

How I dreaded that question, as I'd asked it of myself many times. I was the bookkeeper at the dental practice in our town, although I would never admit such a thing to her. Instead, I feigned the nonchalance of the easy life. "I just drive back and forth to these swim meets."

"So lucky you're within driving distance. The hotels up here are just atrocious." Mimi went on to say how she and Morris had bought a small house in town back when their eldest daughter enrolled. "You can snatch them up for less than our annual co-op fee," she murmured. "Fill it with Pottery Barn and Crate and Barrel—nothing you'd live with normally. But, you know, it's fine for up here. I'll have no trouble flipping it after Justin graduates."

I nodded as if I understood, as if I admired her clever real estate play, but my pulse quickened. Even though we were both mothers and she intended to be friendly, I was stumbling onto foreign soil. Money put her on a totally different plane, true, but it was something else too—it was Mimi's breezy familiarity and confidence with how it all worked. I wouldn't truly appreciate until much later what her access meant: the ability to have a son "home" for dinner, or to provide a place for the tutoring to happen—and even the partying. I'd eventually ask Edward if we might be able to rent something small near Dunning too, but he'd look at me as if I'd suggested cutting off his right arm.

Mimi's high-profile presence must have registered somewhere on campus that afternoon, because as soon as Headmaster Williams entered the pool arena, he took extra large steps over the bleachers toward us. He wore a down vest and turtleneck sweater, an outfit likely reserved for casual Saturdays and making rounds of the days' athletic contests against Easton.

"Mimi." He nodded in greeting, removing a leather glove to take her hand.

"Hello, Brad," she said in droll acknowledgment. Then, almost as an afterthought, she added, "You must know the Webbers? Their son is Sam, Class Four. Is that correct?"

"Yes." I nodded. "I'm Hannah Webber."

"Of course, Mrs. Webber. So nice to see you again. How is Sam getting along?"

"Oh, fine, thank you, Headmaster Williams," I stammered in light of the fact that he and Mimi were on a first-name basis. I bit my bottom lip, smiling as he clapped for the swimmers. He was no longer up on a stage but sitting on the same row as me.

When the meet ended, we gathered our coats and waited for the boys to emerge from the locker room. Edward and Sam said goodbye to Mimi and Justin, but I interjected, "We're going out to dinner, if you'd like to join us."

"So nice of you," Mimi said, taking out her phone, "but we have other plans."

Walking to the burger place Sam had suggested, I took in cold, deep breaths. I wouldn't remember how he'd swum or who had won the big meet. I wouldn't remember any detail except that Headmaster Williams had found us in the bleachers and that I'd made a friend in Mimi Crandall.

I was still smiling when the menus were distributed and our water glasses were being filled. "What a nice afternoon," I said, looking back and forth between Edward and Sam, beaming at the tableau our family made: engaged parents, prodigy son.

"I guess," said Sam.

"I enjoyed meeting your friend," I said.

"Justin's a good guy," said Sam, stretching his arms and yawning.

"And his mother was so friendly. I really liked her. Too bad the season is almost over. I'd love to see her again."

Sam stared at his menu with a blank expression.

After we ordered our food, Edward sat back, regarding Sam's slouch. "Everything all right, son?"

Sam shrugged in response. Edward and I waited for him to speak while he looked down at his lap. I bent to see his complexion reddening.

"Sam? What's the matter?" I asked.

"I dunno. This place is hard. Sometimes I wish I could just come home."

Edward leaned over and patted him on the shoulder.

"But you're doing so well," I said. "And you're making nice friends—like Justin."

Sam looked in my direction, tears welling in his lower eyelids. "Oh, Sam," I said, patting his other shoulder. "Did something happen?"

"Nothing 'happened,' Mom. It's just tiring. Not just the school-work. Making friends. People judge your every move. And when I just want to be alone, Ethan's in the room."

"Winter is always long and trying," I said, remembering the headmaster's warnings about homesickness and Mimi's needing to "buck Justin up."

"Nothing here is simple."

"I know, son," Edward said, nodding and resting his palm on Sam's shoulder.

"Sometimes I just wish I'd stayed home and gone to the public high school."

Edward started, "You can always—"

"Oh, Sam, you wouldn't want to do that," I interrupted, shooting Edward a warning glance. "The education you're getting here is second to none. High school is hard no matter where you are."

Edward frowned in my direction before finishing his thought. "Look, Sam, there's no hard-and-fast rule that says you can't come back home and enroll in the public school."

I shook my head. "You could come home after Saturday classes next weekend. I'll cook something for you."

"It's not the food, Mom." Whatever tears he'd produced were now drying as his expression turned steely.

"Okay, then I'm sure whatever it is will pass. But I want you to know that I'll come pick you up for a weekend visit anytime."

Sam pressed his lips together and nodded. Our food arrived, and Edward inhaled the aroma of his cheeseburger. I poured dressing on my salad and winked at Sam. It was an old game of ours: creating a diversion so I could steal some of his french fries.

Edward saved his thoughts for the ride home. "We need to listen to him, Hannah. Boarding school is more grueling than you can ever imagine."

"Thousands of kids graduate from boarding schools every year, Edward. It's not like it's impossible," I said, looking out my side window. "And of course I listen to Sam. I text him all the time." We were passing the headmaster's house, the white Victorian, and my mind returned to Mimi Crandall and our casual conversation with Bradley Williams by the pool. I'd googled his bio plenty of times, but after he'd moved from the swim meet on to the basketball game, Mimi had provided some color commentary.

Apparently, Williams had started at Dunning as an eager young English teacher while his peers were either being sent off to fight in Vietnam or protesting the war. He'd been a favorite of what was then the all-male student body for organizing off-campus theater outings and literary events in Boston. In fact, he'd been a teacher when Mimi's husband, Morris, and his brothers had attended Dunning.

Williams worked his way up to department head, serving his time in the dorms. His bachelorhood came to an end when he married Victoria Akins. There had been speculation about how Williams had convinced a good-looking woman like Victoria to move her law practice to New Hampshire. The consensus was that their family had arranged it. They were distant cousins, and she had political ambitions best suited for conservative New Hampshire, and he, well, he needed a wife.

Having gained the loyalty of his colleagues, and with an image improved by his new married status, Williams was promoted to dean of faculty. He left the progressive persona behind and adopted an enthusiasm for the classics, asserting, as every head of school before him had, that a true Dunning education included a mastery of the dead languages. It had always been a distinct honor to be awarded a classics diploma and for the headmaster to bestow a laurel wreath upon those special students' heads at commencement. (Not that any of her children had received one, Mimi added.)

Williams proved as savvy a politician as he was an English teacher, eventually moving his young family into the beautiful home in the center of campus. The board of trustees named him headmaster twenty-five years, almost to the day, after he began at Dunning. The men in the Crandall family had held out hope that a former teacher could rise to the occasion, but his lack of business sense and his propensity for handing out financial aid willy-nilly had soured them on the man. Mimi had listened to their complaints around her dining table.

CHAPTER 6

S am leaned against his headboard with Ethan's Beats on, listening to the Doobie Brothers, a band his father had turned him
on to the time they'd varnished the back deck together. The window
was open, but he'd drawn his blind against the sunlight, although
the breeze still carried in the scent of recently cut grass. The vinyl
blew back and forth against the window frame with an irritating
smack that was off beat with the music.

He stared at formulas as music pulsated in his ears. It was a
small personal act of defiance that would have driven his mother
crazy. "Take those things off! You can't study like that," he could
still hear her saying, even though he'd been away from home for
nine months.

"Look," Ethan had said, before going outside to join their
friends, "we've almost made it through our first year, through a
year of Dean Harper's crazy rules, and spring's here. There are loads
of girls outside. Let's go!" But Sam wouldn't budge. Most of the guys
were down on the benches outside the front door, playing Frisbee
and flirting. He thought he'd even heard Andrea's voice mixed in
between balls bouncing on the pavement and the hoots from the
Wiffle ball world series that was now into game seven on the quad.
Of course she'd be down there, fishing for an invitation to prom,

probably showing plenty of skin in her halter top and cutoff shorts, as if it were eighty-five degrees instead of sixty.

Seniors in the dorm had been buzzing for days about slaying their prom dates, their last hookup before summer vacation. Those were the best ones of all, their proctor had boasted. "The girls can get sort of wild, and you won't have to see them again."

Sam didn't want to hear it from the older boys anymore, about how the first-years should "go for it," how they could accumulate points on the laundry room scoreboard. Andrea was the type to walk right into their trap, and it made his head ache. Until a week earlier, he'd considered her his girlfriend. Then, the previous Sunday morning, when he'd texted, "Brunch?" she'd pinged back, "Srry Sam, we're dun."

"Screw her," Ethan had said, looking over his shoulder.

But Sam couldn't talk about it. It was all he could do to attend class. Dunning was like a giant fishbowl with no place to hide. He shut himself in his room to avoid Andrea and her friends.

She was the kind of girl who showed up at Dunning eager to be rid of her childhood. She had zeroed in on him after dinner one night when he was leaving the dining hall with Ethan and Justin. Justin's "Hey, Andrea," was all the encouragement she needed to fall into step with them.

"What's up, Sam?" she asked. The fact that she knew his name surprised him, let alone the teasing manner in which she drew it out.

It was Ethan who told him that was his cue, that Andrea was expressing interest. He helped Sam compose a text that night, confident he'd get a reply right away because it was obvious she was "into him."

It turned out that Ethan was indeed attuned to girls' signals: Andrea did text him back and found him again the next night after dinner. Sam walked her back to her dorm before study hall. "Can you get parietals this weekend?" she asked with a coy smile, referring to permission to spend time in a dorm room of the opposite sex from nine to ten, with the lights on, the door open, and three feet on the floor (since Dunning girls were expected to keep their legs crossed).

She'd carved out a small slice of privacy in her room, where she and Sam made out. He got the feeling this wasn't Andrea's first time.

"I hate the way we have to leave the door open," she said, after the dorm parent cleared her throat loudly and peered in at them. In an attempt to make up for his inexperience, and wanting to impress her, Sam mentioned the setup in the Wilburton laundry room. "I mean, if we want more privacy," he said.

"Really?" she responded, trying on the voice of a sexy kitten.

For the next week, she blasted him with texts: "Do laundry??"

Sam's heart beat faster whenever he thought about the imminent loss of his virginity. He'd always hoped it might be with someone like Nathalie, but she'd had an upper-class boyfriend since the first week of school and was way out of Sam's league. So he had wound up with Andrea, a heavy-chested, made-up girl whose suggestive texts made even Ethan blush. And now he couldn't back down.

The following Saturday night, instead of going to the eighties dance they'd signed out for, Sam snuck Andrea into the Wilburton basement. Justin volunteered to clear his use of the laundry room with the seniors in the dorm, and as Sam folded blankets into a nest on the cement floor, his stomach sank at the realization that they all knew what he was up to. He shut the door before fishing a condom out of the box of detergent on the shelf, his palms sweating. When he looked toward Andrea for some sign of mutual anxiety, she was busy folding up her dress and taking off her bra.

Sam hit all the light switches, then remembered the advice he'd gotten at the dorm grill and flipped the ones by the dryers back on, slipped out of his pants, and sat down with her. He kissed her softly, patting her long hair and inserting his tongue into her mouth. He would have been happy just kissing; he liked making out. Within a minute, however, Andrea pulled Sam on top of her; their kissing became more passionate and their touching more urgent. The sensation of her breasts against his bare chest was overwhelming.

His erection came quickly, but, while fumbling with the condom, he lost it.

Andrea rested on her elbows with an air of amusement. He caught her admiring her upturned nipples and taut abdomen while he stroked his own penis, trying to get hard again. He interpreted her smirking as criticism, and intense heat rushed through his body. Amid his embarrassment and beating heart, he gave up on the idea of intercourse and threw the slimy condom on the floor.

"What'd you do that for?" Andrea asked, her tone more irritated than sympathetic.

"Let's just go to the dance," Sam said, handing back her underwear. They walked to the student center and mixed into the dwindling group on the dance floor, a few kids in neon wigs hopping up and down to Cyndi Lauper.

The next morning, when he texted about brunch, she sent her curt breakup message and Sam threw his phone in a drawer.

He didn't care about being out of touch, but his mother wouldn't like getting sent directly to voice mail. He bristled at her hypocrisy, complaining that teens overused their phones while counting on him to always have his on. He'd preempt her with a punctual call at their appointed time, projecting plenty of enthusiasm in order to get her off his back. She was still easily sidetracked by his mention of the ivy-covered brick buildings, how much he loved his classes, or the headmaster and his daughter.

Sweat beading on his forehead, he turned another page of his physics notebook. With his door shut and the blind drawn, there was little air movement, and the heat from his reading lamp was cooking the skin on his shoulder. Not able to stand it any longer, he got up to crack his door open, and that was when he saw it: a cream-colored envelope on the floor. Had Andrea slipped him an apology? He turned it over in his hands, reading his full name in fancy calligraphy: Samuel Jameson Webber. He studied the lettering and wax seal and sat back down on the edge of the bed. He carefully slit the envelope open with a pen and pulled out a note card.

Sunday, 6/9

Dear Sam,

We are writing to invite you to join something audacious and bold. Your acrobatic stunt was impressive, and your robotic brilliance should be put to use. If you would like to become part of the most important brotherhood in American history, please take the following steps.

Before **9:00** *p.m. this evening, go to the library. Volume 965.12 encompasses the globe, but you need only be concerned with our tiny corner. Books contain many letters, both lowercase and capitals. The clue you'll find should spur your literary juices. The secret to completing this challenge is to be humble—no need to always be the big man.*

Do not speak of this invitation to anyone, or it will be rescinded. Whether you choose to take the next step or not, we request that you destroy this letter in the next **nine** *minutes to prevent it from ending up in the wrong hands.*

Sincerely,

Your admirers

Sam perspired even more, but not because of his sweltering room. There were only a few who knew about his "acrobatics" when, earlier in the term, the seniors had dared him and Ethan to scale the fire escape onto the roof and drop three rotten eggs down Mr. Willis's chimney. It was just a week after all his furniture had been moved outside in the snow, and he was pretty fed up. Sam and Ethan fought to contain their laughter when Mr. Willis paced the halls during study hall, barking, "You little fuckers, I've had it. And don't you think I won't figure out who did this!"

Before he ripped the note to shreds, his eyes lingered on the word "nine," penned in a bolder stroke. He'd always assumed that Max was full of shit when it came to the ways of the secret society, but the possibility was now before him. Grabs might have known what to make of it, but Sam worried somebody could be watching to see if he broke the confidence. Regardless of whether the invitation was real or not, he couldn't be seen as caring too much.

Sam planned to follow the note's instructions while everybody else was at dinner. He'd been skipping meals since the Andrea incident anyway, living on cereal bars from the student center to avoid her gossiping friends.

At five thirty, he swung his backpack over his shoulder and headed to the library. It was another signature Dunning building, five stories tall, constructed with the funds from a reunion class gift. Sam walked through a turnstile at the entrance and past the long circulation desk, where the librarian smiled sympathetically, having probably not seen many kids enter on this beautiful day, and especially not during the dinner hour. After Sam located the small sign on the wall that listed the call numbers, she returned to the magazine she was reading.

The 900s were for history and geography and housed on the top floor. He opted for one of the four corner stairwells, taking the stairs two at a time and emerging out of breath through the metal fire door at the top. The call number was written on the palm of his hand, and even though the ink had smudged slightly, it was also imprinted in his mind.

Volume 965.12 was an oversize book entitled *The Great World Atlas*. He flipped through the pages, looking for Dunning's "tiny corner." He found the page illustrating the New England states and looked extra closely, focusing on the outline of New Hampshire. The label for Concord was circled in yellow highlighter. *Many letters, both lowercase and capital*, Sam remembered. "Concord" was in capitals, and it was the capital of New Hampshire. It must be the next clue.

The Concord that got his "literary juices" going had nothing to do with New Hampshire but rather with Massachusetts. It had been a theme in his middle school as well, the fact that so many important writers came from a neighboring town. In First-Year English, Dunning students traditionally read Ralph Waldo Emerson, Henry David Thoreau, Louisa May Alcott, Nathaniel Hawthorne, and

Margaret Fuller, all natives of Concord, Massachusetts. That had to be the connection, but he was stuck. *To be humble? No need to be the big man?* He went over the books they'd read that year. The elevator call signal chimed, and the doors opened, prompting Sam to close the atlas. He sought isolation in the stairwell and looked at his watch. His mother would be expecting his weekly call, and he'd left his phone in his desk drawer. She might give him ten or fifteen minutes' leeway, but she wouldn't be put off any longer than that. He concentrated on the first-year syllabus, still fresh in his mind, as he'd been studying for the final. Whoever had written the note was giving a nod to Dunning's curriculum.

He closed his eyes. The homework included a lot of reading, some of which they hadn't had time to discuss in class, specifically works by Alcott and Fuller, and he remembered one of the girls challenging the teacher: "Why aren't we discussing any of the women authors?" The teacher replied, "You're welcome to raise any salient points about Alcott and Fuller in our class discussions, in your upcoming essay, or, for that matter, on the final exam."

Sam sat a few minutes longer, then clapped his hand on the book. Of course! *No need to be the big man.* The answer was *Little Women.* Sam jogged down the stairs to the fiction stacks and found Alcott and three volumes of her novel. He pulled all of them off the shelf at once to uncover a slip of paper taped to the gray metal shelf. It read, "Congratulations, Sam. Tomorrow, 3:09 a.m., Wilburton boiler room. Be there."

He headed to the door with a little spring in his step. The librarian looked up again from her magazine as Sam passed through the turnstile. "Have a good night," she said.

"Thanks. You too," he said.

He bumped into Ethan on the steps outside. "Hey, I was looking for you at dinner. Where've you been?"

Sam searched his face for some sign that Ethan might also be embarking on a special errand to the library. He squinted into the lowering sun. The clocks had sprung forward that weekend, bringing an unsettling burst of natural light after the long winter.

Somewhere in the distance, music was blaring, and the echoes of girls' laughter bounced off the brick buildings.

"Oh," Sam said, the heat rising in his face. "In the library."

"Well, yeah, no kidding. That's obvious. But why'd you skip dinner?"

Sam had never been good at coming up with lies on the spot, had never been good at lying, period. "I ate quickly and then came over here to look for a book." He stared at the ground, kicking the toe of his sneaker into the library's marble step.

"For the history final?" They were in the same class, but Sam had been outperforming Ethan all year.

"No, I just needed to double-check something for the essay question in English."

Ethan wasn't buying it. "Were you meeting up with Andrea?" He crossed his arms and nodded his head as if he'd just solved the mystery. "I knew it. That breakup didn't last long."

"Hell no," Sam said loudly. "I told you, she dumped me." Kids coming out of dinner were staring. Sam's nostrils flared. Of all people, Ethan should have empathized with how humiliating the whole situation had been.

"All right, all right. Calm down, dude."

A gust of wind blew the hair from Sam's forehead. Just moments earlier, he'd been elated at having solved the riddle. Now a wedge was forming in the first real friendship he'd ever had.

"What's going on, Sam? I mean, you locked yourself up in our room all day, and now you're acting pretty weird."

"I'm sorry, man," he said, fidgeting with the straps of his backpack. "My mom's on my case again. I've just been dealing with some shit at home." Ethan had met Hannah Webber, so it was a pretty good excuse whenever Sam needed one.

"Sucks."

"Yeah. I'll catch you later, okay? Back in the room?" Sam took off to call his parents, his hunger now replaced by a pit in his stomach at the memory of Ethan's confused face.

....

An invitation to become one of the Nine typically gave rise to a little chest puffing and bravado, but Sam was different, worrying the note and scavenger hunt might be another joke. The boys on their floor had been having fun at one another's expense all year, and the more he thought about it, the more this seemed like the type of stunt Max might pull.

After all, Sam wasn't a legacy, he wasn't great with girls, and there were plenty of kids who were smarter. He had friends, but he wasn't popular. The only area in which he'd distinguished himself was on the robotics team, specifically by clinching the MIT regional championship back in April, for the first time in Dunning history.

And he couldn't take full credit for that either. He and Astrid, a first-year girl in the club, had retreated to the student center after a particularly stressful meeting just weeks before the competition. Opening the door, he'd taken a deep breath, as the student center had the potential to be a social hotbed. To Sam's astonishment, Astrid waltzed right up to Nathalie, who was sitting with some of the boys on the soccer team.

"What are you two up to?" Nathalie looked confused.

"I didn't know you guys knew each other," said Sam.

"Sam, Astrid's my roommate," Nathalie said.

"Huh." Sam chuckled. He'd only talked circuitry with Astrid. Now, standing next to Nathalie, she seemed to reflect some of her roommate's glow.

Nathalie turned to Sam. "So, all Astrid talks about is this MIT competition. I think I heard her murmuring about a cell phone remote in her sleep."

Astrid blushed. "Nathalie, *you're* the one who should be on the team. Sam, she's so good at this stuff."

He raised an eyebrow. "Well, I know she's good at math."

"She won a national engineering prize in eighth grade."

"Seriously?"

"Yeah." Nathalie shrugged. "My sister warned me to keep that on the DL at Dunning. She said it wasn't the image I'd want to project."

"So, you live vicariously through your roommate?" Sam teased.

"Sort of."

"She gives me ideas all the time," Astrid said.

"How's the robot coming along?"

Sam lamented that their progress was way behind schedule.

"Let me get this straight: you have two weeks until game time, and the senior captain told everyone to go figure out the bugs on their own?"

"I know, right?" Astrid said.

"I can get the key to the lab from Mr. Martin," Nathalie said, her green eyes gleaming.

"Wait, you want to help?" Sam asked.

"I mean, if you guys let me, I'd love to tag along."

"I bet we can have a fully operational prototype by Monday morning," Astrid said.

Despite her sister's warnings, Nathalie joined the team while remaining one of the coolest girls in their class. Nathalie, Sam, and Astrid became the core of Dunning robotics.

Winning the regional championship and being applauded onstage had been an exhilarating experience that got them noticed by Headmaster Williams and, more importantly, by Harry Roland, '75, the benefactor of the science center and patron of the school's robotics efforts. He was a pioneering legend of Silicon Valley and a lesser-known contemporary of Bill Gates.

"Congratulations, Sam. I hear you were the mastermind behind it all," Harry Roland said after Sam, Astrid, and Nathalie were recognized during a Wednesday morning assembly.

"It was a real team effort," Sam replied, as Roland shook his hand vigorously.

Sam figured the robotics championship gave him more of a nerd status than any currency the Nine would value. Plus, if it was high-tech talent they were looking for, someone like Grabs would have been the obvious choice.

But if the invitation addressed with his name in slanting script was for real, he was ripe for the picking. He hadn't expected Dunning to demoralize him so early and so often. When he performed well on his first three Spanish quizzes, he was reassigned to a harder section, where he struggled. The coach of the swim team was unimpressed with his efforts, and then there was his disgrace with Andrea.

The Nine would be something of his own, something his parents—specifically his mother—would know nothing about. Attending boarding school had shone an uncomfortable light on how she'd carved herself into him, almost burying a weight he had to carry. Ever since she'd dropped him off, he'd been consumed by a perverse push and pull in their relationship, wanting her to feel his absence as poignantly as he felt hers.

During their weekly calls, he held back on purpose, enjoying the edge in her voice. After their dinner at the burger restaurant, when she'd basically said he couldn't transfer out, he was determined to will his independence forth, to sever the millions of threadlike ties to her one by one. He imagined the Nine providing secretive, dangerous, Harry Potter–like thrills. And while Dunning wasn't exactly Hogwarts, it was similar enough. The Nine had the potential of becoming a true brotherhood, more so than the hodge-podge of first-years he'd been thrown in with on the fourth floor of Wilburton. Six of the Nine would be like big brothers, the perfect antidote to all those long, lonely years of only childhood.

CHAPTER 7

Sam set his phone alarm for 3:00 a.m. and snuck out of the room so as not to wake Ethan. Entering the boiler room nine minutes later, he found Justin Crandall in his pajamas, waiting cross-legged on the floor. Justin's goofy smile and shimmering swimmer's hair were uplit by a flashlight he grasped in front of his chest.

"You?" Sam said, rushing forward in amazement. He couldn't believe Justin was the grand prize.

"Dude! I'm so pumped about this." Justin jumped to his feet and slapped Sam on the shoulder. It was a brotherly, welcoming gesture, Sam's first man-to-man, and despite the unusual setting, it flooded him with warmth.

After the back slapping and laughs, Justin adopted a more serious tone. "I need to lay out all the risks; then you can decide whether to take it or leave it," he said.

He spoke slowly, emphasizing the enormity of the tradition. He described the legacy of the Nine, its history, its exclusivity, and the honor of being tapped. Although his voice was solemn, Justin's face softened, and every so often he winked. "You'll need to take a vow saying you'll put the brotherhood above all else."

Sam nodded that he understood.

"Okay. What have you heard about us already?"

"Just . . . just rumors."

"Well, the active membership consists of three sophomores, three juniors, and three seniors, but the alumni number in the hundreds."

"Yeah, that's what I heard."

"The brotherhood was started by nine students back in 1890. They wrote out the group's mission on an old scroll, which we still have. We'll read from it to begin the first meeting of the fall."

Justin touched on the Nine's major milestones, which seemed to have petered out in the sixties. He said interest in the group sort of fluctuated after that but was resurrected two decades later, in his father's era, when Dunning started admitting girls and increasing the number of minority students. "You see, some alumni feared those changes marked the end of Dunning as they knew it, so they resuscitated the Nine to provoke the administration and regain control."

Sam frowned.

"Don't worry—it's not like that anymore," Justin said. "I mean, of course we still try to undermine the bastards, but now we just pull pranks."

Sam laughed. "There have been some really good ones this year."

"It's gotten tougher since Williams hired Dean Harper. He was brought here to out us, to expose our identities."

Sam shook his head. "But it's like the best-kept secret on campus," he said. For example, Sam had never expected Justin, his clumsy, easygoing friend, to be one of them. In hindsight, it should have been obvious, given all his family connections.

Justin rubbed his eyes. "It's late. We should get back upstairs. But I just want you to know you don't have to worry. I'll be the one guiding you through the process."

"What process?"

"Initiation, but you'll do fine."

Sam's heart raced as he realized his acceptance wasn't a fait accompli. "What happens?"

"There'll be a ceremony and then a little bit of hazing, but it's fun. You'll like it," Justin said. "After you pass everything, we have meetings to decide which missions to move forward with. We've been doing a lot of stuff, but it's not high-tech, not like your robotics." He chuckled. "We want some remote-controlled stuff—stuff that's funny and cutting-edge but doesn't hurt anybody."

"And it's not, like, a protest anymore?"

"Huh?"

"Because of the girls and, like, the minorities?"

Justin stared back at Sam, as if he didn't quite understand or didn't want to deal with so pointed a question at this late hour. In the dim light, with his blond hair askew, he reminded Sam of a dopey golden retriever, with round, searching eyes and a puzzled tilt to his head.

"Nah, I mean, we're in it for the attention, and mostly the laughs," Justin finally replied. "And who doesn't like to annoy adults?"

Sam smiled and nodded.

"We need to let them know who's really in charge," Justin said, regaining momentum. "Williams thinks he *is* Dunning Academy. But nothing could be further from the truth. There are so many brilliant, important people who've graduated from this place, and they look out for their own. Think about it: the way Williams and Harper take themselves so seriously is actually offensive. My father and my uncle always say those two are only here to keep the heat on and make sure the food gets served. We have highly paid, avant-garde teachers and a precocious student body. It's a recipe for beautiful things, but the rules police want to get in the way."

"Like Mr. Willis?"

"Exactly! The Nine bring guys like him down to earth. And our alums support us completely."

"What do you mean?" Sam asked. It wasn't as if he'd ever seen grown men who weren't part of the staff or faculty roaming the campus.

"They challenge us to think big; budgets aren't an issue. If you need expensive electronic parts, that won't be a problem."

Sam felt his pulse quicken. "I'm dying to get my hands on

some new circuit boards. The only ones we get are for the MIT competition."

"That's why we recruited you, Sam. You're the future. We need you to up our game, especially in light of this Faceless group. They're like the whole Occupy movement, exposing privilege and the like. When our alumni council learned about their stronghold on the Dunning campus, let's just say they weren't pleased. But, like I said, Faceless is only online; they don't use the tunnels."

"Wait, back up. What tunnels?"

"Sam, my boy, you have barely scratched the surface of what exists here. After you're officially initiated, Dunning will become your oyster."

Sam sat with that thought for a moment, the idea of accessing places unknown. Before Justin ended the conversation, however, he needed to ask one more question.

"Who are the other initiates in my class?" He held out hope for Ethan.

"There's Raymond, you know, on the football team? His father and grandfather were Nine, so he was guaranteed. And then there's this kid Saunders, who's smart, like you, plays soccer and runs track and is fast as hell. He's also a little bit off the radar. Dean Harper assumes we're all jocks and legacies, so we've picked a few he'd never suspect."

Sam swallowed the backhanded compliment. "Have you considered my roommate, Ethan—"

"Sorry, dude, but we have our reasons. But be grateful I fended off that jerk Max. It was tough—he's a legacy, you know."

Sam exhaled in disappointment.

"Don't worry. You're part of the special forces now," Justin said. "We'll be everything you need." He took Sam by the shoulder.

"Okay, so, what's next?" Sam asked, relaxing under Justin's intoxicating smile.

"Wait for contact to be made. It'll be over the summer. Your orientation materials will be delivered to you before school starts next September."

Sam nodded, already thinking about how he'd keep his mother from snooping through his mail. Justin slapped him again on the shoulder. He was only one year older, but his strength penetrated Sam's back.

"There's one last thing," Justin whispered, as they walked through the door.

"What?"

"It's sort of for security purposes. Just helps keep tabs on everyone." Justin handed him a first-generation pager. "If it beeps, follow the directions and call in. If it gets lost or goes missing, no problem—no data is stored on it; nothing is retrievable. But try not to lose it over the summer. It's how we'll find you. Do you have travel plans?"

"I don't think so."

"They tracked me down on my family's vacation to Italy. Delivered my orientation package with the room service tray one morning in Florence. It knocked my socks off."

Sam's initiation package arrived in August alongside the Sunday paper. It was in a FedEx envelope addressed to Sam Webber, Class Three—the first he'd ever received.

"Something from the dean's office came for you, sweetie," his mother chirped, her curiosity ringing in the air.

Sam lunged for the package across the breakfast table, almost knocking over his orange juice.

"Hey, careful there, bucko," his father said.

"Where did you find it? I mean, when did it come?"

His father eyed him. "I went out on the front stoop to get the paper this morning, and there it was."

"Hmm. Dean Harper must have rewritten the rules over the summer." Sam placed it on the floor by his feet. His mother frowned, undoubtedly disappointed that he wasn't going to open it in front of her.

"Rewriting the infamous D Book—that even makes *my* job sound fun," his father said.

"Since I have you for only a few more days, I'm going to make you some eggs," his mother said, squeezing Sam's shoulders.

"No, thanks—cereal's fine," he said. After gulping down a bowl, he let out an exaggerated yawn, stretching his hands overhead. He picked up the package and tucked it safely under his arm. "I need to go upstairs and finish my summer reading."

"Yeah, you better get on that," his father said. "Only two days before your holiday ends."

In his room, he locked the door, cut one end of the mailer with his desk scissors, and emptied the contents on his bed. After unraveling a few layers of bubble wrap, he found a spiral-bound book, about the same thickness as their community phone directory. Sam flipped open the cover and read the first page.

In the routine world of academy life, where dullness always hangs overhead, pranks bring about laughter, visceral satisfaction, and awe. And they live on for decades because of their retellings. While the administrators may believe that Dunning exists only to serve their careers, pranks are most needed. When a paranoid authority aims to restrict inquisitive youth, the Nine will respond with humor. The Nine give power back to the students, the ones Ezekiel Dunning built the school for in the first place.

Instilling such a mindset has always been the hallmark of a true Dunning education, not just for the Nine but for the entire student body. In life, there are risk-takers and those who admire the risk-takers. You are being enlisted as a steward of a centuries-old institution. Your mission is a noble one.

Sam brightened at the idea of being noble, of being a risk-taker.

"Sweetie, do you have any dirty laundry I can throw in?" his mother called through his closed door.

"No," Sam hollered back, folding his blanket over the book.

The pager Justin had given him beeped inside his desk drawer. He hopped up to retrieve it. It read, "Delivery successful? 1 = yes, 2 = no." He pushed the number 1 and hit SEND. Then another message appeared on the small screen. He had to find his glasses. "Read entire manual before tomorrow's meeting."

Tomorrow? Sam hadn't planned on returning to Dunning for two days. He put on his glasses and began typing on the tiny keys. "I return in two days." A few minutes later, the pager buzzed. "Meeting tomorrow, midnight, in the Tomb. Read manual."

How would he get his mother to drop him off a day early for a midnight meeting? And what tomb? Willis would probably be difficult about letting him move in early, although Sam knew the dorm would be open for the international kids and the preseason athletes.

He thought for a minute, then decided he'd tell his parents he'd been invited to an end-of-summer party hosted by one of the day students. That would make his mother happy—she loved to think he had lots of friends. He folded back his blanket and returned to the manual, searching for directions to the Tomb.

Sam poked his way through prickly branches while thorns scratched his neck. He held a flashlight in one hand and shielded his face with the other as he followed the trail marked by pine cones. He'd convinced himself he was wandering aimlessly, until he spotted the next unmistakable upright pine cone, its tip doused with a touch of Day-Glo paint.

The instructions had been clear: wear gym shorts; keep the hood of his sweatshirt on; and, upon reaching the eighteenth pine cone, stand erect in the clearing, keep his eyes closed, and whistle a short birdlike call.

When he opened his eyes, Justin was standing a few feet away, frowning. "It's about time."

Sam felt heat rise in his face, but then Justin's scowl quickly melted into a laugh. "Just kidding! You made it! Lighten up, dude." He took a step forward and embraced Sam. "Welcome," Justin continued. "C'mon, follow me."

Sam's relief was short-lived, as Justin deftly scampered off and Sam had to hustle after him. He caught up in front of a large outcropping of rocks. The boulders increased in size, and a stone ledge towered above his head.

"In here!" He followed Justin through an opening. He hunched to enter the cave, but the dirt floor descended at a sharp angle, creating just enough headroom beneath a dripping limestone ceiling. Sam proceeded ten feet toward a camping lantern and what appeared to be a large, low altar made of stone. He and Justin joined the circle of boys waiting cross-legged on the ground around a mound of burning embers.

"Okay," the leader's deep voice announced from inside a hood. "Welcome to the Tomb." He went on to explain that the space was so named because alumni often bequeathed a portion of their ashes for scattering around the edges of the dirt floor. "The space in which they gathered," he said, "was sanctified."

Sam sucked in his cheeks to keep his jaw from dropping. He searched the others around the circle for signs of surprise, but the lanterns and hoods cast dark shadows. However, he did eventually spot the solemn faces of Saunders and Raymond, his fellow initiates.

The senior leader of the Nine, Sam would learn, was also called Captain Dunning. He rapped on the altar with a gavel. "It's time to begin the one hundred and twenty-fifth meeting of the Nine," he said. He spread a parchment scroll across the altar. A second boy held a lantern inches above its surface, and the captain began to read its antique script: "We, the Nine, vow to uphold the brotherhood above all else. . . ."

The pagan nature of it all immediately struck Sam. The scroll's wooden handles were a replica of the only other scroll he was familiar with: the Torah. He flashed back to his bar mitzvah, retrieving the sacred paper from the ark and chanting its ancient Hebrew. He remembered the pride on his mother's face. He shivered now, sitting on the damp dirt floor, sweat beading on his forehead amid this unfolding idolatry.

The captain finished reading, but Sam was frozen. It was all so medieval and dreamlike. He sensed the other boys staring at him. Justin pulled him into the circle, closer to the fire. Justin hugged Sam, and before he knew what was happening, the captain took hold of his leg and seared a brand into Sam's thigh with a hot poker. Justin muffled Sam's scream with a hand over his mouth. He then pushed Sam toward a large leather-bound tome open wide on the altar. Justin leaned over his shoulder, pointing to the spot on the page where Sam needed to sign. Sam bit his lip and wrote his name, and Justin pulled him into a close embrace. "Welcome, Brother Webber."

CHAPTER 8

"Did you hear from him today?" I asked one evening, glancing at the empty chair at our table.

"No, why would I?" Edward responded.

"No reason, just thought maybe . . ." My voice faded like the autumn sun outside our kitchen window.

"He'll call on Sunday, like he always does."

Whatever satisfaction we'd once derived from our domestic life was disappearing. I'd always prided myself on rolling up my sleeves and fixing things, but the shifting tectonic plates beneath our household's foundation rendered me powerless. By Sam's sophomore year, our evenings had turned into a rudimentary exchange of information across the kitchen table.

"How was your day?"

"Same as usual."

"Can you take the Subaru in for an inspection?"

"Maybe next week."

After dinner, I'd tackle a rising pile of unfolded laundry and ironing, and Edward would deposit his dirty dishes in the sink with a sigh, then head into the family room, where he'd kick back on his lounger and turn on a movie.

It was mid-September, and Edward hadn't yet registered that the High Holidays were beginning. Rosh Hashanah would start the following sundown, but, given that my husband was oblivious and my son wasn't home, my heart wasn't into making a traditional meal, not even slicing apples to serve with honey for a sweet new year. I'd maintained those traditions for my boy, passing them down as a mitzvah. He'd loved spiraling the dough into a round challah. I taught him that this was the time of year when we atoned for our sins and made a fresh start. He'd look into my eyes, never voicing what he might want to change, and I'd return his gaze, smiling comfort, reassuring him that we all had things we could improve upon.

I remember his little voice asking why the Jewish new year always coincided with a new academic year.

"Because we are the people of the book," I explained proudly. His eyes glistened, and he smiled at my reply, carefully inserting raisins into the raw dough.

Attending Yom Kippur services at the end of the holy days had always been more important to me. Edward made a show of accompanying me when we were first married, but he begged off once Sam's shoulder grew high enough for me to lean on.

Now I needed those Yom Kippur services more than ever. That Sunday on the phone with Sam, I broached the idea of his joining me at temple. Before he even had a chance to reply, I took it back. It was silly to suggest he might be able to leave school midweek. I would attend services by myself.

He said he'd go to hillel services with Vlad, a Jewish boy from Brooklyn who lived in his dorm. Back when we'd toured the campus, the guide had assured me the Jewish Student Alliance was popular, if only for the Dixie cups of wine it was known to serve. Now I questioned how many students would really miss class to observe the Jewish holidays. It was no secret that in the school's early days, it imposed a ceiling on the number of Jews there. I knew the quota system no longer existed, not for Jews, at least, but the place certainly clung to vestiges of the past.

Even though I found comfort in Jewish traditions, I would decline an invitation to my youngest nephew's bar mitzvah to attend Dunning's parents' weekend. I'd become aware of the conflict the summer before but had filed it away with things I didn't want to deal with. Even though I barely knew this boy, having met him for the first time at my mother's funeral, I dreaded calling my sister.

When I finally got up the courage, there was silence on the line for several moments before she said, "We flew out there for Sam's." It was true. My family made up the majority of the guest list at the small luncheon we'd hosted when Sam was called to the bimah in seventh grade. Sam had invited only a handful of friends from school, and it had been an effort to convince Edward's parents to make the trip from Florida.

"I know, I know, and I'm truly sorry. But we can't miss this." I hadn't anticipated the way my life would become a roller coaster, riding the dips and peaks between parents' weekend, Thanksgiving, Sam's swim meets, and eventually winter break. Parents' weekend held the added attraction of peak foliage, invigoratingly brisk air, and kids who were still bursting with promise in the classroom.

There was more silence on the line. "Look, Hannah, I don't know why you can't visit him whenever you want. Parents' weekend can't be more important than family."

"Of course not. You know you're more important. But it's the only time of year they let us attend classes, and it's crucial that we go."

My sister cleared her throat. "The only time?"

"Well, I mean, it's not the *only* time, but they have special events for the parents, and we can schedule meetings with Sam's teachers."

"I see," she snapped. "Look, Hannah, if you can't come for the bar mitzvah, can you at least come for a visit, maybe to help with Dad?"

"Later, Lisa. Let's discuss Dad another time." I would not be guilted into participating in my father's care. He had never supported my ambitions, had even suggested I'd shirked my responsibilities as a daughter when I moved away. Remembering our conversation the day I received my first job offer "back East" still set my teeth on edge.

"I really don't understand," Lisa continued. "First you left for banking; then you gave up banking when you couldn't get pregnant. You finally had a child, but now you've sent him away. Why can't you just come home for a visit?"

Her simplification of my life constricted my throat. I was the only one among my siblings to have left Ohio, and that had caused a rift bigger than the three states between us. It wasn't so much what was keeping me in Boston as what kept me away from them. The eldest of six children, I'd been my parents' built-in babysitter as soon as I could hold a spoon to my brother's lips. They traded my childhood for a big family and their dry-goods business. There was no housekeeping unless I did it, and meals were haphazard unless I prepared them. The only time my parents fulfilled their roles as heads of the family was on the Sabbath. It wasn't so much the forfeiture of my childhood or the fact that nobody ever took an interest in my potential that bothered me; it was that none of them, neither my parents nor my siblings, ever thanked me.

The fact that Edward was uneasy with my family's rituals also caused a divide. "I mean, it's nice when you light candles at home, Hannah," he'd said. "It's just, with all your siblings and their spouses and their children, and your father looming, I feel like an outsider." *Welcome to the club*, I'd wanted to say. A week of sitting shiva for my mother had put him over the edge.

....

Sam called before parents' weekend to say he'd like to return home with us on Saturday evening and asked if I could complete a permission slip for the dean's office.

Music to my ears. I roasted a chicken ahead of time so we could sit down to eat without much fuss after the drive home. I pictured us around the kitchen table, lighting Havdalah candles, constructing a smaller version of the holiday that he'd missed. We'd eat dessert in the family room and see if there was a movie worth seeing. I'd watch whatever Edward suggested, just to be together a little longer.

But when I opened the back door and flipped on the kitchen light, my son announced he'd made plans to meet up with friends in Boston. He said he'd take the subway downtown. I stumbled against a cabinet and pretended I hadn't heard him. I opened the refrigerator and pulled out the chicken, hoping the sight of it might change his mind.

"Hannah, did you hear what Sam said?" Edward asked.

"Hmm?" I kept up the act, hanging my purse on a chair and taking off my jacket.

"Mom, I'm meeting up with some friends in Boston," he said.

"Oh, really? What kids?"

"Friends from Dunning."

"But you see them all the time." My voice was cloying, unattractive. I wanted to cry.

"Yes, but not outside of school and all its rules. There's a kid who lives in the Back Bay who's having people over. I'll be home by midnight."

"Okay, but midnight is way too late—be home by eleven."

He rolled his eyes. "Whatever. Eleven thirty?"

"That'll be fine, son," said Edward.

But I was the one to sit up waiting for him to return, consoling myself that parents with children attending public high school had to do this every weekend. Even if boarding school did trigger an abrupt separation from my son, at least I always knew where he was and that he was safe.

Edward went to bed, and I watched television alone. Sam was true to his word, home by eleven thirty, but instead of lingering in the family room to relay the details of his night, he kissed me hastily and took his backpack up to his room. He slept until almost noon the next day and then sat dazed in front of the television, snacking on leftover chicken, until it was just about time to take him back to New Hampshire.

Edward bowed out of the drive, saying he wanted to turn in early, as he had a week of big meetings ahead. I jumped at the chance to transport Sam north, however—any opportunity to extend our visit. Edward hugged Sam by the back door while I finished loading his crisply ironed laundry into the back of the Subaru.

I flipped on the wipers as we backed out of the drive. The brisk fall weekend had a soggy ending. Wet leaves blanketed the curb, and a hint of winter chill was in the air. Ten degrees colder and it would have been snowing. I dialed up the heat on the console. I glanced to my right with a smile, hoping for something expressive in return, but Sam's stare was vacant.

"Feeling rested?" I asked cheerfully. He grunted something in return that I interpreted to mean, "Not really." We were a *Peanuts* cartoon, and all he heard from me was *waa, waa, waa.*

Was Sam suffering from depression? So many teens were withdrawing, I'd read, getting mixed up in drugs. And then there was *TIME* magazine, pronouncing teen suicides in epidemic proportions. I even tried some of our old, silly jokes, but I couldn't get him to crack a smile.

When we pulled through the ornate iron gates with the school's crest towering above us, he finally spoke. "You can just drop me at Wilburton, Mom. You don't need to come up."

"Sam, don't be silly. Of course I'm coming up. There's that whole basket of laundry to carry." But his stare challenged me. I stared back even more sternly, resenting the role of mere chauffeur. "Look, I could really use a restroom before driving home."

He shrugged his consent.

A group of parents were off in the distance, folding umbrellas in front of the entrance to the main school building. They distracted me so that I practically bumped head-on into Shawn Willis, who was holding the door open to the dorm.

It would have been the perfect opportunity to check in with him, to ask privately whether he'd noticed any signs of depression in Sam. Instead, I pointed to the cluster of people across the quad.

"What's going on?" I asked.

"It's a Q and A with Dean Harper and the college counselors."

"Really?" I said, eyeing Sam scornfully. "You never told me about a Q and A."

"Mom, it's for parents of juniors," Sam said.

"Oh," I said. "Okay." But still—Dunning meted out its invitations so sparsely. I longed for a connection, a conversation with whoever might be able to relate to what was going on with my son. If the meeting was for parents of juniors, then there was a chance Mimi Crandall would be there. Maybe she was staying overnight in her little playhouse; maybe we could grab a cup of coffee afterward.

I kissed Sam's cheek and handed him the laundry basket. I forgot whatever I'd intended to ask Shawn Willis and trailed after the last parents hurrying across the quad against the rain. Even though it was late and the meeting was not intended for me, I had no desire to return to Edward and our empty home.

A few faces turned when I opened the door and slipped in. The panel discussion of college counselors was well underway. I stood in the back until the time was right to take an aisle seat about halfway down.

A staffer passed a microphone to the parents, who asked questions of the panelists: the dean of students, the head of College Counseling, and the head of Health Services. Even to a complete newcomer, their responses sounded predictable and canned, condescending, even: "You should be helpful and supportive of your children; don't put undue pressure on them. There will be a college for everybody; don't get caught up in prestigious names. Admissions are more competitive than they've ever been, especially for our students. . . ."

Dean Harper didn't have an athletic build, nor did he wear tweedy jackets and cashmere V-necks and classic leather lace-ups, like Headmaster Williams. No, Dean Harper wore poly blends and knit ties and inexpensive all-weather shoes. His glasses frames were a silver metal that did not become his round face. He was a definite step down in appearance and class and, I surmised, intelligence.

The audience sat more or less quietly, accepting their fate from this underling. I wasn't so sure I'd be as complacent when it was my turn. This sure wasn't the speech Dunning had given on admitted-students day or move-in day. Back then, they'd boasted about their stellar Ivy League matriculation. Typical—they obviously waited a few years to deliver the shitty news that sending a child to Dunning probably wasn't even worth it. This was exactly what Edward kept telling me—that Sam would stand out more and likely get into a better college coming out of our public high school.

And even though the gist of the evening was that everyone would find the right fit, the subtext insinuated that it was game on. Students should sign up for tutoring sessions and follow a prescribed strategy regarding test dates and locations. An entire industry around college admissions consultancy had emerged, and it was as if the college counseling office was making its pitch.

A well-heeled woman in a Burberry trench coat with a handbag that probably cost more than our Subaru was checking her phone. That's when I realized that most of these people weren't worried—in fact, they were hardly paying attention. They had their own ways of greasing their children's paths to college, ways of throwing money and connections at any obstacle they faced.

What I was wondering that night was, what if your son stopped speaking to you altogether? God forbid anyone ask a question like that. What if your son was depressed? What were the warning signs of suicide?

When a man two rows down asked, "What if my child doesn't get accepted early action to the Ivy of his choice?" the head of College Counseling actually rolled his eyes, as if he'd heard these high expectations a million times and was used to beating them back down into their holes.

"There is nothing special about your child. In fact," the head of College Counseling added, "it gets more competitive each year. You need to set your sights lower." His tone implied that parental involvement was the real menace.

I wondered if Sam's withdrawn behavior was a result of the pressure he felt about college. The people on the panel continued saying different versions of the same thing. "All those dreams you've had for your children? Let them go. Imposing your aspirations on them is bad for their health." After we sent in the tuition, Dunning had a way of treating parents like a bunch of troublemakers. As if the school had hosted this college-counseling panel as a controlled burn of the parental flame, which, without proper supervision, threatened to escalate into a grand-scale forest fire.

Thinking of Sam, so sullen in the car, and of Edward, watching television at home, and then listening to the patronizing information dump in this stupid meeting, I pressed my eyes shut against tears. My dismay stemmed from several things: I wouldn't see my son again until it was time for us to put on a grand charade around the Thanksgiving turkey; it was time to turn the clocks back and enter yet another dismal winter of 4:00 p.m. sunsets; and, in the end, motherhood was just one big heartbreak.

As I filed out of the auditorium with the other parents, I looked down and realized I was dressed in sweatpants and flowered rain boots, having planned to just drive Sam back to school. I picked up my pace and kept my head down, praying not to bump into Mimi Crandall after all.

Approaching Wilburton Hall on the way back to my car, I had a strong urge to hug Sam. As I got closer, I heard Shawn Willis's loud voice through an open window, making announcements. I pressed through the bushes to get a closer look. It was the dorm's weekly Sunday-night meeting. Seeing all the boys gathered together in the common room warmed my heart. I imagined Sam surrounded by friends, boys his age, boys he could probably talk to. After Mr. Willis finished, the group pressed into a circle. Arms stretching across each other's backs, they all swayed. I could make out their voices rising in song and the lyrics to "Lean on Me." I reached out my palm and placed it against a cold pane of glass.

Mr. Willis must have caught sight of my pale, spreading fingers, because he immediately approached the window and knelt to meet my eyes. I backed away, stumbling into the bushes, my hair dripping rain. I jogged back to my station wagon, seeking refuge in the driver's seat.

Sam had a home at Dunning, and he would be all right. What I hadn't yet acknowledged was that I was the one who was homeless. I turned the key, started the engine, and backed into the night, illuminated only by the red glow of my taillights.

CHAPTER 9

Three years at Dunning, and Shawn had gotten lulled into the routine of Coach Schwartz's weekend gatherings. After a week of teaching classes, supervising afternoon practices, and checking the boys into the dorm, Friday nights meant picking up a bottle of white wine for Irene Schwartz and heading to the barbecue. Even though these events marked the ends of weeks that all started to bleed together, he'd never forget his first such evening at the coach's house.

The school year had launched, and posse after posse were shuttling across campus like herds of sheep. Preseason athletes returned first, followed by international student orientation, minority student orientation, and first-year orientation. Already weary of the highbrow academic set, Shawn headed to Schwartz's in search of a crew of his own.

After issuing the invitation on the pool deck, Schwartz explained how to find his house. "It's hard to see at first, but there's a gate inside the hedge bordering the JV outfield. It opens right into my yard." He accentuated that last word, tying himself to New England, specifically hardscrabble, middle-class, dyed-in-the-wool Yankees. He may have made the accent even thicker on this campus populated with imports, in case there was any doubt who'd been there the longest.

Not all faculty could be housed in one of the grand Victorians on Main Street, but the Schwartzes' abode was ample, tucked back on a private cul-de-sac. It was white clapboard, two stories, with a little deck off the back, from which one could sometimes spot Mrs. Schwartz, who was a receptionist in the health center, staring out from the kitchen sink. She had the kinky, tight perm of an older woman who'd given up on her looks, and the puffy, dark skin under her eyes of a smoker or somebody who didn't sleep well, or both.

Once he identified the hidden gate in the hedge, Shawn pushed his way through to find a half dozen men clutching long necks and standing around a grill. The introductions moved fast, and Shawn couldn't remember many of the names, but he did catch on to the fact that the head trainer and the lacrosse coach were Schwartz's sons-in-law. Schwartz had two grown daughters who'd married into the Dunning family and had each produced a couple of kids.

Looking around at the other men, Shawn experienced a moment of panic. When he'd taken the job, it had been a stopgap. But sizing up those thirty- and fortysomething guys—paunches, baseball hats, worn jeans—he wondered what else he'd ever be qualified to do. He knew some guys who'd left hockey to sell insurance, although they called themselves financial planners; even so, Shawn doubted he was smart enough for something like that. Maybe if he saved up some money, he could open a sporting-goods store.

"Ketchup and mustard inside," Fred, the trainer son-in-law, told him. Shawn followed the trail of men as they helped themselves to the potato salad and sliced tomatoes Mrs. Schwartz had put out on the Formica kitchen table. Coach Schwartz loaded up his plate first, then opened a door and flicked on a light, illuminating a steep staircase.

"Somebody tell the new guy to hold on to the banister," he hollered over his shoulder, and Shawn watched as, one by one, the men followed Coach Schwartz down the stairs.

The basement smelled of new carpet and Budweiser, its centerpiece a well-worn recliner that Shawn would learn was Schwartz's throne. The rest of the seating consisted of a couch and lounge chairs that looked like castoffs from a golf club's locker room. Over the waist-high faux-wood paneling, sports memorabilia hung on the wall: baseball pennants and framed, enlarged photos of Schwartz with other coaches, smoking cigars or popping champagne.

One of the guys mentioned that Schwartz was zeroing in on his fortieth anniversary at Dunning. The idea of working at this school, in this small town—hell, anyplace—for that long blew Shawn away. It was practically twice as long as he'd been alive. It dawned on him that, in addition to Dunning providing the coach's livelihood and his home, Schwartz's entire family drew a paycheck from the place. The lacrosse son-in-law looked at home in one of the lounge chairs; the wrestling coach and the basketball coach sat in the others. Shawn took a spot on the end of a couch, balancing his plate on his knees.

"Wow, quite a setup," he remarked, sensing that the finished basement was Schwartz's pride and joy.

Fred stood up. "Beer?" he asked, looking back at Shawn.

"Sure," he said.

Fred walked over to a bar set up on one side of the room and uncovered the tap of a refrigerated keg. He took some Solo cups out of a plastic sleeve and gave the keg a few pumps.

"How old's the brew, Pop?"

"Don't be a smart-ass—you know it came this morning."

Shawn shook his head, picturing Schwartz having his beer delivered every Friday the way other people had a milkman.

Schwartz put his plate down on the TV tray to his left and picked up the remote control. He eased back in his recliner, pointing the remote at the screen like a magic wand. The Red Sox game appeared in high definition. Shawn envied his reception. Schwartz put it on mute. "No score, early innings," he reported.

Despite the fact that their seats were arranged around the TV, Shawn was able to take a mental inventory of everyone's face. There was Schwartz and his two sons-in-law: Fred the athletic trainer and Warren the lacrosse coach. There was Wayne, the tall, gawky basketball coach who had to duck to avoid the ceiling fan. There was a guy named Darren who was the soccer coach and made a big deal about also being a biology teacher when he introduced himself, as if that made him a little superior. And there was a guy named Lou who was the wrestling coach and worked in Admissions—and he had the same scrappy build as Shawn.

"Dunning is a place with an important tradition in athletics," Lou said. "Don't let those intellectual bastards on the other side of campus give you a hard time. This is the side of campus where real character is built."

Shawn nodded, not quite sure how to respond. "They got Buchholz pitching tonight?" he asked, feigning interest in the Red Sox game.

"Yeah, but it'd be a miracle if he lasted three innings," Schwartz said, before finishing off his cheeseburger.

Looking around the room, Shawn noticed a picture on the wall of Schwartz with the late hockey coach. Maybe Shawn had taken his place in the basement. Or maybe this was a tryout too. Shawn surprised himself, feeling a sudden desire to earn a spot on the couch—at least, until he decided he didn't want to be there anymore.

"So, Darren, rumor has it you're up for the dean of students position once Harper is done," said Lou.

"Could be," the soccer-biology guy responded with a grin, his eyebrows arching upward.

"We haven't had a dean in the house in ages," Schwartz said. "Once Darren's in a corner office, I won't have to pump the rest of you so hard for intel."

"That'll be the day," said Lou.

"Any talent for the football team?" Schwartz asked.

"We got a big PG to play quarterback," said Fred, the trainer son-in-law.

"Right—I heard about that kid. He's a rich one too. Father went to Harvard, a real ball-buster. Made them guarantee he'd not only start but be named captain as well."

"He's committed to Harvard but needs a year of academics," said Lou.

"If he's already in, why'd he have to be named captain?" Darren asked.

"You know these parents; they're a bunch of a-holes," said Lou.

"The kid's not gonna make a whole lotta friends. Anderson and Jackson, natural leaders, put in three years on the team. Now they've gotta share the honor with some rich prick," Fred said.

"I usually look out for the PGs," Schwartz said, addressing Shawn. "But I hate the ones who come over from some other private school. It's not how the program was intended, Lou."

"I know, I know," Lou answered.

"We're supposed to give a kid without all the opportunities— someone from a public school or a shitty neighborhood—a fifth year of high school, real college prep. Give 'em a chance at a good Division One, maybe even the Ivies. They used to scout for kids with athletic gifts and academic potential, kids who needed Dunning to rise out of their circumstances. The PG program was never meant to be for kids who didn't give a fuck the first time around at fifty grand a year. This fucking kid'll ride the pine at Harvard anyway—there'd have to be a hell of a lot of injuries before they'd give him the ball."

After Schwartz's rant, Shawn waited for somebody to argue the other side, but apparent protocol on these Friday nights was for Schwartz to get the last word. Shawn wondered if he'd be up against the same type of thing on the hockey team, and if the postgraduate program had really devolved to such a state.

Schwartz wasn't finished. "Lou, why does your office let this shit go on?"

"Why do you think? The father opened his checkbook. You know that pansy Williams—fundraising isn't exactly his strong suit. He'll take the easy money any day of the week."

It always came down to cash. Shawn's father had imparted that wisdom early on: if you want to know why things are the way they are, just trace the money. Shawn's attention turned to Fred, who had stood up in front of the TV, facing everyone.

"Guys, our fantasy football draft is next Friday night. A hundred bucks a head."

And so the conversation flipped to their second favorite topic. This group could dissect any sport up, down, and sideways. It was Shawn's language and afforded an easy connection. Every Friday night, however, they started by gossiping about the kids. As uncomfortable as it was, that was how Shawn learned what went on behind the scenes—behind the whole incident with Harold Chu, for example.

"It was unexpected," Fred said.

"What?" Schwartz asked, without seeming to take his attention away from the TV.

"That a first-year would get in so much trouble so early on."

"What happened?"

"You tell him, Shawn. Didn't it go down in Wilburton?"

Shawn described busting into Harold's room and catching him in a compromising position with porn on the screen, two women rolling around, all oiled up and glistening. "But after I turned the kid over on a silver platter, Harper didn't do much—even after all that talk about coming down hard."

"Explain it to him, Lou," Schwartz said.

"It's 'cause the kid was a Chinese national with ties to big money," Lou said. "See, back in 2006, the headmaster made a public display of dipping into the endowment for more financial aid; then, boom, the stock market crashed."

"Endowment lost about a third overnight," Darren added.

"Yikes," Shawn said.

"We got hit in Admissions too. We had a big pool of applicants who needed aid, but not as many who could pay full freight. So, in order to balance the equation, Williams approved a higher percentage of internationals, who, as a policy, don't receive any aid. The Chinese and the Koreans are all about finding a leg up into the Ivy League *and* have the capacity to pay. We made an Admissions trip to China to meet with a placement firm over there. This whole thing, getting Asian kids into American universities, it's big business."

"Christ" was all Shawn could say. This lecture appeared to be for mostly his benefit, but the rest of the guys seemed to enjoy chewing on a familiar bone.

"Headmaster suggested they take more of them Asians, but the alums threw a fit," Schwartz added.

"He's backed himself into a corner now. You've heard about the lawsuit Harvard's gotten into, denying it has quotas?" Darren asked.

So that was it, the reason Harold Chu was untouchable: his father was a big-time businessman who had the potential to make the kind of donation that would get his name on a building. Dean Harper and Headmaster Williams had told Shawn the procurement of pornography wasn't really hurting anybody anyway. Shawn should have known it all traced back to money.

....

Over his three years at Dunning, Shawn did fine with the guys in the basement and with the no-nonsense athletic director, with his military haircut and his whistle hanging from his neck, but a summons to the academic side of campus made his bad knee ache. Dean Harper never minced words either, writing, "Come see me." And even though the messages didn't state "right away," they didn't need to. The implication that Shawn should drop everything upon request conveyed the dean's disregard for the athletic department.

After receiving one such message, Shawn zipped up his track-suit and trudged toward the academy building, his limp worsening in the cold air.

Harper's secretary looked up from her typing and smiled with fake cheer. "He's expecting you."

When Shawn poked his head into Harper's wood-paneled office, the man was hunched over his desk, the *Dunning Daily* spread open. It was the oldest high school newspaper in the country, and managing its intense print schedule, not to mention maintaining the online version for its worldwide readership, was tantamount to a full-time job. As recompense, teachers gave the editors of the *Dunning Daily* leeway when it came to missed assignments and wrote glowing letters of recommendation for their college applications.

"Have you seen this?" Harper asked, pointing his thick index finger at the front page, not yet bothering to look up at Shawn.

"Uh, no, sir, not yet." Shawn couldn't tell what the dean was reading. He was more familiar with the sports section at the back.

"Did you hear the bells yesterday?" Harper asked, now staring directly at Shawn.

"Yeah, Alice Cooper. That was a good one," Shawn said, chuckling.

Harper scowled. "Vandalism, Shawn. That's what it is. And the *Daily* applauds it. 'Grateful that the Nine have finally struck, and hope they'll delight again soon.' Encouraging more! Egging the scoundrels on."

"Scoundrels?"

"The Nine. A stunt like this has their fingerprints all over it. They think they're so smart. You haven't been around teenagers as long as I have. If we encourage these kids, their pranks get worse. Remember your furniture out in the snow?"

"Yeah, that was a pain in the ass." Shawn had been exhausted, returning from a hockey tournament that first winter to find his living room set up outside on the lawn in front of the dorm. He'd made the boys carry everything back inside, had acted mad as hell, even though it was damn impressive.

"And who do you think coordinated the fish being tossed out onto the ice between periods at the hockey game?"

Shawn nodded, feeling his frown now mirroring Harper's.

"Must have been over a hundred frozen snapper."

"Maybe some trout too, sir." The kids were resourceful.

"Willis, please."

Shawn wasn't like the veteran dorm heads who instinctively knew who got high and who snuck girls into the dorm. Harper had suggested he learn from those people, revert to the law of the jungle and punish boys randomly for crimes, trusting the inner recriminations of communal living to do the job.

"But, sir, nobody's getting hurt." This was also where he differed from these older faculty members. Even though his temper had been tested, he'd maintained some sense of humor.

"The problem with you, Willis, is that you want to be popular."

Shawn inhaled deeply. In the ensuing silence, he used all the restraint he could not to ask why he had been dragged across campus to rehash old theories about the Nine. He backed toward the door. "I've got SPAZ to teach back at the gym," he said, having adopted the widely accepted vernacular for the PE class required of first-years not on a team.

"Not yet, Willis. Not yet." Harper rolled the newspaper into a tube, swatting it on his desk for emphasis. "They need to be stopped. Cede to authority."

"They?"

"The Nine, Willis. Jesus. Haven't you been paying attention?"

"They're behind everything?" Shawn couldn't mask his skepticism.

"Of course they are. They left their marks in the snow a few nights ago, and now this. They're operating out of Wilburton. Right under your nose!"

"Are you sure about that?"

"Don't question my intelligence, Shawn."

He wasn't sure whether the dean was referring to his source of information or to his brainpower. Regardless, Shawn nodded obediently.

"Now, look—the Nine get cute every spring. I guarantee it. If they succeed, they'll take it up a notch."

"Right."

"You still interested in that head coaching job?" Three years in, the athletic director was still stringing Shawn along. It now sounded like Harper had something to do with that.

"Yeah," Shawn said, swallowing a sudden wash of anger.

It was what he had to say, but the place was losing its luster. Dunning wielded a long arm of control. He knew he was expected to live in the dorm for two more years, which meant living under the school's rules, just like the boys, the most painful of which prohibited entertaining members of the opposite sex in his apartment.

"Then don't get complacent. If you deliver one or two of those punks, it will help your cause. Headmaster Williams is concerned about their reemergence. We thought we'd stamped them out last year with that string of expulsions."

Shawn wanted to ask Harper if he'd ever done time walking the halls, whether he'd actually lived in a dorm, making the 11:00 p.m. rounds, whether he could appreciate what they were up against. Shawn was just one guy, and there were sixty-five of them, not to mention that they were brilliant motherfuckers. But he kept quiet, pointing to his watch and turning toward the door. "I've got a class to teach, sir. I need to run."

CHAPTER 10

The Nine were feeling brazen after having left their calling cards in the snow. Sam, Raymond, and Saunders had painted enormous red 9s on the football field, the academic quad, and the lawn in front of the headmaster's house, much to the delight of the student body.

They would reprogram the bell chimes next. Sam downloaded the melody of Alice Cooper's "School's Out," then transferred the requisite code onto a thumb drive that he stuffed in the front pocket of his jeans. Raymond and Saunders would once again be his wingmen, their route a series of tunnels, some tall enough to walk upright, others so small they'd need to crawl on their hands and knees.

Memorizing the map of Dunning's tunnel system was the most urgent assignment outlined in the Nine's orientation manual. The introduction explained that the tunnels were created when Dunning boys still ate in their residential halls and an uppity sort complained about his food arriving cold. His family anonymously funded an intricate underground passage system connecting the central kitchen to the residential halls. The passageways were eventually augmented with smaller utility conduits to the physical plant. When a common dining hall was constructed in the

1940s, the administration shut down most of the tunnel entrances. They'd become notorious places for misbehavior and were taxing to patrol. But that had been many decades before. By Sam's era, their existence was the stuff of urban legend.

The boys emerged from a pitch-black section, and Raymond began to jog ahead, but Sam held out his arm. "Whoa, whoa, whoa," he said, pointing to a light that was not usually on.

"What do you think it is?" Raymond asked, his tired voice reflecting the late hour.

"Probably Maintenance," Sam said.

"Is that an active boiler room?" asked Raymond.

"That's Bennett Hall, Ray," Sam said, not bothering to mask his irritation that Raymond had never memorized the map. He was the typical legacy, taking it for granted he'd be carried along at various points in life, never doing the real work.

"I know it's Bennett, but is it a functioning boiler room?" Raymond asked.

"Yeah," Sam answered. He considered the likelihood that some Bennett girls had been down there partying. But it was most likely Maintenance working on the heating equipment; it had been an unforgiving winter, after all.

"Stay here," Sam said. "I'll go check it out."

He went ahead, keeping to the shadows. He held his breath and strained his ears, scanning the floor. His eyes passed over cigarette butts and liquor bottles before settling on a red LED display. It was the frame counter on a video screen sitting atop a console, reminiscent of the relic VCR his dad kept in the family room to watch his collection of classic movies. Various cables ran from its back up the wall and into a hole drilled in the ceiling. Sam picked up the remote, and the video monitor came alive with the view of a tiled room.

He squinted, leaning closer to the fuzzy picture, tripping on the leg of a chair and knocking over a dirty ashtray in the process.

While he tried to make out the image on the screen, Raymond and Saunders appeared by his side.

"What is that?" asked Raymond.

"I think it's a shower," Sam whispered, following the cable's route into the ceiling above.

"Whoa, there's a video feed into a shower?" Saunders asked, at a higher volume than necessary.

"Shh." Sam glared at him, checking his watch and calculating how long they'd been gone. Five extra minutes put the entire mission in jeopardy. "Guys, we can't risk going to the bell tower now. Let's go back. We can hack the chimes tomorrow night; we'll take the Feeny passage instead of coming this way."

Attempting his bedtime routine, Sam froze in front of the bathroom mirror. Judging by the number of butts in the ashtray, he surmised that somebody had been filming that shower for a while. As he gripped his toothbrush, something settled in his chest, something different than the confusion he was used to at Dunning. This was more like dread, mixed with a pinch of fear. His mind raced as he slipped under his covers. He'd find Justin in the morning. Justin would know what to do.

....

"Tell me again. What did you see?" Justin asked, after the mission to reprogram the chimes had finally been completed. Now a senior and Captain Dunning, he had a deep voice like a man's. He had neither convened a meeting of the brotherhood nor brought in the other two seniors; more and more, he seemed apt to make executive decisions on his own.

Sitting on the edge of Sam's bed, he stretched his feet across the floor to where Sam sat in his desk chair.

"Video equipment, apparently hardwired into Bennett's first-floor showers." Sam ticked off the important details.

"Right."

"A monitor and a recording device."

"Let me get this straight. Was it actually on, in the process of recording?"

"Yes."

"What time was that?"

"About 2:30 a.m. Weird time to be filming the showers."

"Okay. Anything else?"

"There was a chair set up in front of it, a full ashtray, and a few empty cans on the floor."

Justin stood up and began pacing, his face tense with concentration. "Shit, Sam, this is bad."

"I know," he whispered.

Sam's heart pounded as the image of some degenerate training his eyes on innocent girls (possibly Nathalie) formed in his mind. There had been gossip of molestation and sexual advances by teachers toward students over the years. Max, of course, had provided details on the first-year hallway—something about a dorm parent who messed around with kids in the boiler room and photographed it all back in the eighties.

Justin stood, towering over Sam. "There's only one thing to do."

Sam met his friend's eyes, anticipating what he'd say: that they'd be reporting the discovery to Headmaster Williams imminently, that despite their poor regard for Harper and the administration, it was the right thing to do. This was criminal activity, after all.

But Justin crossed his arms against his chest. "We need to go back and dismantle everything. Tonight."

His statement knocked the wind out of Sam. He'd seen enough movies to know it wasn't wise to tamper with a crime scene. The only people who did such things had something to hide. "Do you think that's a good idea? It sort of implies that we—"

"If anybody stumbles upon that setup and turns it over to Harper, he'll pin it on the Nine for sure," Justin said.

Sam hadn't considered that. He nodded slowly, flipping the pages of his chemistry text.

"We'll bring it all back here."

"Just the two of us? But there's a lot of stuff to disconnect."

"We'll cut the wires. We'll see what clues we get from the

equipment; then I'll notify the alumni council. Everything will be stored in a safe place."

Sam sucked in his cheeks and pulled at his bangs.

"You're not sure," said Justin. "Sam, I need you to trust me on this. You do trust me, don't you?"

Sam swallowed hard. "Yeah, I trust you."

After determining the best time to leave, Justin returned to his room and Sam to his chemistry text. His hands trembled with each turn of the page. On top of it all, his mother kept texting. He'd been doing very well, but she never missed an opportunity to remind him that these junior-year grades were the most important for his college applications. He'd balanced schoolwork, swim team, the robotics club, and his rising ascendency in the Nine admirably. And he wasn't one of those kids who'd obtained an ADHD exemption and the Adderall that went with it.

The texts from his mother were always phrased as if she were writing on behalf of his father as well, which was doubtful. He wished he could imagine his parents putting their heads together, but his father was always in the family room, and his mother's domain was the kitchen. Sam's communication with his dad occurred in person, on the occasional weekend home. They'd pull their mitts out of the hall closet and play catch in the front yard. It was on one such weekend that the extra twin bed in Sam's room appeared rumpled with use. When Sam later found his father's paperbacks in the drawer of the bedside table, his heart sank. The discovery validated something he didn't really want to know.

Despite the evident strain at home, his mother carried on texting with playful emojis. "It's time to visit colleges! How about over your spring break?"

When it came to college, Sam had been thinking of someplace big, someplace far from the Northeast, maybe even someplace warm. The proctor on his hallway first year had ended up at UCLA, and he'd heard of a handful who'd followed. Much as they'd planted the idea of heading west in Sam's mind, his mother was stuck on the Ivy League, nothing less than Harvard, Yale, or Princeton for her. At Dunning that triumvirate and its obvious candidates were referred to as HYP. HYPs were smart enough, but it was usually their family connections that got the job done. Sam didn't have the heart to tell that to his mother. Even if he had, she was always so certain he'd be the exception to the rule. And deep down, his ego might have flirted with the possibility that he'd be an outlier as well, though he'd never admit such a thing out loud.

"Sounds like a plan," he texted back.

It took him close to five minutes to read a paragraph of his chemistry book. He closed the cover, hoping to have better luck with his Spanish. From there, he moved on to history, even though he feared nodding off and sleeping through the meeting time with Justin.

Given the workload, it was not uncommon for kids to fall asleep at their desks. He remembered Ethan taking a flashlight into the closet in order to study after lights out. He'd been so paranoid, thinking Mr. Willis was on the hall every night to enforce the rule when he was really just stalking Harold Chu. Sam's head nodded and then sprang back up again.

He moved on to math. After completing a problem set, he glanced at the alarm clock on his bedside table. Its big red digits read 1:45. He emptied his backpack and set it next to the door, along with his black hoodie. He packed the wire cutters from his robotics case and a penlight from his desk drawer.

A knock on his door made him jump. Mr. Willis was the only one who announced himself this way, giving kids only a few seconds to throw bottles or joints out the window. Sam had even heard of girls being zipped into hockey bags.

"You ready?" It was Justin. As a senior, he hadn't gone on a mission all year. Even though the Nine's fixers were good, nothing was foolproof, and there was no need to jeopardize his early admission to Yale.

"I thought we were meeting at the entrance to the tunnel." Justin had the hood of his black sweatshirt pulled over his head, and his blond curls framed his face like a lion's mane. Despite his exhaustion, Sam couldn't help but chuckle.

"Right." Justin blinked. "I'll head down now, and you trail behind."

"Sounds good." Sam turned off his lights after simulating a sleeping body under the covers with his laundry bag.

The idea of one last mission with Justin before he graduated energized Sam, as nothing compared to the stories that resulted from these late-night escapades. Sam imagined his friendship with Justin in the spirit of those lifelong boarding school bonds his father nostalgically referred to. At some future reunion, he and Justin would slap their knees, reminiscing about how they'd mastered Dunning's underworld while the rest of the community slept.

Sam reveled in their efficient movements and the ease with which they maneuvered through the passageways. He slowed before reaching the Bennett connector. The lights were no longer on. He used his penlight to illuminate the remaining stretch of tunnel. Justin crept behind him, his breath so loud in Sam's ear, it could have been his own. Sam's heart hammered against his chest. This wasn't a prank, after all; they were on a mission to confiscate property.

He imagined what his mother's reaction would be if she knew what he was up to—tracking criminal voyeurs at Dunning, habitually breaking curfew—and, worse, that he hadn't gotten a full night's sleep in over a week. It couldn't have been further from the picture he'd painted for her. Despite the fact that she had spent a good part of his childhood imparting the values of justice and righteousness, she never would have wanted him to put himself on the line like this.

The penlight was just bright enough to get the job done. Sam clipped the wires, closed up the monitor and recording device, unplugged them from the wall, and jammed both machines into his backpack. Justin borrowed the light to scan the room. The ashtray was still there, but the beer cans were gone.

"He's cleaned up a little," Sam whispered.

JEANNE McWILLIAMS BLASBERG

"Here, let me take that," Justin said, heaving the loaded back-pack over his shoulder.

They had been gone over forty minutes, and a wave of urgency seeped into Sam's gut. Knowing the perpetrator had been there recently raised the possibility of a confrontation. What if they ran into him? What would he do when he found all his equipment gone?

The tunnel was hotter on the way back. Sam wiped his drip-ping nose on the sleeve of his hoodie. Neither boy spoke, and Sam suddenly had an irrepressible urge to pee, just as he had as a kid playing hide-and-seek.

They crawled on their hands and knees, and when Sam spotted the red emergency light at the end of the dark tunnel, he exhaled. They were almost there. He checked his watch: 3:30 a.m., their plan executed down to the minute. He'd be under the covers soon, with a chance of getting four hours' sleep before first period.

They tiptoed up the stairwell from the boiler room, and when they reached the first-floor landing, Justin tapped Sam's shoulder, whispering, "Good job, Webber. I'll see you at breakfast." He hefted the backpack over both shoulders and saluted before opening the fire door and heading to his room. The door closed slowly behind him, whining on its hydraulic hinge. Sam turned to continue up a final flight of stairs but froze when an unexpected hand grabbed his shoulder. Mr. Willis's expression was almost demonic as his voice rang triumphant. "Stop right there, Webber! I gotcha! Go wait in your room for Dean Harper while I nab your accomplice." Mr. Willis shot past him, pulling the heavy door open in pursuit of Justin.

CHAPTER 11

From the very beginning, Edward and I couldn't agree on how to handle Sam's absence: how often to visit, how often to call, how many teacher conferences to schedule. Edward was a proponent of our stepping back, and, naturally, I wasn't. I hadn't bargained on that at all.

During his sophomore year, the disagreements were made worse when Dean Harper called Edward at work to ask if things were "all right at home." He reported that Shawn Willis had witnessed me standing outside in the rain, peering into the Wilburton common room. So, in addition to the label "overbearing," Edward accused me of being "unstable" too. He even insinuated I might have been drinking.

"You can't risk embarrassing Sam like that," Edward said. "What the hell were you thinking?"

"Don't." I just didn't want to go there. It had been a long time since Edward had shown any interest in what I was thinking, and I hadn't yet struck up conversation with Joy in yoga class. There weren't many people for me to talk to, so I spent a lot of time in my head.

I see now how Edward might have expected my attention to return to him when Sam left for boarding school. But I was actually more absent, like a zombie trying to tune in to a distant radio

JEANNE McWILLIAMS BLASBERG

frequency. I was so focused on what Sam's departure meant to me, I neglected what it meant to us as a couple. I totally missed it, much like I'd failed to recognize Sam's growth spurts until his grandparents remarked on them during our annual visits.

Sam's departure challenged my identity. Sitting in the makeshift space I shared with the office manager at the dental practice, I wondered what type of job I might have had if I'd remained in the workforce after being laid off from the bank. When Sam came along, however, I made him my career. I was 100 percent focused on him, hadn't yet set foot in the Boys & Girls Club or seen the value in serving people outside my family. No, back then, no matter how much I fought it, sending Sam off to boarding school rendered me obsolete.

One dark January morning during Sam's junior year, I woke to find Edward standing in our bedroom, talking on his cell phone. Listening to half the conversation, I deduced it was a person of authority at Dunning, possibly Dean Harper. I sat up in bed, all ears, but Edward offered only headlines before heading off to shower. I followed him into the bathroom, hungry for details.

"He's gotten into trouble," Edward said from behind the shower curtain.

"Sam? What kind of trouble?" The mirror steamed up, and I pulled my hair off my neck.

"Hannah, what teenage boy doesn't get into trouble? They've taken him to the health center to do a drug-and-alcohol screening. They say he left his dorm without permission after curfew and got caught by Mr. Willis."

"Should we drive up there?" I asked, already concocting an excuse to call in to work.

"For Christ's sake, of course not! Why do you always feel the need to drop everything and go to Dunning? Maybe if you weren't doing that at the drop of a hat, making a scene, the kid would develop some sense."

Was Edward really blaming this on me? "Well, it sounds like there are a lot of things to straighten out."

"Yes, Hannah, there *are* a lot of things to straighten out. But Sam will have to man up and deal with them himself. He's seventeen, a big boy. You have to stop trying to solve his problems."

"Okay, let's not make this about me, Edward. I heard you talking about hiring a lawyer. Do you think Sam can do that on his own?" I asked, as he pulled a towel from the rack in front of our bathtub.

"The dean suspects there were drugs involved. He gave me the number of a lawyer in town. Why they have to take legal action, I can't fathom. Anyway, I'll call the guy from my office. Probably his brother-in-law."

"What else did the dean say?" I hated relying on his second-hand version.

While he shaved, Edward gave me a perfunctory description of the case that would be brought against Sam. Now shivering in my nightgown, I struggled to keep it all straight, although it wouldn't matter, because the mechanics of the Dunning disciplinary process would be reiterated over and over. I would live it too. Unlike Edward, I would go to New Hampshire. I had to see my child. Even though it was only a little over an hour's drive, I packed a week's worth of clothes in the back of the Subaru.

Edward rolled down his window as he backed down our drive. "I can't just drop everything, Hannah," he said. "Somebody's got to pay for this. That lawyer is not going to be cheap. And don't think we'll be getting a refund on the tuition if they kick him out."

His final words to me were "Don't make a scene."

....

I arrived at the Lionsgate Inn, adjacent to the Dunning campus, at noon, but Sam said he couldn't meet me until dinner. Sitting at the antique desk in the room and staring at the phone, I thought about calling Mimi Crandall. She had continued to be a friendly presence at swim meets over the years. Justin was now a co-captain of the varsity squad, while Sam was a fixture on JV, so our overlapping was never guaranteed. But I'd hang out, looking for her, hoping to re-create the chumminess of our first afternoon. Unfortunately, when Mimi did attend, she was more consumed by her phone than by the boys in the pool.

"It's Hannah," I'd reminded her just a few weeks earlier.

"Of course. I know that." She'd swatted my shoulder playfully.

"Congratulations! Sam told me Justin got in early to Yale."

"Yes, yes. We're very pleased. Dunning's just gone by in the blink of an eye." She held up two fingers crossed tightly, as if Justin's successful completion might require a measure of luck.

Now, sitting at the Lionsgate Inn, with its colonial-themed wallpaper and four-poster bed, I remembered that tiny hint of vulnerability and hoped, given her history at Dunning Academy, she would have some advice regarding the situation we found ourselves in. I was on the verge of calling directory assistance, then thought twice about it and put down the receiver. How could I ever admit our failing to Mimi?

When Sam finally arrived at my hotel room, he was grumbling. "Everyone just stares at me when I walk into the dining hall."

I went to him with open arms. "Sam, sweetheart." But he wouldn't let me hug him or order food, even though he'd lost noticeable weight.

"Just tell me what happened."

Sam crossed his arms against his chest. "Mom, I was out of my room after curfew, all right? I was coming up from the basement." As if it were as simple as that.

I stood at the floor-to-ceiling window and parted the sheer draperies. The sky had turned a dark gray. "Is it true what the dean said? Were you really using drugs?"

"Mom." He scuffed the heel of his shoe over some salt residue on the carpet. "It's . . . it's complicated."

"It's a yes or no question, Sam."

He raised his gaze and looked at me sternly. His face was

drawn, his complexion sallow, and in that moment, I hardly recognized my own son.

"Look, there's a lot I need to do. I'll go back to the health center if all you're going to do is give me the third degree."

"Don't. It's okay," I said, turning away. Cold air whistled through the window frame.

He needed to write a statement, find a peer to write one, and ask a faculty member to stand up for him. He needed to go to the police station and meet with the lawyer, all while going to class and keeping up with his workload.

"Would you be more comfortable staying here?" I asked, pointing to the bed. "I can sleep on the couch."

"Hopefully I'll be moving back to Wilburton tomorrow." He chewed on a cuticle. "Willis is holding a vote tonight to see if the guys will support me." It was the standard first step in a disciplinary case, a way of gauging whether one's dorm mates considered the accused a good citizen.

What a swing of the scales. Just weeks earlier, Sam's overly cautious college counselor had recommended we take him on a tour of the Ivies. It was no secret that this blemish on his record, a disciplinary hearing, no less, would keep him out of the mix.

A snowstorm hit southern New Hampshire that night. Winter warnings had been all over the news, but I wasn't paying attention. While Sam went to class, I trudged through the snow to meet with any authority figure who'd make time for me. Sam's advisor, the math teacher who supervised the robotics team, said he could spare ten minutes between class periods. He smiled sympathetically, twisting one end of his mustache between his fingers. He said he couldn't imagine Sam misbehaving and assured me everything would be fine. It was clear he had minimal knowledge of the case.

"Oh, and, Mrs. Webber," he said somewhat sheepishly, as the bell sounded, "the bursar's office asked me to give you this." He handed over an envelope with the unmistakable cellophane window of an invoice. "I guess the emails they've been sending have gone unanswered."

The envelope rendered me speechless and gave the math teacher the opportunity to make a deft exit. My first reaction was to call Edward, but there would be no productive communication that began with an unpaid balance. For the rest of my stay, I couldn't help worrying that our being past due would play a part in how the school dealt with Sam.

Next, I met with Sam's college counselor, who could only shrug at our fall from grace. "It happens," he said. "Admissions offices get tens of thousands of applications. They're looking for reasons *not* to consider an applicant."

The irony was that during my stay, the campus was beautiful and pristine, with a foot of fresh snow. I made an appointment in the health center, dodging the grounds crew's army of snowblowers on the way. I wanted Sam, if he was permitted to stay, to have regular appointments with a counselor. However, the head of Mental Health Services informed me that 80 percent of the kids at Dunning were in therapy or on medication or both, and left little room for new patients on the department's schedule. She shook her head, removing her reading glasses from her nose and letting them hang around her neck. She advised me to find a private practice on Main Street, of which there were many. Later, I'd wonder if Mimi had ever sought therapy for any of her children, and whether the head of Mental Health Services had ever brushed her off too. Then again, Mimi was from a family that had a building named after it, a family that paid its bills.

Although I never screwed up the courage to phone her during my stay, I often found myself wondering, *What would Mimi do?* Would she doggedly meet with everyone she could think of, or would she place one simple call to Brad Williams? I knew the answer but persisted nonetheless, sensing the faculty were humoring me, granting me meetings out of politeness, their body language suggesting their minds were already made up.

If the meetings weren't productive in terms of helping Sam's cause, at least they helped me piece together the details of the events in question. In my meeting with Dean Harper, he said that Sam left the dorm without permission sometime after check-in and returned to his room at 3:30 a.m. The school suspected Sam's "outing" involved drug-related activity. Boys were often caught smoking pot in the woods. A group of them, in fact, had been expelled the year before.

"Sam? Using marijuana?" I shook my head.

"I'm afraid so."

"At three thirty in the morning?"

Even Dean Harper had to agree this added up to pretty strange behavior.

"And it must have been below twenty degrees. Was he frozen when he returned?" I just couldn't imagine the allure of drugs in frigid temperatures. I continued shaking my head in disbelief at the scene he painted.

"Mrs. Webber, with all due respect, you might not know your son as well as you think you do." He peered at me through smudged lenses, his Hanes undershirt visible through his thin button-down.

"What's that supposed to mean?" I asked.

"Do you know if Sam is a member of an underground group?"

"What?" I asked, stiffening in my chair.

"Does the number nine mean anything to you?"

"Dean Harper, I don't have any idea what you're talking about. The number nine?"

He exhaled slowly, like he needed time to frame his remarks. "There is a centuries-old secret society on this campus called the Nine. Maybe you should ask Sam about it."

"What? Dean Harper, we're modest people. Sam would be the last person—"

"Listen, Mrs. Webber," he interrupted, "your son left his dorm at a rather suspicious hour. There may have been other boys in his company, although we have yet to confirm that. You might want to find out what he knows about the Nine and report back to me."

As we walked to his hearing in the academy building later that evening, I asked Sam about it. It was only seven o'clock, but the moon hung in the sky as we took measured steps along the path, which had thawed, refrozen, and turned quite slick.

"What's this about an underground group? Something with the number nine?"

Sam stared at me, blank-faced. "Mom, you have no idea what you're talking about," he mumbled.

"Sam, if there were others involved, you should tell the committee. There's no reason to take the blame alone. What were you really doing that night? Were you doing drugs? None of this makes any sense. You need to be completely honest."

Sam breathed deeply, his cheeks chafed and red in the cold. He stared down at his boots, then snapped, "Mom, not now. All right?" He then hurried several steps ahead, leaving me without an arm to balance on.

Other students were making their way to the library, bundled in down jackets, hats, and boots. Back when I was a teenager in Ohio, an accumulation of this much snow would have been heralded with excitement, but the romance of a moonlit winter night was lost on these poor kids, hunched under the weight of all their assignments.

Sam waited for me at the massive wooden door, holding it open with a frown. The *click-clack* of my shoes in the marble entry was the only sound echoing through the foyer. But as we ascended to the second floor, a din of voices became audible. Approximately fifty students had gathered, lining each side of the hallway leading to the committee's hearing room. I recognized some kids from Sam's dorm and the swim team. They hushed as we walked through their tunnel of support. Their presence was for Sam, but they also intended it to make an impression on the committee members.

I choked at the gesture, as my days on campus up to that point had tasted of nothing but bitter loss and disappointment. At the very end of the line of students stood Mimi Crandall's son, that handsome Justin. I had to look away, tears welling up for the first time since all this had started. I pressed at the corners of my eyes, holding back the stream. I couldn't let it start; once it did, it might never stop.

....

I fidgeted on the long, hard bench outside the committee's chamber, still wearing my overcoat. A draft seeped through the auditorium's oversize windows. Given Dunning's massive endowment, I couldn't imagine why the school was keeping the heat down, darkening the hallways, and, most recently, doing away with hot breakfasts. Was it financial prudence, character building, or a green initiative? As the hour grew later, my yawns were harder to suppress and my view of Dunning grew bleaker.

The clock hanging high on the wall above the headmaster's lectern struck eleven. In the past four hours, Sam had made his statement behind closed doors, Vlad Grabowski had spoken on his behalf, and Shawn Willis, whom I'd never really liked since our first encounter, had attested that his poll of Sam's dorm mates had been positive. Last, Sam's math teacher described his robotics acumen and leadership of the team. Now, the committee was deliberating and had been at it for the past hour. I put my arm around Sam's shoulder, but he shrugged it off.

"Why isn't Dad here?" he asked.

My cell phone vibrated with a text from Edward: "Status?"

I showed the message to Sam. "He's working."

I agreed it would have been nice if he had driven up here to be with us for the tribunal. I responded to his text: "Still waiting."

Then, about thirty minutes later, it was Edward again: "Anything?"

I seethed, picturing him watching a movie or reading in bed, his feet hanging over the extra twin in Sam's room. "No," I typed.

Vlad Grabowski sat on the other side of Sam throughout that interminable night. He was an odd kid but a pillar of strength. He'd patted Sam on the shoulder after returning from reading his statement, then looked me squarely in the eye and said, "Don't worry, Mrs. Webber. Sam will be okay. Dunning is the type of place that breaks you, but then it remakes you."

At the time, I smiled at the seeming naivete of his words.

At any moment, the door would open and the verdict would come down for Sam to either withdraw from Dunning or remain on probation. "Verdict," another bit of Latin Vlad had made me aware of, combined the roots of "truth" and "to speak." I sensed that the truth in this situation was buried and complicated and that whatever it looked like at the end of the night would have grave consequences.

I stared at my son, trying to picture what had actually happened that night. Leaving his room after curfew was plausible, but I would never believe he was involved with drugs. The only other explanation I could come up with was that there was a girl. He was handsome enough and must have attracted plenty of attention. And I had been the one, after all, to send him back to school in the fall with a box of condoms. I had done it at Joy's urging, as she had older sons. "He's in eleventh grade, for God's sake! Get your head out of the sand!"

She was right, of course. Sam had told Edward and me that he drank alcohol on occasion and that other kids on campus used drugs. I knew it was only a matter of time before sex rounded out the teenage trifecta.

I felt so "in touch" as I handed over the bag from the pharmacy. He blushed and shook his head, although he did stuff it into his duffel.

I remembered my own high school years, drinking wine spritzers in my boyfriend's pickup. I was a cheerleader, and he was a football player. We were flung together as a stereotypical couple. We had plenty of chances to be alone, as his parents were divorcing and mine were preoccupied with the store. Dating a gentile was an early act of rebellion, one that got my parents' attention and provoked my father's wrath. Besides not being Jewish, the football player took me away from caring for my younger sisters and brothers. I shed a few tears losing my virginity to this boy, both because of his lack of tenderness and because I was certain that as soon as my father came home, he'd be able to see it on me.

I wondered if Sam had similarly traded his loyalty to Edward and me for the love of a girl. Her affection would undoubtedly be more immediate and satisfying than ours could ever be. It was only normal, but it was sudden. After all, I didn't get to answer the door to say hello to this young lady; I had no opportunity to warm up to the idea of her. A mother goes from being the most important woman in a boy's life to languishing at the bottom of the heap pretty abruptly.

Yes, the fact that Sam had become "too cool" for my love was a definite clue. I couldn't remember the last time I'd brushed his bangs off his forehead to kiss him good night. But if this girlfriend could revive his affectionate side, I'd accept her gladly. I'd appreciate any young woman who could make my boy smile.

Waiting for the verdict, I became convinced: Sam was a loyal boyfriend, protecting his girl's reputation. And I should be proud and take solace in the fact that I'd raised a gentleman—even if he was forfeiting his future.

CHAPTER 12

Part of Sam wouldn't have minded getting expelled. Lying awake in the health center, reexamining the past three years through a jaded lens, he felt disenchantment take hold. There was Mr. Willis, whose only interest from day one had been nabbing the boys in his charge. There was that Old Dunning scaffolding, which, no matter how much diversity they tried to drape over it, would always define the institution. The place was conceived, after all, by New England Puritans, who, despite modern-day misconceptions, were intolerant people. And then there was the shattering realization that Dunning was a place where sexual deviants not only existed but were comfortably ensconced in the boiler room of a girls' dormitory.

If that weren't bad enough, there was the confirmation that the adults in charge weren't to be trusted. Dean Harper had manufactured a drug allegation in order to assure his expulsion. It was the only way, since leaving one's room after curfew was not an egregious offense, especially given that Mr. Willis couldn't prove that Sam had even exited the dorm.

Sam first heard about the marijuana charge when Dean Harper grabbed the cell phone out of his hand and conducted his own conversation with his father. Sam hollered, "It's a lie!" while his stomach heaved. He imagined his father in his pajamas, standing in the narrow space between the twin beds of Sam's childhood bedroom, shaking his head at the news.

When Harper ended the call and handed the cell phone back to Sam, he said, "Really, kid? A lie?" His oversize body reclined in Sam's desk chair. Harper smirked in the dimly lit room, speaking softly so as not to wake up the boys on the floor. "Then why don't you tell me where you really were and who else is in this little group of yours?" His expression implied he was willing to cut a deal. "You start naming names, and this all gets a whole lot easier."

But Sam wasn't budging. For one thing, he'd never been a snitch, and silence was the Nine's rule number one. Harper banished Sam to the health center, where they made him pee into a cup. Although Gary in Maintenance was always on call to provide clean urine samples for the Nine, Sam didn't set that in motion; it wasn't necessary.

"It's a lie," he repeated as he entered the health center. "What are you going to do, fake the results as well?" Coach Schwartz's wife was working the graveyard shift at the reception desk and looked on him with pitying eyes. Sam imagined the same sad eyes on his mother when she received the news.

The infirmary was the last resort for kids too sick to go to class. Two girls were sleeping under scratchy gray blankets in the large room when he arrived, and Sam was assigned one of the metal-framed cots next to them. He didn't bother getting under the covers; he sat up instead, waiting for Justin, who would surely be distraught at the possibility that Yale would decide to rescind his acceptance. As the hours dragged on, however, Justin never showed, and Sam imagined his incarceration in a place even more severe than the health center.

Sam watched as the sky brightened through the window. He sat on the edge of the thin mattress, more worried about Justin's future than about his own. Just as the first-period warning bell struck in the tower, Raymond slipped through the door. "Hey, man, how are you feeling?" He stuffed a note into Sam's palm, which Sam immediately unfolded and read:

Close call for yours truly. Harper is swinging blindly. Don't worry about the DC. You'll get probation. Tell them you were down in the laundry room, putting clothes in the dryer, and found some pot, and say you were planning on turning it in yourself in the morning.

"But there was no pot," Sam said aloud, looking into Raymond's blank face. Raymond looked over his shoulder to see who might be listening.

"This is such bullshit," Sam whispered. "Go back and ask Justin why we can't just tell Harper the truth."

The first-period bell cut him off, and Raymond dashed off with an apologetic wave.

Sam was allowed to leave the health center during the ten o'clock midmorning break. The nurse who released him said, "Dean Harper wants you to go straight to his office."

But Sam was hungry, and it was just like Harper to deny food in advance of more questioning. He would make a stop at the dining hall on his way. Exiting the health center via its long central corridor, he passed the med train, a line of kids awaiting their daily dose of ADHD and antianxiety prescriptions.

Walking through the doors to the dining hall, exhausted and a little light-headed, he stood aside while a pack of Class Four girls burst into the food line. Their fresh appearance and cheerful volume struck him. People were carrying on with normal days while his future hung in the balance. Swallowed by the crowd, Sam didn't notice one of the Nine's sophomores approaching him with another piece of paper.

Sam accepted the handoff, then grabbed a bagel before shutting himself in a stall in the boys' bathroom to read the note.

DO NOT mention the video. Can't you see? Harper can't be trusted. He'll blame it on us. Just take your punishment and keep quiet. 1900900.

Leaning against the gray metal stall divider, breathing the stink of misaimed urine, Sam shredded the paper and flushed it. Leaving the stall, he stared into the cloudy mirror over the sink. There were dark rings under his eyes. Stressed or not, he needed to maintain his faith in the brotherhood. Justin and the Nine would know what to do. They had, after all, ruled Dunning long before the likes of Dean Harper and Headmaster Williams.

Harper kept Sam in his office all afternoon. Teachers and students came and went with matters requiring his approval, and they glanced uncomfortably at Sam sitting in the corner. In between interruptions, Harper alternated between describing the harrowing disciplinary process he'd set in motion and offering Sam the opportunity to serve up names to make the whole episode go away.

Sam stared at his shoes, increasingly certain Harper was the bad seed behind Dunning's evil business. It was dark outside when he finally relented. "All right, Samuel," he said, shaking his head. "I see you aren't going to cooperate. Go to dinner, then return to your cot in the health center. You have a lot of work to do before your hearing next Wednesday."

Sam rose from his chair, stiff with exhaustion, and headed out the door. He pulled his phone from his pocket to find a text from his mother:

"Sam, I'm here. Can you come meet me at the inn?"

He typed, "Coming soon."

His mother's presence usually made him cringe, but knowing she'd want to take charge flooded him with relief. She wouldn't be able to help much, but it would be nice to be taken care of.

Before he could see her, however, he had to follow the instructions laid out in the postscript of Justin's note. The original Nine had been the ones to adopt the Dewey decimal system as their special code. They never sent messages with alphabetic characters, only strings of numbers. They were call numbers, preceded by three digits, indicating the time a brother should appear at the appointed place.

Sam made his way to the top floor of the library at seven o'clock and wandered through the 900 section. There were some kids up there, so he had to feign interest in the titles of the books, taking down a volume on occasion and inspecting a weathered spine, inhaling the dust and pulp it was made from. He moved to the History and Geography section, the same place he'd taken his initiation challenge.

Sam startled when the books on the tall metal shelf in front of him rustled apart and Justin's face appeared through the gap.

"You okay?"

It took Sam a moment to respond, and he fought the urge to rush around the shelving and hug his friend. "It's total bullshit. I'm going to go down for using pot," he stammered.

"It's their MO. They always fling a bunch of charges at kids to complicate things and freak out the parents. This is boilerplate Harper," Justin said.

"It's tough. My mom arrived this afternoon. I don't know what to say to her."

"You can handle your mother, but the questions at your hearing are going to be tougher. They're going to dig. You have to know what to say. They'll want you to turn over names."

It might have been because Sam was tired, but there was something about the tone of Justin's voice that didn't sit well. He wasn't the confident, easygoing Justin who'd been Sam's big brother for the past two years. His questions were sharp edged, when what Sam really needed was compassion.

"What happened to you, anyway? Willis never caught you?"

"Oh, he caught me."

Sam scratched his head. He didn't understand why Justin hadn't landed in the health center beside him.

Justin rolled his eyes. "Harper made me phone home, then took my cell once my dad was on the line."

"Yeah?" That part sounded familiar.

"Harper told my dad I'd been caught out after curfew. But my father explained to Dean Harper that he must have been badly mistaken, and that he didn't appreciate getting woken up in the middle of the night. Then my father hung up on him."

"Are you kidding?" Sam asked, his stomach reeling. "So, you're not going to get in trouble at all?" He couldn't imagine his own father taking that kind of tone with the dean, couldn't imagine his own father even knowing it was an option.

"No DC for me, but depends how you define trouble. The alumni council is irate. They're shutting down all Nine activity for the rest of the year. Nothing can happen until I graduate and new recruits are initiated."

Bile rose in Sam's throat. It wasn't that he wanted Justin to suffer consequences, but still, it wasn't fair. His phone vibrated in his pocket. His mother was still texting. She wanted him to join her for room service, but he wasn't sure he'd even be able to swallow. He had a mountain of work to do to keep up with classes and to prepare for the hearing. Sam tugged at his bangs. He was overdue for a haircut.

"Have you written your statement yet?" Justin asked.

"No." He didn't need Justin making demands as well.

"I can write your first draft," Justin said. "I'll have it mesh with my statement. You need to designate me as your peer supporter."

"You? I mean, wouldn't that just be rubbing it in their face? I was thinking of asking Grabs."

Justin went silent and began tugging on his earlobe. "Okay, Grabs will be fine."

"But, Justin," Sam said, slowing the pace of the conversation, "I have a question."

"Shh, keep your voice down," Justin whispered, looking over his shoulder.

"What did the alumni council say? Will I have a fixer?"

Justin nodded. "They'll scare you pretty bad at the DC, then hand down probation. You won't get expelled. It's being taken care of, not that you need much help, with the robotics thing and Harry Roland thinking the world of you."

It was a nice vote of confidence, but Sam didn't feel much relief. He was still absorbing the fact that Justin was immune to the disciplinary process. It might have felt safer to be in trouble together.

Sam took a deep breath. "It's just that my mom's back at the inn. She and my dad are totally unprepared for this. I mean, this was not the plan."

"Hey, you knew when you took the oath that anything was possible."

"Justin," Sam pleaded.

Justin spoke more calmly. "Look, probation will be part of your record. You'll have to report it on the common app."

"But my mother—"

"Yeah, your mother will be upset about that, no doubt."

"You have no idea."

"Willis will come down extra hard, probably put you on restrictions for the rest of the year."

Sam balled his hands into fists. He had no alternative but to go along with Justin's instructions. He needed the Nine, and he needed their fixer.

....

Sam sat between his mother and Grabs in the academy building auditorium. It was a space he associated with school assembly, jammed in with a thousand other students who packed the benches, as well as the balcony above. Dunning had put an end to mandatory chapel services, but every Wednesday morning Headmaster Williams delivered the closest thing there was to a sermon. His signature closing, "to infuse each and every classroom experience and every athletic contest with a higher purpose," had become a well-worn joke among the students.

That night, it was just Sam's small entourage tucked away in a dimly lit corner. As the moon moved across the sky, he stared at the ceiling, avoiding his mother's frown. A night with the disciplinary committee was not part of the plan she'd mapped out. The problem with his father's absence was that if Sam was indeed expelled, he'd be the one holding his mother up instead of the other way around.

The Nine's seniors, Justin, Wigs, and Mumford, had assured him every chance they got that he wasn't going to get kicked out. "Calm down, dude." They used comforting whispers, patting his back, "C'mon, you got this." But they weren't the ones sitting in the auditorium, waiting for Dean Harper's ax to come down. Sam shivered despite the heat radiating off Grabs's meaty torso and his mother's wool overcoat. She had tried to stretch some of it across his shoulder, but he'd pushed her away.

Earlier in the evening, reading his statement to the teachers and two token students who made up the disciplinary committee, he'd searched their faces for sympathy. No one offered a wink of kindness. He wondered which among the eight was the "fixer." He eventually concluded that a real fixer wouldn't sit in on a four-hour deliberation late on a weeknight, and that this was a collection of mere puppets, their strings being pulled from above.

As the hour hand on the large wall clock approached midnight, Sam's mother nodded off. His own head lolled to one side as well, although a caffeine-induced electricity in him prevented true rest. Grabs tapped him on the shoulder and motioned for him to inch closer on the bench. Grabs leaned in and said under his breath, "After you got in trouble, I started poking around. Did you know there's a camera in the Wilburton laundry room? Presumably for filming hookups? I found a bunch of video in a weird Dropbox going back to our first year."

Sam's stomach sank at the word "video," not to mention "hookups" dating back to their first year. The idea of more cameras on campus, let alone one documenting his embarrassment with Andrea, rendered him speechless. Was everything that happened at this place recorded in some way?

"Do you know who did it?"

"Still digging."

Sam turned to observe his mother's slumber, her slack mouth and parted lips. Earlier that evening, in the hotel room, he'd almost confided in her. He would have told her everything, but where to start? When he'd found a video setup aimed at a girls' shower? That would require an explanation of the tunnels and the Nine. But why stop there? Should he tell her of Dunning's stark puritan cruelty and the faculty's entitlement, the way they'd set up nice, protected lives for themselves? A class of teenagers came and went every year, a turnstile of flesh. Sure, Dunning students were musicians and athletes and academic whizzes, but to many of the adults here, they were just meat.

He opted to keep her in the dark. Why rack her with guilt as well? He was the most important thing in her life, and if his mother ever thought she'd done the "wrong" thing, it would kill her. She'd put him at the center of their family, boosting his self-esteem as a child, and since he'd joined the Nine, it had just made his shame worse. He didn't sense that the other boys' stomachs churned like his did over keeping secrets or disappointing parents, and none of them could empathize with the financial stress he'd piled on his dad when he'd had to pay a lawyer.

The door finally opened, and the chairman of the disciplinary committee stuck his torso through the opening, still holding on to the doorknob. "Sam, Mrs. Webber, will you please join us?"

Sam nudged his mother, and she jumped out of her sleeping state, spilling her purse onto the floor.

"Good luck, man," Grabs whispered. Sam straightened his jacket and tie.

His mother gathered the ChapStick, wallet, and phone that had scattered on the floor. She wiped her eyes with a Kleenex. There was nothing Sam hated more than seeing her upset. Forget his rage over the situation, and the weight he'd lost, and the fact that he was probably getting ulcers—seeing his mother cry was the worst.

They entered the room and sat in the two empty chairs facing the committee. Dean Harper sat off to the side, and Sam turned toward him, challenging the man to look him in the eye. It might not be right away, but at some point, Dean Harper would pay.

CHAPTER 13

The morning after we got the verdict, I texted Shawn Willis, asking him to meet me for coffee. I still had misgivings about him, but he lived under the same roof as Sam and was the appointed adult in charge. He was the one who had caught Sam out of his room past curfew. He should know what had really happened.

Dunning, New Hampshire, was one of the few towns Starbucks hadn't invaded yet, and its quirky Cozy Coffee Klatch was at the end of the old Main Street. Although some big-box retailers and an auto mile had sprung up on the way to the interstate, this was a quaint stretch epitomizing postcard New England. A bandstand anchored one end of the green, a white-spired Congregationalist church, the other. Over the past several days, I'd walked from the Lionsgate, past the campus, to Main Street's snowy sidewalks to clear my head. I'd thought about disappearing into the town's single-screen movie theater, but the red letters on the marquee spelled For Sale instead of the title of any new release.

Opening the door to the coffee shop triggered a jingle of bells. The air inside was humid, carrying the warm scent of coffee and fresh-baked muffins. I spotted Shawn at a table for two, a newspaper folded in quarters in front of him. The morning sun cast a spotlight through the window. His clean hair glistened; his fresh shave revealed a cleft in his chin that I'd never noticed before. I waved through the glare before perusing the menu board and flipping my sunglasses on top of my head. Shawn went back to his paper as I waited for the barista.

I'd rehearsed the tone I hoped to strike as I'd dressed that morning. I aimed to be generous and gracious and had repeated those two words over and over as I walked. I was grateful that Sam would not have to leave Dunning, although he'd remain on probation for the rest of the term, a status that would tarnish his record permanently, as would the count of drug possession until Edward could get our lawyer a check for $4,000. *Four thousand* dollars.

I was finally holding down food, knowing that Sam was allowed to stay. Still, it was as if Dunning Academy had betrayed me. I was a jilted suitor, no longer besotted, no longer trusting the school. And, once again, I was preparing to leave my boy in a place my intuition railed against. This time, instead of hearing Headmaster Williams thank me for entrusting my son to Dunning, for bestowing upon him the greatest sacrifice a mother could make, I was reduced to a mere supplicant, thanking him for letting Sam stay.

"Shawn, can I get you anything?" I raised my voice to span the space between us, causing every head in the place to turn.

"No, thanks, I'm all set," Shawn replied, gesturing toward his cup, ignoring the faces that were now trained on him.

The seating options at this coffee shop consisted of overstuffed lounge furniture, chairs, and sofas. Shawn had taken a proper table instead of having us sit side by side in a mock living room—undoubtedly because I was the type of woman who would stand in the pouring rain, spying on a dorm meeting. A sturdy wooden table served as a healthy barrier.

As I made my way to join him, I caught sight of my reflection in the large expanse of window. I'd blown my hair dry and wore a cowl-neck top with slacks that flattered my legs. After deliberating what Mimi might have worn, I had made every effort to carry the air of a put-together Dunning mother, even if my swollen, red-rimmed eyes were a giveaway.

As soon as I sat down, Shawn seemed anxious for our meeting to end. He spoke quickly. "Look, Mrs. Webber, thanks for asking me to coffee. But I don't think you understand the way things work around here. I have zero power. I had none before the DC, and I have none now. After I caught Sam that night, Dean Harper took over."

I nodded, my silence beckoning him to go on.

"The only thing Harper asked me to do was to poll the other boys in the dorm about whether they'd support Sam's staying. You know we operate under a code of trust. Anyway, I was happy enough to wash my hands of it. It's the height of hockey season, and I'm super busy."

A code of trust. I took a sip of coffee, mulling over that phrase. "Shawn, thanks for making the time," I started, but I bit into my bottom lip to prevent a well of emotion from rushing over me. I wiped my eyes with the napkin beneath my coffee cup.

He spoke quickly, as if his enthusiasm might stop my tears. "But congratulations are in order, right?" he said. "I heard Sam is allowed to stay."

I tilted my head. "Congratulations?"

"Yeah, I mean, I know it's been a trying week, but yeah, congratulations."

I coughed into my fist, then took another quick sip of coffee. He just didn't get it; probation was its own kind of death sentence.

Generous and gracious. I concentrated on the words, imagining what Shawn saw when he looked across the table. He'd probably steeled himself for the bitch who'd dropped Sam off three years earlier and grilled him outside the dorm, and now here I was, a blubbering mess.

"Look, I asked to meet you this morning, Shawn, because I'm confused," I said. This time, he nodded for me to continue.

"You're the one who caught Sam that night, right? You were the first one to see him when he returned to his room after hours that night. Is that correct?"

"Yes."

"Were you also the one who found the marijuana?"

Shawn Willis opened his mouth, but no words came out. His cheeks turned red. "Dean Harper was the one who found it, when he went to Sam's room."

"You mean you never saw any marijuana?"

"No, I didn't."

I shook my head. "I knew it. This just doesn't add up. Harper is alleging Sam was in possession of a large quantity of marijuana, and I'm sure he said you found it."

Shawn was silent.

"Sam won't deny it, but he clams up when I ask for details." I gripped the edges of the table to steady myself. I couldn't swallow the tears, everything just started to come, and I cried. It wasn't that Shawn was an especially comforting presence, but he sat still and actually listened to me. I caught my breath, then blew my nose into some fresh Kleenex from my purse. "I'm sorry. I just thought you might help me figure this out."

"No need to apologize," he said, stretching his arm across the table toward mine. I closed my eyes in anticipation of a comforting touch, but it never arrived. No doubt Shawn Willis had been well trained never to make physical contact with a parent.

"Look, Mrs. Webber, I'm sorry about this. I really am. And if there's anything I can do to make you feel better, please let me know." Gone was his hurried tone. He sounded like he meant it.

"Well," I said, "another reason I asked you to coffee is that I fear we got off to a bad start, the two of us, from day one, when Edward and I dropped Sam off."

"Aw, that's ancient history," he said, but I knew it wasn't.

"That's nice of you to say. It's just that I can't help wondering if some of your hostility toward my son is a result of me."

"Hostility?"

"He's told me you aren't very friendly. I think 'short fuse' is the way he described it."

Shawn fidgeted in his chair. "Look, managing a dorm full of boys is challenging. You have no idea what kinds of stunts they pull. Sometimes I lose my patience, but that's with everybody, not just Sam."

"It's just that Dunning has been a much more difficult community than we ever expected it to be," I said.

He nodded. "I'd agree with you there."

"I also thought, since Sam is going to be confined to the dorm for the rest of the year, you're the one adult who will see him most often. And, well, he just doesn't seem like himself. I'm really worried about him. I was hoping you might forgive his transgressions and take a special interest."

"I don't know that I'll be able to—"

I stopped him from finishing that sentence, my eyes welling up again. "Shawn, please."

He looked down at his coffee before meeting my eyes. "I mean, sure. Sure, I'll make a point of looking in on Sam from time to time."

"Every night," I said.

"Okay, Mrs. Webber. I'll look in on Sam every night."

CHAPTER 14

Edward marched around the house, slamming kitchen cabinets, cranky about the lawyer's invoice and a week's worth of microwave dinners.

I only made matters worse. "Edward," I said, handing him the invoice from Dunning. "The bursar's office sent us a letter. Are we behind on Sam's tuition?"

"Oh, for God's sake, Hannah. I just wanted to see how things played out. You can't blame me, can you? You're so easily intimidated."

When I handed him a second envelope, the one containing the receipt from the hotel, I thought he was going to explode. He ranted, waving it in the air. "How could you be so irresponsible?"

"I know. We splurged on room service a few times, but it was easier on Sam."

"Hannah, you just don't understand. When it comes to Sam, it's like you can't think rationally. We cannot afford this." He pointed at the charges on the bill.

"I'm sorry," I said, retreating to our bedroom, where I was sure he would leave me alone. I sat on the bed and wept. Not because I cared about the expense, even though I should have, or because my absence put me on shaky ground at work, but because I missed Sam. I missed him like I'd have missed a vital organ. I missed him all along, sure, but it was now becoming clear that sacrificing our family hadn't been worth it. It wasn't until I was faced with a week of his sullenness that I feared permanent damage had been done.

How stupid I'd been, thinking I could send him off to that fancy school and he'd return every vacation, every summer, unchanged, that he'd never outgrow the clothes I'd packed him off with as a fourteen-year-old boy. I hadn't thought through how he'd turn into a man there, how his life would include experiences I'd never be aware of, and how our paltry family of three wouldn't stand up in comparison.

A few nights later, once it appeared safe to talk to Edward again, I slipped into the family room and asked if he wouldn't mind turning off his movie. He'd just settled into a lounge chair with a bowl of ice cream to watch *The Godfather*. "Or at least can you turn the sound down?" I asked.

He paused the film and stared at me with a hardened face. When had things gotten so bad that he couldn't even smile?

"I think we should talk," I said.

"Hannah, what is it now? I've had a shit day. I just want to relax."

I sat down on the sofa. "I'm sorry you had a shit day. I had a shit day too. I've been having a lot of shit days recently."

His face softened as I mimicked his profanity, the angry words swirling comically around the room.

"I called the lawyer. The one you hired to defend Sam."

"Why in the hell would you do that?"

"I had a question about the hours he billed, and I just—"

"And?"

"And, well, he was very nice. He kept our conversation off the meter, by the way."

Edward nodded, putting his bowl on the coffee table. "What did you talk about?"

"Well, he was happy Sam had gotten probation. But he said a lawyer in his position hears a lot about what goes on at Dunning."

I caught Edward glancing at the television screen, so I took the remote and turned the set off.

"Hannah, for Christ's sake."

"Edward, do you mind? This will only take a minute."

"Then cut to the chase."

"Well, he said that over the past two years, there's been a high degree of inconsistency with how punishments are handed out. Some parents are pretty miffed at Dean Harper and Headmaster Williams because their kids got expelled when others got off. He told me a group of them are contemplating a lawsuit."

"Yeah, but *our* kid got off. Why would we get involved?"

"I would hardly say he got off. The probation and the mark on his record are very punitive. Plus, the story about the marijuana doesn't hold up. Shawn Willis can't confirm it. Dean Harper won't even let me see the results of the urine tests they performed in the health center."

"Hannah, it's time to hang it up and come to terms with the fact that your baby isn't the innocent you think he is."

"I think we should talk to the other parents."

"No. Hannah, absolutely not. This thing is over. Let it die. Sam got caught with some pot. This is not about you."

"But, Edward," I said, "something is wrong. Sam can barely speak to me. There's something going on up there that nobody is telling us. Dean Harper mentioned a secret society and the number nine. I want to find out more about it."

"Hannah, no matter what's going on, Headmaster Williams and Dean Harper are certainly not going to open up if you threaten a lawsuit."

He had a point. But deep down, I wanted to mount a counter-attack, a way to get back at Dunning for ruining my family. Could we sue for false advertising? The catalog hadn't featured pictures of unnerved boys with gaunt skin and sunken eyes, or photographs of distraught mothers crying at their kitchen sinks, praying for a child to call. I'd had to begin a daily email correspondence with Shawn Willis to get reports on Sam.

"Seems fine." Shawn's replies were irritatingly succinct. One day, there was an extra sentence: "Harper is allowing him to go to robotics club, which seems to have him excited."

I brightened at the idea of Sam's being released from his dorm for robotics, then realized Harper's ulterior motive. Of course he'd let Sam build robots—how else would Dunning defend the regional championship? They'd use his brains to their advantage, all the while sullying his school record. There was nothing that headmaster liked more than standing onstage, rubbing shoulders with Harry Roland, '75, all self-congratulatory and victorious.

"I'm going to bed," I said to Edward. As I trudged up the stairs, the volume on the television increased, drowning out the *clink, clink, clink* of his spoon hitting the bottom of his ice cream bowl.

....

The next morning, I set out for the grocery store. I had taken to making care packages for both Sam and Shawn Willis, and I needed more ice cream for Edward. As I stood in front of the dairy case, a woman's cheerful tone greeted me from behind.

"Hannah, is that you?" It was one of the mothers from Sam's middle school.

"Hello, Molly," I replied. She had a boy Sam's age, although they had never been friends.

"I haven't seen you in ages." She pushed her cart perpendicular to mine, blocking my forward progress. She wore those pajama-like blue scrubs with clogs and a long sweater. She had obviously just gotten off work. I smiled sympathetically as I placed a quart of milk and a dozen eggs in my cart, but I was ready to go.

She wasn't moving. "I was actually just talking about you the other day," she said.

"Is that so?"

"Did you know Tricia Foster's son started at Dunning Academy?"

"Really? I hadn't heard. I'll have to ask Sam if he's seen him."

"Tricia mentioned that things haven't been going so well for Sam up there—that he got himself into trouble. Is he going to be all right?"

My body seized at her thin mask of concern. I searched for the words to put an end to the conversation. "I'm not sure what you heard, Molly, but Sam is absolutely fine." Making a series of small turns with my shopping cart as if I were a car trying to get out of a tight parking spot, I accidentally crashed into her cart's handle. Her hand flew into the air, and her shriek and pained expression suggested I might have injured her.

I abandoned my groceries and hurried out the exit. I jumped into the Subaru and sped through the lot, only to encounter a red light that prevented me from turning onto the main street. I checked the rearview mirror, my heart pounding. I was certain it was cosmic retribution. I'd once been a hawk in the middle school's "mommy wars," lording my stay-at-home status over working mothers like Molly. How ironic that a nurse who worked twelve-hour shifts now appeared to have one up on me. I'd actually declined a playdate invitation from her when the boys were in kindergarten, as she'd had the gall to suggest I connect with her babysitter. Then, as the den mother for the Cub Scout troop, I'd driven my point home by requiring all parents to lead at least two meetings, which I'd scheduled for 3:30 p.m. Molly's son had had to drop out after that.

....

That night, after pushing around a spinach omelet on his plate, Edward searched in the freezer. "I thought you were going to get me more ice cream."

"Sorry. I had to leave the store without our groceries."

"What happened?" I thought about telling him about Molly, but chances were he'd blame me for the lack of compassion around town. He hit it off with everybody; everybody loved Edward.

"Crazy thing," I said. "There was a fire alarm, and they evacuated the whole store."

He raised an eyebrow.

The way to Edward's heart had always been through his stomach, but in those weeks, I offered him little. He probably thought I was trying to starve him, but the truth was, I no longer remembered what tasted good.

"What day does Sam come home for spring break?"

Was he really thinking about our boy? The possibility warmed my heart. Could I worry less, knowing we shared the burden?

"March twenty-fifth," I said, taking my last bite of dinner. "His last exam is in the morning, and I'll pick him up after lunch."

"What are his plans for the break?"

I wished we could go back to the days when we all had the same plans and I was the one who made them. Sam had surprised us the year before by joining the Crandalls in the Bahamas over Dunning's long winter weekend. I hadn't considered the possibility that he'd do something like that again.

"Do you think we should still visit colleges?" I asked, trying to control the quiver in my voice.

"Probably not," he said, retreating to the family room and flipping on the television.

Because of Sam's probationary status, his college counselor had sent us a revised list of schools, and it was uninspiring.

"Can you get away?" I asked.

"I should work."

Catching a glimpse of a TV trailer for the upcoming Red Sox season, I remembered the year we'd taken Sam to Fort Myers for spring training—Edward beaming, buying pennants and popcorn and a program with the stats of all the players. I'd been happy just sitting next to "my men," soaking up the sun on my bare legs and thawing out after a long New England winter.

"Why don't we go down to visit your parents?" I asked.

He flashed me a smirk. "You can't last more than forty-eight hours with my mother."

"No, really, it'd be nice to go, and if things get tense, I'll just walk the beach. It's been a tough winter."

"Can you take more time off work?"

"I'll bring a laptop and call in every day. I was once a corporate lending officer, Edward. I can do bookkeeping in my sleep."

He eyed me skeptically, but I spotted a glimmer of hope. I clung to it for the sake of our meager threesome, as well as for our marriage. If we could just board a plane together, I didn't care if it was to a retirement community in Sarasota.

"I'll think about it," he said, turning off the TV and sitting up straight in his recliner. "I'm going to bed," he said.

My mood was lighter than it had been in weeks. And as I followed Edward up the stairs, I lifted my arm to touch his shoulder, to feel the muscles in his back, to feel anything. But he was just out of reach, and when I finally caught up to him on the second-floor landing and tried again, he turned sharply into Sam's bedroom. "Good night, Hannah," he said, closing the door between us.

CHAPTER 15

I put on my yoga clothes and called to Edward in the garage that I was going to meet Joy. He was at his workbench, fixing our mailbox, which had been knocked over yet again by the snowplow. Before I slipped out the back door, I stole the casserole he had his sights on for dinner from the refrigerator.

It was 9:00 a.m. when I reached campus, early enough to guarantee I wouldn't run into Sam or any of his friends. I knocked on the door to Shawn's apartment.

After several minutes, he opened it, wearing a rumpled T-shirt and plaid flannel pajama bottoms.

"I made you a lasagna," I blurted, ignoring his bedhead and bare feet.

"A what?" he asked, backing up into his living room.

"It's a lasagna, Shawn. I asked if you cooked in my last email, and you said you didn't know how."

"Right," he said, stepping aside and opening the door wider. I entered his apartment and set my offering on the kitchen table. He closed the door against the cold.

"I also wanted to thank you for checking in on Sam and for being in touch with me," I said. "There's enough here for twelve. I thought you could invite some of the boys to help you eat it."

Shawn shook his head. "As in Sam and his friends?"

"Exactly. Everybody loves homemade lasagna, Shawn. Look, it's simple," I said, peeling back the tinfoil and revealing a corner. "You preheat the oven to 350 and heat it for about an hour, until it gets nice and bubbly on top."

"My mother used to make casseroles on Sundays." Shawn smiled. He opened the refrigerator and bent forward, shifting around some bottles to make room. His T-shirt lifted enough to expose the soft bare skin around his waist. From that angle, his hockey-player thighs were also especially pronounced. I forced myself to look away. He really was just a boy.

"Sam loves lasagna. I think it will help cement things between you. Again, I appreciate your acting like such a friend—to both of us." That last part was an embarrassing admission, but he smiled in return and I warmed at the understanding we'd formed.

I stared at my feet and made a show of pulling my car keys out of the pocket of my sweatshirt.

"Hey, thanks, Mrs. Webber."

"Hannah."

"Right, Hannah. This looks delicious. I really appreciate it." I couldn't remember the last time somebody had appreciated me.

"My pleasure," I said. "Oh, and if you don't end up eating it tonight, stick it in the freezer."

I was on my way out when Shawn blocked my path to the door. "I know I was the one who started this trouble for Sam, but I hope he knows I'm rooting for him." He might have been a man-child, but at least I had someone in my camp.

"He'll come around, Shawn," I said. "Just spend some time with him and feed him."

....

Edward entered the kitchen the following morning while I was scrubbing a perfectly clean floor and making plans to winnow out the contents of the hall closet. I derived an odd pleasure from discarding our old possessions. I threw away, recycled, and donated objects as compulsively as I'd once dieted, creating newfound space in drawers and closets and on shelves. Edward put on his overcoat and poured coffee into a plastic travel mug with his bank's logo on the side.

Sensing his stare, I stood up from my scrubbing and watched him stir the sugar into his mug. "I think we should go," he said.

"Go where?"

"To Florida, to visit my parents."

"Oh, right! Wonderful!" I cheered, hopping over to hug him.

"Careful!" he said, taking a step back and pointing to his coffee mug. "You still think it's a good idea?"

"Yes, yes! I'll look into flights today," I said. I'd drop everything and find a discount travel website as soon as I got to work. That Edward had agreed to the trip was a positive sign. Maybe we'd walk the beach together, maybe even hold hands. I had a vision of the waves lapping at our feet and the two of us apologizing to each other for having let things get out of hand.

I booked inexpensive flights and was planning to leave work in time to buy a new bathing suit at the mall when I realized I hadn't yet let Sam know. I sent him a text, hopeful the word "vacation" would get his attention. I'd been especially careful to make the message brief, since he'd told me they usually took too long to read and that he didn't realize they required a response. "Break out the sunscreen. Florida for spring break. I'm so excited!"

Florida was a rather pedestrian destination as far as Dunning standards went, but I sensed it would be a breakthrough moment for our family. I hoped Sam would at least dash off a prompt reply.

I checked my phone several times that day and began to worry that his silence meant something. Cleaning out the basement was the best outlet for my nervous energy. I swept cobwebs out of the corners and placed Sam's Little League equipment in cardboard cartons to take down to the Boys & Girls Club. I wondered if some little boy could use a worn mitt, maybe a little boy who still held his mother's hand.

I called Sam late the following afternoon on my way home from yoga.

"Mom?"

"Sam?"

"Mom, what's up?"

"Just wanted to hear your voice."

"You couldn't wait until Sunday?"

"You didn't reply to my message."

"I didn't see one."

"About Florida? About going to Florida for spring break?"

"Huh? Oh, cool."

He sounded distracted, and I sensed the window for our conversation closing. "How are you holding up?"

"I'm actually in the robotics lab. MIT is around the corner."

"Wow! Well, good luck. I'll be cheering for you."

"Thanks. It's not until after break, but I've started fiddling with some ideas."

"Anything else going on?" I resisted asking how he was doing in his classes.

"Nope. I'll talk to you Sunday."

"All right, Sam. I love you." But there was no "I love you too" before the line went dead. When I arrived home, I went to the medicine cabinet and took a Valium, then lay atop my bedspread. I brushed a longing hand against Edward's crisply ironed pillowcase and imagined his head once again lying next to mine after a week of Florida sunsets.

CHAPTER 16

S hawn picked up a tin tray of brownies from the bakery on Main Street to take to the coach's barbecue. When he arrived, Irene Schwartz was cleaning up the buffet of chips and potato salad on the kitchen table. "Hey, Shawn," she said, returning to the dishes in the sink.

"Hey, Irene," he said. "They all downstairs?"

"Yup," she said, bending over to put a bowl away in a lower cabinet. Shawn had once assumed their weekly invasions were a strain on the coach's wife but had come to realize a full dose of Coach Schwartz was what wore on a person, and that Irene most likely appreciated a peaceful living room in which to read on Friday evenings. Shawn waved the tin of brownies in the air. "Would you like me to put these on a plate?" he asked, enjoying the homines of her kitchen.

"Did ya bake them yaself?" she asked, with a good portion of sarcasm and a husky smoker's laugh. Take away the Boston accent, and Irene was a lot like his own mother.

"Yeah, in my free time I do a lot of baking," he said with a wink, turning the knob on the basement door. But before his foot hit the first stair, Fred opened the back door, letting in a blast of cold air, and handed a tray of burgers to Shawn while he removed his jacket. With the burgers in one hand and the brownies in the other, Shawn headed carefully down the stairs.

When he landed at the bottom, all heads turned, as if they were basketball fans following the arc of a jump shot. Shawn sensed there was more to their interest than seconds on grilled meat.

"Well, look who showed up," Schwartz said, giving him a sideways glance. "Thanks for gracing us with your presence. I've been waiting all day to hear what happened to that kid in Wilburton, the swimmer who got in trouble."

Shawn took a little extra time crossing the room, setting the tray on the counter and fixing a burger. He slathered on ketchup, thinking what to say, feeling slightly protective about the situation in his dorm. "His name's Sam Webber. I caught him coming in around three a.m."

"Shit, that's late," Fred said. "Meeting up with a girl?"

Shawn shrugged. "I have no idea."

"Partying?"

"Dean Harper says he had pot on him," he said.

"Uh-huh. I'll bet he did. Was he alone?"

"Yeah. Well, no. Sort of."

"What the hell does that mean?" Schwartz asked.

"I saw Justin Crandall sneaking back into his room at the same time, but he's been granted immunity or something."

"Are they part of the Nine?"

"Harper thinks so, but how the hell would I know?"

"They scanned the security films; there was no sign of anyone using the doors," said Darren, the biology teacher who was supposedly in line for Harper's job.

"They must be in the Nine, using the tunnels and not the doors. Surprised Williams hasn't installed cameras down there too," the lacrosse coach son-in-law said.

"Are you kidding?" Schwartz said. "He can't risk what goes on down there being caught on film."

Shawn couldn't contain his curiosity any longer. "I've been

down to our basement, the laundry room, and the boiler room, for Christ's sake, but where are these tunnels?"

"The boiler room in Wilburton has a connection. That's the one they use," Schwartz said, staring directly at Shawn. The room grew silent as they all chewed their last bites of meat.

Shawn remained skeptical. "So, they crisscross campus undetected?"

"Not just that," Darren said, looking down at his plate.

"What? They party down there too?"

"No," Darren said. "It's not just the kids." A collective chuckle and eye roll went around the room. Schwartz shot Darren a look of warning, then turned back to Shawn. He would always be the "new guy," but Shawn hoped he'd demonstrated enough loyalty over the past two and a half years to warrant being filled in.

"You tell him, Coach. It was before our time," Fred said.

Schwartz knocked back the contents of his Solo cup, let out a belch from the side of his mouth, and wiped his face with a paper napkin. He shifted around in his recliner, then shut his eyes, as if conjuring up a memory. "There was an English teacher back about twenty years ago, head of the department, a theatrical guy named Whittaker. He was also a dorm parent." Schwartz opened his eyes and looked directly at Shawn. "Rumors spread that he'd had his way with a boy in the shower, but the school hushed it up and he was never officially charged."

"What?"

"Probably had something to do with the fact that the kid was a senior, already eighteen. Well, Whittaker must have gotten a scare after that, so he took his predatory practices underground."

Shawn crinkled his brow in disbelief. This was terrible enough, but Schwartz went on. "He was a flamboyant guy and never careful. Finally, the school asked him to leave. Created a bogus position— emeritus chair of theatrics—and sent him off on a sabbatical year in Rome without a return ticket. Williams was dean of the faculty at the time, and he dealt with the evidence. The mother lode was hidden in the tunnel below the dorm—boxes with all sorts of weird paraphernalia and pictures of him with boys and pictures of boys together."

"Jesus. So, did this Whittaker end up going to jail?" Shawn asked, his skin rising with goose bumps.

"Uh, no," Schwartz said.

"What? Why?" Shawn practically screeched.

"Because Williams never called the cops. He opted to escort the guy out quietly."

"Never called the cops?" Shawn was floored.

"It was rumored they were good friends, if you know what I mean." Schwartz winked, his tongue pressing against the inside of his cheek.

"What? But Williams has a wife."

"That's always been more of an arrangement than a marriage."

The lacrosse coach son-in-law let go of a stifled laugh, snorting like a pig. "If a teacher went to prison, the press would find out. God forbid anyone caught wind."

"If it wasn't made public, then how do you know the details?" Shawn was hoping it wasn't as evil as all that. Maybe the story had been embellished over the years as it had been passed on from one person to the next.

"Who do you think was the maintenance guy who found all that sick shit?" Schwartz's eyes were now open wide, a sardonic grin spreading across his face. "Who was the one who notified Williams and led him to the scene of the crime?"

"You?" Shawn ventured.

Schwartz tightened his arms across his chest and nodded slowly. "And not long after, Irene and I got this nice house, and I became the head football coach. They added baseball a few years later."

"Are you kidding me?"

"Nope. The students and their families made some noise, but they went away in the end. I've never been sure if it took threats or a payoff or both. School had a lawyer who implied the students had homosexual tendencies of their own."

"The school paid off the families?" Shawn asked. That would mean complicity among the treasurer and the board, or maybe some wealthy alumni.

"Willis, haven't you learned that the most important thing around here is protecting Dunning's good name? The economy was in a slump, and the last thing the school needed was bad publicity. Everyone knows a scandal is bad for enrollment, not to mention fundraising."

Shawn hung his head and closed his eyes, collecting his emotions. He pictured a dorm parent, like him, with sinister intentions. It was the kind of thing horror movies were made of. He flashed back to the distress on Hannah Webber's face, the likelihood that Dean Harper had manufactured the pot allegation, and the fact that Sam was taking all the punishment while that golden boy Justin Crandall was untouchable. Those offenses were nothing compared with Williams's having quietly ushered a sexual predator out the back door.

"It wasn't just Williams who wanted it dealt with quietly," Darren added. "There were other gay teachers who were afraid of a backlash. They'd come so far and had a nice lifestyle at Dunning. They fought to keep it quiet as much as anyone. This was almost thirty years ago, remember."

Darren let out another snort-like chuckle. "Yeah, and there's been nothing but exemplary behavior ever since."

Shawn felt disgust spreading across his face.

"You see," Schwartz said, "once it became clear that there would be no consequences and that the administration had an incentive to keep the authorities at bay, well, let's just say a few more risk-takers came out of the woodwork."

"And they had to guard against a whole different sort of temptation once girls were admitted. They were really outnumbered in the beginning and treated kind of like diversions let in to make the winter a little warmer," Darren said.

"And Harper knows about all this?" Shawn looked back at Schwartz. For a few seconds, their eyes met.

"I'm not exactly sure how much Harper knows. He's on the Nine's trail, that's for sure. But I'd guess Williams doles out information on a need-to-know basis."

Shawn left his half-eaten burger on the paper plate and climbed the stairs to the unlit kitchen. Irene must have already gone to bed, because it was dark in the living room too. He grabbed his coat and let himself out.

As he passed through the hedge in the outfield, the campus spread out in front of him in a different light. What had once been formidable beauty now appeared as a flimsy veneer. Crusted over with gray salt and mounds of hardened snow, the street and sidewalks had become the callused skin of a heartless beast. Never before had Dunning felt so remote, an island operating under its own set of rules while its far-off patrons and the parents of its students assumed that the adults in charge, who included Shawn, had nothing but the kids' best interests at heart.

CHAPTER 17

"Sam," Mr. Willis called into his room during evening rounds, "Harper says it's okay for you to go to robotics club."

"Uh, thanks."

"And swim team also."

Sam greeted the second bit of news with a frown, and when he showed up at the pool on February 1, the season almost over, the coach told him not to bother. It was something he'd stopped enjoying anyway. Swimming felt more like a habit than a passion, something he'd done his entire life and kept at only because attending Dunning as an athlete put him on better footing than a NARP (nonathletic regular person). Once, he'd raised the idea of quitting with his parents, but the "q" word was something his mother wouldn't hear of.

Fiddling with circuitry, however, still lit him up. With no swim practice and the Nine's activity temporarily suspended, Sam had more time for robotics. His weeks at Dunning had always revolved around the club's Wednesday evening meetings, but now that was the case more than ever. Sam ate dinner quickly his first week back in order to get to the lab early.

Raj was already diagramming some circuitry on the whiteboard when Sam arrived. He'd taken over running the meetings once Sam's probation had rendered him ineligible for leadership positions. Although the robotics team had never operated under a formal hierarchy, everyone had looked up to Sam as the de facto leader. He'd been the one to stand at the front of the room and had been the assumed recipient of the prized summer internship at Harry Roland's software and robotics firm in Silicon Valley. It was a position awarded every year during the Prize Day ceremonies to the outstanding junior in the field of robotics. Both Sam and Raj had been nominated, and now Raj was clearly operating under the assumption that his primary competition had been eliminated.

Disqualified and outside the frenzy, Sam had begun viewing his classmates' résumé building with amusement. Dunning now seemed like nothing more than a holding pen where students tried to set themselves up for a happy life in the future.

Since he was no longer pitted against his classmates for highly sought-after senior leadership positions, they treated him differently. Kids who'd never opened up before entered his room like it was a confessional. Even Max sat on the edge of Sam's bed, admitting that Dunning was getting to him, that he wasn't living up to his brother's success and was afraid he might crack. Junior year was the infamous tipping point. The workload, combined with standardized tests, had everyone buried in books, and never before had the stakes felt so high. Sam listened intently to what was invariably the same story over and over again: his friends felt trapped by the high expectations they'd been raised with and believed that no matter how much they achieved, it wasn't enough. Their parents were never satisfied, and the school was always shifting the playing field. He'd endured the pressure too, but he was now able to shed it like a heavy winter coat.

While Raj busied himself at the front of the lab, Sam raised his head every time the door opened, hoping to see Nathalie or Astrid enter the room. They hadn't had a private moment since his DC, and he craved their lighthearted rapport. When the girls finally entered, however, it was with grave expressions on their faces.

"Cheer up," he said, summoning his most charming voice. Astrid hugged him first. He rested his chin on her shoulder and locked eyes with Nathalie.

When Astrid let him go, he made his way to Nathalie. "It's so good to finally see you," she said, wrapping her thin arms around his shoulders. She held him for an especially long time.

"Do you believe in love at first optical recognition, or should I ambulate by your location again?" he whispered. It was his Poindexter impersonation, a private joke, inspired by the nerds at the MIT competition. Sam breathed a sigh of relief at her giggle, its normalcy, and the way she held him for an extra beat.

They broke apart, and Nathalie searched his eyes. "I was so worried about you," she said, her tone implying something more than casual concern. Sam cocked his head. If Nathalie was about to reveal feelings for him, this fall from grace was coming with a serious silver lining.

Mr. Martin began calling everyone to attention. The room was humming. Like cars revving their engines, waiting for the green flag to drop, the robotics team was on the verge of being let loose. Tonight, along with dozens of other teams in the eastern region, they would listen to the MIT tournament director announce the design expectations via webcast. It was the nation's biggest regional competition, sponsored by Boeing, GE, and NASA, and the winner would qualify for nationals in San Diego a few weeks later.

After receiving tonight's instructions, they'd have six weeks to assemble a robot using only the motors, batteries, control system, construction materials, and automation components included in the official package.

When their screens came to life, the tournament director described the parameters: Their robot would have to pick up Wiffle balls and deposit them into buckets, then climb up a metal ramp, where it would rescue plastic figurines and send them down a zip line to safety. Teams would be judged on speed, accuracy, number of balls collected, execution of the mission, and number of figurines successfully rescued. His last slide outlined the dimensions of the ramps, zip line, and obstacle course. On the day of the contest, they'd be allowed to make minor adjustments in the pit.

Their screens went black, and Raj whooped. "We're gonna kill them this year!" He pumped his fist. Even though his lanky, wiry frame marked him as a nonathlete, he gloated that robotics was the "varsity sport for the brain." He was especially jazzed because Headmaster Williams had invited him up onstage at that morning's all-school assembly. "I'm clearing a special spot in the trophy case. Wouldn't it be nice if this was the year Dunning brought home the national championship?"

Raj had never been in the spotlight or called out in front of the school. As the kids shut down their laptops and started congregating in small groups, he said, "I'm going to have special sweatshirts made for us this year. Everyone come back on Saturday with your design for the cell phone controls and circuit board interface."

Sam had already started scribbling down notes. He glanced at his watch—two hours before check-in, and he didn't want to return to the dorm until he'd sketched out an initial design with Astrid and Nathalie.

"Working in groups results in mediocrity, Webber," Raj said, gathering his things. "Everyone knows that true genius emerges in solitude."

Sam shook his head. "Sure, Raj. Whatever you say." He pulled his stool up to the whiteboard alongside Nathalie and Astrid and began outlining the logical order of operations. Several first-year students hung back to watch.

They could practically complete each other's sentences. "Wiffle balls will be fairly easy to gather and pick up, so I'm not as concerned about the mechanics," Nathalie said, using a green marker to draw an arrow in her schematic.

"Right. It's the control and rotor design that will have it moving efficiently around the course. Accuracy is a higher priority this year," Sam said.

Rookies would spend excessive time on the design of the robot itself, but their special sauce had always been the code Sam and Nathalie wrote for the circuitry boards. A few first-years hoping to align themselves with a winning design asked questions. Before he needed to leave, Sam snapped a picture of what they'd sketched out on the whiteboard.

"Sorry, guys, I've got to go check in."

"Will you be able to get out at night to work with us?" Astrid asked.

"If I can get it cleared," he said.

Astrid collected her things and swung her long black hair behind her back.

"If I can't get out, can we share the code in a Google doc?" he called on his way out the door, but Nathalie didn't lift her head to answer him.

CHAPTER 18

S hawn passed the library every evening on his way to and from
the dining hall. Looking through large windows at the students
illuminated by green-shaded table lamps, he breathed relief that
his life had moved on from memorizing facts out of books. No one
would ever catch him going back to school.

Sidestepping the turnstile at the library's entrance, he caught
his breath at the height of the ceiling and the overall enormity of
the space. It was even more impressive on the inside. The paneling was carved mahogany, on which grand oil portraits depicting
the sixteen Dunning headmasters. A lit image of Ezekiel Dunning,
with his jutted chin and fierce gaze, was at the center of them all.
Despite the progressively modern eras in which his successors held
office, there was something of Ezekiel in all of them. Even Williams,
standing erect, clasping a volume of Arthur Miller's plays to his
heart, wore the requisite severity as if it was an occupational hazard.

Shawn shuddered at Ezekiel's stern visage, approaching the
reference desk and the woman sitting behind it. It was Angeline
Florentine, new to the staff and dubbed the "hot" librarian by the
boys in Wilburton. His heart skipped, and he found himself grinning. He hadn't smiled since he'd heard Schwartz's story.

"Hi. I'm doing a project on the history of the hockey team, for its one hundredth anniversary. Can you point me to the old yearbooks?" he asked.

"You the hockey coach?" she asked, putting away a magazine. She must have known who he was. After they'd won the championship, his picture had been in the *Dunning Daily* regularly.

"That's me," he said, extending a hand. "Shawn."

"Hey, I'm Angeline."

"Nice to meet you."

"Yeah, you too." Their eyes met before he had to look away. She got up from her desk, swinging her long curls behind her back. "Yearbooks are in the basement. Let me show you."

Shawn followed her to the corner stairwell, fixating on the delicate way her slender hand grazed the banister. Her nails were long and bright red, a detail that stood out in Dunning, New Hampshire, a place where women wore short, practical haircuts, little to no makeup, and layers of woolen clothing.

Not only did he notice Angeline's fingernails, but they turned him on. It wasn't her perfect, round ass, her full, glossy hair, or her big brown eyes. No, it was her manicure that did it.

She pointed to the yearbooks.

"Thanks a lot," he said, but before he picked out a volume, he turned toward her. "Hey, would you ever want to grab a bite sometime?"

"Sure," she said, smiling. She jotted her phone number on a scrap of paper.

"Great. Okay. Thanks." Shawn smiled again before sucking in his stomach and stuffing her phone number into the front pocket of his jeans.

"All right," she said, her eyes twinkling under the fluorescent lights. She let out a happy laugh, then made her way back to the stairwell, her hips swaying with a little extra sass. If Shawn hadn't been so intent on hunting down information on Whittaker, he would have followed her back upstairs.

Instead, he spread the yearbooks from the early eighties across a table. When he flipped the first one open, he couldn't help shaking his head. All the people had hair that was blown out and feathery. The men wore funky mustaches and sideburns. And even though the kids were pictured for the most part in class dress, the athletics pictures featured short shorts and white tube socks with dark horizontal stripes yanked up to the knee. Flipping through these pages made Shawn feel like whoever Whittaker was and whatever he'd done was ancient history, from a black-and-white era when people weren't as sensitive to the rules as they were now. He scanned all the senior pictures, recognizing family names that were still around.

The yearbooks from the early part of the decade pictured Headmaster Williams as chair of the English department. He'd been a handsome guy—robust, even. Then, toward the middle of the decade, there was a switch. Whittaker was chair of the English department, and Williams was dean of the faculty.

Shawn flipped to the pages where departmental faculties were photographed together. There, sitting at the head of a table, flanked by colleagues on either side, was Arnold Whittaker. His hands were clasped on the table. In the grainy image, his facial features weren't clear, but he did wear long sideburns, thick-framed glasses, and a turtleneck sweater under a blazer.

Shawn opened the following year's volume, in which Whittaker was pictured at a chalkboard in what was obviously a staged candid, which revealed a better sense of his size. He was a tall, slender man with a goofy smile, yucking it up for the camera. His glasses were scrunched up on his nose, and his dark, thick eyebrows sprouted ungroomed strays.

Shawn found the first volume in which Whittaker was abruptly absent and Schwartz was pictured as the assistant football coach: 1988. He wondered how Williams might have spun that—a janitor promoted to head football coach. Wouldn't there have been a lot of speculation? Or at least pushback from the boosters?

Shawn returned to the reference desk to ask Angeline where back issues of the *Dunning Daily* were housed.

"Sure. What year are you looking for?" She smiled, clicking her fancy long fingernails against her keyboard.

"Late eighties—like, eighty-eight, eighty-nine."

"You want all of them because they came out, like, daily," she said.

"Jesus, that's a lot of paper."

"Don't be a wise guy. They're scanned."

"Right."

Angeline expertly navigated various links on the library's website and loaded all the issues from two years in a few minutes. Shawn wondered how smart librarians needed to be. Was Angeline more like the academic faculty, or was she more like him?

Shawn opened up the first file and clicked on the sports page. "You can type in keywords to search, ya know." He hadn't realized Angeline was looking over his shoulder.

"You can just type in 'hockey,'" she added.

"Oh, okay," he said, shutting down the computer. "I think I'll do this later, but thanks for showing me how."

"Sure," she said, looking worried she'd done something wrong.

"I've gotta run," he said. "I'll call you."

....

"A draft beer," said Angeline.

"Make that two," Shawn said to the waitress. McGrory's pub on Dunning's Main Street was a locals' watering hole that was also popular with the younger faculty.

Even though she'd been late to arrive, causing Shawn ten minutes of doubt, he was now beaming. He'd taken some extra thought with his appearance, and when Angeline removed her coat to reveal tight jeans and a silky, low-cut blouse, it looked as though she had as well.

They relaxed into conversation about work over a second beer and a plate of chicken wings.

"Yeah, I'm the interim head coach, which means I have all the responsibility and half the pay."

"And I work for an old spinster who staffs me, like, every Sunday." They couldn't stop laughing, agreeing that their titles and departments were different but the politics were the same.

Shawn smiled when Angeline ordered a burger. It might have been for show, because she was pretty thin.

"Italian metabolism," she explained.

She wasn't shy with the fries either, picking them up between those long fingernails, now painted a softer shade of pink, and placing them suggestively on her tongue.

Angeline would confess it had been against the rules for her to leave the reference desk unattended to show him the yearbooks in the basement, but it was the first time she'd seen Shawn in the library, and she didn't know if he'd ever return.

He'd confide what he had been up to, how Schwartz had gone from the maintenance crew to football coach overnight and why researching this Whittaker character had become his obsession. He'd wait a while into the relationship to tell her how he was a regular in Schwartz's basement and had learned about the sexual misconduct that had occurred in the 1980s.

"Are you kidding? Everyone at Dunning knows about you guys. People joke about what must go on in Schwartz's basement on Friday nights."

"Just guys eating burgers and talking sports."

"Maybe a little sex too?"

Shawn grimaced. The idea of Schwartz or any of his crew having sex was enough to make him lose his appetite.

....

Angeline lived with her mother and sister in the house she grew up in, about fifteen miles away, so, after a few dates, when she and Shawn were at the point of wanting to rip each other's clothes off, he snuck her into his apartment. But he received an email from Harper the next morning reminding him that it was against the faculty code of conduct for two unmarried persons of the opposite sex to spend time alone in dormitory lodging. He wondered who had tipped off the dean.

It was likely one of the punks in the dorm, instilling payback. Shawn bit his lip before replying to the email, resisting the urge to write something to the effect that molestation of minors was okay—it was people like him and Angeline that Dunning had to look out for.

So they reverted to spending time in her car, as if they were in high school as well, fogging up the windows and contorting in awkward positions, but they also sometimes just talked in there. Shawn learned that Angeline had earned good enough grades in high school to get a scholarship to the University of New Hampshire. She paid the rest of her way working in the university library.

"I really like it—I mean, the order, and the way things are classified."

"What's that called, again?" Shawn laughed, wondering why, now that Google existed, anyone would bother going to a library to do research.

"The Dewey decimal system?" She swatted him.

"Yeah."

"Call me a nerd, but I like stacks of books—all the information, all the stories. I like the enormity of what a collection represents, everything that's ever been written down, all under one roof. And then there's the smell: old, musty volumes, and new books with protective plastic covers. I guess I also like to help people find what they're looking for."

Shawn swallowed, realizing this was not the time to tease. She was smart and thoughtful and had just opened up to him. Shawn couldn't remember a time that had happened before. He looked into her eyes, and she continued.

"One of the older librarians, one of my supervisors back at UNH, suggested I think about library science as a major."

"That's really cool. My major in college was hockey. I didn't pay much attention in class. After I blew my knee out, I was in a real funk. Barely scraped together enough credits to graduate."

"But now . . . I mean . . . ," she said, "coaching hockey and all—you're back doing what you love, aren't you?"

"Me? No. My passion was playing, not coaching. I don't think I have what it takes to relate to the kids."

"Seriously?"

"Yeah." He looked away.

"I'd say—I mean, just by watching you on campus—they treat you like you're one of the guys."

"Don't get me wrong. My teammates, man, they were my life—it's just these *kids*." Shawn wondered whether it was too late to start fresh. Could a little lasagna make a difference?

"I'm supposed to be an authority figure, ya know? A coach and a dorm head, but I can just tell . . ." He caught himself and straightened in the driver's seat.

"What, Shawn? You can just tell what?"

"I don't know," he said, his gaze melting into hers. "I just feel like they don't respect me. I'm new, I'm young. They're smarter than me." That last part was hard to admit out loud, but once he did, his quick temper began to make more sense.

"Jeez, I don't think of respect as something that comes with age or intelligence. Human beings owe it to one another."

"Yeah, I guess, ideally. But that's not really how the world works, Angeline."

She nodded. She had to know. She couldn't tell him those privileged little geniuses didn't show her a bunch of attitude when they strutted into the library.

Shawn surprised himself by having more to say. "At a place like Dunning, when you're not on the academic side and you're pigeonholed as a jock, monitoring the rowdiest dorm on campus, it's like nobody . . . Well, it's not just the kids who don't respect you."

"Shawn, listen, I don't want to butt in or anything, but I don't see that."

He turned the key in the ignition, and the radio came back on. The digital clock on Angeline's dashboard glowed green. It was time to get back to Wilburton for check-in. "I do," he said.

CHAPTER 19

"Whoa, Sam. I have an appointment with my college counselor," Nathalie said, pulling away.

"Give me five minutes, Nat." He tried to meet her gaze, but she stared impatiently over his shoulder. "You've been avoiding me."

"You're, like, locked up in your dorm. I'm not the one avoiding you," she said.

It was a few days after the robotics meeting, and he'd been waiting outside her art history seminar in the newly renovated fine-arts building. They had fifteen minutes, the midmorning break that Dunning built in to give the student body a chance to catch its collective breath. Most kids used it to grab breakfast or go over homework. Sam had always used it to seek out Nathalie.

He guided her to an exit and pushed the door open, wanting to be alone even if it was out in the cold. They sat on a granite bench, and Sam jammed his hands into the pockets of his jeans. His feet numbed quickly in the harsh temperature, as he wasn't wearing any socks. It was a thing at Dunning, underdressing in defiance of the season. Nathalie went sockless as well, and Sam resisted the urge to wrap her fragile ankles in his sweater.

"This won't take long," he assured her. He looked at the ground, trying to summon the speech he'd rehearsed. He couldn't meet her gaze, afraid he'd go off script once he saw those rosy cheeks and glossy lips. "Look, the thing is," he said, "I need you to believe me here. I'll tell you what I can, but I can't tell you everything."

"Okay . . . ," she said, with a rising inflection. Still, he didn't look up.

"Nathalie, you know the real me. You always have. It's just that I've discovered something weird, and if it's what I think it is, it's pretty bad. There are people at this school who can't be trusted."

"Like a drug ring?"

"Nathalie, be serious. I'm a robotics geek. I'm not into drugs." There were kids at Dunning, red eyed and cotton mouthed, who were stoned most of the time, and Sam couldn't help but laugh at the idea of being one of them.

His laugh made her smile.

"Anyway, something isn't right at this school, and it's a lot more serious than me getting a DC."

Her eyes widened.

"I need your help."

"Wait, Sam—I can't afford to get mixed up in any trouble."

"No, no, no," he said, shaking his head insistently. "I would never put you at risk. I just need a tour of Bennett. We would do it straight up, get permission and everything. But I need to get inside your dorm and have a look around."

She squinted. "This has something to do with Bennett?"

"Possibly." Sam hoped that her mind, wired for problem solving, would find it hard to resist a real-life mystery.

"So, all you want me to do is show you around my dorm?"

"Yeah, that and one more thing."

She raised an eyebrow. "What?"

Sam exhaled. "Believe in me. Please. If you . . ." And he had to stop because his lower lip was trembling and heat was rising in his cheeks.

"Shh, it's okay," she said. And before Sam realized what was happening, Nathalie started rubbing his back as if he were a baby in need of soothing.

He swallowed hard. "If I lost your friendship, I don't think I could last here another day." The wind bit into his chapped lips, and his backside ached on the freezing stone, but there was no way he was going to stand while Nathalie had her hand on his back. After several minutes, she leaned against him, and his cheek brushed against her soft hair. She may have been seeking only body heat, but it was the best moment of his life.

Sam would look back on that morning out on the cold stone bench whenever he needed a reminder of how life could surprise him. Sitting close to Nathalie like that produced a high made even more extreme because it followed such a low. He'd been spending time alone in his room, doubting his allegiance to Justin and the Nine and feeling guilty for disappointing his parents. Although the biting wind meant it was still undeniably winter, that morning his heart swelled with the promise of spring.

....

Nathalie completed the online form requesting parietals for the coming Saturday. They chose a time when the athletes would be at their games, and a bulk of the girls at the library.

Despite his grinning politely and shaking hands with the Bennett dorm parent, she looked Sam up and down as if he were a bad person. She delivered the scripted speech about leaving the door to Nathalie's room open and three feet on the floor. God, how he wished he'd come to test those boundaries.

"Thanks very much," Sam said. If only she knew that just below her apartment, a pedophile had set up shop.

Sam and Nathalie walked down the hall together. Entering her room, Sam couldn't help noticing the framed pictures of her friends on the walls, her plush lavender duvet, and the bright pink throw pillow atop a lounge chair. Being in the midst of her belongings infused him with an intimacy he hadn't been prepared for. He wanted to spend more time looking around, cataloging her tastes and interests.

"What now?" Nathalie asked, putting her hands on her hips.

"Right. Let's get to work." He started pacing out the footprint of the boiler room. He concentrated on his steps in relation to the windows. Doing so led out into the hall, to the bathroom door.

"Can you check that the coast is clear?"

Nathalie pushed the door open and confirmed that it was empty, then let Sam in to survey the row of toilets, sinks, and shower stalls.

"Is this the bathroom you use? Where you shower?"

Nathalie rolled her eyes. "No, I trudge up to the second floor." She paused. "Of course this is the bathroom I use. What's going on? You're freaking me out."

"Are there any security cameras on this floor?" Sam asked, scanning the molding by the ceiling.

"Yeah, by the entrances and in the stairwell, and then one about halfway down the hall." She pointed to one that was easily visible and revolved, capturing the ins and outs of every dorm room.

"But nothing in the bathroom?" he asked.

"Ew," she said. "That would be weird."

Sam continued his search, checking the walls, high and low.

"Holy shit," Nathalie said after a minute. "You think whatever weird thing is going on at Dunning has to do with our bathroom?"

"Maybe. Are the ones on the top two floors in the same location on the hallway?"

"Yeah."

"Then it might not be this bathroom. It could be one of the others, or it could be all three."

She looked at him as if he was crazy. "What are you talking about? And why haven't you reported this?"

Sam had been wondering the same thing but was still giving credence to Justin's instincts. "Wait in the hall and keep watch. Warn me if someone's coming. Please, Nathalie, just trust me on this."

"Okay," she said, peering one way and then the other, scanning the closed doors along her hall.

Sam turned toward the tiled room. He looked for obvious cracks, drilled holes, any fixtures that had been tampered with or refit, anything newer than the rest. It was altogether possible that the pervert, upon discovering that his video equipment had been confiscated, had already removed the actual camera and taken back every scrap of incriminating evidence. In that case, Sam was also looking for signs of a hasty removal, even more cracking or dislodging.

He scanned the interior wall of the bathroom with his penlight, shining it up by the ceiling and down by the floor. Nathalie cracked the door and whispered, "Are you almost done?"

"Have you noticed any workmen in here? Anything that might have been added or removed?"

"Um, no," she answered quickly, and shut the door.

He searched the showers. There were three stalls, each with its own opaque nylon curtain. He pulled the curtain to the first stall taut behind him. The door to the bathroom opened.

"Jenny!" Nathalie called.

An upperclassman entered, sleep still in her voice. Sam held his breath in the shower stall. His heart beat a little harder than usual, but, after she urinated, the girl flushed the toilet and left.

"Sam, Jesus. How long is this going to take? This is really weird," said Nathalie.

He didn't answer, focusing on the showerhead and its connection to the wall. It was an obvious angle. As he reached up to pull on it, his elbow knocked into the shampoo dispenser adhered to the tile. The plastic square, clean and new and filled with a pink gel, came loose. Sam took it in both hands and pulled it from the wall, exposing a blue cable running out of its back. Sam snipped it with a pair of clippers he carried in his back pocket. He plugged the hole in the tile with a bit of putty.

Sam rapped on the bathroom door to notify Nathalie that he was coming out. He concealed the plastic box under his sweatshirt and walked briskly back toward her room. She followed a few steps behind.

Once they were inside, he uncovered his find. "Look," he said, holding the dispenser out to her like an offering.

"Shampoo?"

"A camera." He pointed to the dime-size lens embedded in

the dispenser's chrome frame, but his discovery no longer felt like success. He watched as the implication of what he'd found dawned on Nathalie. Her eyes opened wide, and she began walking in a series of small circles around her room, thumping her hand against her chest, repeating, "Oh my fucking God," in a whisper-scream.

He stared silently at the apparatus, not quite ready to broach what it meant. Nathalie rummaged a tote bag out of her closet to put it in, to get it out of sight, then covered it with a towel. Sam's heart raced with adrenaline and the desire to figure out his next move.

Nathalie reached out and grasped his arm, as if she could read his mind and didn't want to be alone. Her eyes swelled with emotion. "Are you going to robotics tomorrow?" she asked.

"Of course. I'll be there. Will you?" He tried to reassure her with an easy smile that things could go on as normal.

"Yes," she said.

"Great. We have lots to do before MIT. And the rest of this stuff . . ." He pointed at the tote bag. "Don't worry. I'll get to the bottom of it. Everything will be okay."

While she continued to search his face for consolation, Sam wrapped his arms around her in a reassuring hug.

He carried the tote bag across his middle like a football through the dark, quiet halls of Wilburton. As with a cat proudly delivering a dead bird to the feet of its master, Sam's first instinct was to bring it to Justin, but then he reconsidered, remembering that Justin was staying at his family's home in town that weekend. Besides, Sam was not in the mood for one of his outbursts over why Sam couldn't seem to leave the subject alone.

He passed Grabs's bedroom door and heard the unmistakable sound of fingers tapping away on a keyboard. He poked his head in, hoping his friend might not be too busy. Grabs was typing furiously, wearing noise-canceling earphones and jumped in his seat when Sam waved an arm across his line of vision.

"Sam!" Grabs shouted. "Shit! Don't do that. You scared me." He took off his earphones and closed his laptop, then folded his arms in front of his chest and leaned back in his chair. Cold silver light beamed through his window, casting a shadow on the wall behind his bed.

"Sorry to interrupt. Gotta minute?"

"Sure," he said, pulling the quilt over his rumpled sheets and neatening a space for Sam to sit. Sam locked Grabs's door.

"What's going on?"

"I need your expert opinion," Sam said, unwrapping the shampoo dispenser from the towel and placing it on his lap.

Grabs crinkled his fleshy brow, taking the plastic contraption, now oozing pink gel, in his hands and tugged on the cable running out of its back.

"Is this for your next prank?" He eyeballed the small camera lens in the front of the soap dispenser. "You'd better be careful, Sam. Invasion of privacy is a federal offense."

"Very funny." Sam paused and looked at Grabs with an expression devoid of humor. "I was just wondering if you'd seen anything like this before."

"Well, they get pretty creative with cameras these days. But yeah, I think I've seen one advertised—not on a respectable site, however."

"How does it work?" Sam asked.

Grabs had a series of facial expressions reserved for stupid questions. "Seriously, Sam? It's a camera."

"No, I mean, how would someone control it?"

"Probably like any other remote device: this cable runs to a video monitor and/or recording device, allowing the operator to turn it on and off when they want to."

"Do you think the lens moves around or only gets one angle?"

"You're the robotics whiz, man. Why don't you take the thing apart and find out?"

"Yeah, I could do that." But the truth was, Sam didn't want

to spend any time handling this thing. He didn't want to think too much about what it had been used for. "What did the camera you found in the laundry room look like?"

"Definitely not as James Bond. It was just a small plastic device taped to one of the shelves over the dryer." Grabs packed the shampoo dispenser back in the tote bag. "Where'd you find this?"

"There's some sick stuff that goes on in this place," Sam said, shaking his head. He still flinched at the way kids shared their social lives on Snapchat. Somebody videotaping private moments in the shower was too much.

"Was it actually in use somewhere?" Grabs asked.

"The Bennett showers."

"And you dismantled it yourself?"

"Yeah."

"Who else knows you took it?"

"Nathalie." Hidden cameras weren't just Nine business—he'd have to share some information if he wanted help.

"Nathalie's fine, but did you sign in with the dorm parent?"

"Yeah," Sam said, instantly regretting the trail he'd left.

"You need to be more careful."

Sam didn't need to be told. "Back to the camera—I don't think it's been in operation for a few weeks. The recording device was dismantled. The wires were cut."

Grabs nodded slowly, then locked eyes with Sam. It would have been so much easier if he could have told Grabs about his Nine mission and the tunnels and how he'd discovered the monitor and cable hookup. Their friendship had survived two years of secret keeping because neither of them pushed. Grabs had secrets too. He was likely a major player in Faceless and deep into covert cyber-activity of his own.

"Unless the sicko is using the video for his own personal entertainment, he's probably selling it, uploading it to a porn site," Grabs said.

"Do you think that's what happened with the laundry room video?"

"Possibly, but my guess is that those videos were more for the amusement of the upperclassmen in Wilburton."

Sam's stomach lurched. During their first year, when Grabs had proffered late-night access to the Internet, Harold Chu hadn't been the only one who'd purchased online porn. Listening to the upperclassmen at the dorm grill brag about sex had spiked all the boys' hormonal urges. One night, their proctor had egged them on, and a group of first-years had gathered around Max's monitor, watching as he clicked on one site after another.

Even harder to admit was that Sam hadn't pulled his eyes away. Not even when Ethan took it one step further and started watching in their room. Ethan was obsessed with a site called Girls Who Suck. He watched hours of oral sex, enormous breasts taking up a large part of the screen. Sam had never imagined women taking visible pleasure in doing such things with their tongues.

Sitting on Grabs's bed, Sam felt his head aching with those memories. Besides what Ethan was into, the video that had seared itself into his mind had been shot via hidden camera. Their proctor had said that unknowing subjects were premium. The girls were less whorish, and the whole concept had a peeping-Tom thrill to it.

Sam wasn't proud of the way late-night porn had gotten him and Ethan speculating about their female classmates in a vulgar way. After lights out in their bunks, they'd muse about the size of the girls' nipples, whether they shaved, what experiences they'd had. Now, Sam sat in Grabs's room with the tote bag and felt his face growing hot—he might as well have been an accessory to the crime in the Bennett showers.

"You know there are tons of these sites online," Grabs said, nodding toward his laptop.

"Right. But I need to find out exactly who took pictures with this camera and where they are now," Sam said, pointing the tote bag.

Grabs shrugged. They both knew that if something was posted on the Internet, he'd be able to track it down, but a little more to go on would be helpful.

"Can you get me some of the footage?"

Sam shrugged as he gathered the bag's handles. "I'll try."

He'd witnessed Justin and the seniors in Wilburton. They'd been in a celebratory mood ever since they'd finished their last exams before graduation. Justin was likely hosting a party that night and would soon be leaving on spring break. The last thing Sam wanted to do was bother his friend about the whereabouts of the backpack.

CHAPTER 20

I wove around the double-parked Range Rovers, wondering behind which tinted window Mimi Crandall sat. It was the end of March and winter exams, and I was at Dunning to retrieve Sam. Seeing a boy I thought was Justin loading his luggage into a trunk, I slowed to a stop and started rolling my window down so I could wave at Mimi. But one of the black town cars hired to chauffeur kids to the airport started honking at me. I tapped the gas obediently, all the while swearing at the aggressive New York manner with which everyone jockeyed for parking places. *Just get me out of here.*

Our flight to Florida would depart the next morning, and as I reviewed our packing list against the steering wheel, Sam loaded his bags into the back. He moved slowly, making multiple trips to his room and saying drawn-out goodbyes while I rapped my fingers on the dash. I looked right past the brick and ivy and scowled at Sam for having turned this place into a battleground. I thought about all he had given up. All our work—my work—down the drain.

Before I looked back at my list, Shawn Willis appeared on the path, walking in our direction. I waved through my window, hoping he'd keep a safe distance, not wanting to let on to Sam that we'd formed a familiar relationship over email. But I needn't have worried, because it turned out he was focused on somebody else.

JEANNE McWILLIAMS BLASBERG

An attractive young woman with long spiral curls was leaning against the hood of a dated sedan in the spot behind mine. I checked her out in the rearview mirror: camel-hair coat tied snugly at her waist, tight jeans tucked into suede high-heeled boots, a big red smile, and whiter-than-white teeth.

"Who's that?" I asked, as Sam slid into the passenger seat.

"Willis's girlfriend."

"I see," I said, with a surprising pang in my chest. "She's certainly dressed up. Where do you think he imported her from?"

"Mom, she works here. She's a librarian."

I swallowed. "Oh." The idea of Shawn making a life for himself on the Dunning campus had a curious effect on me. I'd always thought of him as an ally, believed we were up against this weird world together. In our emails about Sam, I had revealed some of my most private concerns. Shawn knew much about what obsessed me, and I assumed I'd gotten to know him pretty well too. But he'd never mentioned a girlfriend.

"So, how'd it go?" I asked, driving through the campus gates.

"Mom, our robot is going to be so amazing this year." He was chatty and animated. "Astrid and I just figured out how to—"

I couldn't fight the urge to interrupt. "No, I mean, how did your exams go? These are some important tests," I chided.

Up until then, I'd been extremely forgiving of Sam's mysterious escapade. But for some reason—maybe the combination of the honking town car and Shawn's ignoring me—I chose that moment to lose it. I interrogated Sam about his finals as if acing them might catapult him out of the hole he'd dug. All excitement vanished from his face, and he sank back in his seat and turned toward the window. He carried the same posture onto the airplane and all the way to Florida.

Edward's father met us at baggage claim in the late afternoon. The humidity hit me like a wall, stifling any extraneous conversation as we pulled our roller bags through the parking lot.

"Smooth flight?" he asked.

"Very," Edward answered.

His mother greeted us at their front door, the aroma of dinner filling my nose the minute I crossed the threshold. Whereas my parents ran a business together, Edward's had always divided the tasks. It was his mother's place to stay home and cook the roast, as it had been for the past sixty years.

I'd once ridiculed her old-fashioned ways, her gray coif sprayed tightly in place each week during her standing appointment at the beauty parlor. But seeing her aged, frail frame on that afternoon suddenly filled me with a compassion I'd never been able to access before. Edward was her Sam, after all, the son who'd left home and barely communicated anymore.

As she stood, thin and nervous, watching my husband shuttle in our luggage, I understood her anxiety over the meal she'd prepared and whether it would satisfy him. Given my recent lack of culinary inspiration, I was confident it would, but she was wringing the oven mitt she'd carried to the front door from the kitchen. She hadn't seemed to worry about her appearance, however, not until her husband pointed to her waist, saying, "Sandra, your apron."

"Oh, my heavens. I'm sorry." She pulled it over her head and popped into the powder room to fix her hair and apply lipstick. There were a thousand little ways in which I found Sandra and Howard odd, so different from my effusive parents, who hugged and fussed and talked loudly whenever a rare visitor came calling. But that day, all Edward and I had in common with his parents dawned on me. Even though they had two sons and Edward and I had only Sam, they had sent theirs to boarding school as well. Howard had worked long hours, managing an insurance agency, and Sandra chaired the ladies' auxiliary at their church. When I'd first met them, I'd been wide-eyed and impressed during dinner at their country club and at the WASPy way in which they all fit in. Now I was a part of their reserved, understated family.

Our first dinner in Florida, it didn't take long for the conversation to turn to Sam's education. They were familiar with the drill. Their other granddaughters had graduated from UC Berkeley and

Pomona. All people seemed to do in their retirement community was brag about their grandchildren.

Howard poured the wine, including a token amount in Sam's glass. "So, Samuel, do you have this thing all wrapped up? Where do you plan to go to college?"

Sam stuttered, "Gramps, I haven't even finished my junior year."

I wanted to jump to his defense, but Edward caught my eye and put a finger to his lips. I took a bite of roast beef and chewed it laboriously, pushing overcooked green beans around my plate.

"Oh, I guess that's right," Howard said.

"I won't be applying until next fall."

"Early decision?"

"Still figuring it out."

Thankfully, that ended the discussion. But Howard turned to me, most likely expecting a postscript. Apparently, everyone in the family was used to my speaking on Sam's behalf, to my broadcasting the headlines of his life. Instead, I asked what I thought was a safe question: "Is the forecast good for the next few days?"

Sandra grinned at my attempt to shift the subject. "They're saying unseasonably cold," she said.

"Oh," I said. "Well, that's all right. We didn't come for the weather; we came to be together."

CHAPTER 21

Sam stretched his arms overhead, yawning in a beach chair. He never slept well on the hideaway in his grandparents' living room. He wished he could flip a switch and doze on the beach like his father, but his mother's restlessness was contagious.

"Want to go for a walk?" she asked. She'd been peering over her sunglasses as if his dad's snoring were the reason she hadn't been making headway in her novel.

"Sure," Sam said. His father had declined a walk before falling asleep, and Sam didn't have the heart to refuse her as well.

He wondered why he always fell back into the role of dutiful only child without thinking about it. He should have still been irritated with his mother. Her nagging about his final exams was still fresh, but striding side by side, step for step, did its job to forge a silent truce.

In years past when they'd visited Florida, he and his parents had built elaborate castles in the white sand, his mother asking him where the drawbridge should go or how deep the moat should be. These experiences had led him to believe that even though he was the child in the family, he held the special power of constructing their world. The spotlight was on him during times like that, but it was also cast on him during trying times when he swayed attention away from their troubles.

Sam and his mother walked at least a mile without exchanging a word, until a seagull squawked overhead. "Ready to turn around?" she asked.

It was the kind of flat, glistening beach that stretched toward the horizon. Despite his lack of sleep, Sam could have continued walking forever. What he really wanted to do was aim for the distant, hazy line where the sky met the sea and never return to the reality of his cold life.

"Sure," he said.

When they finally returned to their chairs, his father was just walking toward them with three cups in his hands. "The ice cream man came by. I couldn't resist," he said.

Midweek, his father announced at the breakfast table that he'd purchased three tickets to a spring training baseball game.

"Cool," Sam said.

Excitement lit his mother's face until his dad quickly added, "I was thinking it could be a boys' day. I've invited your grandfather to come along."

His mother crossed her arms, rubbing the bare skin below her short sleeves, and turned abruptly toward the window. Sam felt her disappointment but simultaneously flashed a grin of appreciation in his father's direction. His mother pushed back from the kitchen table and began shuttling breakfast dishes to the sink.

Sam ached for her as they pulled away from the condo, but there was something primal about sitting in the ballpark, watching the warm-ups: three generations of Webber men embarking on yet another baseball season. The pastime had been at the center of so many of their interactions. The routine of batting practice and infielders throwing the ball around the diamond took Sam back to his childhood.

After they stood with their hands over their hearts for the national anthem, his father bought them all hot dogs. As Sam squirted mustard out of a small plastic packet, his father leaned closer to him, out of his grandfather's earshot, and whispered, "I know you've come off a terrible time at school, and I hate to think it's been made worse by the strain between your mother and me."

Sam squinted his eyes at his dad.

"Well, what I wanted to say is, just don't forget how much I love you." His father put his hand on Sam's shoulder.

Sam looked at his feet. "Dad, I . . . I worry about Mom. Is everything going to be okay between the two of you?"

"I'm not sure. I've been thinking about making some changes."

"I want . . ." Sam choked on his words before kicking the metal base of the seat in front of him.

"Look, we'll find time to discuss this later, when your grandparents aren't around. But I just want to say you're a great kid and you're going to be just fine."

His father, sporting a salty Boston Red Sox cap and well-worn T-shirt, was the only one who could give him this. While his mother strode stoically around the tension in the air, his father put words, albeit minimally, to what was going on. And only his father could let Sam off the hook, granting him permission to be less than perfect. His mother might have been the one to cheer more loudly from the sidelines and to give him pep talks before big tests, might have been the ever-present one in his life, but she never showed any of his father's quiet acceptance, an ability to take life a little less seriously.

The sun melted the tension knotting the back of Sam's neck. It was rare for him and his father to speak face-to-face. Their family had grown used to his mother's being at the center of every conversation, as the clearinghouse of information, the one who called, often reporting on behalf of his father because he was working or not able to come to the phone.

That afternoon at the ballpark, his father disrupted the norm by confiding his intention to leave his marriage. And even though this direct communication was liberating, once his father turned back to his salty popcorn and the next man at bat, a lump lodged in Sam's throat. The innings of the baseball game sailed by, clouded by the betrayal of knowing his mother's destiny before she did.

....

It didn't matter that warm weather wouldn't arrive in northern New England for several more weeks; after spring break, kids at Dunning dressed to show off their suntans. The baseball team had gone to Arizona, the lacrosse team had been to South Carolina, and the hockey team had visited Disney World to celebrate winning the league championship. Justin's family had hosted a group of seniors at their home in the Bahamas, where, when not cruising on the Crandalls' yacht, everybody zipped around to the local bars in golf carts. Sam had been Justin's guest the previous winter, and it hurt his feelings to see glimpses of the fun on his Facebook feed.

While most of the Wilburton boys were caught up in a campus-wide game of Assassin, Sam was still on restrictions. When he wasn't in the dorm, he was at the robotics lab. That first Saturday after spring break, all he wanted to do was take his spiral notebook filled with ideas and hide out there. He shivered walking across campus, his light jacket and Bermuda shorts a sorry defense against the wind. He decided to grab a quick cup of coffee in the student center, hoping he might bump into Nathalie.

Instead, he spotted Justin waving him over. When Sam joined him in line, Justin said, "Hey, Robot Man! Dude, what's up? Are you still alive?"

Sam's chest fluttered at the attention and realization that this might present an opportunity to ask Justin for access to the video. "Nah, I'm not playing Assassin."

"No? I, for one, am determined to leave this place on top. But I have some important killing to do today." He fluttered his eyebrows. When Sam didn't reply, he said, "Hey. It's good to see you."

"You too. How was your break?" Sam asked, although he really didn't want to hear about how he'd been overlooked or how all

Justin had planned for the day was hunting someone down, getting them alone, then whispering, "You're dead."

"Awesome. We had a little pregraduation fun in the Bahamas," Justin explained. "It was all seniors; otherwise, you know I would totally have invited you." He might not have meant it, but Justin always knew how to make Sam feel better.

"Yeah, I get it," Sam said. "Anyway, I had to visit my grandparents in Florida."

"Cool. Sounds chill."

"The epitome of chill." He hoped spring break had put some distance between the present and what had happened back in January. "Hey, Justin, you think I can get a look at those videos?"

Justin froze. "Jesus, Webber! Do we have to talk about this right now? There's only six more weeks until I graduate. C'mon, just relax, okay?" He clasped Sam's shoulder and added, "Let me get you some food."

He ordered two cheeseburgers, handing over his student ID like a platinum credit card with no limit, and led Sam to a table in the corner.

"So," Justin said once they sat down, breaking into his signature smirk, "I hear you're making headway with Nathalie."

News spread fast. "Maybe," Sam said, bowing his head.

"Ha ha, wow, I knew it," Justin said, pumping his fist and raising his hand in the air for a high five. "That's my little bro. Way to go, dude. I knew you had it in you." He was smiling so hard, he'd forgotten about his burger, and the red juices were dripping down his wrists. "She's hot," he said, with a smile and a nod that implied some knowing.

"Yeah," Sam said, fidgeting and assuming Justin meant it as an off-color compliment. "Listen, Justin, it's crunch time," he said. "Thanks for the burger, but I need to take it to the lab."

Later that evening, after checking in with Mr. Willis, Sam put on sweatpants and headed to the bathroom. He ran into Ethan brushing his teeth at the row of sinks. Sam looked down at the porcelain, turning on his own faucet, avoiding Ethan's reflection in the mirror. They'd never talked about the trouble Sam had gotten into. Ethan hadn't been one of the guys who'd offered him sympathy or unloaded in Sam's room. Instead, he'd acted as if Sam had deserved what he'd gotten, should have seen it coming, and never should have thought he could make it as one of Justin Crandall's crowd.

Rinsing the toothpaste from his mouth, Ethan asked, "So, Willis let you out?"

"Robotics lab," Sam said, staring ahead into the mirror.

"Of course—they can't go on without you. God forbid the team doesn't bring home the gold. Are you cleared to go to San Diego too?"

"No."

"Oh, man, and to think you're going to miss a trip with that hot piece Nathalie."

"Fuck off, Ethan." If only Ethan understood how much Sam missed their friendship.

He passed by Grabs's open door on his way back to his room and heard his friend call out, "Hey Webber, you want to play some chess?"

Sam smiled. His chess games with Grabs were just like bonding over baseball with his father.

"Sure," he said, but when Sam entered the room, there wasn't a board set up at the end of the bed. Grabs closed the door, turned the volume up on his music, and sat down. Sam could practically see the gears spinning in his friend's head.

"What is it?"

Grabs half smiled and balled one hand into the palm of the other, cracking all five knuckles. He pushed the bridge of his glasses up his nose. His white skin was oily by this time of day, and he smelled a little strong.

"Jeez, did you find something online?" Sam winced, bracing for an image of showering girls, or even his own naked body, coupling with Andrea, on a site somewhere.

"No, but I've been doing some investigating." Grabs paused, breathing deeply. "I'm not sure I should be sharing this, but since we're best friends, I'm going to."

Sam sucked in his breath with a measure of guilt. Sure, he'd asked Grabs to speak on his behalf at the DC, but there had also been long stretches when he'd been too busy with Justin to give Grabs the time of day.

"I know you're one of the Nine, along with Justin and Raymond and Saunders—"

Sam held out his hand and said, "Wait."

Grabs continued in another vein. "Okay, I know Willis busted you and then Harper took over. I know a representative of the Nine was on the committee and arranged your probation."

"What the hell?"

"I can even tell you what you got on your chemistry midterm."

"Grabs, are you fucking kidding me?"

Sam laughed. It was comical. All the sneaking around, talking in code, and passing notes in the library, all the middle-of-the-night shit, the black hoodies, the meetings in the Tomb, and fucking Grabs had known all along.

"Listen, Sam, I've known for a long time that Harper is hell-bent on catching the kingpin of the Nine. He put Willis on your trail."

The back of Sam's neck prickled. "What are you saying? You could have warned me."

"I had to let it play out."

"What? Why? Letting it play out has me totally fucked."

"Look, this was hard for me too. I don't want to get personal, but we've got a problem with your group. The Nine are so yesterday, not to mention elitism personified."

"Grabs, you might be able to hack information, but you don't know what you're talking about. We were sticking our necks out. We were dismantling a pornography operation."

"Look, when you brought that bogus shampoo dispenser in here, I thought you were asking for my help."

Sam scowled. "If you'd really wanted to help, you could have warned me Willis was stalking me."

They faced each other in silence, Sam crossing his arms at his chest.

Grabs bit his bottom lip and started anew, in a calmer tone. "You know I track a lot of online activity?"

Of course he did. Grabs was a social misfit who spent every minute he wasn't in class in front of the two computer monitors he'd rigged up on his desk. He was most likely behind the recent leak of married faculty members' online dating profiles, accompanied by the message that Faceless would continue exposing the hypocrisy of 1 percenters.

Sam's head spun. "Yeah, you track a lot of online activity. You spy on people."

"I know things, Sam."

"What kinds of things do you know?" Sam snapped.

Grabs crossed the small room to his electric teapot. He brewed strong black tea in the evenings. God only knew when the kid slept.

"For example, I know Willis and your mother exchange emails every day. Would you like me to read them or just guess what might be going on?"

Sam felt dizzy for a moment. "Fuck you. You're lying."

"Believe whatever you want."

He hated to think it was true, but his mother had a knack for crossing boundaries. His head pounded. He turned around. "I don't know, Grabs," he said. "All that Faceless shit—maybe you're the one who should be careful." Reaching for the doorknob, he continued, "I hear Williams has ramped up cybersecurity."

Grabs smirked. "That'll be the day."

They were shouting over the music and didn't hear Mr. Willis's knock before he opened the door.

"Jesus! Webber, Grabs! Turn it down."

While Grabs killed the music, Sam took two steps back at the sight of the man, facing Mr. Willis with scorn, questioning his right to invade a dorm room—or to communicate with his mother behind his back, for that matter.

"Look, I'm sorry to interrupt," he said. "I was looking for you guys. If you're hungry, I made nachos, and the Red Sox are on."

The robotics club dynamic had a way of turning political in the weeks leading up to the MIT tournament.

"This is one weird team," Astrid said, clutching the notes their trio had worked on together.

"It's Dunning, where we all get along and care deeply about one another. Now, go break a leg," said Sam. He and Nathalie had nominated Astrid to present their design at the whiteboard.

"Ours is the best," Nathalie whispered in Sam's ear.

"Of course it is." He winked. The interface between their cell phone control and the circuit board was clean. Their design's accuracy would be boosted with larger claw pins and a more stable ramp.

Confident that the rest of the team would eventually come around, Sam led Nathalie to the back of the laboratory.

"You okay?" he asked.

"I've been racking my brain to remember how often I used that shower stall and when that shampoo dispenser first showed up."

"Have you mentioned it to anybody else?" he asked.

"No, I'm not that dumb. But I'm pretty sure it's been there all year."

"It was probably installed over the summer." If so, there would be about six months' worth of recordings. Sam wondered if the pervert had focused on a special girl and whether she was now a celebrity on the dark web.

"Astrid uses that stall all the time." Nathalie hung her head.

Nathalie was upset, but he knew she would recover, just as he would rebound from whatever video was out there showing his backside in the laundry room. However, Sam wasn't so sure about Astrid. She was shy and modest, unaware her digital image was likely out in cyberspace, copied a thousand times over. There was no way to undo it, like trying to put toothpaste back in the tube. And what about the other girls on the hall? Given that ten of them lived on that floor, there were plenty of other potential starlets.

Sam tried to picture the cameraman. He had to be aware that his equipment had been confiscated; maybe leaving it behind had been not careless but bold. What if he was in a position of authority and didn't fear getting caught?

Astrid's presentation was ending, and Raj began firing objections. "It's too complex. We won't have time to run test scenarios."

Sam ignored him and walked to the supply closet. He stepped onto a footstool and brought down a large plastic bin from the uppermost shelf with a broad smile, his eyes trained on Nathalie. Watching her jaw drop made his weekends in the lab worthwhile. Sam set the robot on the floor and turned on a switch. Its red lights, installed only for effect, blinked excitedly.

"Here he is," Sam announced to the room. "Everyone, meet Dunster!"

CHAPTER 22

When Sam was in middle school, I was involved with all his science fairs. Hell, I practically constructed the exhibits. However, I never imagined the likes of an East Coast regional robotics competition. Of course, I was giddy when Sam first mentioned MIT—the prestige of it, the idea that it might even be the university Sam would attend. I'd bragged to the woman who cut my hair, but robotics at MIT didn't seem to impress her. I added that Sam was on the swim team too, all-around athletic *and* brilliant.

When he was a first-year at Dunning, I pried the details out of him during one of our Sunday phone calls. When I expressed concern that his voice sounded tired, he let it slip that he'd been spending late nights in the robotics lab, preparing for a tournament. And, of course, once I heard that, I wouldn't give an inch. What competition? Where? When? He pleaded with me not to come and embarrass him, saying none of the other kids' parents would be there.

When we got off the phone, I went online and found out all the details: the event began on Friday morning and went through the weekend, and it was open to the public.

"Edward, it says that the final rounds begin at noon on Sunday and the championship trophy will be awarded at three o'clock."

"Hannah, he asked us not to go," Edward said, shaking his head.

"We'll sit in the bleachers," I said, not even sure there would be bleachers, but I pictured it as something like a swim meet. "He won't see us. I really want to go. I want to see what it's all about."

"Hannah, what are the chances you can be in the same building with Sam without calling out his name?"

"Edward, this robotics stuff really intrigues me." There was no way I was going to let this opportunity to watch my son's mechanical prowess slip by.

"Well, go if you like, but I won't show up someplace after Sam's specifically asked me not to."

That was how I found myself alone, driving to Cambridge. If my husband, Mr. Negative, wasn't going to be a part of it, I'd attend all three days by myself.

A big banner advertising the East Coast Regional Robotics Tournament and its sponsors hung over a double set of glass doors. I needn't have worried about my anonymity, because a mass of humanity swallowed me as soon as I entered the hall. Groups of teenagers in matching T-shirts dominated the center of the gymnasium, which had been arranged into an android obstacle course. There were ramps and ladders and zip lines, little white balls, action figures and robots of all shapes and sizes.

I made my way to the side of the hall where there were, in fact, bleachers full of people. I climbed over piles of coats and bags to the top row in order to get the best perspective. I searched for kids wearing Dunning's telltale crimson, and specifically for Sam, but it was a mob scene.

An older gentleman sitting next me was thumbing through a program. "Excuse me," I said, leaning toward him.

He turned his head in response, letting out a yawn.

"I'm sorry, I didn't notice programs when I came in. May I take a peek at yours?"

"Sure," he said. "Have it. My grandson's team was just eliminated. The next round is about to start. See the four teams down there in the pit?"

"Oh, thank you so much," I said, following his pointed finger.

I scanned the floor for several minutes, then spotted Sam. His long hair hung across his face, and his T-shirt blended in with the others, but his gait was unmistakable. I recognized the bounce in his toes and the pumping of his arms from his days as an excited kindergartener.

He huddled together with his team, waiting to be introduced. He stuck close to two girls which piqued my curiosity. One had long, black, shiny hair. The other girl was fair skinned and thin, with what my generation would have called a pixie cut. I might have mistaken her for a boy if it hadn't been for the bangle bracelets on her arm. She wore a denim button-down over her team T-shirt and hung back from the group. What I felt for those girls bordered on envy, not because they were close to Sam but because they were courageous enough to pursue mechanical engineering. It was a possibility I'd never even considered when I was their age.

Sam and the girls seemed like an island unto themselves. I giggled, indirectly experiencing their laughter, their nervous anticipation. I imagined the tenor of their anxious yet confident conversation. My heart overflowed with appreciation for the opportunities Sam was being given at Dunning.

The excitement in the building mounted on Saturday, but I kept my eyes trained on my son and those two wonderful girls. He was actually smiling. On Sunday, I cried tears of pride and jumped to my feet, clapping as ferociously as my arms would allow, as Sam and the girls balanced together on a podium built for one and hoisted a huge silver cup high in the air. I snapped pictures that I wouldn't share with anyone.

The next year, when Sam was a sophomore, I marked the dates of the MIT competition on my calendar as soon as they were published. I didn't let on to Edward where I was going that weekend, wanting the same experience as the year before, from high on my perch. Again the Dunning team won, and again I feigned surprise at the news during our Sunday call. Sam was unusually jovial, spilling over with a play-by-play description of the final round. I had to restrain myself from adding any detail, as, once again, I'd created my own version of the drama.

During Sam's junior year, I took a program and expertly found my place, spotting the Dunning team right away. But my stomach sank as I scanned the faces with my binoculars. I should have known they wouldn't let him travel, and when I focused in on that pretty girl with the pixie hair, her glum expression confirmed my fear. My first instinct was to leave, to climb back down over the people and coats and bags, but I watched anyway, hoping Dunning would lose without Sam.

I dug a package of peanut M&M's out of my purse. I sucked on each piece of candy, dissolving the sugary coating first, then the chocolate, before cracking into the peanut middle with the full strength of my molars. Fury rose in my chest at the thought of Sam back on campus, confined to that depressing dorm. After I'd eaten every single M&M, I found my phone and sent Shawn Willis an email. "They wouldn't even let him attend the competition? It was his fucking robot."

....

With summer vacation closing in and our spring break in Florida having not resuscitated anything, repairing my relationship with Edward became more urgent than ever. The Monday after MIT, I left work a little early to broil steaks and bake potatoes. When Edward got home from his office, the scent of sizzling fat juices greeted him, along with candlelight, cloth napkins, and wineglasses set on the kitchen table.

"What's gotten into you?" he asked, hanging his suit coat in the closet.

"I thought you might like a nice dinner." I smiled.

"Smells great," he said.

I poured red wine and served the meal. Edward cut into his meat immediately and then went to the refrigerator in search of A-1 sauce. He pounded the small, dark bottle with the heel of his palm, completely dousing the New York strip I'd blown our weekly budget on.

Between forkfuls, he looked at me with what I assumed was gratitude and also hoped was a sign of reconciliation. My plan was working. Maybe if I served a delicious dinner every evening, we'd eventually stitch together a life independent of Sam.

I wasn't concerned about the lack of table conversation, as Edward was genuinely enjoying his food. When he took his dish to the sink and proceeded directly to the freezer in search of his ice cream fix, however, it was evident that the routine of sweets in front of the TV would be a hard habit to break.

"How was work?" I asked. I ate the skin of my potato while he scooped out one serving of chocolate and one of cookie dough.

He looked at me sideways from the counter and shrugged. "Long day," he said.

I nodded in understanding. When he departed for his lounge chair, I placed my glass and bottle of wine by the sink. I ran the hot water, biting my upper lip as I doused the dirty dishes with blue detergent.

Wearing a yellow rubber glove, I gripped the stem of the wine glass and took a long sip. I had never been a drinker while Sam was living at home, but the warm buzz was nice, and I wondered why it had taken me this long to start.

Once I had straightened up the kitchen, I stood behind Edward's chair and put a hand on his shoulder. I leaned close to his ear and whispered, "I'm thinking about a nice hot soak." Early in our marriage, when we'd made love night after night, trying for a pregnancy that would stick, my running the bathwater had been his cue.

"Take a bath; it will help you relax," my abundantly fertile sister had suggested. I'm not sure anything could have truly made me unwind, but the sight of my body emerging from the tub had certainly aroused Edward. While my breasts were still pert and pink, my thighs glistening with emollient oils, he'd bend me over the vanity and take me from behind, unable to wait the ten steps to our mattress.

"Good night," he mumbled, aiming the remote control at the television screen. His voice was tired but held no contempt. I may even have discerned a twinge of gratitude for the steak in that brief exchange.

Once upstairs, I took care to clip my hair on top of my head, leaving a few strands wild. Examining my reflection in the mirror, I was grateful to have avoided a postmenopausal thickening around the middle, even if it was the result of all my fretting, a nervous melting-away.

I mixed bubbles with hot water, then rose oil and lavender crystals. My head was still light from the wine as I bent my legs and submerged my shoulders below the surface of the bathwater. I left the door to the bathroom wide open, hoping the sound of the faucet would trigger a Pavlovian response buried deep in Edward's core.

After Sam was born, I resisted lovemaking. At first it was because I was sore, and later it was because I was exhausted. When Edward reached for me in bed, I'd tell him no, and he'd roll over onto his side. He was sensitive about the weight he'd gained and his demotions at the bank. When I remembered how he'd winced at my rejection, I knew he'd been silently asking me, then more than ever, to build him up. I can see now how it must have seemed as if all I really wanted from our marriage was a child.

The water cooled, and I drained the tub, patted myself dry, and slipped into a long silk robe, which I left lazily untied. The television downstairs was off. My heart skipped when I spotted a crack of light under Sam's bedroom door. It was only eight o'clock. Perhaps Edward had come up early to do a little personal grooming of his own. I lit a vanilla-scented candle on the bedside table and lay on top of the covers, trying to read my novel. When thirty minutes passed and I was still alone, I poked my head into the hallway, only to find that Edward's light was out.

I was determined not to let the evening end that way. I sprayed his favorite perfume between my breasts and stood in the hallway, gathering my nerve. I turned the knob on Sam's door, opening it just enough to glimpse Edward, a hulking mass on a mattress meant for a child. He was on his side, his back to me, curled under a frayed patchwork quilt. I pulled the covers away, and he started, flipping onto his back in confusion. That was when I straddled him.

"Hannah, what the hell?"

"Edward, shh." I pressed my fingers to his lips.

"Hannah, don't," he said, more firmly this time.

I lay on top of him, his body clad in cotton pajamas. I rested my cheek against his chest and sensed his quickening heartbeat. His body stiffened, guarded, but at least he had enough compassion not to push me off.

In those disgraceful moments before I retreated to my room, where I would take an extra sleeping pill for good measure, I scanned Sam's desk through my tears. When he first left for Dunning, I'd treated his desk like a shrine, approaching it with a dust rag under the pretense of cleaning. I'd fondled the swimming and baseball trophies that lined the shelf from which several science fair blue ribbons hung. A photograph of the three of us taken on his first day of kindergarten sat there as well. In it, I was smiling, terribly ignorant of how quickly my happiness would come to an end.

CHAPTER 23

Justin tugged on Sam's shoulder, holding him back after the Nine met in the library. They had just finished vetting which first-years to tap. After the last brother made his way down the stairwell, Justin turned to face him.

"How are you doing?" he asked.

"I'm okay," Sam said, wondering what the agenda was. Justin hadn't been making much time for him and had to want something. He seemed to feed off the imbalance of power in their friendship and its decreasing significance as graduation loomed.

As they stood together between long rows of books, Sam's emotions rose to the surface. He felt his lower lip beginning to tremble. Justin could be confusing, but *Goddammit, not now. Fucking man up*, he commanded himself. He could only hope Justin interpreted his emotional display as year-end wistfulness.

"I guess I'm not entirely okay," Sam said, sniffling into the back of his hand. "Did you see Harper's email?" he asked, buying time to dry his eyes. There had been an all-campus alert that morning saying, "Because of the recent discovery of drugs on campus, Security will be conducting a full search of dormitories with the aid of scent-catching dogs."

"He loves a police state."

"Yeah." Sam scuffed a toe against the carpet. He couldn't look up yet.

"Hey," Justin said, gripping Sam's shoulder firmly. It was about as much physical contact two adolescent males could afford. "What's the matter?"

"You're graduating, going to college and everything. But it's over for me; my future is fucked," Sam said, recalling the desperation on his mother's face as she'd driven him back to school after spring break.

Justin laughed. "You are definitely not fucked." His hand slipped to Sam's bicep. "Listen, they roughed you up a little bit, came down hard with the restrictions, but you're gonna be fine."

"My mother is spinning her wheels with ideas," Sam said. "She wants me to go to all my teachers and offer to do extra work, like probation is reversible." The frequency of her texts rivaled only that of the international mothers who came down hard on their kids over every grade.

"Well, your mother hasn't seen the way the Nine can move mountains," Justin said, exaggerating his smile. "What you need for your college applications," he continued, "is an impressive summer internship and a Pulitzer Prize–winning essay."

Sam tilted his head. "Are you for real?"

"My mother is the founder of the Make All Your Dreams Come True Foundation. You can work at their offices in the Bronx this summer. Live with me at my brother's apartment on the Upper East Side and come up to Long Harbor with us on the weekends."

Sam stood, staring. This was Justin's grand solution? Moments ago, he had anticipated his friend's imminent disappearance from his life altogether, but now here he was, asking Sam to become a member of his family.

"Sounds cool, but I haven't had time to think about summer yet." That was a lie. Sam had intended to mow lawns back home, maybe repay some of the legal bills, but it was the type of suburban mundanity he'd never admit to Justin.

"Sam, the summer before your senior year is crucial. I'm handing you an internship on a silver platter, loaded with all that community-service bullshit. You'll thank me later."

"I'll have to let you know."

Justin glowered. "Do you know how many kids have hit me up for a summer job? Mimi has never been willing before."

Sam inhaled deeply. "I'm still wondering what you did with the backpack and, you know, all the evidence."

"Jesus, Sam," Justin seethed. "It's in a safe place. That's all you need to know."

"But it's the only proof. I want to figure out who's responsible so I can clear my name."

"That's not important!" Justin hissed. "Clear your name with who? Harper? He already knows you're innocent. It's not to his advantage for you to clear your name."

"Were you aware that somebody was filming our hookups in the laundry room?"

Justin stepped backward, scrunching his face in confusion.

"Do you think it's all related?"

"I have no idea," Justin said.

"There might be footage of me," Sam said, glaring at Justin. "From the night *you* reserved the room on my behalf."

"Shit, look, I don't know what you're talking about, but while you're still on restrictions, you need to lie low."

"But you should see the way the teachers look at me, and, you know . . ."

"What?"

"The other kids, and . . ." He didn't want to bring up Nathalie's name.

"And what?"

"Justin, it's my mother, okay? I just can't stand the idea of her thinking I did drugs."

Justin shifted his eyes to the stacks of books, making it easier for Sam to continue: "My family's not like yours. Dunning's been a real stretch for my dad. That I'd waste the opportunity, well, it's a huge slap in the face."

Justin nodded as if he understood, even though Sam didn't think he possibly could, what with his family's ski jaunts and their yacht in the Bahamas.

"Okay, I understand that you want to clear your name." Justin kicked the toe of his running shoe lightly against the metal bookshelf. "But there's something else going on here with Dean Harper and Headmaster Williams. We have to play our cards right."

"Will that be anytime soon?" Sam's voice lilted upward. "I mean, you're going to graduate in a month."

"I know it's hard, Sam, but I'm asking you to put the brotherhood first. You'll understand why next year, when you're in charge. Then be my guest—bring the assholes down."

"Me? Captain Dunning?"

"Yes. Be patient. The alumni council doesn't want us to turn in the video now. They have a plan. And there can't be another DC on my watch."

Sam's skin tingled. He'd taken an oath in the Tomb, but he'd never imagined how much the whole loyalty-to-the-brotherhood thing would be put to the test.

He tried another angle. "Justin, have you ever watched them?"

"Jesus, get off it," Justin implored. "Just come spend the summer with us. The internship will be good for you, and the weekends by the ocean will be even better."

Sam couldn't imagine an internship and a well-written essay were enough to solve his problems. Still, he didn't like being at odds with Justin's interpretation of the way the world worked. His head throbbed. He would have given anything to rewind the calendar six months and forgo that stupid mission to the bell tower.

How could he tell his mother that he'd be living with the Crandalls for the summer? Even though she had a weird infatuation with Mrs. Crandall and had always looked for her at the swim meets, she would be crushed if he didn't return home.

Justin shifted his weight from one leg to the other in mounting impatience. He kept looking over his shoulder to make sure nobody was entering the stacks.

"C'mon, man," he finally said. "I know the idea seems sort of sudden, but it's the next step on the road to fixing things for you."

Sam bit his lip. "Who's doing the fixing?" he asked.

"There are all sorts of higher-ups coming out of the woodwork for you."

It still didn't add up. "You talk about 'higher-ups' and 'something bigger going on,' but I'm feeling out on a limb."

Justin shook his head, his blond curls sweeping across his forehead. "You are not the only one out on a limb." Anger rose in his voice, and his face reddened.

Sam nodded, wanting to agree, not necessarily because he was ready to but because Justin's anger frightened him.

"When you come to Long Harbor," Justin said, "you'll see. You'll meet my uncle. He was class president and Captain Dunning, class of eighty-five. He'll have some insight into what's going on."

"Your uncle?" Justin's father and grandfather had gone to Dunning, but Sam had never heard about any uncle.

"Yeah, my father's younger brother. He's divorced and sort of had an early retirement, so he spends a lot of time at the family house."

"I'm not sure, Justin." Sam had been looking forward to the prospect of his father's returning from work on a summer afternoon, surprising him with tickets to a ball game. It was their thing, going to Fenway a couple times each summer. If Sam lived in New York, he'd miss all that. Hell, his father would probably never leave work.

"Sam, please. You can't say no." Justin shook his head, as if warding off a nightmare.

Sam had also considered his going home the one thing that might keep his parents together. He'd feel terrible for his mother, but the way she was obsessing over his college options and repeatedly invading his privacy made Justin's invitation more appealing. Sam bit his lip again and looked at the clock on the wall.

"C'mon, Webber. Say yes."

Sam took a few long breaths before meeting Justin's eyes. "Okay," he said. "I'll do it."

Justin pumped his fist and clasped Sam in a quick hug before leaving the library.

Sam ducked into the men's room to slap water on his face. He assessed his reflection in the mirror and adjusted his baseball cap, bending the bill into a well-worn curve to hide his red eyes. On his way to the main doors, he passed Shawn Willis, chatting up the new librarian.

"Hey, Sam."

"Hey, Mr. Willis," he said, without slowing down. He pointed to his watch. "I'm heading back to Wilburton now," he said, aware he had ten minutes until his curfew.

Shawn tapped his knuckles on the librarian's desk, then called after him, "Yeah, Sam, don't stress. I'll walk back with you."

As they crossed the quad, Shawn said, "If you get hungry later, come by my apartment. I've got some good snacks." These offers of food were piling up. The boys in the dorm had noticed Mr. Willis's recent efforts to make over his hard-ass image, but Sam couldn't forgive the fact that he was his mother's freaky pen pal.

"You trying to put the dorm grill out of business or what?" Sam asked.

When they got back to Wilburton, he headed straight down the hall to his room. Once inside, he locked the door and dove face-first onto his pillow.

....

Milder weather had the student body hanging out on outdoor benches for the hour between dinner and study hall. For Sam, however, restrictions meant staying inside the dorm.

Besides wondering who Nathalie might be spending time with, Sam was preoccupied by the approaching need to call home. It was Sunday evening and time to deliver the news about his summer plans.

While an improvised outdoor speaker system blared music in the distance, Sam sat on the edge of his bed, procrastinating with Facebook. He checked the time. His father would be in the den, watching his programs, and his mother would be up in her bedroom, reading.

His mother answered when he called, enabled the speaker-phone, and joined his father in the family room.

"Having a nice weekend?" his father asked.

"Yeah, but I have something to tell you."

"You're not in more troub—"

"No, Mom, it's not that."

After Sam finished describing the internship and how he would be moving to New York City, there was silence on the line.

"The Crandalls invited you?" his mother asked.

"Justin did, yeah."

"For the entire summer?"

"Yeah."

"Well, maybe I should call Mimi," she said, with an uptick in her voice.

"You don't need to do that."

"Well, I think she might expect me to."

"Mom, it's not like I'm a kid and you need to arrange my playdates."

More silence. Almost immediately, Sam regretted having resorted to cruelty, but when his mother got insistent, he needed to shut her down. He couldn't explain exactly what the Crandalls were offering. He couldn't put words to what their wealth and connections could do, and didn't want to admit that they were the type of family he needed at the moment. Instead, he told his parents that most of his Dunning classmates got these types of internships during the summer before their senior year, and that as far as the top colleges were concerned, it was practically expected.

CHAPTER 24

"So, you going to your men's club tonight?" Angeline asked, sitting up straight at the reference desk, her hands folded in front of her. Shawn smiled at the prim act, the way she played the bookish librarian by day.

"Nah, I was thinking you and I could go to McGrory's instead." He could no longer keep his romance with Angeline a secret, as the boys in Wilburton teased that he seemed to find time every day to check out the sports page in the library.

They made plans to meet up at the bar, and as Shawn walked back to the dorm, he smiled at the waning orange glow in the sky. The campus buzzed with the anticipatory energy of Friday afternoon morphing into the weekend. When he stepped out of the shower, every boy in Wilburton seemed to be lined up outside his apartment, waiting to sign out for the evening. Every boy, that is, except Sam Webber.

Checking sixty-odd names off on his clipboard took longer than expected. He glanced at his watch. "Fuck," he said, fumbling in his pocket. Before he met Angeline, he needed to go through the rigmarole of locking his door.

He had installed a double bolt and a padlock after all his furniture had been put out in the snow. Around the same time, the kids, who had always left their doors wide open in Wilburton, had started locking up as well. Shawn wasn't sure if it was to guard against each other or him, or because of the potential for random searches by Harper and his scent hounds, but the atmosphere in the dorm had gone from one where boys swayed in song after dorm meetings to a cell block where he was the prison guard.

Shawn stuck his head in Sam's door on his way down the hall.

"I'm in for the night, Mr. Willis."

"Lots of work to do?" Shawn asked, hoping Sam would say he was bogged down with assignments.

"Nah, I think I'll just download a movie."

He'd witnessed Sam earlier that day standing by the driveway to the main school building. The robotics team had been loading onto a Dunning minibus for the ride to Logan Airport, where they'd fly to the national championships in San Diego. Headmaster Williams had even boomed their send-off at Wednesday's all-school assembly, God-like, into the microphone, turning his solemn weekly ritual into a pep rally of sorts. As the minibus had prepared to pull out, Sam had reached up to an open window and pressed palms with one of the girls.

Shawn entertained the idea of hanging out in the dorm with Sam, maybe ordering pizza and watching a baseball game with him. That kid had more than paid the price for whatever beef Harper had with the Nine. He was on the verge of suggesting it when his phone buzzed in his pocket. It was Angeline: "At the bar where are you?

"Uh, all right. Check out the new *Blade Runner*. It's a good one."

Shawn hurried to the exit, and as the fixed spring on the fire door closed behind him, it let out a long, slow whine that matched the feeling in his gut.

It wasn't just Sam's probation that was excessive; it was what he was up against at home. Since Shawn had been on the receiving end of Hannah's emails, he understood the way she latched on to a worry and couldn't let go. She had berated him for not having let

Sam attend the robotics competition, saying, "It was his fucking robot." Sometimes he didn't know how to respond to her rants, so he kept his replies short and positive.

She couldn't have been more different from his own mother, who barely looked up from her soap operas when he entered a room. After he'd turned ten, it had been as if being a boy relegated him to his father's realm, and the kisses she'd once showered on him were saved for his sister.

When he entered McGrory's, he was surprised to see Angeline's sister, Phyllis, sitting on a barstool. She was older by three years and lived in the same town, except not with Angeline and her mother. Still, they were best friends, and Shawn knew making a good impression was important. Angeline had asked Shawn once if he knew of anyone at Dunning they might fix Phyllis up with. "It could be fun," Angeline had said. "We could double-date."

Shawn ducked into the men's room and called Lou. He was the one single guy Shawn had formed a bond with in Schwartz's basement. It didn't take long for Lou to enter red-faced and sit down next to Shawn just as the girls were returning from the restroom. Phyllis was attractive when you looked at her alone, but alongside her sister, you couldn't help but compare the two. They had the same genes, the same black curls, but in Angeline's body things had come together much better. Phyllis was a fun one, though, and with no affiliation to Dunning Academy, she could afford to be a little louder, a little more crass.

Shawn signaled the bartender for another round. Lou raised his beer in the air. "To the snow finally melting." The four clinked glasses.

Shawn looked up at the television set behind the bar, where the local news was just coming on. A still shot of Dunning's academy building grabbed his attention. His mind raced, as if a crime were about to be reported—maybe another pervert teacher. "Hey, turn the sound up on that, would ya?" he asked the bartender.

But the reporter spoke about a local robotics team having won the regional competition at MIT and heading off to nationals for the third year in a row—"That's right, from our very own Dunning, New Hampshire."

"One of the kids in my dorm is the star of that team," Shawn boasted, pointing to the screen.

"Really?" Phyllis seemed impressed.

"He didn't go to the competition himself, but he probably designed the thing from his room. Kid's a robotics genius."

"Coach Schwartz still has it in for him, though," Lou said. "He's a little too smart for his own good."

Angeline leaned backward on her stool, and Shawn caught her winking at her sister behind Lou's back. He wondered what it would be like to have such a close connection with a sibling. Things might have been different if he'd had a brother. He'd never been close to his sister like that.

Phyllis was laughing at Lou's jokes making fun of hockey players. Shawn had a sense of humor about it. "How can a guy who wrestles make fun of me?"

They laughed even louder, the alcohol making everything funny. Shawn ordered a plate of nachos, and they all ate a few, not wanting the evening to end. If only Lou and Phyllis would pair off, he and Angeline could be alone. He was buzzed enough to consider taking her back to his apartment at Wilburton.

The local news cycle ran the robotics team story again, and Shawn remembered Sam, back at the dorm alone. He privately vowed to make a display of throwing away his padlock in front of the boys at Sunday meeting. In that crystal-clear way ideas and solutions popped into his head when he was drinking, he envisioned ending the mistrust and darkness. He'd start by ignoring the sustainability initiatives and turning the fucking hall lights back on.

He glanced across their faces: Angeline, Phyllis, and Lou were all elated. He was having a normal evening, for once: he and his girl and her sister and a work colleague, all around the same age—well, except for Lou, who might have been in his thirties. But whenever

Shawn could point to an occasion that felt basically normal, it made him smile. He ordered another round.

"Thanks, buddy," Lou said. "I really owe you for tonight." He gave a thumbs-up toward Phyllis.

The next thing that should have happened, if things had continued normally, would have been for Shawn to take Angeline back to his apartment and make long, passionate love to her. He leaned over and kissed her cheek.

But Angeline pointed to her sister, saying, "I should get her home," which made Shawn's heart sink. Phyllis had been keeping up with Lou drink for drink, but Angeline was driving and sober. She'd stopped laughing along about thirty minutes earlier. Phyllis gathered her purse and coat, and Angeline kissed Shawn. She whispered, "I'll call you tomorrow," and before he knew it, the girls were headed out the door and it was just him and Lou left at the bar.

Shawn finished his beer silently, wondering what had gone wrong. "Thanks a lot for coming out," he said, after settling up the tab.

"She's great," Lou said, as they walked back to campus.

"Yeah, nice girls," Shawn said. His manner had gone from happy to subdued, stuck in a situation that was no longer normal, walking back to his apartment in a fucking dormitory, with a balding, divorced guy instead of his girlfriend.

"Hey." Lou turned toward Shawn as though he needed to confide something. "Like I said before, Coach started going off on Sam Webber being in the tunnels again tonight. He thought he'd made it clear that you were to follow him, check on him, keep him from messing around down there."

"What the fuck is in that tunnel anyway, and why does Schwartz care so much?"

Lou shrugged.

"Hey, I have an idea," Shawn said. "Let's go check it out."

It was spontaneous and impulsive, but Shawn still had a good amount of energy and wasn't ready for the night to end.

Lou laughed, taking a swig from the beer bottle he'd stowed in his jacket pocket, and they picked up their pace.

They stopped in Shawn's apartment to have a few swigs of Jack Daniel's from the bottle he kept hidden in his room.

"Leave your jacket here," said Lou. "It can get pretty toasty down there."

Descending the stairs to the basement, Shawn craned his neck to check whether there were any kids fornicating on the floor of the laundry room.

The tunnel entrance, waist high on the wall, reminded Shawn of the door to a pizza oven. Lou hoisted himself up. Shawn followed and was only a few seconds in before he checked himself, thinking, *Shit, I am actually doing this.* He was usually too immersed in routine at Dunning to have that kind of thought in the present moment, his first night with Angeline being an exception. Maybe it was his intoxication, but crawling through the tunnel on his hands and knees took him back to playing Indiana Jones as a child. As his eyes adjusted to the dark, he strained to see how far the tunnel stretched. He giggled with childlike wonder.

Shawn turned his smartphone flashlight on, casting a white beam ahead. Lou let out a long, exaggerated burp and rolled up his sleeves. The air carried the faint scent of stale beer mixed with exhaust and humidity. The metal surface radiated heat beneath his hands. There were pipes running along both sides of the tunnel, and Shawn scraped his shoulder on a clamp.

"Just don't fart," he joked, wanting to gauge whether Lou was still having fun or now regretting their decision.

Shawn's stomach lurched with beer and a twinge of hunger. Those nachos hadn't done the trick, and all of a sudden it was as if every bodily function were making a call.

Lou stopped suddenly, and Shawn did too, hanging his head. When he closed his eyes, his head spun.

"What's the matter?" he asked Lou.

"My knees hurt."

What had started out as comforting warmth was quickly becoming stifling, a prime opportunity for an episode if a person happened to be claustrophobic.

"Keep going," Shawn urged. "It can't be much farther. When Schwartz described the tunnels, I never imagined anything this tight."

"They're not all like this."

They continued, heads down, sweat dampening the backs of their shirts. They finally reached a door. Lou tapped the metallic surface with his bulky class ring, then scooted back a few inches. Sitting on his rear, his hands reaching up to protect his head, Lou punched his legs against the door. Shawn understood why Security wanted no part of monitoring these things—they required the flexibility of a ten-year-old.

Another pizza oven–like door swung open. A faint red light lit a room similar to the Wilburton boiler room in size and shape. Lou lowered his feet to the floor, and Shawn was right behind him, gulping in the air.

Lou unzipped his fly and faced a corner. "I thought I was going to wet myself." Urine streamed across the floor.

"Jesus, that's gross," Shawn said, but within a few seconds he was standing next to Lou, relieving himself too.

Shawn kicked some liquor bottles against the wall and asked, "Where the hell are we?"

"The Bennett basement. It was the quad butt room back in the seventies, a place where the seniors could all hang out and smoke, back before people knew smoking could kill you. If you go through that door and up some stairs"—Lou pointed—"there's an exit, but it's been bricked up. Or you can go that way"—he pointed down a hallway—"to get to the dorm's common room."

Shawn was zipping up his jeans when he noticed Lou dragging a chair across the linoleum floor toward an abandoned AV rack. To his amazement, Lou stood up on the chair.

"Be careful, dude. You aren't too steady."

Lou tugged on clipped blue cables that hung from the ceiling, then rubbed the frayed ends between his fingers. "Odd, right?" he asked.

"I guess."

When Shawn had discovered condoms and a scoreboard in the Wilburton laundry room, he'd jumped to the conclusion that mischief occurred only in a boys' dorm, but if there was anything that night's touring of the tunnel system taught him, it was that misbehavior at Dunning was widespread. Almost every basement they landed in showed signs of partying or clothes left behind.

"I can't believe I never knew about the tunnels before," Shawn said, after they returned to Wilburton.

"Don't feel stupid," Lou said. "They're a well-kept secret. The maintenance guys know; it's sort of their job security. Schwartz knew because he was one of them. One Friday night somebody called bullshit, made a bet that he was lying, so he sent the sons-in-law down."

"And they showed you?"

"Something like that. Anyway, the kids party and mess around in their basements, but they don't know about the connectors."

It was true—the doors were well concealed and neither well lit nor welcoming. Most of the passages were dark and tight because of the utility conduits that ran through them. "Except Sam Webber?" Shawn asked.

"Except the Nine. They've handed down a campus map for decades. Those kids know the underground routes better than anyone."

Shawn remembered the night he'd caught Sam. He'd been perspiring and wearing only a sweatshirt. He'd probably been sneaking underground to visit his girlfriend. The fucking boys in Shawn's charge had more sex than he did. He recalled the way Sam had looked up through the window of the robotics team bus. He couldn't be sure, but he thought the girl was Nathalie de Witt, Class Two as well. Shawn made a mental note to look up which dorm she lived in.

Besides being a connector between dorms, the tunnel system would have been a dream for any kid who relished manhunt or spy games. But as soon as Shawn recalled what Schwartz had implied about the tunnels' being a playground for pedophiles and deviants, he sobered up quickly.

"Harper and Williams must know all about the tunnels too, right?"

"According to Schwartz, they've inspected all the wider parts, but they don't comprehend the expansive nature of the web. And they've been focused on Wilburton for so long, they only worry about that connector."

"Then why doesn't Williams just fill it up with cement?"

"Because it's functional," Lou explained. "The heating systems and water main for all the dorms run through it." Shawn nodded, starting to understand. To reroute the utilities would be a huge expense, not to mention require an excavation that would risk exposing the secret passageways to others.

Back in his apartment, flipping the channels, Shawn considered Schwartz. There had to be a reason he wanted anyone who used the tunnels watched carefully. He recalled that creepy butt room underneath Bennett and the expression on Lou's face when he'd come across the snipped blue wires.

CHAPTER 25

Justin stood at the Tomb's altar, a candle flame flickering in front of him. It may have been the quality of the light, but his eyes seemed especially sunken inside his black hood, and his face had taken on the quality of a skull. Sam and his other seven brothers sat cross-legged in a semicircle, as if waiting for a ghoulish story time to begin. The sophomore class hadn't seen much action after Sam's DC in January, but they were spirited nonetheless, having applied war paint like streaks of mud to their faces. It just went to show that belonging mattered more than what the Nine actually did.

Saunders beat a steady bass line on an African drum while Justin spread the scroll across the rock altar. Wigs drank from a silver chalice filled with vodka-spiked grape juice before passing it around the circle.

Glancing frequently into the eyes of those seated at his feet, Justin read the scroll's preamble, outlining the Nine's origins and mission. When he was finished, he rolled the scroll into a spiral and placed it in its velveteen cover. He then asked Wigs and Mumford to read the names and bios of the three proposed initiates.

If they could pass the test in the library, they would be invited to next fall's first meeting to be branded. Sam winced at the memory. "Calm down," Justin had said. "When you get to college, all the

207

fraternities do it." Sam had learned that hundreds of men out in the world had the number nine seared into their inner thigh. If only Harper knew, he'd have stripped down the boys on campus and checked the skin behind where their balls hung.

After the bios were read and a vote was taken, Justin cleared his throat. It was now time to announce his successor, the next Captain Dunning. Even though the idea of wielding a branding iron nauseated Sam and he cared less and less for the other traditions—the Tomb, the scroll, and drinking from the chalice—the idea of playing a supporting role to either Raymond or Saunders made him crazy.

What was more, if he were appointed captain, he'd be in a better position to investigate the videotaping. He'd have foot soldiers, access to Gary's keys, and influence—over what, he wasn't sure, but Justin always implied it was far reaching. Being captain would mean added work, but he'd be on the inside for once.

"It's not all fun and games." Justin had once complained that he was often up late at night, sifting through the multitude of messages from the alumni council instead of studying. "But there are perks," he'd added. "Each captain becomes a member of the alumni council, and those guys look out for each other *for life*. I just got my first invitation: box seats on the first-base line at a Yankee game."

On the other hand, having spent the past few weeks hanging out with Nathalie, Sam's eyes were opened to the serenity of living inbounds. There was a peace to simply studying together in the library or exchanging ideas in robotics. All that time by her side had rendered Sam a tad ambivalent about future risk-taking escapades. He couldn't help remembering Grabs's words either: *The Nine are so yesterday.*

Justin was still talking, making a grand production of all that had gone into the deliberations. On one side of Sam, Raymond, whose father had served as captain in the seventies, was beading up around his hairline, while Saunders stared blank-faced into a candle flame.

Justin walked behind them and, after a pause, maybe to elevate the suspense or maybe to telegraph that it had been a tough decision, placed his hands on Sam's shoulders. His voice echoed throughout the cave: "Congratulations, Brother Webber. You are hereby named the next captain of the Nine!"

....

Once he emerged from the woods, Sam texted Nathalie.

"What's up?"

"In student center."

"Come to Wilburton."

"Is that allowed?"

He knew it was stretching the rules, but he was a little puffed up after leaving the Tomb and wanted to test whether sitting on the benches outside Wilburton might fly. "All OK," he typed.

It was twilight, the gift of daylight savings ending and the hemisphere creeping toward the longest day of the year. Some stars were almost visible, and the crescent moon hung low in the sky. He searched for Nathalie's silhouette across the freshly mowed quad while he inhaled the well-manicured scent of impending commencement and reunions.

Sam smiled at the idea of being captain. Maybe he'd detoured from the path the rest of his classmates had taken, but he was going to find a way to beat this place. He clung to the faith his father had expressed in him at the spring training game and to the boost of confidence the Nine had given him. A mixture of the two must have shone on his face, because when Nathalie arrived, her expression was curious.

"What? You're not used to seeing me out on a Saturday night?"

"Not just that. You look like the cat who ate the canary."

Sam broke into an even wider grin. She used old-fashioned expressions all the time, claiming it was because she spent summers with her grandparents. She picked at the label on a bottle of iced tea, and Sam took it from her and helped himself to a sip. A group of boisterous junior girls walked by, their voices ringing with popularity, a sound that would have made Sam run the other way his first year.

With only a few more papers to write and a few final exams to sit for, the girls were prematurely assuming the tenor of Class One. The transition would be made official on the athletic fields the week before graduation, when their entire class would run maniacally around a bonfire while the underclassmen cheered them on.

"Nathalie," he moaned, pulling her closer.

She smiled, acquiescing to his tug. "What happened to your shyness?"

He closed his eyes and tilted his head, hoping. Nathalie met him halfway, and their lips connected in a kiss. When they parted, Sam wrapped her in his arms.

Applause, catcalls, and jeers from the band of girls erupted in the background. It would not take long for news of this kiss to spread. A public display of affection was as loud a statement as there was that Sam Webber and Nathalie de Witt were officially a couple.

He'd been out of the social scene all term, and his reemergence was big news for these onlookers. If Sam had enough resilience to survive the strong arm of Dunning, then they all might make it. His resurrection was a testament to the fact that you couldn't keep kids down. Flying high and bulletproof, Sam went so far as to salute the girls. It was a cocky move and didn't really feel like him, but they shouted their approval before continuing along the path.

Nathalie rested her cheek on Sam's shoulder and giggled. He'd never been the type of guy she'd have gone out with, and Sam wondered if he was giving off a different vibe now, maybe a secret power. But just as he was about to kiss her again, Mr. Willis appeared. Sam and Nathalie immediately stood up.

"Forget to check in, Sam?"

"I knocked, sir. You weren't there."

"Aw, I'm just messing with you." He winked at Nathalie and gave Sam a friendly punch on the shoulder.

"Hi, Mr. Willis, I'm Nathalie de Witt," she said, extending her hand.

"Yeah, I know who you are."

"Where are you coming from, Mr. Willis?" asked Sam.

"Oh, I was just down at McGrory's." Mr. Willis was half in the bag—Sam could smell it on him. "Why don't the two of you go enjoy yourselves? Come back and check in at midnight with the rest of the upperclassmen."

"Are you sure?"

"Absolutely. I'm happy you're out on this beautiful evening instead of sneaking around underground." Mr. Willis chuckled.

"Sir?" Sam asked, cocking his head in confusion.

"It's okay, Webber. I know. I've been down there," he whispered, pointing to the ground.

"What if Dean Harper is out patrolling?"

Mr. Willis shrugged. "Up to you. Just trying to be a nice guy."

There were so many things Sam wanted to say, but he kept his mouth shut. He and Nathalie sat back down on the bench and watched Mr. Willis return to his apartment.

"That was weird," Sam said.

....

Nathalie took Sam's hand and led him across the street to the baseball field. He put his arms around her waist as they both stared out at the fresh red clay. The base paths, raked with bright white chalk, were a sure sign of spring, but all Sam could think about was what the hell Mr. Willis was up to.

Nathalie changed the subject. "I wish you'd been in San Diego with us."

"Me too." That didn't make him feel any better.

"In two weeks, your probation will be over and you'll be done missing things." She smiled and nuzzled his ear.

They kissed again. In contrast with the urgent and frenetic making out he'd experienced with Andrea, Nathalie was as calm as a deep, still lake. He felt no rush, no impatience, as though they had the rest of their lives to get where they were going.

"I should head back," Sam said.

"Okay," she said softly.

Sam walked Nathalie back to her dorm, but she stopped short of Bennett's doors, pulling her hand away. "Sam, I need to tell you something," she said.

He pulled on his hair and cast his eyes to the ground.

"You seemed so happy before, I didn't want to break the spell. But I heard something today."

He sucked in his cheeks.

"One of the girls on my hall walked in on Justin snooping around our bathroom. She was just about to take off her robe and get into the shower. He ran away when she screamed, and nobody else saw him."

"Did she report it?"

"No, she's got such a crush on him that she'd never dream of it."

CHAPTER 26

Edward and I drove to Dunning together at the end of the school year to pack Sam's dorm room and bring him home. The sight of both of us emerging from the car was probably the first clue that something was wrong. The second came on the drive home, when we made a detour off Route 1 for soft serve. Sam trained his eyes on me while Edward paid the girl at the window. Sitting on a sticky picnic table while cars whizzed by, Edward cleared his throat. "Sam, your mother and I need to talk to you. . . ." He paused and looked down at the ground.

Sam looked back and forth between us, his stare resting on me, as if to ask, *Are you really letting him do the talking?*

"We wanted to tell you that we've decided to experiment with a separation."

Sam inhaled deeply and looked down as well. Edward rubbed his shoulder and nodded like he understood. I tried to hug him too, but holding my dripping cone made it difficult. Sam used the napkin wrapped around his sugar cone to wipe his eyes, eventually licking the drips of chocolate from the tender skin between his fingers.

Every time I tried to open my mouth during the drive home, I froze. Adding words to Edward's succinct explanation felt like a dangerous betrayal of our agreed-upon script, while moving the conversation off-topic felt trivial. I was caught between a desire to project calmness, a hope that my acceptance of the situation would usher Sam along his own road to recovery, and a desire to talk it all out, in the spirit of not sweeping my feelings under the rug. The former, reserved approach was the norm on Edward's side of the family, while my roots were more emotional and confrontational. I could imagine that if my father had ever sat us all down to make such an announcement, there would have been plenty of crying and fist pounding.

I turned to face Sam in the backseat. In the absence of the right words, I could only hope the angle of my eyelids and their blinking moistness might convey my surrender and ease his mind.

I continued to smile those two weeks before Sam went to Rhode Island, because Joy informed me that my resting expression had become a frown. "Just look at that vertical crease between your brows," she'd said. With that, I realized, it didn't matter how much time passed—parenthood was etched permanently on my face.

I wanted Sam to be happy at home. I saved any remaining tears for bedtime. I was done clinging to my edge of the mattress and began spreading out into the middle, using Edward's pillow as a bolster under my knees, like I sometimes did during Savasana. It was strange, but once I made good use of his pillow, I began to sleep better.

I dug out the log-in credentials and surfed through Dunning Academy's online parent directory until I found it: Mr. and Mrs. Morris Crandall III (Mimi). Their Park Avenue address was listed, as well as a home phone number but no cell, no email. I'd already composed the perfect paragraph to Mimi, a combination of appreciation and assurance that our Sam would be the best intern she'd ever had. Now I would have to call her and worried I wouldn't be able to make the same points without getting nervous.

The third ring sounded, and then the fourth, as if anyone picked up their land line these days. "You've reached the Crandall residence. Please leave a message." I hung up.

I popped my head into Sam's bedroom. "Sam, sweetie, would you ask Justin for his mother's cell phone number?"

He looked up from his computer screen, irritation painted all over his face.

"I'd like to call her to express my appreciation for having you this summer."

"She's not *having* me, Mom," he shot back. "I'm working for her foundation and rooming with Justin in his brother's apartment."

"Well, you mentioned you'd be spending weekends at their summer home."

"Mom, be serious. I know you just want an excuse to get in with Mimi Crandall."

"*Get in* with her? Sam, show me some respect."

He held my gaze before relenting. "Okay." He punched out a text on his cell phone. His "are you happy now" expression suggested that the request had been issued and I was free to leave his room.

Down in the kitchen a few minutes later, my cell phone buzzed. I shook my head at a text from Sam with Mimi Crandall's number. When I was his age, we hollered through the house, calling each other to the phone or to relay messages. It might have been raucous and aggravated, but at least we were talking to each other.

I pulled out a chair at the kitchen table and inhaled deeply before entering her number. Mimi's phone rang only once before she answered.

"Hello?" she said. It was more a question than a greeting.

"Mimi? It's Hannah Webber."

"Who?"

"Sam's mother, Hannah Webber."

"I'm sorry, I can't hear you that well." There were other voices in the background, like I had caught her in a store or at a luncheon.

"Sorry," I said, more loudly. "My son, Sam, is a friend of Justin's from Dunning Academy. I was just calling to thank you for the invitation and, well, all you're doing for him."

Mimi didn't respond right away, her confusion obvious, but,

with masterful social grace, she recovered quickly. "Of course, of course. Sam the swimmer, the boy who joined us in the Bahamas last year. You'll have to forgive me, as I'm the last one to learn of my children's plans."

My stomach dropped. She had no idea.

"I wanted to call because Edward and I truly appreciate everything. We don't know how we can ever reciprocate your kindness." I was following my script, despite the direction of the conversation.

"Oh, dear, don't be silly." There was the warped sound of her putting a hand over the receiver, telling the company at hand she'd be right back. When she returned, she said, "I'm sorry. Our kids have people in and out all the time. But if I recall correctly, that poor boy of yours had quite a year."

So she did remember us, identifying Sam as the boy who'd gotten in trouble.

"Well, yes."

"These kids. Make us crazy, don't they? And he'll be helping at my foundation, I hear."

"It's—"

"Look, Anna, thanks for the call, but I've got to run."

"Oh, Mimi, it's actually Hannah. And I was hoping we might sit down to chat when I drop Sam off in Long Harbor." It wasn't until I stopped talking that I realized she was no longer on the line.

....

Besides keeping up a cheerful presence, I avoided saying anything that might set Sam off. Any brightness in his mood could deteriorate as quickly as the June weather. He'd lost all patience with me, but he was home for such a short time and I had to jam in his doctor and dentist appointments.

All I wanted was my family, and to overdose on Sam and shower him with the love he'd been deprived of at Dunning. I wanted to cook big breakfasts, wanted to fold his laundry. His T-shirts and shorts, now so oversize that I couldn't believe I'd given birth to this young man. I wanted to reconnect, talk about his friends, the school year, his classes, his teachers. I wanted to talk to him about the impressions of Wilburton Hall that Shawn Willis had given me in his emails, and I wanted to talk to him about Dean Harper.

I just wanted him around. I wanted to say good night to him as he stayed up to watch the late innings of a baseball game. I wanted to see his size 10 shoes by the back door. I wanted him to devour all the food in the refrigerator.

We assembled a modest wardrobe for his working in New York and weekends in Long Harbor. I was much more generous in the stores than we could afford to be, adding more debt to our credit card balance and caring less and less about Edward's parsimony. I hoped Sam would recognize this generosity as my faith in him, as love. I was running out of ways to show it.

I encouraged Sam toward the pastel and plaid button-downs, but he insisted that wasn't the right look for the MAYDCT offices.

"It's in the Bronx, for God's sake. It's a nonprofit."

"Well, then for your visits to the Crandalls' on the weekends. I've heard Long Harbor is dressy. Maybe we should get you a pair of boat shoes."

Sam rolled his eyes but didn't resist when the salesgirl brought out a few boxes. She smiled up at him from one knee, like an old-fashioned proposal in reverse. "Are you in college?" she asked, then acted surprised when he told her he was still in high school. I enjoyed watching an attractive young girl lavish attention on my son, and the resulting embarrassment that spread across his face.

The bounce she put in his step led to a better second half of the day. He let me get him two pairs of Bermuda shorts and a belt. We bought everything name brand, no knockoffs, which also made Sam take notice. It had probably been hard on him at a place like Dunning, not having certain things. Although I could remember my sisters pining after Jordache jeans, I had underestimated how boys also cared about labels.

"I don't want you to feel out of place with those people," I said.

"I'll be fine," he said, shrugging it off. It was the same easy shrug he displayed on the first day of school or before his first sleepover. We both knew the clothes he wore barely scratched the surface of the ways in which he might not belong.

After the mall, we swung by the barbershop. "You can just leave me here," he said. "I'll walk home."

So our afternoon ended like that, just as our rapport was becoming natural. Those two weeks he was home, our encounters sputtered from the awkward to the uninhibited in a choppy sort of way.

Before I knew it, it was time to deliver him to Long Harbor. On the morning of our departure, Edward came by the house so the three of us could have one last breakfast. Sam, in his sleepy state, may not have understood the significance of the meal, but I registered Edward's uneasiness at the kitchen table. That was when I realized that my husband's move was not experimental but forever.

Sam wore a DUNNING SWIMMING T-shirt with a pair of Bermuda shorts and new leather flip-flops. Even though he'd kept his bangs long in front, the sides were cut above his ears, and he looked good, fresh, like a clean start might be around the corner. He'd look even better after spending some time in the sun. Edward stood up from the table once he'd drained his coffee. Sam was still sopping up egg yolk with a piece of toast. "Work hard and do a good job," said Edward.

Sam stood up slowly and wiped his eyes. Edward gave him a hug. I envied their wordless affection.

"And have a little fun," Edward added, as they continued their embrace. I couldn't remember the last time either of them had held me. I swallowed the unfairness of it all. I had tried so goddamn hard.

Watching them, I envisioned Sam choosing his father and an apartment closer to Boston over me and this little house. I bit my lip, thinking once Sam had a taste of New York City, he might never come back to Massachusetts at all.

I assembled a gift basket of fruits and cheeses for Mimi. Even though our phone conversation had been awkward, I wouldn't have my son arriving empty-handed.

I had practiced what I might say when I handed it to her: "First you take Sam to the Bahamas, and now this. Edward and I just can't thank you enough."

We drove south on I-95 and were halfway between Boston and Providence when I turned down the volume on the radio. "So, Sam," I said, in my most upbeat tone, "I've been wondering if there's a special girl in your life."

He offered no reply.

"It's just that if you lived at home, I'd know your friends, whether or not you had a girlfriend."

"I get that, but you'd never know everything. You think you might, but you never would."

I took my eyes off the road for a second and turned toward him. "I love you, sweetheart. I want you to be happy. I was just curious if you had a special someone."

"It's more like you're nosy, Mom," he said, staring out the passenger-side window.

"I just care about you."

"God," he said, shaking his head. "No, I do not have a girlfriend."

"But Shawn Willis mentioned something about your spending time with a girl."

"See what I mean? Why the hell have you been emailing him every day?" Sam yelled. "What the fuck is going on?"

His outburst leveled me. I guided the Subaru into the slow lane, my hands trembling on the wheel. "I was worried about you. I needed to make sure you were all right."

"So you asked for reports on me?"

"Not reports—he just let me know how you were doing."

"And that's all?"

"Yes!"

I cracked my window, the car overflowing with his hostility. "I'm sorry, Sam. It's just that I've felt so cut off, and now you're leaving for the summer, staying with people I barely know. I was desperate to find out what was going on in your life." I sputtered out the last words.

Tears welled in my eyes, and I had to pull over into the breakdown lane. We sat there, shaking in the fragile shell of our car every time a tractor trailer whooshed by.

"I'm worried about you too," he said.

"Oh, Sam, I won't deny how hard it's been," I said, placing a hand on his knee. "I guess it seems sudden to you, but your dad's moving out has been a long time coming."

Sam pressed his lips together and nodded quickly, another tic I recognized from his childhood. "Yeah, I guess I've known too. It's just hard to be home and see it." He wiped his eye.

"Oh, Sam. I love you." I did my best to smile reassuringly, even if, for the first time in my life, I could no longer project what our future held. I patted his knee. "Won't you please fill me in on your summer plans?"

Sam nodded and inhaled, then turned to meet my eyes. "I've never met Justin's brother, but he works at a bank. His roommates have moved out, and the new ones won't be moving in until September, so Justin and I get to share that room. You know he's going to Yale next year? His father got him a job working on the set of a movie that's being filmed around Central Park. When that gig's over, he'll be hanging around Long Harbor."

He finished the longest monologue he'd offered in three years, then gave me another "are you happy now" smirk. I smiled back and shifted the car into drive.

"Thanks."

"Sure."

"But no girlfriend?"

"Mom!"

"Then who's Nathalie?"

"Oh my God! She's a friend from the robotics club."

It was a joust, but it was playful, the type of back-and-forth honesty we'd shared years earlier. After a few moments of silence, almost as if he were reading my mind, he added, "I'll call you every week, okay?"

"Could you manage twice a week?"

"You are too much."

A tastefully carved white sign welcomed motorists to Historic Long Harbor. And just as we passed it, the clouds cleared and the sun blazed through the windshield. I pulled off the road again and rolled down my window. "Why are you stopping?" Sam asked.

"Do you have their address? Directions to their house?" I asked, fumbling through my purse, looking for lipstick and my hairbrush.

"Yes." He turned his phone screen in my direction. "The same directions we've been following the whole time."

Perspiration rings were forming in the armpits of my cotton jersey, and I turned the air-conditioning on.

"Wow, it really got warm all of a sudden," I said.

"Yeah." Sam laughed. "Justin always says Long Harbor is in its own little bubble."

Obviously, I'd never been to Long Harbor before. I'd only heard mention of the tony summer community on the news in the fall, when hurricanes threatened the coast and weathermen stationed their film crews near its expensive oceanfront real estate, susceptible to rising tides and rogue waves.

I had assumed our drive past old, shingled cottages and privet hedges would culminate in the Crandalls' driveway, where Mimi would be waiting, maybe to invite me to come inside and stretch my legs after the long drive. I pictured her calling to me from a porch, inviting me to join her for a glass of iced tea.

"Oh my. I have a long trip back, but why not?" I would say. "That would be nice."

However, the only person to greet us when we rolled into the crushed-shell driveway was Justin. He shook my hand while Sam unloaded his luggage. Justin was polite enough but didn't think to invite me in. I searched the windows for a trace of movement. Maybe Mimi feared I'd ask for a tour of their home. All I wanted was to look her in the eye before turning over my son.

I was on the verge of asking Justin if I might use a bathroom when a gentleman in golfing attire and Gucci loafers walked through the privet.

"Oh, hello," I said. "I'm Hannah Webber, Sam's mom."

He shook my hand and smiled. "Henry Crandall, Justin's uncle." Funny how I assumed then that this man's presence was mere happenstance. I didn't realize he'd been the one to summon my son.

Sam kissed me on the cheek. "Bye, Mom," he said, before following Justin into the house. I was left standing in the driveway with Henry Crandall, suntanned and radiating the air of a bon vivant. He swirled ice cubes and spent wedge of lime around a plastic cup. A needlepoint belt, heralding the same clubby insignia as the cup, cinched his golfing shorts below a generous paunch. Reddish hair glistened on his legs and arms, and there was more in both those places than on his scalp.

"I take it we'll be seeing a fair bit of Sam this summer," he said, his gold-rimmed sunglasses reflecting my image.

"Yes. It's most kind of you all. I was actually hoping to thank Mimi," I said, retrieving the gift basket from the backseat and holding it against my chest.

"Oh, you just missed her. She headed off to tennis a few minutes ago." I found it hard to fathom anyone's going to play tennis when she was expecting a guest.

"Oh well." I feigned indifference and handed the cellophane basket to him.

He held it under one arm and tore through the cellophane,

grabbed an apple, and took a bite. "So, where do you folks spend your summers?" he asked while chewing.

"Oh," I said, trying to ignore the gift card that had fallen to the ground. "We head to the Cape when we can." It was the best I could come up with and still be honest. I wouldn't apologize for being middle-class, and I didn't want to play the who-do-you-know game with him.

He was merciful. "Well, I'm sure your son will enjoy himself here."

"It's very kind of you to have him. He could use a nice summer. Junior year, you know . . . Well, it was all they were warned it would be, and then some."

"Yes, Justin told me. Sam had to face the DC this winter. No Dunning experience is complete without being dragged across the carpet by the dean." He laughed, like it was a case of the chicken pox.

The wound was still too fresh for me to join him. "Well, the whole thing put a few gray hairs on my head, that's for sure."

The sound of deep barking interrupted us, and two chocolate Labs trotted excitedly through the opening in the privet. One of them aimed his snout directly into my crotch. I pushed his wet nose away, but he redirected himself into my rear end.

Henry raised his eyebrows in amusement but didn't chastise the animal at all, as if the scent I put off were canine. He threw the apple core onto the lawn, sending the dogs chasing after it. I caught a glimpse of rosebushes and white peonies in full bloom, most likely well tended by Mimi.

"Well," I said, backtracking toward the car, "I should really be heading home." I'd rather have braved a gas-station restroom than spend another minute with this man.

He slung a melting ice cube into his mouth, crunching down on it. "All righty, then. Drive safely. And don't worry, we'll take care of your boy."

It came across as a benign remark at the time. But as I thought about it on the drive home, it seemed more of a commentary on our family's ability to provide. I didn't know back then why the Crandall family was taking Sam on as a special project. I didn't know the first thing about the Nine, or how the men in that family ruled the fraternal order.

I fumbled with the GPS to make sure I could get out of that town. Backing up, I hoped to catch a glimpse of Sam, maybe his shadow in the window. Pulling out of the driveway and leaving him with that fair-haired family was another in a long line of parenting mistakes. Sam certainly wouldn't be kindling the Sabbath lights in this land of gin and tonics.

Driving north, I recalled the way my mother had always spread out a picnic for my siblings and me on summer Saturdays. Eating in the backyard during the Sabbath, maybe with watermelon or ice cream for dessert, had been the epitome of fun. Plus, it had been the one day neither of my parents worked and I had help supervising my brothers and sisters. My father had often presented me with some token of appreciation for minding everyone, usually closeout merchandise from the store, ribbons or scarves that I'd inevitably pass off to my sisters to dress their dolls.

Despite how much I enjoyed those simple, peaceful days in Ohio, I had always plotted my escape. I had been so eager to replace my family of birth with a family of my own creation. I had craved a deliberate, orderly household, not the chaos of so many children and a mother unable to keep up with the cleaning.

Edward and me and then Sam—that became my family: a small triangular composition, pure in its simplicity, its fundamental geometry. The problem was that I'd allowed the foundational bond, the one connecting Edward and me, to sever. Our triangle was now three segments, still connected but with the two on the ends swirling about in space.

The three of us used to spend summer evenings laughing together at the movies. Sam's face beamed with pride when Edward handed over the spatula and the burger-grilling responsibilities to him. After a long day cutting lawns, Sam often rode his bike to the town pool to meet up with friends. He saved his money, filling his bank account slowly and nobly. Were those memories the equivalent of my girlhood Saturday picnics? Even though Sam had seemed to relish our company at the time, had he also been plotting his departure?

I pulled off at a filling station, driving into the full-service bay in defiance of our belt tightening. I relieved myself in the dirty toilet, thinking how Mimi Crandall probably kept scented soaps and linen hand towels in her powder room.

Sam was in search of another family. Of course he was. Still, it shouldn't have been so easy for him to leave. After all the drop-offs at Wilburton Hall, we'd become too accustomed to saying goodbye. As a twenty-two-year-old, I had cried when I'd boarded that plane at Cleveland Hopkins. At just seventeen years, however, Sam was a pro at departure.

CHAPTER 27

Viewing his mother alone with Henry Crandall in the driveway through Justin's bedroom window made Sam's jaw clench. It wasn't for fear she'd find a way to embarrass him but rather because Uncle Henry didn't offer the best impression of the Crandalls. He wasn't warm or welcoming, not the type to humor his mother with a tour of the grounds, not even the view of the ocean from the back lawn. Henry was a man with too much time on his hands, although he'd never have enough time for somebody like Hannah Webber. He epitomized the snobbery she had warned he'd face in Long Harbor. Sam's mother had broached the topic while they'd been clothes shopping and at the dentist, but now he saw it for himself. The real world, unlike Dunning, shone a starker light on his family's differences. Sam needed to work; Justin didn't. Sam wanted to save money, while Justin never thought twice about spending it. Sam knew how to prepare simple meals in the apartment; Justin ordered takeout. They even rooted for rival baseball teams.

Sam made a point of figuring his own way around New York, anxious to be rid of his daily dependency on Justin. He found an ATM on his network near the subway and checked the balance in his account. Viewing even that modest three-digit number on the screen made him feel better. No, he'd never be able to afford rent, but he wouldn't be the Crandalls' charity case either. He would find a part-time job, save money, and grow his balance. He just needed the Make All Your Dreams Come True internship on his résumé—that and the Crandalls' connections.

Sam sent emails to his college counselor at Dunning, forwarding him the scores he'd earned on the standardized tests he'd taken that spring. They were excellent. The grades that came from Dunning were as well. "Nice work, Sam," the counselor replied. "This summer would be a good time to work on your essays."

He got a night job at a diner down the block from the apartment on the Upper East Side. He bused tables for minimum wage, but the waitstaff tipped him out after the dinner rush.

"Wow, not a very fun way to spend your evenings," Justin commented, upon learning about the gig.

"I don't have a choice, Justin." He practiced his Spanish with the guys in the kitchen and kept the bill of his baseball cap down, in the event that Dunning kids who hailed from the neighborhood stopped in for the restaurant's famous french fries.

When his shift was over, he'd call Nathalie, who was home in California with her family. He'd joke about the way Mrs. Crandall sautéed ground beef for her chocolate Labs, how she freaked when people didn't take their shoes off but let those two animals shit all over the place, how Uncle Henry picked at his stray nose hairs when he thought nobody was looking.

His second weekend at the Crandalls' summer cottage, dubbed Salt Spray, Uncle Henry invited Justin and Sam to play golf. It was a Saturday morning, and Mr. and Mrs. Crandall had stayed in Manhattan the night before for a fundraiser.

"I'm not much of a golfer," Sam said, having planned to spend the day drafting his college essays. The Crandalls' housekeeper, Cecile, bumped around them, clearing away the breakfast dishes.

"Fine. We'll talk here," Henry said, scraping his kitchen chair closer to Sam. He tapped his coffee cup against the table, and Cecile came over with the pot, her thin body lost inside a gray uniform.

Henry lit a cigarette and inhaled deeply. Justin refilled his cereal bowl, although Sam was conscientious about taking seconds.

"I didn't want to discuss this in front of your parents, Justin," Henry said, flicking his ashes into a china saucer, "but your mother's had it with all this Nine business."

Sam couldn't mask his surprise at Henry's mention of the Nine, and in relation to Mrs. Crandall, no less. "Don't look so surprised, Sam," he continued. "Why else do you think you're here? If you're to be Captain Dunning, we've got to start working together."

Justin cast a glance in Sam's direction that was both an apology and an *I told you so*. So, it wasn't the family's generosity that had brought him here but an opportunity for Uncle Henry to establish his chain of command.

The kitchen filled with the smoke from Uncle Henry's cigarette as he continued, "Now, now, I know what you're thinking." He didn't give Sam a chance to voice his surprise. "But we do need to get to know each other better, build a friendship. There's never been a captain without familial ties to the council, and we lobbied hard on your behalf. I told them you were practically family. Al Raymond put up quite a protest."

"I-I..." Sam couldn't put the words together. "I had no idea..."

"Of course you didn't. I was Captain Dunning back when we wore proper capes, not hooded sweatshirts. I've been leading the alumni council for years, and now that Justin's graduating, I need the next captain to be somebody I can trust."

"Oh," Sam said. "I thought I was here so you all could help with my college process."

Uncle Henry smiled, nodding his head, his flaccid double chin bobbing. "Don't worry about college, son. If you do a good job in the fall, the Nine brotherhood will make sure you have your pick of schools."

"Even with the stain on my record?"

Henry smiled. "Look, Sam, the council has been trying for some time to remove the headmaster. He's been able to stay because of support from the board of trustees." Justin was staring intently into his bowl, fishing for the last morsel of cereal. "We're building a case against Williams. We should have enough evidence to support his termination by the October trustees' meeting."

"I don't understand why you can't just wait for the old guy to retire," said Justin. "It can't be very far off."

"That's what we thought five years ago, but he hangs on. Think about it. Where else would he go?"

"And how would building a case against Williams involve me?" Sam's voice cracked.

"The Nine, Sam. You will direct one very important mission this fall." Henry rolled his eyes in Justin's direction. "Something Justin here couldn't follow through on."

"Uncle Henry, I told you! Dean Harper had Mr. Willis patrolling the place night and day."

"Well, Raymond told his father that it wouldn't have been that hard."

"Raymond doesn't even have the tunnels memorized," Sam said, rushing to Justin's defense.

"And you do?"

"Yes."

Sam's confidence made Uncle Henry smile. "That's the ticket, Sam. I knew you were the right man for the job." He patted the top of Sam's hand.

Sam looked back and forth between Justin and his uncle, for the first time putting a face to the man who sent the orders. The Nine truly was much bigger than what he saw on campus. Finally in the presence of true authority, Sam summoned the courage to ask the question that continued to haunt his sleep. He turned to face Justin. "Did you tell your uncle what we found?"

Justin's face froze, and Henry interjected, "Yes, yes, I know all about the recording devices, and I've stored that evidence in a safe place. And you showed true loyalty to the brotherhood by keeping it mum and taking your punishment."

Sam swallowed and nodded.

"Those tapes will come in handy, as I said, at the October trustees' meeting."

"Do you really think Headmaster Williams was behind the filming?"

"The important thing, Sam"—Uncle Henry paused, gazing through a window—"is that they were made while he was at the helm."

"Then who actually did the filming? Who sat at the controls?"

Henry patted Sam's shoulder. "Look, Sam, it was just a setup to make Williams look bad."

Sam inhaled deeply, pondering Henry's explanation. "Why would somebody want to set him up?"

"People are disappointed. Williams has a history of cover-ups."

"It's happened before?"

"It goes way back," Henry said. He crushed out his cigarette in the saucer, then explained, "Back to when I was in Class Four and Williams was the dean. There was this English teacher named Whittaker who got caught diddling boys. Turns out Williams protected him."

Sam went silent. This was more far reaching than he had ever imagined, in terms of history and in terms of actors. It made his head hurt. While Justin put his dish in the sink, Uncle Henry returned to the matter of golf. "How about teeing off after lunch?"

But Sam spoke up quickly. "Wait, where are the tapes now? Have you watched any of them?"

Justin crossed his arms and jutted out his chin. "Jesus, Webber, you've *got* to let this go."

"It's okay, Justin." Uncle Henry's tone was placating. "They're in a safe place. Nobody's going to watch them," he said.

Sam hung his head, trying to compute it all.

"Cheer up, son," said Henry, patting him on the back. "You should feel like you're on top of the world. Being one of the Nine is the best part about Dunning. I can assure you it's a fraternity made up of the finest men."

How Sam wanted it all to be so. But there was something about the way Justin wouldn't meet his eyes and about Uncle Henry's casual dismissal of the videotaping that didn't sit right. Whoever had gone to the trouble of hardwiring a camera into the shower with a line to the boiler room was creating more than a setup. There was also the fact that Justin had been seen looking for something in the Bennett bathroom.

"And do you know anything about the camera in the Wilburton laundry room?"

"What?" Henry said, glaring at Justin.

"Don't look at me," Justin said, leaning against the marble countertop. "I don't know what he's talking about."

"I certainly hope you don't," Henry said. "I've never known a generation more infatuated with sexting and dick pics. You boys are really crude."

Sam felt himself flush. The Labs roused themselves on the floor, stood, and barked in that low mock howl of theirs, wagging their tails in the direction of the front door. Seconds later, tires crunched on the driveway. "It's Morris and Mimi," Justin said with a sigh. "They're home." He ran a hand through his hair and left the kitchen.

....

At dinner that evening Sam asked Mrs. Crandall if he could help, maybe set the table. She was tickled, muttering, "If any of my own four children ever pitched in." When it was time to eat, she insisted Sam sit to her right while the rest of the family jockeyed for positions at the other end of the table, closer to their father.

"I've already received glowing reports from the office about you, Sam," Mimi said, beaming.

"Oh. Thank you. I mean, I'm glad."

"And Justin tells me you're busing tables at the Second Avenue Diner in the evenings?"

"I need to return to school with spending money."

"Well," she said, her pink lips spreading into a thin smile, "I'm very impressed. Your parents must be proud of you."

Sam rose early the next morning to swim in the ocean while Justin snored, tangled in his sheets on the other side of the room. As Sam ran down to the beach, he remembered Mrs. Crandall's compliment. The night before, he had been able to verbalize only a simple "Yes, I believe my parents are proud," but as far as his mother was concerned, it wasn't garden-variety pride. From as young an age as he could remember, she had read books to him with drama in her voice; she had taken him to the library and accompanied him on all his school field trips; she had been the class mother, the den leader—she'd said yes to anything that put her in his orbit. Of course it was because she loved him, but she was so invested. She was worlds apart from Mrs. Crandall, whose children seemed to take up only a fraction of her life. Sam could never imagine his mother running a foundation of her own.

Still, after everything he'd put his family through, Sam was determined to make it up to her in some way. His father would be satisfied for him to be a content and productive member of society, but his mother had always hoped for more. She needed him to break through a ceiling, get into a great college, allow her to ride his coattails.

As he kicked and pulled through the swells, he realized how wrong his mother had been to think Dunning would elevate their family to a higher social class of people. She didn't realize the academy wasn't the thing that brought these people together; it just happened to be where they sent their kids to school. They were connected long before Dunning by blood and social ties, including summering together in places like Long Harbor. They weren't looking for new friends. They'd never exchange holiday cards with Hannah and Edward Webber.

All the same, they were happy to host one of their son's disadvantaged schoolmates for the summer, especially one who behaved like a perfect houseguest. Sam's mother had taught him proper etiquette: where to set the bread plate, how to place a knife with the sharp edge facing in, what a salad fork looked like. He was grateful for that training now, noticing how Mimi Crandall took stock of such things.

Even though he couldn't easily join in on the tennis court or the golf course, Sam demonstrated athleticism by swimming a mile parallel to the beach on weekend mornings. His ability to weather the bracing temperature and ignore occasional shark sightings impressed his hosts. Even though his lips turned blue in the cold, it was a good antidote for the Crandalls' hold.

Fourth of July weekend found Justin and Sam on the back lawn with Justin's father and Uncle Henry, who had started on cocktails early. The brothers were sparring verbally, one of their favorite pastimes. Henry espoused his libertarian views, his mistrust of government, and the citizenry's right to privacy. Morris gave up rebutting and goaded his brother on. Henry's face turned red. "Regulation and intrusion! Come now, Morris—as one of the nation's great capitalists, you must be on my side here. The government has encroached upon every facet of our lives."

Morris Crandall shook his head at his younger brother's fervor, then peered into the distance toward the porch, where Mimi and Celeste were preparing for company.

"We deserve privacy and freedom to live as we please," Henry said.

"That's why you fit in so well in New Hampshire, Henry. Live free or die," Morris teased.

Sam and Justin, sipping Cokes, laughed.

"The one person, however," Henry chortled, "who needs constant monitoring is Bradley Williams."

"Oh, Henry, can't you get over that old grudge?" Morris asked, rising in response to Mimi's waves from across the lawn. "I'd better go help before I end up in the doghouse."

Henry continued his rant for the boys, indignant that Williams treated the largest endowment in secondary-school history like his own private checkbook. "His need-blind financial aid policy is an outright redistribution of wealth. Who the hell does he think raised that money, anyway?" He claimed that under Williams, the number of gifts to the school was in decline. "There are about twenty thousand alumni. Every year, the graduating class offsets the number who die. Back when I was the chair of the alumni fund, fifty percent of us gave. Now it's below thirty." Henry also had a strong point of view on the new admissions policies. "Do you boys know what the discount rate means?"

Sam and Justin shook their heads.

"It's the percentage of students who pay full freight—and last year it was less than half! Just don't get me started on that imbecile." He paused and then asked, "Have you ever thought about infiltrating his office?"

Justin shook his head in defeat. "I told you, Uncle Henry. That's damn near impossible."

"But I don't think we've ever tried," Sam said, looking back and forth between Henry and Justin.

"See, Justin," said Henry. "you need to adopt more of a can-do attitude, like Sam here. I'm sure Gary can get us the blueprint of the alarm system and security cameras in the headmaster's suite."

"And the keys?" Sam asked.

Uncle Henry guided Sam away from Justin, toward the bar set up on the lawn. "Of course—he's got all the keys. What else would you need?"

Sam's train of thought was interrupted. Guests were arriving for the family's prefireworks party, and Mrs. Crandall was escorting a group of young women onto the lawn.

"Sam! Justin!" she called out cheerily. "Come say hello. Look who's here! It's Rae Stern, Becca Fitzpatrick's granddaughter!"

While Sam smiled in the girl's direction, Henry whispered one last thing in his ear. "Sam, my boy, I'll make you a hero on that campus, a Dunning legend, and the toast of the brotherhood."

....

Mrs. Crandall breezed into the MAYDCT office once every other week that summer, popping her head into the office of the executive director, who stopped whatever she was doing to greet and update her patroness. One morning, as Sam was working on an initiative to install MAYDCT in Mount Sinai Hospital's pediatric wing, Mimi paid one of her visits.

Mount Sinai had a long-standing relationship with the competition, but one of its young cancer patients had recently been stranded in the Orlando airport on her return from Disney World. The distraught family had been all over the local media, causing a public relations nightmare, and a friend of Mimi's had immediately texted her a link to the story. Mimi saw this as an opportunity to pounce, exclaiming, "A dream can't really come true if you're a sick child stuck in an airport."

"Do you think we can guarantee seamless travel?" the executive director asked.

Sam heard her cautious tone, followed by Mimi's exasperated response, through the office's glass partition. Mimi's voice raised a few decibels. "Of course we can. It's our in. I'll have Morris's Gulfstream fly back and forth if I must."

The executive director must have raised an eyebrow or shown some other sign of skepticism, because Mimi snapped, "Look, I want MAYDCT to be the only organization making fucking dreams come true at Mount Sinai. Period."

Mimi's expletive rang through the small office, giving the few, meek employees a reason to put their heads down. Sam was licking envelopes he'd stuffed with Disney brochures when Mimi stopped in front of his desk. "Sam, darling," she said, "care to grab a coffee with me before I drive back to Rhode Island?"

"Oh, sure," he replied, expressing mock surprise at her sudden appearance.

They walked down a sidewalk that radiated midsummer heat.

She turned into a coffee shop that smelled of bacon and eggs and made Sam's stomach growl. She placed her order in a gruff New York manner, and gestured for him to do the same.

"It's for here," she added, ducking into a small booth.

"Sam, I want to talk to you about Justin." She voiced her frustration over the fact that he had dropped out of the film crew. He'd complained that the hours were too long and the work too arduous. "I need to relax before college starts, all right?" was what he'd said, and, as a result, he was now spending all his time in Long Harbor.

"Morris agreed right away, but I'd sort of hoped Justin would engage his mind over the summer." Mimi stirred sugar into her coffee slowly, and Sam sensed some sort of request forming. He missed having Justin around the apartment too, not that he could afford what Justin usually had in mind for entertainment. Living in New York City was expensive.

"Justin and Henry were hoping you might beg off early and come to Rhode Island this afternoon."

It was only Wednesday, and Sam had two shifts at the diner before the weekend. "Oh, jeez, today? No, I can't do that."

"They'll be disappointed."

"I can't keep up with them on the golf course anyway."

"I know. Golf's a bore, Sam. But I'm worried about Justin."

Sam didn't know what to say. A friend's mother bestowing a confidence was a delicate situation he'd never found himself in before.

"He's been quiet," she continued, "and avoiding his regular crowd. He's spending an awful lot of time with Henry."

"Hmm." Sam bit his lip. "I mean, he seems like the same old Justin to me." But that couldn't have been further from the truth. Sam picked at the torn vinyl on the banquette and wondered if he'd even want Justin as a friend if he met him now. Ever since the night in the Bennett boiler room, he'd stopped being a floppy-haired goofball, easy to smile, the first to tell a joke or ride Sam on his handlebars across the quad to dinner. Then again, Sam hadn't been the same either. If Mimi Crandall and Hannah Webber had bothered to compare notes, they'd have had a lot to discuss.

"What has Henry gotten him into? Gotten the two of you into, I'm afraid?"

"Into?"

"Look, I know about the Nine. Morris was a member back in the day. He's told me all about it. But Henry, a grown man, just can't seem to let it go. I can't fathom it."

"Well, look, Mrs. Crandall. I'm in a bit of a tight spot. I'm not supposed to talk—"

"Oh, Sam. Morris keeps telling me it's just schoolboy fun and games, but I think something bigger is eating at Justin. And now I take it you're going to become Captain Dunning, or whatever they call it, in the fall?"

Sam nodded.

"I love Morris's family—the Crandalls are all good people—but Henry is . . . Let's just say he's never quite found his place. As the youngest son, he's sort of lost and comes across as a bully, and, well, the two of us have words. I never thought Justin was particularly fond of him. I can't get my head around why they're joined at the hip all of a sudden."

Sam shrugged and sipped his coffee, though he knew his lack of an opinion might irritate Mrs. Crandall even further. Her comments, however, did validate his instincts about Uncle Henry.

He changed the subject. "Mrs. Crandall, I was wondering, why is it always Disney World? Don't you think some sick kids might want to go someplace different? Maybe a one-of-a-kind experience would be a better idea?"

Mimi took a sip of her coffee. "Like what?"

"I don't know, like a hot-air balloon ride, or going up in a helicopter, or horseback riding, or white-water rafting?" At least, those were the types of things Sam would have wanted to try.

Mimi smiled. "Sam, you're an interesting kid."

"Mrs. Crandall, when I get up to Long Harbor this weekend,

I'll get Justin to do something fun. I'll suggest we hang out with the other kids on the beach."

Mimi smiled again. "Thank you, dear. We're so lucky to have you."

....

August weekends took on the air of celebration. Besides coming for the perfect weather, the Crandall siblings wanted to give the baby of the family a proper college send-off, which meant sneaking Justin and Sam into the local bars.

Sam had fun on those outings, publicly wrapped up in the big Crandall family. But when they returned home one particularly sultry Saturday night, the partying went on a little too long. Uncle Henry came down from his room near the attic, found them in the game room, and went drink for drink with his nieces and nephews. Sam even caught him checking out Justin's sister as she leaned across the pool table. Claiming he had an early swim planned the next morning, Sam tried to beg off when the shot glasses came around, but Uncle Henry forced one into his hand. "We haven't toasted your inauguration yet."

Sam lifted the small glass between his thumb and forefinger.

"It's a big deal, Sam. Don't you understand that?"

"I get it. That's not it. I'm just tired. It's been a long week."

Uncle Henry blew smoke in the air, then put out his cigarette in a crystal ashtray before raising his shot glass in Sam's direction. "To the brotherhood," he said.

"To the Nine," Sam said, before gulping the bronze-colored liquid. Justin and his brother caught on and joined in with raucous excitement, clapping Sam on the shoulders and huddling around him and Uncle Henry. They all started chanting as if they were inside the Tomb, beginning in a low voice that built to a full crescendo. "Nine, nine, nine, Nine, Nine, *Nine, Nine, Nine!*" Justin and his siblings were much more inebriated than Sam. They turned the music up and danced around the room, jumping on the couch and waving their arms in the air. They were making so much noise, Sam was afraid Mrs. Crandall might come through the door at any minute. But she never appeared at night; she preferred to save her disappointment for the breakfast table.

Just as he'd anticipated, the vibe was rather frosty the next morning. Sam had slipped into the dining room to grab a banana from the sideboard and caught snippets of the adults' conversation.

"Acting like one of the children again, Henry?"

"Acting like my mother again, Mimi?"

"That's enough, you two," Morris said, playing referee.

Even though they didn't acknowledge him, Sam felt trapped, as if he couldn't leave without saying something. "Beautiful day, isn't it?"

The three of them looked up from their newspapers, and Sam noticed their eyes. Justin's father's were accusing, his mother's red-rimmed, and Uncle Henry's even puffier than usual.

Sam walked across the lawn to the ocean, breathing in the fresh sea air and squinting at the rising sun. As he dove through the waves, he didn't find the cold as shocking as he had on those first summer mornings. He made long, strong strokes underwater, disappearing into the ocean's vastness for as long as he could hold his breath.

CHAPTER 28

Sam showered the greasy residue from the diner off his body, collapsed on the couch in front of the air-conditioning unit, and flipped on the game. It was an added thorn in his side that the Red Sox games weren't televised in New York and he was left watching the hated Yankees. He stayed tuned as a sociologist might, stuck in a foreign world, the place where the archrival lived.

It was the end of August, and Sam was counting down the days until he could return home. Boarding the train for Long Harbor at Penn Station on Friday afternoons had become a hot, sweaty chore. He had to make up ways to avoid Uncle Henry, who wanted only to plot his destruction of the headmaster. He was just about to go to bed when his phone buzzed.

"Come to Brooklyn this weekend?" It was a text from Grabs. "My mother wants to make you her famous borscht."

Sam perked up at the invitation; this was the first he'd heard from Grabs since their argument the prior spring. It would be a legitimate excuse to avoid Uncle Henry, as well as an opportunity to apologize properly to his friend. There couldn't be a place on the East Coast more unlike Long Harbor than Coney Island.

Sam immediately accepted the invitation, then sent Mimi Crandall an email excusing himself, saying he didn't want to intrude on their last weekend as a family but that he hoped to thank her in person for all she had done at the MAYDCT offices the following week.

"Oh, bosh!" she wrote back. "I was planning a game night and hoped you would be my partner in charades. Please consider yourself family, Sam. But I understand—we've been monopolizing all your free time, and I'm sure you have other friends to visit. Do have fun. Xo, M"

When Friday afternoon came around, Sam boarded a Q train and rode it to the end of the line. When he made his way out of the station, it took a few seconds to adjust to the heat. The weather had attracted throngs of people, traveling not just in ones and twos but in big groups. Many of the men wore sleeveless T-shirts and denim jeans with high-top sneakers. The women were more scantily dressed but not in a way that suggested they'd be going swimming. The colorful array of store-front signs served as a backdrop to the scent of cotton candy drifting through the air. The tinny sound of carnival tunes from the arcades competed with hip-hop music blasting from the shops.

Sam stood on the boardwalk and spun in a slow circle, gaining his bearings and searching for a street sign. Grabs had texted him some basic directions, but the noise and the heat and people jostling about were disorienting. Momentarily longing for the expansive cool grass of the Crandalls' lawn, Sam recognized how quickly their orderly world had co-opted him.

He swung a backpack containing swim trunks and a towel over one shoulder, laughing to himself at the presumption he'd made while packing that he and Grabs might spend the afternoon cooling off in the ocean.

Using the map on his cell phone, Sam finally found the right apartment building. He pushed the buzzer, setting in motion heavy footsteps above. He chuckled, watching through the glass in the front door as Grabs pounded down the stairs, one hand on the banister and the other on a belt loop, holding up his pants.

"Sam!" Grabs exclaimed, after opening the door and catching his breath.

Sam clasped his friend's hand, surprised by the emotion that rose in his chest. Instead of speaking right away, he hugged Grabs.

Once upstairs, Sam greeted Mrs. Grabowski, handing her a small box of candy. He'd met her only a few times at Dunning, where she seemed out of place. However, she glowed in this environment, the odor of roasting poultry filling the apartment. She bustled back and forth from the kitchen, and Sam recognized the same line of perspiration above her lip that Grabs sprouted when he exerted himself.

Their furniture was heavy and dark, some upholstered in red velvet, all with a very old-world feel. Grabs took Sam into his bedroom, where he dropped his backpack. Sam's eyes popped at what appeared to be a mini control center. He pointed at all the equipment.

"What? You think I can afford to take the summer off?" Grabs joked.

They left the hot apartment, rushing down the stairs and into the melee of revelers. Grabs bought a couple of bags of roasted peanuts from a vendor on his corner and tossed one to Sam. They munched on the salty snacks as they meandered back toward the boardwalk.

"I'm so glad you're here," Grabs said, once they reached the railing overlooking the crowded beach.

"Hey, thanks for inviting me."

"My mom wanted to meet my best friend, and I needed to speak to you in private." Grabs launched in right away. "It couldn't wait until Dunning and couldn't be over a phone line or SMS."

Sam turned to face his friend. "Yeah, and I need to say a few things too. Grabs, I'm sorry I acted like such a jerk last spring."

"That's okay. I implied some mean things too."

They stood in silence for a moment, watching people splash through the water up to their big, overweight knees.

"Did you ever find video of me in the laundry room?"

"Yeah, but you weren't recognizable. Neither was Andrea. It was an amateur effort, and I wiped out the Dropbox. Looked like only a couple of kids had access anyway."

"I owe you."

"More importantly, I think I found the shower videos for sale," Grabs said.

"I knew Henry was lying."

"Henry?"

"Yeah, Justin's uncle. He said it was all just to frame Williams and that the recordings were safely hidden."

Grabs raised an eyebrow, his glasses slanting across his face. It was the same expression he'd worn the first time he'd run the chessboard on Sam.

"I know, I know," Sam said, having been caught, yet again, believing something stupid. "Tell me what you found."

"It's on Thor, the dark web. Everything is anonymous and encrypted. There are videos available for sale called *Boarding School Babes*. There's no question it's the girls in Bennett. I'm trying to trace who the seller is, but because of the encryption, it's going to be tough. I think I've found another way around it, but it's just going to take some time."

"Is Nathalie in any?"

Grabs turned back to look at the ocean. His silence was the answer Sam feared.

"You're sure?"

Grabs nodded in the affirmative, with eyes wide open. "The advertisement called them 'not yet legal' and 'hot, wet teens.'"

Blood surged through Sam's veins. He leaned over the railing, on the verge of vomiting.

"There's been a lot of email communication between Williams and Coach Schwartz. They've been mentioning a teacher named Whittaker and a 'replay of what happened in the eighties'—something about the tunnels. Schwartz accused Williams of screwing up again."

"Coach Schwartz?" That was a name Sam wasn't expecting. He didn't have much history with the guy, but it was common knowledge that Shawn Willis spent every Friday night in his basement. Was it possible he screened dirty movies for that creepy gang of coaches each week?

When they returned to the Grabowskis' apartment, the dining table was set with lace linens and candlesticks. The sun was setting, and Grabs's mother accentuated the atmosphere by pulling the brocade drapery across the bay of windows in the living room. Grabs's father emerged from the bedroom in a black suit over a starched white shirt. "Sit down, boys. Time to light the candles and say our prayers."

Sam basked in the warm glow of his mother's traditions. It was the first time he'd observed Shabbat with another family. Mrs. Grabowski seemed pleased that he was able to recite the kiddush in Hebrew.

CHAPTER 29

I ran the length of the platform as soon as Sam hefted his bags off the train.

"My city boy! You're home!"

Overflowing with questions, I chattered most of the car ride, commenting on how healthy he looked, how grown up. I asked about the Crandalls and whether they'd given Justin a big send-off to Yale.

Instead of answering, Sam turned toward me with a question of his own. "How's Dad?" he asked.

I took a breath. "He's coming for dinner," I said, nodding reassuringly. Sam nodded too, then gave me brief reports on New York, Long Harbor, and Brooklyn. "But it's really good to be home," he said, as we pulled into our drive.

My heart swelled at that comment, and I flashed back to an afternoon almost thirty years earlier when my father warned me, "You can flee to the ends of the earth, Hannah, but you will never leave home." I'd been determined back then to prove him wrong, but now here I was, hopeful that my son would always be tied to his roots.

I'd had to convince Edward that it was important to provide Sam with the familiar comforts of home before he went off for his senior year of high school.

"He's going to have to get used to our separation sooner or later, Hannah," Edward had said.

"But not before his senior fall. Don't you realize how much pressure he's going to be under?"

"Hannah, he'll only be under pressure if you apply it."

"Me?" I rolled my eyes, but I resisted a blowup on the phone. "One last meal, Edward. Come at six thirty."

When he arrived, Sam was already upstairs. I sensed him surveying the countertops for everything I'd changed since he'd moved out. For one thing, I'd thrown out his clutter, including the magnets he collected on the refrigerator, holding pizza menus and baseball schedules.

"How's the old car holding up?" I asked.

"I take the subway these days," he answered, with a hint of self-righteousness. I'd driven past his apartment complex, a building notoriously full of divorcees and widows, four stories, long and low, tan-colored brick, modest landscaping, and conveniently across the street from a subway stop.

"Oh," I said, emerging from the open refrigerator with two juicy New York strips wrapped in butcher paper. "Would you like to fire up the grill?" I gestured toward the steaks with an apprehensive smile, hoping he wouldn't recall what had happened the last time I'd made his favorite meal.

"Sure, looks great for you and Sam, but I've stopped eating meat," he said. "I'll be fine with a baked potato."

I looked at him through new eyes. Taking public transportation and not eating meat? He might have been trimmer too. His hair was a tad longer, and . . . I don't know, there was something else about him. I daresay he looked happy.

"Hmm. Sounds like you've made a few changes."

"Yeah, I'm hoping to look for a new job too." I froze. We couldn't afford any financial risk when Sam was about to enter college.

"Don't worry, I won't do anything crazy," he assured me. Leaning against the sink, he asked, "How have you been?"

I could have colored the past two months in different shades of terrible, but that wouldn't have been entirely fair. There was no denying I'd brooded the first several weeks, dwelling on how he'd abandoned me, but a person can cry only so many tears. And since Sam and Edward were off trying new things, I'd looked for ways to be useful as well. I went to yoga more often, started going for coffee with Joy.

"Oh, the dentist office keeps me busy. And when I was delivering books down to the Boys and Girls Club, I saw a flyer that they needed help. So I'm a reading tutor in the afternoon." I had always loved reading aloud, first to my brothers and sisters and later to Sam, tucked into my lap.

Unbeknownst to me, Sam had been listening in the doorway. "That's so cool," he said. "Mom, seriously, you'd make a great tutor."

"Thanks, sweetie. The kids have been enjoying some of your old favorites."

Edward nodded in approval. "That's good, Hannah. That's really good."

CHAPTER 30

Sam found a cell phone wrapped in a rubber band and a yellow Post-it at the bottom of his duffel. It was an older-generation flip-top like his father kept in his briefcase. The note read, "This is how I will contact you. If you need me, speed-dial #1. BTW, we still need to discuss first meeting in Tomb.—HC"

Sam wadded up the paper and whipped it into his trash basket. He recalled how he'd looked up to the seniors when he was an initiate, and wondered if Uncle Henry had orchestrated everything they'd done as well. After his summer with the Crandalls, being Captain Dunning no longer felt like a cool honor; it was nothing but a strange masquerade.

Sam was putting his clothes away when his father pulled in. He started for the stairs, but the Henry phone started vibrating on his bedspread.

"Hello?" he said, flipping it open.

"Webber, tell the brothers your first prank will be in Williams's suite right after parents' weekend."

Sam chewed on his thumbnail while he listened to Henry's instructions. What he shouldn't tell the brothers was how an envelope would be hand delivered to campus and planted in Williams's drawer while the prank was being carried out. Uncle Henry also confirmed that Gary in Maintenance would provide the necessary keys.

Exactly what the prank looked like was up to Sam. He decided on something good-natured: filling the headmaster's en suite powder room with Ping-Pong balls. Breaking into the headmaster's office was dangerous enough; they didn't need to push their luck.

He looked forward to getting that mission over with and Uncle Henry off his back. Then he'd be able to start his real work: investigating how Headmaster Williams, Dean Harper, Mr. Willis, and Coach Schwartz might have been involved with videotaping the girls in Bennett and trafficking in child pornography.

....

After dinner, Sam sprawled across his bed, jotting down notes amid piles of clothes and bins of school supplies, when he heard a knock. "Come in," he said, sitting upright, anticipating his mother's horror at the sight of the mess.

But it was his father who slipped through the door. "Hi." Sam brightened. "I thought you'd left."

"Your mother and I had some things to discuss."

It was strange to stand face-to-face with his father in this bedroom, knowing it was where he'd taken refuge in the extra bed for such a long time, maybe even long enough to start thinking of it as his own.

"Sam," he said, holding out his arms for a hug. His father had never been one for physical contact when he was young. Now it seemed like all he wanted to do. "I came up to say goodbye."

"Oh, okay."

"Can I drive you back to school this weekend?"

"Won't Mom mind?"

"We'll both take you."

"Really?"

"Yeah, and I'd love to swing you past my new apartment." His father seemed oddly proud.

"Sure, sounds great," Sam said, recognizing a new brightness in his dad's eyes.

CHAPTER 31

Sam balanced on his bed frame, tacking up posters. He didn't have enough to cover the walls, as the senior single he'd drawn was the biggest he'd ever seen, twice the size of the double he'd shared with Ethan as a first-year. As he struggled with a roll of Scotch tape, he rehearsed what he planned to say that evening from behind the Tomb's altar.

His phone buzzed, and he dropped the tape on the bed and let the poster float to the ground.

It was Nathalie: "Parents leaving soon." They had been apart almost three months, and even though they had talked on the phone, texted, and FaceTimed frequently over the summer, her proximity on campus got his heart pounding.

"LMK."

Ten minutes later, she wrote again: "In quad."

Sam jumped down to the floor and jogged out the Wilburton door to find Nathalie waiting for him across the green, swaying slightly from side to side. She'd grown her hair to her shoulders and wore eyeglasses he hadn't seen before.

"Oh, Nat," he said. He buried his face into the crook of her neck and inhaled deeply. The pressure of her arms against his back nearly made him cry. They pulled away and looked into each other's eyes.

"What's with the glasses?" Sam laughed.

"Got them to make me look smart."

Their conversations over the summer hadn't been burdened with the weight of this place, and being back at Dunning was a heavy reminder of the previous year's trials. Seeing Nathalie here, in front of her dorm, reminded Sam of the vow he'd made to root out the pervert.

"Our senior year," he said, forcing a smile.

"I know." Her voice quavered. Senior fall was notoriously as brutal as junior year. Plus, there was all that anxiety over what would come next. Parents were waiting with bated breath for news of college, and their classmates were already acting coy when it came to discussing their own hopes. This semester's grades were the last ones college admissions officers would see on their transcripts. Yes, the vibe in the air was fun, filled with everything starting up again, but the inevitable intensity put a pit in Sam's stomach.

"This place hasn't broken us yet," he said.

"Not for lack of trying." She sighed.

He took her in his arms again and whispered in her ear, "Nathalie de Witt, we are in this together."

She took his hand and squeezed it, leading him out of the quad and toward the playing fields. The fall teams were already practicing, and the sounds of whistles and laughter pierced the air. They found a secluded spot on the top tier of the football stadium, sat down on the concrete, and kissed.

Several perks came with being a senior at Dunning: first-floor dorm rooms; reserved seating areas in the dining hall and the student center; a thirty-minutes-later check-in; and, of course, the senior lawn, a square section of grass in the center of the quadrangle, bordered by walking paths. The only ones allowed to step on the grass, besides the grounds crew, were members of the senior class. In the spring, they would cover it with sand, bring in beach chairs, and sunbathe to surfing tunes.

It was funny how these benefits seemed to matter so much. Watching older kids lord them for three years resulted in a hunger among every rising senior class to do the same. Maybe it was also because making it to senior year at Dunning was an accomplishment worth noting, not so much for the kids who'd arrived sophomore and junior years, and most definitely not for the PGs who'd just shown up, but as a testament of endurance to those like Sam, who had survived the place since age fourteen.

....

Sam, Nathalie, and Grabs found seats together at the first Wednesday morning all-school assembly in the rows reserved up front for the seniors. An a cappella group opened the meeting while Headmaster Williams beamed from the stage. He made a show of introducing the dozen new faculty members and then recited his expectations for the class of 2014.

"I have always admired this special group of young men and women, not just because my lovely daughter is a member." The audience laughed as the headmaster grinned at Mary in the front row. "But I have gotten to know you all a bit better because you are her friends. I view you not only with the eyes of a head of school but with the heart of a parent.

"With that in mind, please indulge me for a moment. I'm urging you to relish every last day on this fine campus, because the end will come sooner than you think." Williams's stare seemed to move from his daughter's face to Sam's. Sam turned to Nathalie and Grabs to see if they perceived this as well, but they just slouched with boredom.

"You students have lots to complain about while you're here," the headmaster continued. "But as soon as you graduate, you'll see—you'll become fanatic alums, remembering Dunning as the Garden of Eden. You'll recall these years as the ones that made you."

Nathalie rolled her eyes.

Williams invited Mr. Booker, the head of IT, onstage. Everything else in the assembly had been standard issue, but this got people's attention. Booker had the complexion of a man who worked in the basement. His ashen skin blended with his white hair. He had wild eyebrows and wire-framed glasses, and he shrank back when Williams put the microphone into his hands.

"Uh," he stuttered, "there's been a bug we've discovered—a, uh, virus—and it's come from those laptops that were issued in 2010. So all of you in Class One will have to come down to my office to have your hard drives scanned." He handed the microphone back to Williams and got down off the stage quickly.

"You will each receive an email with your appointment time," Williams added. "In the meantime, make sure all your work is backed up."

The administration told the students to back up their data every day, the same way others urged them to cover their coughs or use condoms, because nobody would ever forget the meek girl who had jumped to her death from the roof of the library several years earlier when her hard drive had crashed during exams.

"Booker's announcement was intended for me," Grabs said, as they exited the auditorium. "Such a pain. I'm going to have to wipe so much stuff offline before I go down there." The huge cache of backed-up data had been a treasure trove for Grabs when it came to hacking information. "But if Williams thinks Booker is any match for Faceless, he's dumber than I thought. I mean, did you see that guy?"

Grabs didn't believe anybody over thirty could truly understand computers or the Internet. He had also never forgotten when he'd asked, as a first-year, if helping out in IT was an option for his financial aid campus job, and Booker had politely turned him away. Joining Faceless and making Booker look like a fool had become one of Grabs's primary diversions.

He went on, "Making everyone bring in their laptop is just their way of letting Faceless know they mean business. It's a message to you as well, Sam."

"Why?" Had Grabs noticed the way Williams's stare had drilled into him?

"Williams and Harper are making it clear they're coming out with guns loaded."

Sam's email from Booker arrived later that morning. After his appointment, he went directly to Grabs's room and handed him his laptop. "Check it out. Booker might be old, but he managed to install spyware in less than ten minutes," he said. Sam had homework to do, had been doing the minimum since school began, as tracking down what the administration was up to had become his highest priority.

Grabs handled the black rectangle like a fine diamond, holding it up to the light and rotating it on its axis, wearing the type of magnifying glasses that jewelers wore. He never failed to impress Sam with the breadth of gadgets he had within arm's reach.

Grabs powered it back up and went through the program code that ran Sam's operating system. He began to nod slowly, having obviously found what he was looking for.

"Those bastards," he said. "Sam, we'll have to find another laptop for you to use. We're shelving this one. If they think they're going to watch you, it's going to be a pretty disappointing show."

CHAPTER 32

In early October, a hurricane traveled up the coast, dumping an extraordinary amount of rain and keeping kids in the buildings they'd dreamed of escaping all week. But when the boys dashed through the downpour back to Wilburton after brunch on Sunday, they found invitations from Shawn Willis taped to their doors. "Come for pizza and soda during the Patriots game. Bring your quarters for the pool."

Gambling was against the rules, but Shawn figured the boys played poker in the hallways, and just about every male on campus had bought into a fantasy league.

Angeline had helped him plan everything, had even copied the invitations in the library. But this whole evening was really now possible because of Dean Harper's generosity at the beginning of the school year.

Shawn had heard a knock on his door a few days before orientation activity had begun in September.

"The dean sent us," said a guy in a dark blue mechanic's jumpsuit.

"Why?"

"To install cable in your apartment," a second guy said, brushing past Shawn, coils of blue cable looped over his shoulder.

Shawn typed a quick email to Harper. "Thanks for the cable hookup. Boys will be really pumped."

A few minutes later, he got a reply. "Not too pumped, I hope. All common rooms are receiving upgrades, so Wilburton is nothing special, but yours is the only faculty apartment, so keep it quiet. I'm also sending over an extra flat-screen monitor from the renovation of the science building. Have fun bonding with your boys."

It was like Christmas morning in September. Shawn didn't know whether to jog over to Harper's office to kiss him or to act like a normal adult whose boss had treated him nicely. He returned to the living room and pointed to the spot where he wanted the technician to set up the TV.

Generations of Dunning students had pleaded for a modern-day menu of channels. They were isolated enough, and to not be able to watch the news made it even worse, they argued. Yeah, right—news. It wasn't CNN they were after—more like ESPN. Regardless, somebody had finally heard them.

He flipped open his cell phone. "Hey, Angeline," he cooed when she picked up. "Hi, sweetie. Wanna come over to my place tonight to watch a movie?"

"On what, your laptop?"

"Someone just got a brand-new, forty-eight-inch flat-screen, smart-ass."

"Does it get reception?"

"Can you say 'premium cable package'?"

"Ooh, Shawn. I love it when you talk dirty. I'll bring the popcorn."

....

For the football game, Angeline had suggested he serve pizza.

Max and Ethan were the first to arrive, grabbing prime seats on the couch and propping their feet on the coffee table. They assumed an air of collegiality with Shawn, having been appointed fourth-floor proctors. The three of them had meetings often, Shawn needing to reinforce the importance of being good role models for the first-years. Sam would have been a better proctor, but nobody ever asked Shawn's opinion.

By the time Sam and Grabs arrived, it was into the first quarter, and Shawn had a full house. The pizza was being delivered, so they were the ones to help him set up all the food on the kitchen table.

"Thanks for doing this, Mr. Willis," Sam said.

"It's about time, right?"

"Yeah, what do you think got into them, upgrading the televisions and hooking us up to cable?" Grabs asked.

"Natives were getting restless?"

Just then, there was a loud howl from the couch as Tom Brady connected on a long pass. It made Shawn smile—normalcy again. This was what a Sunday afternoon in America was supposed to sound like. He made sure the door between his apartment and the hallway was wide open, hoping the cheering and laughter would lure some of the more studious kids out of their rooms, or at least set a new tone in Wilburton, one with plenty of spirit.

Shawn grinned as tomato sauce dripped off his chin. He couldn't wait to tell Angie how well it was going—she'd be proud too.

He dumped chips into a bowl and opened a few packs of Oreos. The sweets had been her idea, and he could tell it was a good one as he watched the boys dreamily unscrew the cookies of their youth and lick up the cream filling. The practice elicited a few raunchy comments, but Shawn didn't shut it down, since the afternoon was turning out just as he'd hoped—somewhere between locker-room banter and brotherly camaraderie. If only these kids had been of age, he would have loved to crack open a few beers.

Grabs returned to the kitchen table, helped himself to another slice, and then leaned back against the kitchen counter. He seemed more interested in checking things out than he was in the game. His eyes wandered around the apartment as if he were taking inventory, noticing the few books Shawn kept on the shelves, the dirty dishes in the sink. He might have even looked at the closed bedroom door, imagining Shawn's sloppy, unmade bed. Shawn scratched the back of his neck while Grabs continued his slow, deliberate survey. Grabs then walked behind the television stand and fiddled with the wiring in the back of the cable box.

"You sizing up that monster for some gaming?" Shawn called to him.

"Oh, sure," he said. Shawn wasn't sure which was cool these days, PlayStation or Xbox, and was just about to throw out that question for debate when Brady threw another touchdown pass and three of the boys let out a whoop, jumping to their feet and high-fiving each other. This was turning into a slaughter, which prompted Max to grab the remote and flip to another game.

"What the fuck?"

"Max, you're a fucking asshole. Turn it back."

"That game is over."

Ethan jumped on top of Max and started wrestling him for the remote. Max's slice of pizza dropped onto the couch.

"Jesus," Shawn said, lunging for a lamp that was about to be kicked off the side table. It hit the floor, smashing the shade and knocking out the light. "Goddammit!" he yelled.

The boys quieted.

"Why the hell do you guys always go overboard and wreck things?" Shawn's voice was now as loud as the one he used on the ice—the sound of fun coming to an end. He bent over to pick the mess off the carpet. "Shit, I mean, really. This is my fucking apartment I've invited you to, and this is how you behave?"

He regretted the tone the minute the words came out of his mouth. The boys suddenly took on the expressions of puppies threatened with a rolled-up newspaper. Max and Ethan disentangled and sat up straight. Max handed Shawn the remote. Sam stood, saying, "Thanks, Mr. Willis, but I should go." He headed for the door.

"No, no, guys. You don't have to leave yet," Shawn said.

"I actually have some work I need to get started," Sam said. And once the word "work" was mentioned, everyone's posture became rigid, as they were collectively reminded of everything they needed to finish before first period on Monday.

"Okay, but do you want to take the pizza?" Shawn asked.

"Nah," Sam said.

"Well, at least take the leftovers to the common room," Shawn said, fumbling with the remote, trying to get the Patriots back. Despite his attempts at hospitality, the boys were filing out the door, all except for Grabs, who lingered behind.

When the boys were a distance down the hall, he closed the door to Shawn's apartment.

"Mr. Willis," Grabs said, leading him to a corner of the kitchen and turning toward the refrigerator. Shawn surveyed his large frame, his untucked T-shirt and messy jeans, the way his coarse black hair grew aggressively all over the back of his neck, the oil on his nose around the bridge of his glasses, and wondered why this poor kid had never made more of an effort to fit in.

"Yeah?"

"I just wanted to give you some advice." He spoke in almost a whisper.

"Advice?"

"Well, I know you're pleased about the big monitor and the cable hookup, but I think you should be careful."

"Don't worry, kid, I'm a big boy. I know when to turn off the idiot box."

"I mean, it looks like there's a camera embedded in the top of the monitor, and the cables running into your wall aren't all for getting shows. Looks to me like spyware."

Shawn's immediate reaction was to go over and check it out, to see which wires he was talking about, but Grabs held him by the elbow.

"Don't do anything rash. Don't let on right away that you know—just be careful. Big Brother is watching you."

As Shawn went to the kitchen table to clean up the pizza boxes, all he could think about was how excited he'd been to receive the television, and the night he and Angeline had broken it in.

CHAPTER 33

I was the one to call Edward. Mr. Public Transportation acted like it had never occurred to him to carpool up to parents' weekend. "I'll pick you up six thirty Friday morning," I said.

"Right, okay." His curtness gave away his irritation with my interminable need to build in a hefty cushion.

Although I still harbored resentment toward the school's punitive system, I'd always admired Dunning's teaching philosophy. Even if all the rest of it—the dining hall, the discipline, the social life, the residential life—was torturous bullshit, the inner sanctum of the classroom was the one feature that made Dunning worthwhile.

Our first parents' weekend had made a huge impression on me. I'd put together a smart fall ensemble outfit that I'd admired on the cover of a J.Crew catalog: black leather boots and a gray wool skirt. I'd even invested in a violet pashmina to wrap around a white turtleneck sweater.

When we gathered in the theater for Headmaster Williams's welcoming address, he commented that, despite our coming from all walks of life, we had one most important thing in common: our exceptional children. I beamed, extending his statement one step further to mean we were exceptional parents. I imagined all of us, rows and rows of adults, in our lit-up houses or high-rises, farms or condos, sitting with our kids, the sky black outside, quizzing them on math facts and reading them bedtime stories.

When we found his algebra class, Sam and the other kids were diagramming solutions on the board. The teacher, an older, bespectacled man in tweed, fit the mold. I'd loved the idea of Dunning for a long time, but this was the moment when I first witnessed its academic rigor, and it swept me off my feet. The respectful way in which the teacher joined the kids at the table and started the discussion made the classroom feel more like a boardroom. He didn't talk down to them, or really even acknowledge the parents, for that matter, as most of us were lost anyway. There was the assumption that this was a valuable class period with work to be done and that they wouldn't be dumbing it down just because they had an audience.

I came away certain that Dunning students were the absolute best, and I continued to hold on to that view, adding to it the conviction that the school's graduates gained wisdom beyond their years from the hard knocks they'd survived. Resilience was the special ingredient Dunning mixed in, and I hoped, even though Sam's DC was painful when it happened, that we'd be able to appreciate it after we'd gained some distance.

Sure, our interactions with the lawyer and with Shawn Willis, and the stresses of the college process, had been wearying. Yes, my interactions with the Crandall family and the knowledge that my friendship with Mimi had never gotten off the ground had wounded me. Even though all of that had bruised me, I really looked forward to Sam's last parents' weekend—to being with Edward and to spending a day in those wonderful classrooms as if we were still a family. I wanted to return to the crisp neatness of the campus, mulched and planted with chrysanthemums, and bask in the vastness of Sam's intellect.

I also wanted to bring him a package of scholarship applications I'd copied at the town library. I knew he could find them at College Counseling, but I wanted to make sure he got started right away. Wherever Sam went to college was going to be expensive, and now that Edward was paying rent for his own place, our monthly cash flow was even more stretched. After the back-and-forth with the bursar's office and the unpaid balance the previous spring, I feared Edward was dipping into Sam's college savings to finance this last year at Dunning.

....

I sprang out of bed when my alarm went off at 5:00 a.m. Ironing my hair straight, I smiled at my image in the mirror. I had a new dress on and looked forward to Sam's and Edward's seeing me pulled together. Maybe we'd go to Sam's burger haunt "one last time."

I texted Edward from the parking lot of the apartment complex because he wasn't waiting outside. When he finally got in the car, he sighed and said, "Good morning, Hannah," without meeting my eyes.

"It's going to be a great day," I said, turning onto the main road. He flipped on the radio, but I spoke over it. "I probably should have booked us some rooms at the Lionsgate Inn."

"Too expensive," he said. "Besides, I'm not even sure I'll go back up tomorrow. Sam and I have been talking about having him come home tonight to stay with me for the weekend."

That statement sucked the oxygen out of the car. There was so much wrong with it. First off, since when was Edward's shitty apartment considered home? Second, he knew how much I longed to spend more time with our son. If Sam had the ability to leave Dunning for the weekend, we should both get to be with him. And third, it wasn't like Edward was alone in betraying me on this either. When had Sam decided he could spare a weekend to sleep on his father's couch? When I'd asked him about dates when he might take the SAT subject tests or when we might visit a school or two to determine where, once and for all, he'd be applying early, he'd said he couldn't spare the time.

"Really?" was all I could say to Edward now. And not a run-of-the-mill "Really?" I said, "*Really*?" with that sarcastic twang that captured everything I wanted to say without having to spew the profanity that was filling my mind.

Edward simply nodded.

And so I was silent for the rest of the drive, turning up the volume on the radio. Even when traffic came to a complete stop on I-93 because of an accident, neither of us commented on the delay or the time, or on the solidity of my suggestion that we leave nice and early.

As we got closer to Dunning, the stream of cars holding fellow parents thickened. License plates from Massachusetts merged with those from New York, Connecticut, and New Jersey. As we made it through the series of traffic lights on Main Street, the signs became visible, as well as the maintenance crew and campus security officers who had become parking attendants for the day. I checked the digital display on the dash. We had agreed to skip Williams's nauseating welcome speech, but there were only fifteen minutes before Sam's first class, and I cursed under my breath at the slowness of the other cars—first-year parents with no clue; or international parents, for the love of God, the worst drivers known to man; or people with SUVs so big they took up multiple parking spaces. And why did people have to roll down their windows to have conversations with the attendants? Weren't we all trying to make a first-period class? Weren't we all running a little late? Edward shook his head, always critical of my anxiety, yet if it hadn't been for me, he would have never gotten anywhere on time.

Once I maneuvered the car into a spot, I grabbed my purse from the backseat and bolted. Edward had never been one to act urgently, so I left him behind. I didn't have to turn around to know that he was shaking his head. I didn't care if we walked into Sam's class together, and I wouldn't care if we ate lunch together or went out to dinner. If he and Sam had made weekend plans behind my back, well, then screw them both.

Edward probably hadn't printed out the schedule the night before, like I had, probably didn't know where to go for Sam's first class. He would have to go register at the main school building, where he'd receive a folder that included Sam's schedule and a campus map. Then he'd wander off, get coffee, likely get lost, and show up at the first class fifteen minutes late. I, on the other hand, knew Sam had Advanced Calculus first period, and I knew exactly where the building was. I would show Sam which of his parents truly cared.

Perspiration soaked my back as I entered the classroom. The teacher was already speaking, so I took the first seat by the door. It took me almost a full minute to realize I was in the wrong place. I went back out into the hall and checked the room number.

Rushing through the math building, I peeked through the windows set in all the doorways. I shuddered hearing the classes get underway, panicking that neither Edward nor I was there for Sam.

I reached the end of a hallway where the corner classroom had a large glass partition instead of a wall. Students and parents sat around the oval table and were well into a conversation. I did a double take because not only was Sam diagramming the solution to a problem on the whiteboard, but Edward was there, his arms folded atop one knee. I couldn't bring myself to open the door. Instead, I just watched Sam and put my palm to the glass. He waved for me to come in. It would have been fine to arrive late, but I couldn't do it. I couldn't walk in and suffer Edward's smugness.

So I retreated to the lobby of the math and science building, where a makeshift café had been set up, offering complimentary coffee, tea, and scones. I poured myself a cup and sat at a small square table for two. When I looked up, Henry Crandall was sitting across from me.

"Hello, Hannah," he said, with surprising familiarity.

"Oh my. Good morning, Henry."

"I never go to the math classes either," he said.

I bit my lip. "Do you have a child at Dunning? I mean, is there another Crandall, a niece or a nephew?"

"No, Justin was the last of them—as far as I know." He chuckled.

I smiled in response, not in the mood for company or his crude humor.

"No," he continued, "I'm here for some meetings. The trustees always meet right after parents' weekend."

"Do they? And I take it you're a trustee?"

"Well, not exactly. Let's just say I'm on a subcommittee of sorts. Hey, how's Sam doing? He fled Long Harbor without saying goodbye."

"Oh, he's doing well. Thank you."

"Where will he be applying? Early-action deadlines are in a few weeks. He must have an application just about finished."

"Oh, well, you know Sam—he keeps these things under wraps."

Henry looked at me with squinty eyes. In the Crandall family, most likely, where one went to college was not a matter of individual choice. One was expected to follow a certain path, to do things the way they'd always been done.

"Well, as I told him this summer, I'd like to be helpful. But I'll need a little heads-up. He needs to tell me whether he wants Harvard, Yale, or Princeton. I'm happy to make a call."

I took a slow sip from my cup. Was he for real? Had we been, once again, fools to follow College Counseling's guidelines, when all we needed to do was put a call in to Uncle Henry? How cozy had Sam gotten with this character? And why hadn't he indicated to me that Henry's help was at his disposal? The morning certainly was full of surprises.

"Well, that's very kind of you," I said. "I'll be sure Sam gets in touch."

"Soon. He's a great kid. He should know I'd do everything possible for him."

The same man who had made me feel so uncomfortable in their driveway last June now seemed nothing but kind. I finished my coffee and checked my watch. The bell would ring soon, and I wanted to catch Sam and Edward coming out of class. There was still time for him to reconsider applying early somewhere. If he really did intend to come home for the remainder of the weekend, then we could work on it together. Edward and I could help him submit an application before I brought him back to Dunning on Monday morning.

....

While Sam waited in line for food, I pulled Edward aside to tell him about Henry Crandall's offer.

"Do you really think that's what Sam wants?" he responded.

"Well, I don't know. Harvard, Yale, or Princeton? I thought we should talk about it. You know, be united in our approach." It was all I could do not to shake him by the lapels of his standard-issue blue blazer. Wasn't it a parent's job to push offspring toward the best possible outcome? I hated how he stood there, searching my face as if I had lost my marbles.

"I mean, if he comes home this weekend, we can talk, and he'll still have time to submit an early-action application."

Edward nodded. "Possibly."

It was like somebody was holding out a winning lottery ticket and he was loath to accept it. I was still pushing, I knew, but an instinct for my offspring's upward mobility was at the core of who I was as a human being. Maybe it was my parents' immigrant sensibilities, so elemental to my DNA that they had me approaching everything in a Darwinian manner. But where would our species be if a bunch of Edwards populated the world?

I thought back to the desperation I'd felt in the wake of Sam's DC, all the disappointment. Henry Crandall's offer was a second chance. I took back all the unflattering things I'd thought about him and was suddenly grateful that he and Sam had spent the summer under the same roof. He really must have made a wonderful impression.

Sam returned to our table with his bagel, but he didn't sit down.

"Uh, excuse me for a second, guys," he said, walking toward the alcove housing the restrooms. I followed Sam's course toward Henry Crandall, who stood there, waving. Once Sam reached him, they shook hands; then Henry clapped Sam on the shoulder. It was a happy greeting, and my insides warmed. I tapped Edward on the hand and pointed to the affection on display between Henry and our son.

"That's the guy?" Edward asked.

"Yes."

"Does he have a kid here? I mean, what's he doing here?"

"He's come for alumni meetings."

We observed the interaction from across the room. Henry's back was now turned to us, and he loomed over Sam, who was pinned against the wall. Henry had taken on a threatening posture and was waving an envelope in front of Sam's face.

Edward jumped to his feet. I tried to hold him back, but it was no use. He was halfway across the lobby when Henry pounded his fist against the wall over Sam's shoulder. The noise attracted everyone's attention, although they likely mistook the scene as an eruption from an angry father over his son's bad grades. Then the bell sounded and people went back to talking and dashing toward the exits, juggling backpacks and coffee cups. I quickly followed Edward across the room, prepared to intervene if I had to.

"What the hell is going on here?" Edward barked into Henry's bloated face. It was the first time I'd seen my husband this passionate about anything.

"You must be Mr. Webber," Henry said, holding out his hand. But Edward was assessing Sam, who was looking down at his shoes. He was doing the thing he used to do, shaking his hair in front of his eyes. The only problem was, his hair was no longer long enough to hide anything. It made me want to cry, to scream, but most of all to take Sam in my arms and hold him. Henry, that big walrus of a man, then turned his attention to me. "Hannah," he said, "your husband seems to have lost his manners."

"Henry, forgive us, but it seems as if you were expressing some hostility toward Sam."

"*Forgive us*?" Edward barked. "Who the hell do you think you are, threatening my son?"

"Dad," Sam said, and I could tell he was uneasy, that the volume of Edward's voice was drawing more attention. "Dad, c'mon, Mr. Crandall wasn't threatening. That's just the way he is. C'mon, we should head over to the planetarium. I don't want to be late for Astronomy."

"Mr. Webber." Henry extended his hand again. "Sorry to scare you. I can get dramatic. You must know Sam and I are old friends."

Edward clenched his teeth and brushed past Henry into the men's room.

"Are you all right?" I whispered to Sam.

"I'm fine," he said.

Edward was still in the lavatory, but Sam and I started off in the direction of the planetarium. I was happy to be in step with him once again, to be the one accompanying him. Edward could catch up to us this time.

During the parents' weekend lunch in the dining hall, the head of development rose to the podium. I could have delivered his speech myself: describing how tuition made up only a fraction of the real cost of a Dunning education, and how all students attended with a built-in subsidy provided by previous generations. "If you don't need that subsidy, then you should contribute to closing that gap. That gap, by the way, is thirty thousand dollars per student."

Every year was the same. Edward always went nuts after the fundraising pitch, lambasting the arms race these schools were in, outdoing each other's science centers and theaters and indoor athletic complexes. "What kind of fiscal management is in place to run a thirty-thousand-dollar deficit per student? Liquid gold must flow through the pipes."

It was lucky Dunning turned out such an inordinate number of Wall Street financiers. They were the ones to perennially pony up, if not because they remembered Dunning with such fondness but because doing so greatly elevated their chances that when the time came, their own children and grandchildren would be admitted.

At the end of the day, the three of us were happy to be driving back to Boston. Edward took the wheel, and Sam stretched out in the backseat like he used to when we went on long drives. He was quiet, preoccupied with his phone, and I was determined to let him be. I left Edward alone as well, turning on the radio instead of filling the silence with conversation. I waited until just before our exit to ask, "Do you want to drive to your apartment first? The two of you can get out, and I'll come by tomorrow, if we all think it makes sense to—"

"Nah," Edward interrupted. "My kitchen isn't stocked. He'll be more comfortable with you."

Our eyes met, and I smiled my thanks. "But you'll come by tomorrow? To help with the application?" I made a point of using my kindest tone for Sam's benefit. It was important for him to know that his parents were figuring out the new landscape of their relationship. We pulled into the parking lot of his building, and Edward let the car idle.

"Sure, and I'll bring donuts," he said. The cider donuts from the local orchard had always been Sam's favorite.

"Oh, in that case, will you also bring me a candy apple?" Sam's voice rang childlike from the backseat. He'd been denied all sorts of treats during middle school because of his braces.

"Sure, kid." Edward chuckled. "I'll go crazy and get you two."

CHAPTER 34

"He's fucking spying on me!"

Unleashing his anger on the Friday-night crew was out of character, but there was nobody else for Shawn to talk to. He couldn't tell Angeline about the spyware. She'd be mortified to know that the dean had been a voyeur of their most intimate moments. There was no love lost for Harper in Schwartz's man cave, so he expected all the guys to share his rage.

"Of course he is," Schwartz said, without moving from his reclined position in front of the television. "You of all people should know Harper plays dirty."

"But against *me*?"

"Why are you so surprised?"

"He installed a television in my apartment with a fucking camera in it and has been spying on me since September."

Schwartz shrugged, and the others shook their heads as if they weren't surprised at all.

"How'd you find out?" Lou asked.

The heat rose in Shawn's face as he remembered how he'd stomped into Harper's office the Monday morning after Grabs had tipped him off.

"Dean Harper, about the television."

"You're here to thank me?"

"Not exactly."

"You want more channels? What is it?"

"Dean Harper, the television isn't just . . . I mean, does it have other functions?"

Harper's irritated expression disappeared. "Well, Shawn, yes. I've heard of people playing DVDs on their televisions, and maybe even video games. What do you have in mind? What kind of thing would you do in front of your new television?"

Shawn searched the dean's eyes. They were unflinching, but a wicked grin was spreading across his face.

"I thought you'd be happy to have it. You've been asking for one ever since you arrived."

"Is this some kind—"

"Look, Shawn, it would be a shame if you missed out on the head hockey coach position because you continually break the rules. They were planning on naming you before the season begins."

Shawn left Harper's office feeling the same irritability that had consumed him as a hotheaded hockey player thrown in the penalty box. The idea that Harper had invaded what little privacy he had at Dunning, and the fact that he had violated Angeline, made Shawn shake.

Shawn let his guard down further, confessing to the men how quickly and easily Grabs had figured out what was going on. "He's a fucking computer whiz."

"Jesus."

"It's criminal, isn't it? I mean, isn't spying on people in their homes against the law?"

"It's school property."

"Are you defending him, for Christ's sake?"

"Not defending him, just telling you what he'll say."

Shawn stopped cursing and sweating and took the beer Lou held out for him. "I mean, maybe the apartment is school property, but doesn't an employee have rights? Don't human beings have basic rights?"

"Good question," Schwartz said, waving his arm across the room and inviting the rest of the guys to weigh in.

"I mean, what would you do if you found out Harper had installed cameras in this house? It's school property too, isn't it?"

Everyone turned to stare at Schwartz. He nodded, silently contemplating the question. "What would I do?" he asked.

"Yeah, what would you do?" Shawn challenged him, the tough guy who knew so much.

"First thing I'd do would be to sit up in this here chair, look straight into the camera, and give the man the middle finger. I'd tell him I had some friends at the ACLU who would be interested in what was going on. But wait, I'd say, maybe before I called the lawyers, I'd go to Channel 7, which might also find his tactics newsworthy."

"And how do you think Harper would react?"

"How would you want him to react?"

Thinking through the scenarios made Shawn's head hurt. Twenty-five years earlier, Schwartz had exchanged his discovery in the tunnels for lifetime employment and a home for his family. The guys in the room waited for Shawn's response.

"There might be a pretty sweet payoff in it for you," Schwartz added.

"If you're comparing my situation to what you discovered twenty-five years ago, it's not the same. Somebody is spying on me. I'm not a minor, and I'm not being exploited for sex."

Schwartz laughed. "Sure it is, kid. So much for doing what's right and exposing evil. Let's see what kind of moral high ground you take when *you* get a chance to line your pockets."

Schwartz's smug laughter drove Shawn back to the bar. He could hear his father's voice, the same one that asked him every week if that head coaching job was his yet. "For fuck's sake, Shawn. Why are they taking so long?"

He had a sudden desire for fresh air. He didn't even bother

with polite goodbyes. As he walked home across the outfield, Shawn tried to exhale the ache that had taken up residence in his chest. He'd never been a victim before, but to work for Harper, for Dunning, and to give so much of himself, only to discover spyware in his living room—where was the code of trust? And what were they trying to catch him doing? Was it all about him and Angeline, or was there something else they were looking for?

He returned to Wilburton to find Grabs lurking by the door to his apartment. It was still pretty early on a Friday night, and the dorm was quiet, but it was no surprise this kid didn't have plans.

"What's up?" Shawn asked, reaching for his doorknob.

"I was wondering if we could talk."

"Sure. C'mon in." It took everything he had to switch back into responsible-adult mode. The institution had split his personality. He didn't like the Shawn Willis who busted kids, and he didn't like the Shawn Willis who hung out in Schwartz's underground on Friday nights, but it was tricky to transform into the Shawn Willis who had an easy rapport with the boys.

He threw his jacket over a chair. "You want something to drink? I have some Cokes."

"No, thanks," Grabs said.

Grabs's face was concerned; Shawn could tell by the way his cheeks were flushed. "Over here," Grabs whispered, leading Shawn back to the corner of the kitchen that he must have deemed safe, out of the scope of the camera.

Grabs whispered, "I think you understand that I'm good at figuring these things out."

Shawn nodded.

"You're not the only one being watched. We've found more spyware."

"We?"

"Faceless."

"You're Faceless? Of course you are. I should have guessed," Shawn said, shaking his head.

Grabs ignored the comment. "I'll need to hack into that device in order to find the IPN address of whoever's watching you."

"I'm pretty sure it's Harper."

"It could be multiple people. I can't do it tonight, but keep everything intact for me."

This boy genius had appeared just when Shawn needed a savior. While his instinct had been to rip all the wires out of the back of the TV and smash it against the floor, Grabs had shown up with a better plan. He was the kind of person who was five chess moves ahead before his opponent even opened.

....

A few days later, Shawn called Irene Schwartz to ask if she might help him learn a recipe so that he could cook dinner for Angeline. Irene's tone softened on the phone, assuming a motherly air when it came to Shawn's love life. "I always like to see two nice young people get together. Makes living in this town more agreeable." In fact, since he'd started dating Angeline, Shawn had paid closer attention to stories about members of the faculty who'd met and fallen in love at Dunning. There were even some who divorced and married other teachers while coexisting with their castoffs on campus. If Dean Harper really cared about enforcing the rule against interfaculty dating, he wasn't the first offender.

Shawn told Irene that he wanted to have a little dinner party and prepare a roast for Angeline, her sister, and Lou. Irene said, "Ah, and I love Lou like a son. It would give me double pleasure. I'll make it myself and deliver it to you in time for dinner."

"No, no," Shawn backpedaled. "I want you to teach me. It's about time I learned how to cook for myself."

When he entered her kitchen, Irene was watching a small television set on her Formica counter, the volume turned up loud. She had the Home Shopping Network on, and she didn't seem to be paying attention until a price was announced and the personality began throwing in giveaways. Irene bit her cuticles, assessing the value of each item out of the corner of her eye. She grumbled something under her breath before reaching into the refrigerator's crisper.

She handed Shawn some potatoes and the peeler. As he stood at her kitchen sink, he spotted Sam and his sidekicks waiting in the shrubbery that bordered the outfield.

A bell sounded on HSN to notify viewers that it was the beginning of a fifteen-minute "two for the price of one" promotion on an ivory bracelet. Irene lunged for her wall-mounted kitchen phone and dialed the 800 number.

"I've been meaning to see if I left my cap downstairs," Shawn said, resting a peeled potato on the edge of the sink. "I'm just going to pop down and check."

"Sure," she mumbled, twisting the telephone's long cord around her hand and turning to face the small screen.

Shawn hurried down the stairs and headed straight to the hatch window, where three sets of running shoes and the ankles of denim jeans waited outside. After kneeling on the coach's bar, he unlatched the glass easily and helped the boys down.

"You should have about twenty minutes," he whispered. "We still haven't put the roast in the oven."

Sam and two younger boys nodded in their black hoodies. They were like professional hit men—not a trace of nerves. The boys' merciless expressions freaked him out. They pulled penlights out of their pockets and then, with a simple gesture toward the stairs, dismissed Shawn to his post in the kitchen.

"I don't know where I left that thing," Shawn said, back at the sink.

"Didn't think you'd find it," she said. "I was down there this morning after last night's ruckus."

"Ruckus?" he asked. He hadn't attended, having opted to go to the movies with Angeline instead. The defiance he showed by not always attending Friday nights seemed to heighten Irene's impression of him.

"Yeah, Lou and Fred got into it."

"Really?" That was unusual; there had been little infighting all the times Shawn had been around.

"Stupid—they act like children down there. Sounded like furniture getting toppled over, and the next thing you know, Lou came up the stairs with a bloody mouth."

"Holy crap. Did Coach tell you what it was about?"

She held her gaze on him an extra beat, with the knowing eyes of a hardened woman. She knocked a cigarette out of the pack she kept in the kitchen drawer. "Of course not, but if I was you, I'd be happy to have Angeline—it's a perfect excuse not to come back." She pointed the tip of her long carving knife at the basement door. Shawn swallowed.

"You have a roasting pan?" she asked, tossing chopped onions and celery around the edges of her raw meat.

"Uh, I'll have to pick one up."

"The oven's been heating at 375. Sprinkle the meat with some seasoned salt."

He feigned a desire to commit the canister's label to memory.

"Do you have a meat thermometer?"

"No. I'll get one of those too."

"So, it goes in the oven, and the juices and all the vegetables will make a nice gravy."

Shawn pulled out a chair from her kitchen table, crossed his arms across its clean surface, and smiled at her, thinking how nice it would have been if his mother had ever let him into her inner sanctum like this.

"What are you doing?" Irene surprised him with her question.

"We wait while it cooks, right?"

"Honey, that's going to take a few hours. You're not going to sit in my kitchen all afternoon, are you?"

"Oh, jeez. I guess not." He looked at his watch. It had been only ten minutes since the boys had entered the basement. He couldn't leave the house while they were still down there. He stood up slowly and smiled. "Well, I just can't thank you enough, Irene."

"Anytime." She was heading toward a hook inside the cupboard and removing her apron.

"Uh, Irene, before I leave, do you think I could just write down all those steps? I don't have a very good memory. What size roast should I buy for four people?"

She snatched a piece of paper by the phone and scribbled some lines. "It's the easiest thing in the world—even you can't mess it up—but you'll need that thermometer. The inner temp needs to be 140 degrees. Then let it sit before you carve." She handed him the instructions and took a long drag on her cigarette. He wasn't sure if her squinting was suspicious or due to the smoke swirling around her face, but before he could decide, manicured hands held up a faux-pearl necklace on-screen, and the television lured her attention away. Irene leaned into the counter, the tip of her nose almost touching the TV.

CHAPTER 35

"All right, that was a little taste. But tomorrow you'll join me on a real mission, the type the Nine are famous for." Sam and his foot soldiers walked across the baseball outfield to the quad.

Miles and Seth stopped in their tracks. "Just a prank this time?" Miles asked. They had been understandably nervous about breaking into Coach Schwartz's basement.

"That's right." Sam eyed the sweat rings under their armpits. The Nine's recruiting was never perfect. No one could predict who would panic when it was go time, who might become crippled with anxiety, just as no one ever knew who might blossom underground. Sam liked to think he had taken to it right away, although he had certainly benefited from Justin's boundless encouragement.

Standing on the path with these younger boys, he felt some of Justin's early compassion return to him. "There are no bad recruits, just bad captains," he had once said. And even though Sam accepted the title with a measure of ambivalence, he recognized it as an opportunity to mold the next generation, to show leadership.

"Look, guys, I know it feels dangerous and your heart rate might accelerate, but it makes you ultra-alert. You'll see, it's like a drug. You'll start to love it. Meet me Monday at 0200 hours in the tunnel connection between the library and the main school building. Don't forget the balls."

Seth and Miles nodded.

"You remember how to get there?"

They nodded again, still silent. Sam clapped them each on the shoulder. "It'll be fun. You're doing a great job."

Sam grabbed the manila envelope Uncle Henry had given him on parents' weekend. The handoff had turned into an altercation when Sam had expressed his reservations. When he'd announced the idea in the Tomb, the pushback had been severe. "Look, Mr. Crandall," he'd tried to explain, "we're a little uncomfortable breaking into the headmaster's office."

"Goddammit, Sam," Henry had yelled, smacking his fist against the wall above Sam's shoulder. "You already agreed!"

"But the envelope showing up at the same time as the Ping-Pong balls? He'll know it was the Nine."

"He'll know you were the messenger. But when he sees the contents of this envelope, he'll know he has bigger problems."

Sam wasn't going to put an envelope in the headmaster's desk without knowing what was inside. So, upon returning to campus the Sunday after the eleventh-hour effort his mother led to submit an early-action application to Princeton, he brought it directly to Grabs's room. Grabs steamed it open over his teakettle and emptied the contents onto his bedspread. A dozen or so Polaroids taken in what had once unmistakably been the Bennett Hall butt room spilled out. The lighting in the pictures was dim, but a sign that clearly read SMOKING CLUB was in the background. Each photo featured the same two men striking poses, with ridiculous expressions on their faces. The images were fuzzy, but it was possible to make out naked teenagers, both boys and girls, reclining sleepily on the furniture in the foreground. Sam didn't recognize either man, but one of them could have been a much younger Williams.

Grabs shook his head, not so much in disbelief as in dismay. "Unbelievable," he said, "although, after everything I've discovered at this place, I don't know why I'm still surprised." He singled out one of the photos and stashed it in his desk drawer before sealing the rest of them back into the envelope.

....

Raymond had been in charge of procuring the Ping-Pong balls on Amazon over the course of several weeks, so as to not arouse suspicion in the mailroom. When Seth and Miles met up with Sam, they carried garbage bags filled with them. One of the juniors had been charged with tipping off a photographer from the *Dunning Daily*. If all went as planned, Williams would greet the prank with good humor and would ultimately pose for a picture knee-deep in balls. When it appeared in the next day's paper, the student body would know that the Nine were off to the races.

A hoax at the headmaster's home base would undoubtedly raise his ire, but he wouldn't be able to fly off the handle in the presence of a student journalist. He'd have to wait before yelling at his secretary to summon Harper, before flailing his arms in the air and shouting profanities, ordering the dean to get to the bottom of everything. It would be even later, when Williams sat down at his desk to finally deal with the day's business, that he would notice that his pencil drawer had been forced open. He'd inch it toward him to find the envelope filled with Polaroids. This was where Sam's imagination failed. He couldn't be sure what would happen at the trustees' meeting or how this would lead to Williams's resignation.

Uncle Henry had insinuated that there were skeletons in Williams's closet, but a faction on the board looked the other way. He said their keeping Williams also had to do with some agreement they'd signed with his wife, who was now climbing the ranks of the Democratic National Committee and had political aspirations of her own. Henry said the board members would receive their own copies of the Polaroids. He was confident they couldn't be ignored.

Williams was the sixteenth headmaster in Dunning's history, and Uncle Henry had told Sam that the academy's leaders were typically one of two types: those who rose up from within and had the support of the faculty, and thus kept the peace on campus, or those who were brought in from the outside because they were good at raising money. Williams was the former. He'd never enjoyed the dog-and-pony show of soliciting alumni for donations and, frankly, didn't have the right wardrobe for Manhattan dinners. Even after investing in custom-made suits, he didn't have the right haircut or shoes or cuff links. He didn't make the right conversation. He'd shrug off his shortcomings, however, reminding whatever audience he'd been put in front of that he was just a simple English teacher who, first and foremost, cared about the students. He and Vicky, dressed handsomely and looking fit, exuded attractiveness as a couple that made up for his lack of polish.

In light of his fundraising deficiencies, the board of trustees hired a smooth head of development who pumped donors' hands unapologetically. Under him, the development office became a machine that, even Williams had to admit, could manage the capital campaign without him.

"Two hundred million of the two-hundred-fifty-million-dollar goal was raised in the silent phase alone," Henry asserted. "No, they don't need Williams hanging around any longer. They're just being kind. The old guy is terrified of the world outside Dunning's walls. He's spent his entire adult life in a little universe of his own making.

"And he can't stand the idea of leaving his creation in 'inferior hands,' or maybe he's just concerned with covering his tracks before leaving office." A changing of the guard, especially involving an external candidate, would inevitably make his cover-ups susceptible to discovery. Williams was guarding his skeletons.

Emerging into the boiler room of the academy building, Sam checked his watch. Seth and Miles were visibly antsy, shifting their weight from one leg to the other. Even though kids at Dunning were typically jacked up on caffeine, adding adrenaline to the mix made it impossible for them to stand still. "Be silent and stay alert," Sam reminded them.

Sam had sent two different juniors on recon missions earlier in the week, to check things out during bogus appointments with the headmaster's secretary. Grabs had been following Harper's server activity and figured out which locations sent live video. Of all the cameras he'd detected, not one was inside the headmaster's suite, which made Sam feel better. Dean Harper had his eye on a lot of people and places but was ironically nonchalant about his own suite of offices.

Sam gave Seth and Miles a short pep talk before they left the tunnel. "When a mission is thought through and planned well, the execution is very fast, almost anticlimactic." They stretched their fingers into surgical rubber gloves, and Sam pulled out the keys Gary had left him.

"Why does Gary always help us? What's in it for him?" Miles asked.

"The alumni council pays him more than the school does. It's no wonder his loyalties rest with us," said Sam.

While Miles and Seth poured Ping-Pong balls into the small restroom, Sam picked the lock on Williams's desk drawer and placed the envelope front and center.

Once the last little white ball was in place, Miles and Seth turned to Sam with wide grins on their faces. He remembered the excitement of his first prank too but maintained a stern expression and put his index finger to his lips, reminding the rookies that they weren't in the clear yet.

CHAPTER 36

Sam's essays were in pretty good shape. There were several short questions on the application that needed some thought, but the afternoon was not as arduous as it might have been. He assured me that he had texted Henry Crandall and that his letter of recommendation would be mailed promptly, in addition to the ones Sam had already obtained from his teachers. Hitting SEND on the Princeton application was like pushing the release valve on a high-pressure gas cylinder inside my core. In that single instant, it was out of our hands. I was lighter, able to push the chair away from my computer with little effort.

Edward patted Sam on the back, then placed a hand on my shoulder. "Why don't I drive him back?" he said. "It's late."

I thanked him. I was tired, but I could breathe more easily than I had in a long while. I hugged both of them, then padded up the stairs. I smiled at my reflection in the bathroom mirror. We'd done it.

As I ran the tub, I felt grateful for Edward's offer to make the two-hour round-trip drive. He was actually more involved in Sam's life now that we were living apart, and there was no denying he was happier and healthier. We would make it. We'd even discussed drawing up an amicable divorce settlement.

"I'm not in any hurry, Hannah," he'd said, "but the house is quite valuable. We could put a chunk aside for Sam's education, then split the proceeds. We'd each have enough to make a good, fresh start."

"Hmm," I'd said, massaging a sore muscle in my back.

"I'd be able to leave the bank and try my hand at being a film critic." He'd smiled sheepishly sharing this last bit, his dream, with me.

"Really?"

"Yeah."

"Wow. I had no idea."

"I guess I never thought I could tell you. We were always so strapped, keeping up this suburban act."

"Okay, Edward. I see your point," I'd said, reaching for his hand. "But it's taken a while to get used to Sam being gone and our marriage ending. Don't make me give up the house right away."

"I understand. But will you think about it?" He'd been good not to push me.

"Of course."

Before I got into bed, I fell back on an old habit and sent an email to Shawn Willis. "Wow! Sam's senior year. He just submitted a college application. I can feel it all coming to an end." Now that Sam was off the swim team, I would have no more excuses to visit campus until the spring, when senior festivities would begin.

"It's gone by fast," he replied a few minutes later. "I'll miss Sam. Nice kid."

I smiled. Shawn may have been a man of few words, but he was a kind person.

I switched off my lamp, and Mimi Crandall's face appeared in my head. It was probably because of our interactions with her brother-in-law over the weekend, but I couldn't help wondering how she was. I'd searched for her on Facebook, thinking we might become friends that way. I wanted to see her pictures. What must it have felt like to have had four children and to have seen them all through Dunning and off to wonderful colleges? I wondered how often she and Morris visited Justin at Yale and whether it was much different than seeing him at Dunning. But I never found her profile, was never able to send her a friend request. I concluded Mimi wasn't the type of person to be reduced to Facebook.

However, if Sam were indeed admitted to Princeton, I would make a point of sending Henry a large fruit basket of his own as a thank-you, and I'd write Mimi as well, breaking out my fancy Crane stationery for the occasion. I would thank her for everything she'd done for Sam. Surely she'd be interested in his college plans. She would probably even invite him for a weekend in Long Harbor.

CHAPTER 37

Eight o'clock on a Saturday morning was an ungodly hour for a knock on the door. But Sam was awake, lying in bed, reading the same paragraph from Milton's *Paradise Lost* over and over again. Amid the Nine's activity, Uncle Henry's texts, and his mother's latest college scholarship findings, not to mention his collaborations with Grabs and Mr. Willis, he'd been falling behind in his classes, and his midterm grades were at risk of being the worst he'd ever received. He was plowing through some particularly dry reading in the hours before he met up with Nathalie for brunch.

But a knock was always cause for alarm. He sat up, hoping it was Grabs, but Mr. Willis entered. Sam wasn't quite used to their newfound alliance. Grabs had spent a lot of time convincing Sam to forgive their dorm parent's shortcomings and accept his help. "I know he's not very smart, and he did you a great disservice, but just think about the access he can provide."

"But he could be in on it," Sam had exclaimed.

"Sam, think about it. Mr. Willis has been violated too. He's never been the sharpest tool, and you've seen the way Harper treats him. He's not 'in' on anything."

Closing his book, Sam swung his feet onto the floor. "What's up?"

Mr. Willis picked a T-shirt up off the floor and threw it at Sam. "Put some clothes on."

"Why?"

Mr. Willis's hands shook, defying his casual manner. "Don't worry, I'm sure it's all going to be fine, but law enforcement is here, wanting to ask a few questions."

"What are you talking about?" Sam's heart beat in triple time.

Mr. Willis ducked his head through the door to the hall. "Just a second, all right?" He closed the door more securely.

"The police? What do you mean? In the hallway?" Sam's voice rattled, imagining Dean Harper's drug-sniffing German shepherds.

Mr. Willis whispered, "He's not wearing a uniform. Says he's FBI."

"What?" Heat rose through Sam's body. It had to be Henry's goddamn envelope. A second later, the special Uncle Henry phone started to buzz in Sam's desk drawer. It had been conspicuously silent all weekend, just when Sam had been expecting a report on the trustees' meeting and a message of appreciation.

"I think he's a little perturbed. He said getting called this early on a weekend to drive up from Boston came out of the blue. The Williamses must be cashing in some real chits."

Sam's breath quickened as he got out of bed and pulled on a pair of pants. He pictured his parents, his father's calm voice. What would he advise in this situation? Sam wasn't yet eighteen, a point that the attorney his father had hired for the DC had emphasized. "Never answer questions without an attorney present, no matter how low-key the authorities try to act." Ironic that it would turn out to be the most practical bit of learning he'd receive at Dunning Academy.

Sam opened his door.

"Why don't you all use my apartment?" Mr. Willis said. "We don't need the other boys catching wind of this." Max's and Ethan's heads both poked through the bathroom door.

"That won't be necessary," Sam said, emboldened by the high ground on which he was certain he stood. Mr. Willis crossed his arms and looked back and forth between Sam and the tall man dressed in a dark business suit.

"I'm Sam Webber," he said in a low voice, reaching out his hand and looking up into the face of this expressionless agent.

"Good morning, Mr. Webber. I was hoping we could have a little chat, that you could help me understand a few things."

"Why me?" he asked.

"There's been a break-in at your headmaster's office. I want to ask you some questions about your association with a Mr. Henry Crandall."

Blood rushed into Sam's eardrums, and a dizzying sensation forced him to extend one arm against the wall to steady himself. No matter how confidently he wanted to act, he could not fend off the heat that was now swarming through his body. But after several deep inhalations, he gathered the words he needed to speak, his tongue now completely dry. "I won't be able to have a conversation unless my attorney is present. You'll be in breach of interrogation-of-minors laws if you question me."

The tall man sighed. "All right, kid, all right." He looked at his wristwatch. "Is there somebody you want to call?"

"Well, first my parents, but it might take some time." Sam looked to Mr. Willis for moral support, glad to have him witnessing what was going on.

Max and Ethan now stood in the hallway, bath towels around their waists, holding toothbrushes and toothpaste. The tall officer stared down their boyish curiosity before taking a business card from his breast pocket and pressing it into Sam's palm.

"I've got to get going, but you'll be hearing from me on Monday. Get that lawyer. I'll be in touch."

Delivering news that would require another attorney would be a blow to his father. The positive side was that he'd get the call in his apartment away from his mother. Sam couldn't bear the thought of telling her; she'd go off the deep end. It had been less than a week since they'd sent his application to Princeton.

He hated having to do this, but he locked himself in his room and pulled the Uncle Henry phone out of his desk drawer. Henry's text message had read, "Call me." The timing couldn't have been coincidental. Sam hoped Henry would tell him what to do next. But the phone rang and rang until Sam tossed it against the wall. Uncle Henry had promised he would always be reachable.

Sam opened his door and almost bumped into Ethan and Max, who were loitering outside his room. It wouldn't take long for the news of what had just happened to spread across campus; indeed, a few seconds later, a text came through from Nathalie on his personal phone.

"R u OK?"

"Yes," he typed back right away, hoping she might quell the shit storm. Their friends would believe her if she claimed nothing was out of the ordinary. Thinking about her slowed his heart rate, if only momentarily. He redialed what he thought was Henry's number but was surprised when she answered.

"Hey!" she said.

"Oh, whoops, sorry," he stammered, "I dialed the wrong number."

"Huh?"

"Sorry, Nat. I'll call you back. Gotta go."

His hands shook. He was a mess again. He picked up the Henry phone from the floor and ran to the bathroom, just making it to a toilet in time to throw up.

Ethan followed him in and was standing by the sinks when Sam emerged from a stall.

"Sam, what the fuck is going on, man? Are you all right?" A true look of concern spread across his face.

"Yeah, no, I'm not, but thanks." Sweat rings had formed in Sam's armpits. He clutched the Henry phone and ran the length of the hall to Mr. Willis's apartment, rapping his fist against the door.

Mr. Willis opened it a crack and, upon seeing Sam, pulled

him inside. Grabs was on the living room floor, in the process of disassembling the television and the cable box.

"Wait, what are you doing? I thought we decided—"

"It's time to play our cards," said Grabs.

"It was the effing FBI, Sam," said Mr. Willis. "Look, I think we're running out of time."

"I've uncovered the identity," Grabs stated flatly.

"Seriously?" Sam asked.

"I found the computer server that offered *Hot Wet Teens* for sale." Even though it was the information he'd been waiting for, Sam wasn't ready to hear who it was.

"It's an IPN in Manhattan, Upper East Side."

"And?" Sam asked.

"What?" said Grabs.

"I mean, do you have the name of the guy?" Sam raised his voice.

"Not yet. But I have a digital address."

"And what the fuck good does that do me?" Sam was almost screaming. Was he going to have to catch the next bus to New York City and track down the owner of a specific computer there?

Grabs looked offended, as if he'd just unveiled a masterpiece to an unappreciative audience. "This is where the Faceless network comes in," he assured. "I'll have it narrowed down to a physical address in the next few hours, and then a basic Google Maps search should uncover the degenerate."

"Follow the money," Mr. Willis said.

"What?" Sam asked.

"Just something my father told me."

"If only these guys dealt in money. Most of the transactions were in cryptocurrency."

"Crypto-what?" Mr. Willis asked.

"Never mind," Sam said, glancing at his watch. Just a few hours earlier, he had been nestled under his covers, reading an English assignment. Now, he paced back and forth in the kitchen while Grabs and Mr. Willis watched. Using them as a sounding board to sort through all the information, he began to think aloud. "Okay, so, we'll have that identity, which is huge, only because it's immediate proof that the Nine aren't responsible. We won't necessarily have proof that Williams knew about it and chose to cover it up."

"But we'll have proof that a criminal act took place on this campus for some time. Besides the seller in New York City, there must have been accessories on campus," Grabs said.

Mr. Willis spoke up. "And we have a trend: Schwartz found evidence of sexual abuse and racy photos in the tunnel thirty years ago, which is similar to what you discovered in Bennett. Schwartz told Williams about it then, and Williams did nothing, so why would anyone have reason to think he's changed his behavior?"

Now Grabs, gaining momentum, added, "And we have knowledge of all the covert cameras and spyware that have been embedded on campus, including in our laundry room, on Sam's laptop, and here, in Mr. Willis's living room. And we have the shampoo-dispenser camera that was installed in the Bennett showers."

"And," Mr. Willis said, "we have proof that Harper is a liar."

"What?" Sam asked.

Mr. Willis took a moment. "When I caught you in the stairwell last year, Harper said that I found you with marijuana. That was a lie. Oh, and he conveniently ignored the fact that Justin Crandall was with you. That was a pretty shitty move, letting you take all the blame."

Sam checked Mr. Willis's face for a hint of sarcasm, but he was dead serious. The absurdity of that statement rubbed Sam as hilarious. Mr. Willis began to chuckle as well, and then Grabs joined in. Pretty soon, the three of them were roaring. A year earlier, facing the DC and receiving probation had seemed the worst possible fate anyone could experience on the Dunning campus, but now here they were, face-to-face with an FBI agent, blackmail, and several cases of sexual misconduct.

"Okay," Sam said, once he regained his composure. "Let's write it all down, then sign our names on a clear, comprehensive statement." If he were able to document the history of the crime, maybe his father wouldn't have to hire another lawyer.

Grabs and Mr. Willis rubbed their chins, considering Sam's request. It wasn't until Sam sat ready with pen and paper at Mr. Willis's kitchen table that he recognized what he was asking of these two. Grabs's name on a statement would expose his hacking activities and certainly jeopardize his standing at Dunning and his college admission. Then there was Mr. Willis, who'd lose his job—assuming, that was, Williams and Harper weren't terminated first.

Sam finally broke the silence. "Okay, I get it. You have too much to lose." He started writing anyway. He needed to assemble the truth. Once all the cover-ups were exposed, Williams, the board of trustees, or whatever other higher power was out there safeguarding Dunning's integrity might even forgive him.

The Henry phone buzzed in his pocket.

Sam answered it immediately. "Henry?"

"Listen, Webber." It was Uncle Henry shouting over a fuzzy connection. "Things have turned out badly. If anybody comes asking about me, don't say a thing."

"Henry, an FBI agent came to question me this morning."

"Jesus. What did you tell him?"

"Nothing. I told him I wouldn't talk to him without a lawyer present."

There was silence. Sam asked, "What happened at the trustees' meeting?"

"Things didn't go as I had hoped. Look, I'm on my way out of the country. I might be difficult to reach for a little while."

"Henry, I need to know."

"What?"

"Is Williams going to lose his job? Are the trustees going to report him?"

Sam could barely hear Henry over the static. "He's scared. A picture's worth a thousand words, all right. But that Victoria is more shrewd than I gave her credit for."

The line went dead. Sam pictured Henry Crandall in a car racing to Teterboro, where Morris's Gulfstream would be waiting, the one Mimi had boasted could Make All Your Dreams Come True. Sam wondered if Uncle Henry would board the plane alone or if Justin was carrying his bags.

After Sam looked up from his call, he noticed Grabs and Mr. Willis, their heads together in the kitchen.

"That asshole," Sam said aloud.

Grabs crossed the room and took Sam by the arm. "Let's go back to my room and see if my guys have the address yet."

Grabs put on his white-noise machine and flipped open his laptop. Sam sat down on his bed while Grabs typed some characters to the right of a blinking cursor. Sam felt sick after his conversation with Henry. His hands were still trembling.

"Ah," Grabs said. "I was afraid of this."

Sam recognized the address immediately. "Shit, that's where Justin and I lived last summer."

"Looks like the FBI will be able to pin this on one of two people, then."

"Either me or Justin?"

"Look, Sam, I've been reading a lot of email communication on Williams's account. This confirms my suspicions. I think Henry Crandall had Justin set you up, invite you to his ritzy summer home and to stay in New York so they'd have further proof that you led the pornography ring. Who knows—maybe he even quit his job on the film crew to make sure you were alone in the apartment."

"Fuck. Why me?"

"My hypothesis is that Victoria and Bradley Williams were coming down hard on Henry. Even though they'd negotiated some weird coexistence, they wanted Henry out of those tunnels so they could retire in peace. But he fought back, and he needed a scapegoat. He had Justin send you on a mission to 'discover' the video equipment. Weren't the lights on in the Bennett boiler room? He made sure you wouldn't miss it.

293

"I don't mean to say that Justin had it in for you from day one, but his uncle had him wrapped around his finger. And, you must admit, *you* were wrapped around Justin's finger."

Sam retched into Grabs's wastebasket. Punched in the stomach didn't even begin to describe it. How did a person spend his whole young life feeling like one of the smart ones, only to realize he'd been played?

He'd loved Justin like a brother. Despite all that had transpired, he'd always believed Justin was good on the inside. Sam had once hoped they could use the Nine to promote the values espoused on the Dunning crest, *veritas irradiant*—to shine light on the truth. Even though the place was cold and harsh and unnecessarily tough at times, he had never given up on the notion that there were people in charge who would do the right thing.

"Sam, you've got to act fast," Grabs urged him. "This IPN address doesn't back up your story. The porn has your fingerprints all over it. Henry's on his way out of the country, and the FBI will be back tomorrow."

CHAPTER 38

I was on the front lawn, raking leaves, cursing Edward's retreat to apartment living. There would soon be snow to shovel, and if leaving me with all his chores was a ploy to convince me to sell the house, it was working. I went inside for a glass of water and noticed two missed calls on my phone.

The first one was from my sister, checking in and wondering whether she should make reservations for Sam's graduation. "We'll be booking inexpensive flights, and Dad really wants to come too."

The second message was Edward, saying we needed to talk about Sam. My first thought was that it had to do with his college application. I was certain that Henry Crandall's letter of recommendation boosted his chances of getting into Princeton. In fact, the whole prior week I'd regained my old energy, convinced the nightmare was over—nothing but a close call intended to wake me up.

"Withdraw?" I fell back into one of those rickety kitchen chairs when I called Edward back and heard what he was suggesting.

"It's his only hope."

"But if he withdraws, he won't graduate."

"Oh, Hannah, you've got to listen to me now. Whether or not Sam graduates from Dunning is the least of our worries."

An orange Princeton sticker would never be adhered to the rear window of the Subaru. An orange-and-black pennant would never be pinned to the bulletin board above Sam's desk.

Edward asked me to pick him up at his office the next morning and drive to Dunning. Headmaster Williams had asked to talk to us alone in his office, without Sam. He said that some serious charges were being thrown about and that it was best to get the adults in the room. Edward had considered having the same attorney who had gotten Sam's drug possession charges dismissed meet us there but then figured it would appear too adversarial.

When we arrived in the headmaster's suite, though, it soon became evident that more than just the three of us would be at this meeting. Gone was the scenario I'd concocted where we'd put all the craziness aside, Edward warming up Bradley Williams with some small talk, all of us laughing about the juvenile shenanigans of the group called the Nine.

Williams's administrative assistant picked up her phone to say, "Yes, Mr. and Mrs. Webber are here." A few minutes later, Shawn Willis appeared breathless in the reception area, followed by Dean Harper, who walked coolly over from his office across the hall.

When we entered the headmaster's office, he shook our hands, ever polite, but his charming smile was gone. His skin was pale, and he had more gray hair around his temples. His necktie was askew, as if he'd been tugging at the knot. "Mr. and Mrs. Webber, take a seat, won't you?" he said, pointing to the chairs facing his mammoth desk. Edward and I obliged, leaving an empty chair between us. Shawn remained standing next to me, and Dean Harper stood at the side of the room, his hip propped on the credenza. A family portrait of the headmaster with his wife, Victoria, and their daughter, Mary, was framed in silver on the bookshelf behind him. A clock ticked somewhere while Edward and I waited for him to begin.

"Your son," Headmaster Williams bellowed, standing at his full height behind his desk. He stopped and coughed into his fist and began again, at a lower volume: "Unfortunately, your son has gotten himself caught up in some dangerous business."

I turned toward Edward. "Go on," he said.

"I cannot remember a time in Dunning Academy's history when a student's actions have prompted a visit from the Federal Bureau of Investigation."

My head exploded. Did he mean Sam had broken actual laws beyond the school's rules? Beads of sweat broke out on my forehead and began rolling down my back. I slumped in my chair and pressed my palm against my forehead. A scenario in which we might recover from this was officially blown to pieces.

Out of the corner of my eye, I noticed Edward, sitting upright and calm in the face of the terms Williams was throwing at us: "cybercrime," "pedophilia," "pornography," "dark web." Oddly, just when things couldn't get any worse, a rush of tenderness swept over me—something I hadn't felt for my husband in many years. I never could have handled this alone.

"Hannah, are you all right?" Shawn Willis knelt beside me. The other men in the room appeared less concerned and more intrigued by Shawn's chivalry.

"Will you bring me some water? It's awfully hot in here."

Edward stared at me, his brow furrowed with impatience. I knew that face to mean, *Let's not choose this moment to have a breakdown, okay?* I managed a quick smile in response, *I promise to pull it together.*

A few moments later, Shawn handed me a glass and I made a show of emptying it, as if it hadn't been a frivolous request. I handed it back to Shawn, and he patted my shoulder. The men on either side of me had turned into unexpected sources of support. I would let Edward take the lead, although I wore my silence as loudly as a scream.

"Mr. Williams," he said, "what part are you suggesting Sam played in all of this?"

Williams wasn't the one to answer that question. Instead, Dean Harper came forward, standing next to the headmaster to list Sam's transgressions. His face turned red, as he emphasized each point with oversize hand gestures. My head spun, and I zoned out for a minute, but I heard Harper cap his monologue with "And we have reason to believe this ring of crime extends far beyond Dunning Academy."

Edward met that statement with a raised eyebrow.

"Mr. Webber, Sam has been trafficking in child pornography," the dean said.

"That's the craziest thing I've ever heard."

"Look, an FBI agent from the cybercrime unit made a visit to your son Saturday morning."

That's when Edward stood up and shouted at them, "Are you telling me that law enforcement questioned Sam on this campus without our knowledge?"

"He was never formally questioned," Dean Harper said. "I suppose they didn't want to risk notifying you and having Sam disappear."

"Disappear?" Edward asked. "Why would they think he'd do that?"

"Because his friend Justin Crandall has mysteriously vanished from New Haven, and his uncle Henry Crandall is long gone as well."

The room fell silent. Edward collapsed in his chair.

I, however, found my voice. I clenched my fists and stood up. "I don't believe any of this," I said, staring directly into the headmaster's eyes. I had once revered him, but now I was channeling the savagery of a lioness, daring him to come any closer. Remembering that group of parents who had considered suing Dunning over their children's unfair punishment, I gained courage. I imagined displaying a set of fang-size canines for these men. "You have no proof of anything. You never have. I'd like to have Sam join us. I want to hear what my son has to say."

Headmaster Williams looked surprised by my volume, my strength, and took a step back. He looked to Dean Harper, who shrugged his acquiescence. Williams pressed a button on his intercom and asked his assistant to summon Sam Webber, Class One.

About ten minutes later, Sam joined us in the office, sniffling and carrying a backpack over his shoulder. I waved for him to come sit between Edward and me.

"Sam," I said, turning toward him. "Can we please hear your side of this story?"

Sam stood erect, taking the floor as if he'd been waiting a long time to tell his story. He emptied the contents of his backpack on the headmaster's desk, spreading out half a dozen grainy photographs. He then opened his laptop and played a very shocking video.

"What in the world?" Edward asked.

"This is the type of thing that goes on here. And Mr. Williams knows all about it."

"Son!" Williams pointed an accusing finger across his desk.

"Henry Crandall was blackmailing you for years with these!" Sam pointed to the Polaroids on the desk. "You let him set up shop in the tunnels."

Dean Harper stepped forward, as if to confiscate the evidence.

"Don't you dare," Sam said, extending a protective arm over his cache. "You have plenty of images of your own, you paranoid lunatic. You've embedded spyware all over this campus."

"Sam!" I interjected, more out of surprise than in any condemnation of my son, but it stopped him short. When he slowly turned to face me, I recognized his reproachful stare as something he'd perfected at Dunning. I didn't need any further reminder of my role in it all. I had handed him over to the wolves.

....

It was time to pack Sam's room, time to say goodbye to Dunning. I was a fool to have equated this beautiful campus with truth and knowledge. This place, which I had once mistaken for paradise, had revealed itself as my hell.

When we walked down Sam's hallway, Shawn Willis was

outside his room, leaning against the wall. His face was painted with concern, but I couldn't forgive him for not having warned me about what was going on. I could count at least a hundred email exchanges between us, yet Shawn had never once mentioned a secret group or tunnels or videotaping or malware or hacking, or any of these terms that had just sailed over my head. As he approached us, I could only scowl.

Granted, he'd tried to help Sam in the end, but he wasn't losing his job at Dunning, at least not right away. He had a winning hockey team and a local love interest to keep him busy through the rest of the school year.

It didn't take long for a cluster of boys to gather in the hallway. Sam ignored them all except Vlad Grabowski. They hugged and had a short, hushed conversation; then Vlad patted Sam's shoulders and muttered something that sounded like, "Don't worry, it will all come out."

A boy named Raymond came by the room, and Sam passed off some boxes to him. He accepted everything with an air of satisfaction.

That pretty girl, Nathalie, was waiting by our car. We exchanged sad smiles as I walked around to the passenger door. Sam led her to the edge of the parking lot. They held each other for a long time, most likely assuming they were out of view, but I could see everything from my side-view mirror. When Sam finally got in the backseat, I could tell he'd been crying.

CHAPTER 39

After the Webbers cleared out Sam's belongings and drove away in their Subaru, Shawn punched a wall. He wasn't sure why he had been spared—probably just Harper wanting to keep his enemies close.

Even now that the spying had stopped, living in that apartment in Wilburton Hall gave Shawn the creeps, and the thought of reporting to Harper became unbearable. But he needed to orchestrate his departure on friendly terms—he'd need a good reference.

He wanted Angeline's advice, but she was out with her sister. He left a message with her mother. Then, while waiting for her to call him back, he received a call from Schwartz.

"We need to talk," the coach said.

He was the last person Shawn wanted to hear from. Shawn was convinced that if Sam and Grabs had had time to dig a little deeper, they would have figured out how Schwartz was involved.

"Look, can you come over?" Schwartz wasn't asking; he was demanding.

"I-I-I'm not sure."

"Willis, get over here, for Christ's sake. I'd come over there, but your apartment is probably still wired."

The reminder made Shawn's veins pulse. He wanted to wrap his fingers around Harper's thick neck and squeeze.

"Shawn, are you there?" the coach shouted into the phone.

"Yeah, I'm here," Shawn replied. "I'll be over in a minute."

Sitting in the man cave, across from the same hatch window that Webber had crawled through a few weeks before, was strange. He was accustomed to the blue glow of the TV monitor, not to daylight illuminating the room. Stains on the couch and carpet were visible, as were dust motes suspended in the air.

"Listen," Schwartz started, "I knew about it; I knew about the camera in the Bennett boiler room, about the videotaping."

"You fucker!" Shawn jumped up and grabbed him by the shoulders.

"Wait! Wait! Stop! Hear me out."

"How could you let that shit go on again after the Whittaker scandal?" Shawn hung his head, his rage turning to despair.

Schwartz rubbed his eyes and spoke more calmly. "Look, Shawn, I found out about the camera around the same time Sam Webber stumbled upon it. Gary in Maintenance came to me. He was afraid, said it had gone too far and he wasn't sure what to do. The Nine paid him a lot for his cooperation. That's why I asked you to keep an eye on the Webber kid—I didn't want him to get hurt."

"You were *worried* about Sam?"

"Well, it didn't turn out so good for him, now, did it? But it could have been a lot worse."

Shawn closed his eyes, his dull headache made worse by the dappled light bouncing off the ceiling.

"Shawn," Schwartz continued, "I knew about the camera, but I didn't know who was behind it."

"So? What difference would that have made? You knew people were being violated, and you didn't do a thing to put an end to it."

"Okay, but the way Gary described it made it seem like there may have been willing actors using the shower stalls as well. I needed to figure out how Williams was involved so I could know where to take it."

Shawn nodded.

"You'll see, after you've been at Dunning for as long as I have and seen the things I've seen . . . Well, it's not obvious who to trust."

"That's a problem at a school that's supposed to operate under *a code of trust*."

"Shawn, stop expecting Dunning to be any different than the rest of this sick, messed-up world."

"Maybe it's even sicker."

They sat in silence for several minutes. Shawn didn't want to dissect the situation any further, but he didn't want to walk back across campus either.

"You have to understand," Schwartz said, pointing to the ceiling and the kitchen above, "I'm a few months from retirement, and keeping this house, being close to the grandchildren, is real important to Irene."

Shawn crossed his arms and nodded. Schwartz provided a nice living for his family by trading in whatever currency Dunning handed him.

CHAPTER 40

The chairman of the board of trustees arranged for us to meet off campus, in the all-glass conference room of Dunning's Boston law firm. Sam stayed home, however, shaking his head at what he said was bound to be an inadequate understanding of the facts.

"Their lawyers are meeting with you and Dad and your lawyer—it's ridiculous. No Williams, no Harper, no Willis. What about Grabs and me? We should be the ones in there, explaining what really happened."

"Sweetheart, I think it's about time your father and I took over," I said.

"But you have no idea."

"I wish you had come to us sooner," Edward said. "We could have gone straight to the police when you first came across the camera."

"I asked you to tell me what was really going on last winter, before the disciplinary hearing, and you lied to me."

"I never lied."

"By omission."

"I just wish you had trusted us." Edward's voice was layered with fatigue.

Sam's nostrils flared. "It seems obvious now, but it was complicated as it all unfolded, and you two were busy splitting up. I

304

thought I could solve the mystery on my own. I thought I could salvage things." He closed the door to his bedroom.

....

Dunning's baritone spokesman began the meeting by expressing his willingness to forgo Sam's implication in the pornography scandal in exchange for several things. I stopped breathing when I heard "felony," "prison," and "FBI," and Edward slumped in his chair. Gone was the erect posture he'd displayed in Headmaster Williams's office. He put a hand on my forearm, needing, I think, to feed off my strength this time.

The lawyer Edward had retained cleared his throat, filling the silence that took over our side of the long mahogany table. "Now, now, my client inadvertently discovered some filming equipment and got mixed up in something he had no understanding of." He was a colleague of Edward's father, and the tremor in his voice revealed his age. I cringed, knowing Edward's parents were now privy to the details of our downfall, and for what? This old-timer was no match for the big guns Dunning had on retainer.

Their side responded, "Dunning quite obviously would like to avoid publicly exposing such a terrible scandal and the ruination it would bring to your son."

"Our son?" asked Edward.

"You see, the sale of child pornography can be traced back to the IPN address of his summer residence. His fingerprints are all over the recording devices. The camera that was installed in the shower was discovered in his closet. We can also provide testimony about his infatuation—one might say *stalking*—of one Nathalie de Witt, a girl living in the dormitory in question, a girl who frequented the shower stall being photographed."

"You bastards," I seethed. They were my only two words of the morning, although I wanted to rant about the hypocrisy of a school hell-bent on ruining a boy's life while harboring pedophiles. I wanted to scream and claw and act out on all the protective instincts that were boiling just below my skin.

I doubted our lawyer even knew what an IPN address was, but he was attuned to the maelstrom he was up against and was aware that I was about to blow. He placed his cool hand on my arm. With Edward on my left and this frail old man on my right, both holding me in place, I inhaled deeply, then exhaled, hoping to alleviate a cramp that had formed in my side. The dour-faced attorneys across the table were not the real culprits. The men who really deserved my tirade were safe in their little realm at Dunning Academy. Making a scene here would do us no good.

Our lawyer would eventually negotiate a cash settlement in exchange for silence. I insisted we refuse, but Edward argued we were due reimbursement for the spring tuition he'd already paid. I'd just put down a nonrefundable hotel deposit for graduation weekend as well. "And now with these legal bills . . ." He had pleaded with me just to go along with it, as if Dunning would inevitably win in the end.

Before our gag order went into effect, however, Dunning's lawyers directed Sam to make a statement exposing the Nine and the criminal behavior of its alumni council. He would have to specifically implicate Henry Crandall, who would be arrested not on pornography charges but for coercing minors, for manipulating the actions of boys on campus.

Mercifully, Henry pled guilty once they found him on a beach in the Cayman Islands. Mimi and Morris helped turn him in in the end, apparently furious that he had taken Justin on the lam.

After Sam implicated the Nine and Henry Crandall, he met with a reporter from *Vanity Fair*. The magazine was given an exclusive exposé titled "The Nine, Uncovered: A Century-Old Cancer Removed." Headmaster Williams was painted as the hero, Sam as an innocent victim.

When the issue hit the newsstands, it featured a cover photo of Sam standing in front of the academy building and sold like crazy. I pictured Molly and the other mothers in town scrambling for their own copies. The feature told the story of the Nine, showing pictures of the beautiful Dunning campus, as well as the brotherhood's secret cave in the woods, called the Tomb. Guilt may have been Sam's first reaction when the magazine editor demanded step-by-step directions to the Nine's sacrosanct meeting place, but he'd later snicker at the poetic justice of betraying his "brothers" by means of photography. Sam went on to describe how initiates were hazed and fed the reporter lots of colorful anecdotes, without mentioning the tunnels, as Williams insisted their existence be kept quiet.

A picture of Mimi and Morris Crandall pulled from the *New York Times* society pages was embedded in the article. I imagined Mimi in her tennis whites, taking refuge from the fallout in her rose garden, her enormous dogs as companions. I wondered if she would now be the one to contact me. Would she apologize, or did she expect me to say how sorry I was for Sam's role in her family's downfall? I wasn't sure.

The chairman of the board of trustees was quoted as saying, "We are extremely grateful that Headmaster Williams has eradicated Dunning of the Nine, a dangerous, subversive group determined to ruin our fine institution."

....

The first Monday morning he woke up in his own bedroom, Sam proposed enrolling in the public high school in order to graduate on time and attend college in the fall. He said he felt terrible about all the money we'd spent on Dunning. "There'll be time for that. Sit tight," Edward had advised him. I agreed.

I was finally listening to my maternal instincts. Sam needed my care, and there would be no way to protect him from the spotlight outside our walls. By the time the lawyers had hammered out a deal, however, he wanted to disappear. He stopped caring about a high school diploma, or the Ivy League, or the Little Three, or any of those other New England badges of success; he just wanted to get as far away from Massachusetts and New Hampshire as possible.

In addition to the monetary settlement, our agreement with Dunning provided for Sam's employment as a robotics engineer for

Harry Roland, class of '75. Dunning's attorneys liked to take credit for his employment, but Roland had had his eyes set on my son ever since the first MIT victory. Just before Thanksgiving, he flew Sam to San Francisco, where a furnished apartment was waiting for him. When I sensed Sam's misgivings about the distance, I piled on my encouragement: "It's a great idea. Go to California. Build robots. It will be good for you."

....

Amid all the back-and-forth with the Boston law firm, the *Vanity Fair* reporters, and Harry Roland, and because negotiating the terms and conditions of Sam's settlement took several months, nobody ever thought to notify College Counseling. So you can imagine my surprise when a letter arrived in mid-December, inviting Sam to join Princeton's class of 2018. Admission was contingent upon his graduating with an exemplary record, so it was already moot. Still, holding the letter in my hands was breathtaking.

No matter how perverse it seemed, I called Edward to share the good news. He was still the only one I could talk to about Sam.

"Does it make you feel better?" he asked quietly.

"No. Well, yes, sort of." I couldn't help laughing. It was true—it was all I'd ever wanted.

Edward started laughing too. "Why don't you mount the letter on the wall, Hannah? Go ahead and frame it," he teased.

"Edward, stop." I laughed some more, actually shedding tears.

"I know." He chuckled. "Call your family in Ohio and tell them Sam was accepted to Princeton but has decided to take a position in Silicon Valley." He cracked up at his own joke, even though the thought had actually crossed my mind. I had been putting off the phone call to my sister to let her know that Sam wouldn't be graduating with his class and that she should cancel her reservation.

"Well, okay." I sighed. "Enough of that. I just thought you'd want to know. Your parents might want to know too."

"Oh, Hannah, please. Really. Throw the letter away and forget about it."

After I hung up, I went to the bookshelf in the family room and tucked the letter inside Sam's baby book, along with his first tooth and lock of hair.

My boy would get the last word in the end. While Edward and I were holed up in that lawyer's conference room, Sam was stationed at his childhood desk, carrying out Grabs's final plan. He wrote the best essay of his high school career. And he had great material, as Shawn Willis had convinced Coach Schwartz to agree to a phone interview about what he had discovered thirty years earlier.

In its precocity, the *Dunning Daily* had log-in credentials with the Associated Press, which Grabs hacked into on Easter Sunday, downloading Sam's revelatory article. The next week, "Dunning's Headmaster Williams Sits atop Child Pornography Ring" was picked up all over the country. It was positioned as a "Faceless leak" in response to the *Vanity Fair* article, and it went viral. The *Boston Globe* latched on to it, sending to Dunning the same Spotlight team that had exposed the Catholic Church's history of sexual abuse. Even *60 Minutes* came knocking.

The article alleged that Henry Crandall had forged a relationship with the headmaster during Henry's time as a student in Williams's First-Year English class. It outlined their friendship with Whittaker as well and the crimes the three had committed in the 1980s. The leak went on to describe how the Nine brotherhood functioned and how Henry asserted control from afar. Sam also provided a map of the tunnel system.

Henry Crandall may have been a ne'er-do-well in the real world, but he was king of the universe he'd developed on the dark web. Although the leak described Henry's reliance on an "obedient insider" to direct the Nine in ways that aided his cause, Sam would never report what he and Grabs ultimately discovered: Justin had been the person stationed at the video screen, smoking cigarettes. He had been the one enthralled by the girls in the showers, the one who'd transferred all the salacious footage onto a thumb drive and mailed it to his uncle. He had even taken it upon himself to set up the camera in the Wilburton laundry room, as an underclassman's ingratiating attempt to impress the older boys in his dorm.

Sam cried when he learned that last bit of information, and then he kicked his door. However, despite being angrier than he'd ever thought possible, he decided to keep Justin's name out of the article. He'd lived with the Crandalls, with Mimi and Morris. He'd witnessed the way in which his friend had withered in the shadow of his parents' busy lives and his older siblings' success. Uncle Henry, also the youngest in a large brood, had recognized a void in Justin's life and taken advantage of it.

Grabs used the grainy Polaroid of Williams that he'd filched. A harbinger of the egocentric "selfie," it was scanned and embedded at the top of the file. He'd confirmed that the freakish figure posing in front of a half-dressed student was indeed Williams, at the age of thirty-two.

Sam quoted from personal email correspondence between the headmaster and Uncle Henry, which Grabs provided to him through the safety of the US Postal Service. The exchange painted the picture of a tired headmaster with a furiously ambitious wife who had told Henry their run in the tunnels was over and asked him to please go away quietly. Henry had rebutted with a reference to Polaroids and to how Williams had enjoyed a cut of the proceeds over the years. Most troubling, the messages alluded to the fact that artistic adult-film productions had also been staged during the wee hours in the Bennett showers and that capturing girls shampooing was the mere pastime of an amateur.

Suffice it to say, being told to go away didn't sit well with Uncle Henry, especially not when it came from Williams's wife. They lobbed all sorts of threats back and forth in their correspondence until Henry devised an endgame that might allow all of them to come off unscathed. Enter Samuel Webber.

Because Sam kept Coach Schwartz's identity confidential, he and his wife would receive the title to their house as a retirement gift from the trustees. Schwartz's lacrosse coach son-in-law would even be promoted to athletic director.

The PR firm the school hired suggested that the celebratory pageantry surrounding Dunning's two-hundredth anniversary and the successful Define Dunning campaign be put on hold.

Williams announced that he would retire at the end of the year, playing the part of a befuddled old English teacher with the media. I sipped wine at our kitchen table, watching him on the news, pleading with the press to act decently. "These are unfounded, unsubstantiated leaks," he said. "I'm requesting that the media respect our students' privacy."

Dunning's applications might drop, but they'd bounce back eventually. The academy was much bigger than any one incident. It was an ivy-laden, Teflon-coated brick fortress.

Shawn Willis wrote me an email asking for forgiveness. I responded right away: "Granted." What I received in return was the longest message he had ever sent me. He told me Dunning had finally offered him the permanent head hockey coach position, although he hadn't accepted it. He said that during the final exam period in December, he had put on his crispest shirt and his pressed trousers and visited the library.

Angeline was manning her post at the reference desk, the same place she'd been the afternoon they'd met.

"Wow, you look nice," she said.

He walked around her desk and got down on one knee. Out of his pocket, he pulled a velvet ring box containing a diamond solitaire, one Irene Schwartz had helped him pick out at the mall.

Angeline let out a scream that sent kids on all five floors out of their seats. She jumped up and down. "Yes, yes, yes!" she said before he could even get the question out.

A week later, they packed up her car and drove to Wisconsin. Good for him. I wrapped up a sterling silver serving tray Edward's mother had given us as a wedding present and sent it to them, with my best wishes.

....

Sam forwarded me an email he received from Mimi Crandall. "Wow, Sam. Despite what the *VF* article, not to mention the Faceless leak, has done to our family, I must say, I admire you. You landed on the right side of this nightmare. I wish I could say the same for Justin. He won't be returning to Yale. He's traumatized, to say the least, and Morris finally put his foot down and told him to get a job. He's living in Long Harbor and working on a commercial fishing boat based out of Point Judith. Tell your mother I regret not having gotten to know her better. She raised you well."

I shook my head but saved Mimi's email address. I took the next several days to compose a letter from one mother to another. Despite her money, multiple residences, household help, and many children, I tried to empathize. "There is nothing more worrisome than a disheartened child," I wrote.

I called my sister and my father. I don't know why I was hesitant. My sister had never heard of Dunning before Sam attended, so his withdrawal before graduation registered more as an inconvenience than as anything cataclysmic. "Kids these days take all sorts of different paths," she said, generous with her comforting words.

My father just sounded all-around confused. "Hannah? Can I still come see you?" His voice was weak and small.

"Oh, Dad," I said, my knees almost buckling. "It's not the best time. But I'll come home soon. I promise."

The following Sunday, instead of killing time waiting for Sam to call, I rang my father again. It wasn't clear at first that he knew who I was, but toward the end of our short conversation, he referred to me as his "dear Hannah."

....

I questioned the brains at Dunning after the Princeton screwup, and because the development office hadn't taken us off their email distribution. That's how I ended up reading the newsletter describing the commencement exercises for the class of 2014. It included pictures of a long trail of girls in white dresses, holding red roses, and boys in blue blazers and crimson ties marching behind a kilt-clad bagpipe player. I wept upon learning that Vladimir Grabowski had been named valedictorian and that Nathalie de Witt had won the math prize. I chuckled, reading on that Miss de Witt planned to study mathematics in her home state, at the University of California, Berkeley. Sam would win her in the end.

But I'd never experience Sam standing between his best friends at graduation. I'd never have a photograph with my arm around him in his cap and gown. He'd never pose, cigar in one hand, diploma in the other, between his beaming parents. There'd be no post ceremony lunch with Nathalie's parents. We'd never whisper tidbits of what we'd gleaned about their budding romance.

Instead, Sam was transported to the Wild West, where you were only as good as the robots you designed and the code you wrote, and nobody cared where you'd gone to prep school or college or if you'd even graduated. He was staffed on a team that built better prosthetics for amputees, primarily veterans and survivors of traumatic injuries. Harry Roland paid him handsomely, reminding him that when it came to creativity, the only rules were that there were no rules. When Sam relayed that philosophy to me on the phone one Sunday, I said, "Well, that couldn't be more different from where you came from."

We had to joke, brief quips all we could manage. I didn't dare venture into more serious topics, like whether he was happy or whether he liked the job. Nonetheless, our phone conversations were filled with evidence of his moving forward. "I rode a bike over the Golden Gate Bridge with a guy from work," he'd say. Or, "I took a ferry over to Alcatraz for a look around." He didn't seem to carry the same loss I was carrying, and the disconnect struck me. I used to take it for granted that our desires were intertwined. I assumed he'd absorbed them in utero, just as he shared my blood and my oxygen.

Edward and I put our house on the market, and I went back to clearing out our possessions. Happily married couples coined it "downsizing," but for us it wasn't a fun, empty nest–driven activity.

I began with the bookshelves, from *What to Expect When You're Expecting* to *Awaken Your Genius* to *The College Hook* and all the dozens in between. I had been sold a whole bill of goods, including the fact that there was such a thing as child-rearing success. If she did it all by the book, a woman would be saluted for mothering perfection. I'd read a tome for every step of the way and every deviation (God forbid) from the norm. I packed them all up into boxes to donate to the local library's annual paperback swap. I thought about sticking warning labels on their covers: "Beware: Advice held within is a guideline only. Following it to the letter does not guarantee a damn thing."

Staring at four cartons of books, I remembered the story of Hillel, who was able to paraphrase all the teachings of the Torah while standing on one foot: "Love thy neighbor" was the bible's message distilled into three words. I knew all the details of those parenting books, but I missed the point. I wish I'd known, back as an insecure, nervous mother, that it just came down to love—love for Sam, love for Edward, and even love for myself. I had been so caught up in doing the right thing that I hadn't done what was right. I'd taken everything so seriously, I had never listened to my heart. Maybe if I had been more human and less like the robots Sam built, more spontaneous and less driven, our little family would have survived.

I stashed the cartons of books in the back of the car to remove them from my sight. The bookshelves had large gaps, dusty imprints left behind, like an elderly mouth with missing teeth. I picked up more boxes the next day from the U-Haul store in town. There was not much left in the house that I wanted to take with me to a new apartment. I had given Sam everything that mattered.

I flew to San Francisco in June, my mother's candlesticks in bubble wrap inside my carry-on. I took a taxi from the airport to Sam's apartment, which he'd told me was in a neighborhood called Dogpatch. As the car sped along, I marveled at the city's playful colors in the fading evening light, recalling everything I'd seen about San Francisco in movies and on television. But when the cab came to a stop and I stepped onto the sidewalk, I was struck by the grit and trash blowing about. Sam's building was a converted industrial warehouse devoid of all the suburban characteristics he'd grown up with.

I rang the buzzer, and he came down in the elevator and wrapped me in a firm hug before I had a chance to kiss him. He had arranged for all sorts of things for us to do, ranging from visiting museums to hiking in Muir Woods, craning our necks in admiration of the majestic redwoods. He treated me like a special guest, giving me his bed and sleeping on the couch.

Nathalie had just returned to her home in the Bay Area after a week of Dunning graduation parties. She came to the city one evening, and I roasted a chicken for the three of us. The smell hung in the air, making the sterile space feel more like my kitchen in Boston. Sam turned on some music, a band he'd once listened to with his father.

Nathalie entertained us with stories of senior spring, the unlikely pairings, and, of course, the pranks. Though Sam smiled the whole time, she was careful not to go on too long. His amusement could have been at her stories, but I guessed it was due to the simple fact that she was there, in his kitchen, sharing a meal with us.

I, on the other hand, had to grip the counter while listening to her describe the year-end celebrations. I changed the subject to Cal, but when Nathalie told us of her plans to attend freshman orientation and concentrate in applied mathematics, that stung too. After doing the dishes, I disappeared into the bedroom and left them alone.

My week culminated in a makeshift Shabbat dinner, again at the kitchen counter, just Sam and I. We recited the prayers and drank the wine and were watching the candles burn to their conclusion when Sam told me it was time for me to go home. "I'd like you to come again, but when you're not so sad," he said. He sidled up to me, putting his arm around my shoulder. The physical contact and warmth of his body were stunning. I was surprised I had any tears left, but they came, flowing down my cheeks. I didn't even bother drying them anymore.

"Oh, Sam," I said. "It's just, your whole life got fast-forwarded, and I don't know what to do. You're barely eighteen, and you're already an adult."

"You always said I was more advanced than the other kids."

I swatted his knee, laughing and crying at the same time.

"But seriously, Mom, I know this isn't how you wanted things to turn out."

"But it shouldn't have been about what *I* wanted. When your dad and I were trying to get pregnant with you, I promised God I'd be the best mother ever. I vowed to raise a child who would achieve great things. Now I see that's probably not what God cared about. I should have been satisfied with the mere miracle of you. Your existence should have been enough."

Sam nodded. "It's not exactly how I thought it would turn out either."

"Remember when I read *The Lord of the Rings* trilogy to you? I'm not surprised you couldn't back down. Good overcoming evil is in your bones."

He chuckled, then said gently, "Go back home, Mom. Those kids at the Boys and Girls Club need you." He was using the same tone I used on the phone with my father, telling him to get out more, to go play bingo at the senior center.

"I will," I said. "They actually asked if I'd like to work there full-time."

"With the kids? That's great!"

"I know. I'd be the academic coordinator. I'm sort of excited."
I shrugged. The dentist said I could continue bookkeeping for him
on the side, so my income wouldn't be all that bad.

He hugged me. "Those kids don't know how lucky they are."

My tears started again. "Sam, I'm sorry."

"I'm sorry too," he said.

"For what?"

"For cutting you off. I guess the whole time I was at Dunning,
I was so focused on how hard it was for me. I thought it was my
experience to bear. Now I understand that Dunning happened to
all three of us."

I smiled on the inside, relieved that Sam would rebound from
what had happened these past few years—from the bulk of his childhood, for that matter. For the first time in a long while, I envisioned
my son's future expanding in front of him. Maybe mine too. A new
job. New friends.

....

A few days later, I started my journey east, having rebooked my
flight to Boston and added a layover in Cleveland for a long-overdue
visit to my dad and my siblings. The apartment I left Sam in was far
more upscale than the one-bedroom I'd rented in our old neighborhood. The California weather was milder as well. I wondered
why I felt so tied to New England, to its hardened work ethic, its
harsh winters, its liberal values and focus on academia. Maybe I felt
at home there *because* it was hard and salt crusted. But after what
Sam had been through, his best chance for healing was California.

The last thing I said, while the taxi waited on the street below,
was, "I love you, Sam."

"I know you do, Mom. And I love you too."

As the cab sped toward the airport, it became clear that no
matter what I did or how often I visited, I'd never be able to make
it all better. What had happened to Sam at Dunning would always
be a part of his life. There may have been some bad characters, but

he'd found Nathalie and Grabs there too. Dunning was the place where he'd discovered true friendship and experienced first love. Sam had always been smart, but the school had made him resilient and taught him that not everybody can be trusted. I clasped my hands and held them to my heart, bowing my head in a brief prayer of gratitude because, somewhere along the way, Sam had acquired the grace to land on his own two feet.

ACKNOWLEDGMENTS

I set out to write a novel about a mother and her son, inspired by the story of Hannah in the Book of Samuel. It also turned out to be greatly influenced by recent revelations on many educational campuses in the United States. Therefore, the first acknowledgment I must make is to the real victims of sexual misconduct, to the children whom the adults in charge took advantage of, overlooked, and did not listen to.

To those parents with whom I shared a long, cold bench during a late-night disciplinary committee hearing, I will never forget your kindness. And to the teenagers who made age-appropriate bad decisions, I am sorry that the consequences had to be so extreme. The memory of our episode was something I could exorcise only on the page.

To Rabbi Elaine Zecher and the modern midrash class at Temple Israel Boston, studying Torah with you over the years has turned our ancient scroll into my greatest inspiration. Thank you for being a guide through this ageless text and challenging me to fill its empty spaces with my own stories.

Inspiration only takes you so far, and then you have to get down to the business of writing. Completing this work of fiction would not have been possible without the support of many teachers and fellow writers. Thank you, first, to Grub Street. To Sophie Powell, Lisa Borders, and all the members of our Novel Generator class, you were the ones who convinced me this was a manuscript worth sticking with. Thanks to Melanie deCarolis, Evelyn Herwitz, James LaRowe, and Judy Goldman, for helping me refine the structure of this work and encouraging me to push on. Thank you to Anna Williams for the only-child connection and your millennial expertise. Thank you to Henriette Lazardis, Ben Russell, Michael Marano, Kristina Watts, Susan Evans, Marti Webster, all Grubbies to the core. And many thanks to Eve Bridburg and Chris Castellani for creating this incredible place I now call home.

I'm grateful for the wonderful team of support I've found in Anna Levitan, Devon Lee, Peter Magnusson, Marnye Young, Stephanie Brownell, Florrie Everett, and Larry Zevon. Many, many thanks for the hard work of my agent, April Eberhardt, who pushed me when I needed to be pushed.

Thanks to my editor, Annie Tucker, whose enthusiasm for this story was just what I needed. I have so much gratitude and admiration for Brooke Warner who has created a one-of-a-kind publishing company and to Cait Levin for ushering *The Nine* through the process. To all my She Writes Press sisters, especially the ones I have collaborated with over the past two years, I never imagined such a well of generosity—just knowing you are out there made this second novel possible. To Crystal Patriarche and the fabulous team at BookSparks, I'm so glad to have hitched my wagon to a team of go-getters!

To my early readers, thank you! Your various expertise and sharp eyes made *The Nine* so much better: Suzanne Berger, Stacey O'Rourke, and Katrin Schumann.

Thanks to my family, for embracing my writing life and all the love and space you've given me. To my dad, as always, and to Heidi, for making connections as only you know how, I can't thank you enough. To my children, who read and commented and discussed the plot with me ad nauseam, and to whom this book is dedicated, thank you for your encouragement and also for sharing your stories with me. I promise everything won't end up in a novel someday.

Most of all, thanks to John. You are my first reader, my last reader, and everything in between. I love you.

ABOUT THE AUTHOR

Jeanne Blasberg is the author of *Eden: A Novel*, winner of the Beverly Hills Book Award for Women's Fiction and finalist for the Benjamin Franklin Award for Best New Voice in Fiction and Sarton Women's Book Award for Historical Fiction. After graduating from Smith College, she embarked on a career in finance. Though she worked primarily with numbers, she was always reading and writing. After holding jobs on Wall Street, at Macy's, and writing case studies at Harvard Business School, she turned her attention to memoir and fiction. Blasberg founded the Westerly Memoir Project. She sits on the board of the Boston Book Festival and Grub Street, one of the country's preeminent creative writing centers. She and her husband have three grown children and split time between Boston, MA and Westerly, RI. She loves to travel, play squash, ski, and take in the glorious sunsets over Little Narragansett Bay.

Author photo © Hunter Levitan

SELECTED TITLES FROM SHE WRITES PRESS

She Writes Press is an independent publishing company founded to serve women writers everywhere. Visit us at www.shewritespress.com.

Cleans Up Nicely by Linda Dahl. $16.95, 978-1-938314-38-4. The story of one gifted young woman's path from self-destruction to self-knowledge, set in mid-1970s Manhattan.

The Rooms Are Filled by Jessica Null Vealitzek. $16.95, 978-1-938314-58-2. The coming-of-age story of two outcasts—a nine-year-old boy who just lost his father, and a closeted young woman—brought together by circumstance.

Stella Rose by Tammy Flanders Hetrick. $16.95, 978-1-63152-921-4. When her dying best friend asks her to take care of her sixteen-year-old daughter, Abby says yes—but as she grapples with raising a grieving teenager, she realizes she didn't know her best friend as well as she thought she did.

True Stories at the Smoky View by Jill McCroskey Coupe. $16.95, 978-1-63152-051-8. The lives of a librarian and a ten-year-old boy are changed forever when they become stranded by a blizzard in a Tennessee motel and join forces in a very personal search for justice.

Arboria Park by Kate Tyler Wall. $16.95, 978-1631521676. Stacy Halloran's life has always been centered around her beloved neighborhood, a 1950s-era housing development called Arboria Park—so when a massive highway project threaten the Park in the 2000s, she steps up to the task of trying to save it.

Bittersweet Manor by Tory McCagg. $16.95, 978-1-938314-56-8. A chronicle of three generations of love, manipulation, entitlement, and disappointed expectations in an upper-middle-class New England family.

CPSIA information can be obtained
at www.ICGtesting.com
Printed in the USA
BVHW071829300719
554626BV00002BA/4/P